THE OATH

Preetha Rajah Kannan is the author of *Shiva in the City of Nectar,* an enthralling collection of stories based on the revered Tamil text, *Thiruvilayaadal Puranam.* This was followed by *Son of Shiva***,** narrating the exploits of the warrior-god Kartikeya, commander-in-chief of the heavens and epitome of wisdom and valour. Her third book, *Hounds of Shiva,* is a treasure house of tales detailing the impassioned, heroic acts of sacrifice, devotion and service in the life and times of the Shaivite saints, the Nayanmars. Her next book was *The Warrior God: Ayyappa of Sabarimalai,* the fascinating story behind the renowned Sabarimalai Temple. Then came *Dance of Shiva***,** a collection of sthalapuranams, narrating the precious legends linked to our temples. Her sixth book is *The Tiger Throne*, an English retelling of Kalki's epic, *Ponniyin Selvan.* She is also the editor of *Navagraha Purana,* a translation of the eponymous Telugu work on the mythology of the nine planets, by V. S. Rao. Kannan has contributed extensively to newspapers and magazines, such as *The New Indian Express* and *The Express School Magazine.* A homemaker and grandmother, she lives with her family in Madurai, Tamil Nadu.

THE OATH

Kalki's *Sivagamiyin Sabatham* Retold

PREETHA RAJAH KANNAN

JAICO PUBLISHING HOUSE

Ahmedabad Bangalore Chennai
Delhi Hyderabad Kolkata Mumbai

Published by Jaico Publishing House
A-2 Jash Chambers, 7-A Sir Phirozshah Mehta Road
Fort, Mumbai - 400 001
jaicopub@jaicobooks.com
www.jaicobooks.com

THE OATH
ISBN 978-81-19792-01-6

First Jaico Impression: 2024

Page design and layout: R. Ajith Kumar, Delhi

Printed by
Thomson Press India Limited, New Delhi

To my husband,
K. Vetrivel Kannan—
for the good times.

Contents

Author's Note

RAMASAMY AIYAR KRISHNAMURTHY (1899–1954) or Kalki, serialised *Sivagamiyin Sabatham* in his eponymous magazine from 1944 to 1946. It was then published in four volumes in 1948.

In his inimitable style, Kalki takes some historical characters and events as his skeleton and fleshes it out with his prodigious imagination. He paints the poignant love story of an emperor and a beautiful dancer against the backdrop of the rivalry between the Chalukyas and Pallavas in the early seventh century.

Mamallan and Sivagami's love is caught up in a whirlwind of brave warriors, beautiful women, emperors in disguise, assassins with poisoned daggers, master spies, floods, sinister monks and intrigues. In the background, the exquisite sculptures of the Mahabalipuram Shore Temple take shape.

Dear readers, after giving you *Ponniyin Selvan* as ***The Tiger Throne***, I automatically picked up *Sivagamiyin Sabatham*. Captivated by Kalki's brilliant tale of love and war, I now give you ***The Oath***. As always, I have tried to come up with a compact version of the novel while staying true to the body and soul of Kalki's narrative.

I hope that you enjoy every page of ***The Oath*** and go on to read *Sivagamiyin Sabatham* in all its original glory at https://www.tamilpdfbooks.com/download.php?id=18501#pdf.

Happy reading to you all!

Preetha Rajah Kannan

Main Characters

Aayanar	Master sculptor
Asuvabalan	Pallava palace stable keeper and spy
Bhuvanamahadevi	Emperor Mahendran's queen
Dhurvineedhan	Kanga king and Chalukyan ally
Gundodharan	Pallava spy
Hiuen Tsang	renowned Chinese traveller
Kamali	Sivagami's friend and Kannapiran's wife
Kannapiran	Pallava royal charioteer
Kalipahai	Pallava general
Mahendran	Pallava emperor
Maitraiyan	Chalukyan spymaster
Manavanman	Sri Lankan prince
Naganandhi	Buddhist monk
Narasimhan/Mamallan	Pallava crown prince
Navukkarasar	Saivite saint
Paranjothi	Pallava general
Pulikesi	Chalukyan emperor
Ranjani	Kapalika
Rudracharya	Mahendran's guru
Sarangadevan	Mahendran's prime minister
Sasangan	Pulikesi's commander
Shatrughan	Pallava spymaster
Sivagami	Master sculptor Aayanar's daughter
Sivanesan	doctor and Paranjothi's uncle
Umayaal	Doctor Sivanesan's daughter

Vadivazlagi	Paranjothi's mother
Vanamadevi	Pandyan princess and Mamallan's queen
Vishnuvardhanan	Emperor Pulikesi's brother

PART 1

THE EARTHQUAKE

The Travellers

ONE SPRING EVENING, two travellers walked towards Kanchipuram on the highway along the shore of the Mahendran Lake. One was a Buddhist monk in saffron robes. Over six feet tall, his body was toughened by penance or hardship. His face inspired fear. His companion was a short, handsome boy of eighteen. The exhausted travellers had clearly come a long way.

"How far is the capital?" the young man asked.

The monk pointed. "There it is, Paranjothi."

Paranjothi stared at the palaces and roofs visible through the dense trees. "That is about half an hour away, right? I will rest for some time. If you are in a hurry, carry on." The boy laid his bundle and staff on the roadside and sat facing the lake.

The monk sat beside him. The setting sun whirled like Vishnu's chakra on the horizon, setting the clouds on fire. The lake's calm water shone like molten gold. The northern hills threw shadows on the vast lake. The exhilarating sight of a flock of cranes drifting in the dark blue sky brought one close to God.

Paranjothi said softly, "This majestic lake should be called the Mahendran Sea."

The monk stood up. "Right now, the water level is low. You should see the lake brimming with rainwater in *Aippasi* and *Karthigai*—it is truly a sea then."

Paranjothi shouldered his bundle and staff and followed the monk. The traffic increased with lines of carts carrying passengers and grain. Rice fields stretched on one side of the road. The scent of harvested rice and straw filled the air. As they crossed a pretty village, they were flooded by the smell of jasmine. The dazzling white flowers twinkled like stars in the dark fields, interspersed with golden chrysanthemums.

A snake slithered across the road and disappeared into the field.

The two men walked on in silence.

Paranjothi suddenly laughed. "Swami, this afternoon, you killed a snake and saved me, didn't you? But you are a monk: isn't it wrong to kill?"

"Mustn't I protect you? You saved my life. In return for that …"

"I saved your life! When was this?"

"Three hundred years ago … in a previous birth."

"Oh, forgive me! I forget that you are a sage who knows the past, present and future …"

"Shall I tell you something?" the monk asked. "A terrible war is coming. It will turn the Mahendran Lake into a lake of blood."

"Aiyo! That is frightening." Paranjothi paused. "But what do I care about the kingdom? Tell me something about myself."

"You will get into trouble tonight."

"Shiva, Shiva! Can't tell me something good?"

"By the grace of Buddha, you will get through that trouble."

"But I am a *Shaiva*. Will Buddha bless me?"

"Buddha's compassion is boundless."

In the dim evening light, they saw a strange figure coming towards them. The newcomer was short and wore only a loincloth. He carried a corded hoop with a *kamandalam* and a fan of peacock feathers. He had a small mat under his armpit.

"Who is that?" Paranjothi asked.

"Can't you see? That is a Digambara Jain monk."

"Are there still Jain monks here?" Paranjothi wondered.

"Most of them have left the Pallava kingdom for the Pandyan kingdom. The remaining will leave soon."

The Buddhist monk greeted the Jain: "*Buddham saranam gacchami.*"

"Praise to Arugan's holy feet," the Jain replied.

"Where are you going as night falls?" the Buddhist asked.

"Thondaimandalam has become the cremation ground in which Shiva dances—I want nothing to do with it. I am going to the Pandyan kingdom."

"Is there any news?" the Buddhist monk asked.

"Yes, there is: I heard that the fort's gates are to be shut." The Jain hurried on his way.

The monk said, "The Jains once controlled the Pallava kingdom. Emperor Mahendran Pallava would not dream of defying them. Now Shaivism and Vaishnavism are celebrated in the Pallava kingdom."

"Oh," said Paranjothi. "And what was that about the fort's gates being shut?"

"Look," said the monk.

They turned a corner and saw Kanchi Fort's southern entrance. The massive gates were closed.

The Capital

BORDERING THE FORT'S wall was a huge moat, about a hundred feet wide, filled with dark water. The highway diverged into two roads here. A narrow wooden bridge crossed the moat, leading to the gate. Signaling to Paranjothi to follow him, the monk walked across the bridge. He picked up a wooden rod and beat the gong hanging by the gate.

A man called out from the terrace above: "Who is there?" His face was hidden in the dark.

"Marudhappan, it is me," the monk cried.

"Naganandhi *adigal*, it is you! I am coming, swami."

The gate opened, creating a gap wide enough for one person. Naganandhi led Paranjothi through it and the gate closed behind them. Paranjothi stared at the city which blazed with the light of torches. The buzz of thousands of voices filled the air. He had never seen such a large city and was stunned by its magnificence.

Naganandhi asked, "Marudhappan, why is the city so quiet? Why are the gates shut so early?"

"I do not know, swami. This morning, the city was in a festive mood … Sivagami was to give her debut dance recital in the emperor's court."

"Which Sivagami is this?" Naganandhi asked.

"Who else but Aayanar's daughter, Sivagami," the guard replied.

This caught Paranjothi's attention. "Who? Aayanar the sculptor?"

"Yes," said Marudhappan. He stared at Paranjothi. "Who is this boy, *adigal*?"

"My disciple. Go on: what happened next?"

"I heard that a messenger came with urgent news in the middle of the recital. The emperor left the court at once, followed by the prince and the council of ministers. At sunset, I was ordered to shut the gates. That is all I know. What do you think, swami? Is it war? But there is no king on earth strong enough to fight the emperor of Kanchi now ..."

"Do not say that, Marudhappan. Emperors wearing gem-studded crowns today, may tomorrow ... but why talk about such things now! How is your son?"

"By your grace, swami, he is fine."

Marudhappan's son once lay dying of snake bite. Using snake-stone as an antidote, Naganandhi had saved the boy. Marudhappan was devoted to the monk for this.

"I did nothing, Marudhappan. It was all Buddha's compassion. I will be on my way."

Paranjothi followed the monk. "Swami, how come the guard let you in?"

"It must be the glory of these saffron robes."

"If these robes command so much respect under the Pallavas, why is it that the Jains ..."

"Unlike the Jains, we do not interfere in matters of state. We have nothing to do with kings. Leave that aside. Are you coming with me to the Buddhist monastery?"

"No, swami. My mother has ordered me to stay only at Navukkarasar's *matham*."

"In that case, we must part ways here."

"Swami, how do I get to Navukkarasar's *matham*?"

"Go straight down this road and ask for directions to the Ekambar Temple. The *matham* is on the same street. Careful, my boy. These are dangerous times." The monk went his way.

Kanchi was then the greatest metropolis of the south. The streets were wide enough for chariots. The houses were palatial. Wide earthenware pots stood on stone pillars, holding lamps which burned brilliantly

The crowded streets hummed with people. The endless market stalls displayed flowers, fruits, sweetmeats, grains, precious gems ….

The awed Paranjothi walked along, taking in the sights. He heard people talking about Sivagami's dance recital being stopped half-way and the fort's gates being shut. He stopped every few minutes to ask a passer-by, "Where is the Ekambar Temple?"

Although Paranjothi kept going in the direction pointed to, he did not reach the temple. He was not bothered by the delay. Fascinated by the capital, he walked leisurely along the streets.

Suddenly, he heard alarmed shouts: 'The temple elephant is in musth! Run! Run!' People ran in all directions. Children and women wailed, horses neighed, carts rattled and doors banged.

Paranjothi froze. As he considered whether to run, and in which direction, a palanquin came towards him. A beautiful young girl was in it, along with a man who looked like her father. Hearing the shrieks, the bearers hurriedly put down the palanquin and ran away. At the same time, the earth shook under the elephant's feet—the mad beast was close behind Paranjothi!

Paranjothi hesitated for a second. Then he quickly opened his bundle and fit a spearhead to his staff. Even as he raised the spear, the elephant was upon him. Paranjothi hurled his spear with all his might. The spear pierced the elephant's thick hide and penetrated close to its left eye. The beast trumpeted horribly, plucked out the spear and stamped it. It flung the spear aside and turned towards Paranjothi.

Paranjothi ran away from the palanquin. By the time the elephant moved its huge bulk, he was well ahead of it. He looked back—the animal was trumpeting and charging behind him. He turned into a side street and ran non-stop until he came to a wide road once more. He saw a group of elephants coming towards him, urged on by their mahouts. *These animals are on their way to control the mad elephant.* Paranjothi slowed to a walk.

He became aware of his racing heart and sweat-drenched body. Tired by his day-long journey, he was now exhausted. He stumbled and shivered from shock. *I must rest.* He sat on a roadside platform. The full moon shone in the sky and a gentle breeze caressed his tired body. *Why did I throw my spear at the elephant? What if the beast had killed me? I am life itself to my beloved mother. I would have never seen her again.* He thought of the young girl and elderly man in the palanquin. *I did it to protect them. Could the girl be the Sivagami whose dance recital was cut short? Could the elderly man be her father, Aayanar?*

Paranjothi fell asleep on the platform.

Saved by God

AAYANAR AND SIVAGAMI saw the young man throw his spear and run, with the elephant chasing him. Amazed at his courage and worried about his safety, they got down from the palanquin. The street was deserted.

Aayanar drew his young daughter close and asked tenderly, "Are you scared, Sivagami?"

"No, *appa*. What would have happened to us if that young man had not distracted the elephant?"

"The palanquin would have been shattered. That is why I told the bearers to run. We too could have dashed into one of the nearby houses, but I must admit that we were in danger."

The people who had run away trickled back. The silent street buzzed with excited chatter. "It is Aayanar and his daughter. Thank goodness God saved them!"

Aayanar and Sivagami thought that even if it was God who had saved them, God had come in the form of the young man. *Who was he? What had happened to him?* No one knew.

Aayanar walked to the spot where the elephant had stood. He picked up the broken spear and a bundle which lay a little distance away and came back. Sivagami fingered the spear in fascination.

Aayanar said, "Sivagami, let us not waste time. Let us go. Things will be clear tomorrow."

As they were about to get into the palanquin, they heard horses. They saw two majestic men on white horses, followed by five or six lancers. The company stopped by the palanquin.

The crowd respectfully moved away shouting, "Long live the great Mahendran Pallava! Long live Prince Mamallan!"

The riders were Emperor Mahendran and his only son, Narasimhavarman, known as Mamallan.

Sivagami stood modestly behind Aayanar, her large, dark eyes fixed on the prince.

The emperor dismounted from his horse. "Aayanar, what is this I hear about an accident?"

"By the grace of Lord Ekambar, we escaped, my lord," Aayanar replied.

Mahendran asked affectionately, "Sivagami, are you annoyed with me because I left in the middle of your performance?"

Sivagami smiled shyly but remained silent.

Aayanar protested, "My king, is Sivagami a fool? Doesn't she understand that it must be something very important which called you away?"

"It was something very important," the king replied. "I will explain later. Why the hurry to leave?"

"I did not want to waste a day, my lord," Aayanar explained. "The moonlight is as bright as day—it is convenient to travel."

"Sculpture is a sacred vocation for you: you cannot stay away from it even for a day. This moon makes me want to come with you, but that is not possible. I will come tomorrow."

Mamallan effortlessly jumped off his horse and stood by his father. The prince asked Aayanar, "Who is this young man who threw his spear at the elephant? Where did he go?"

"I know nothing," Aayanar said. "After throwing his spear, he vanished like lightning. That is why he survived. He looked like a stranger."

As the prince spoke to Aayanar, his eyes were fixed on Sivagami. Sivagami, who had stared at the prince while he was on his horse, now stood with her head bowed. The broken spear had slipped from her hand and lay on the ground.

Mamallan stepped towards her. "Sivagami, what is this?"

Sivagami picked up the spear and held it out to the prince. As Mamallan took it from her, his fingers brushed hers. They jumped apart as if stung by scorpions.

The prince hid his embarrassment and turned to Aayanar. "Is this the spear?"

"Yes, my prince ..."

Mamallan cut in, "*Appa*, we must find this spear's owner. If not for his courage, the Pallava kingdom would have lost its greatest sculptor."

Mahendran added, "The Pallava kingdom would also have lost its *Kalaivani*." He smiled at Sivagami. "My child, your dance was marvellous. If only I could have watched the full performance!" He turned to her father. "Aayanar, there are many things I must discuss with you. I will come to Mamallapuram soon. It is late. Safe journey to you." The emperor mounted his horse, followed by the prince.

Mahendran Pallava ordered a soldier: "Keep the young stranger under custody tonight and bring him to the palace tomorrow morning. Pass on my command to the captain of the city guards."

The emperor and the prince rode away. Aayanar and Sivagami climbed into the palanquin and made their way to the fort's entrance with an escort of soldiers.

A Bad Omen

NOT FIVE MINUTES after he fell asleep, Paranjothi was startled awake by voices.

"They say that the temple elephant went wild because some stranger threw his spear at it ..."

Paranjothi was worried to hear talk of the elephant being driven to madness by his spear. He remembered that he had dropped his bundle in the middle of the street before running from the elephant. *My letters to Navukkarasar and Aayanar are in the bundle, along with my clothes, food and money. I must find the bundle.*

Paranjothi climbed down from the platform, guessed the direction from which he had come, and started walking. The streets were deserted, doors closed and lights extinguished. Luckily, the full moon threw its milky light on the city. He walked a long way, searching the streets, but he could not recognise the place where he had met the elephant and dropped his bundle.

By the moon's position, Paranjothi realised that it was midnight. He could walk no further; all he wanted was to lie down somewhere. *It is useless to search for my bundle. It is enough to find Navukkarasar's matham. But how can I find it? There is no one on the street to ask directions. Am I going to spend all night wandering like this?*

Two men came around the corner, talking. They looked like city guards. They stopped.

"Who are you? Where are you going in the middle of the night?" one man asked.

"Sir, I am a stranger …"

The guard interrupted: "A stranger? Where are you from?"

"I am from Sengathankudi, a village in Chola Nadu. I reached Kanchi only today. I am here to study Tamil at Navukkarasar's *matham*. I have been searching for the *matham* since this evening."

The guard chuckled. "We are going in that direction. We can take you there."

Paranjothi thanked the guards and followed them. They came to a building with high walls. It did not look like a *matham* and there was no temple nearby. The walls and the huge lock on the gate made Paranjothi suspicious. One of his companions went to the guard at the gate and said something in a low voice. Immediately, the door was unlocked.

"Come, my boy."

His heart racing, Paranjothi stepped inside. They took him down a narrow passage, stopped and opened the door to a room.

"Stay here. Everyone in the *matham* is asleep. You can see them in the morning," a guard said.

Paranjothi peered into the dark room. There was some straw and a rush mat on the ground. A pot of water stood in a corner. He turned back to the guards and asked, "Is this a *matham*?"

"Of course, my boy. Do you have any doubts?"

The exhausted Paranjothi just wanted a place to sleep. He walked into the room. "I will stay here."

One of his escorts said, "My boy, this is a *matham*: but not Navukkarasar's *matham*. This *matham* belongs to Emperor Mahendran." He shut the door.

Paranjothi heard the key turn in the lock.

The Pampered Child

PARANJOTHI'S ANCESTORS WERE from the ancient Mamathirar clan. They were army commanders when the Cholas ruled a vast kingdom from Uraiyur. When the Cholas lost power to the Pallavas, the Mamathirars gave up their careers in the army and the border patrols and became farmers.

Paranjothi lost his father when he was an infant. He was his mother, Vadivazlagi's, pampered child. He grew up to be a wild ruffian. With the blood of his brave ancestors, he enjoyed fighting and had a natural gift for battle strategies. He mastered wrestling, along with the cudgel, spear and knife.

Paranjothi was life itself to his mother, but she was worried by his wildness. Vadivazlagi came from a learned family of Shiva devotees. Her brother, Sivanesan, was a well-known, skilled doctor living in Thiruvenkadu. Umayaal, Sivanesan's eldest daughter, was good and beautiful. She was learned and devoted to Lord Shiva. Deep down, Vadivazlagi hoped that Umayaal would marry her son. *But will my brother let his beloved daughter marry my unruly son?*

Vadivazlagi did her best to educate Paranjothi, but every teacher she hired gave up and said, "Lady, your son is a genius: he understands the most complex problems at once. But it is impossible to get him to focus even for an instant. I just cannot teach him." Any teacher who tried to use the stick on Paranjothi was forced to leave the village at once.

One year, Vadivazlagi and Paranjothi celebrated Pongal at Thiruvenkadu. Paranjothi overheard his mother and uncle discussing Umayaal's marriage and worrying about him.

Back in Sengathankudi, Paranjothi came home one day to find his mother crying. He sat down by her mat, without questioning or consoling her. "*Amma,* I am going to Kanchi to study."

The startled Vadivazlagi sat up. "But, my darling, can't you study here?"

"As long as I stay here, I will never get an education. I hear that Kanchi is the greatest center of learning and art in Bharat." Paranjothi paused. "*Amma*, until I return from Kanchi, you must see that Umayaal does not marry anyone."

Although she was sad to part from her only son, Vadivazlagi shed tears of joy over his decision.

Sivanesan was delighted. Advising Paranjothi to learn sculpture along with his Tamil studies, the doctor gave him letters of introduction to Navukkarasar and another old friend, Aayanar. Reading his nephew's heart, Sivanesan promised to give Umayaal in marriage to Paranjothi when he came back home a scholar.

At that time, Kanchi had schools teaching the Vedas, Buddhism, Jainism and Tamil. It had colleges devoted to sculpture, music and art. Above all, Kanchi was the birthplace of Navukkarasar's glorious Tamil revival.

Navukkarasar, born Marulneeki, turned to Jainism and became the famous monk, Dharmasena. Later, under the influence of his sister, Thilagavathi, he renounced Jainism and became an ardent Shiva devotee. Marulneeki composed a flood of sweet Tamil poems, drenched in Shiva bhakti. Lost in these divine verses, Emperor Mahendran exclaimed, 'I am the king of the nation and you are the King of Words (Navukkarasar)!' Mahendran also renounced Jainism and became a *Shaiva*. Under the emperor's patronage, Navukkarasar established a *matham* in Kanchi to teach Tamil, along with his compositions.

At an auspicious date and time, Paranjothi left for Kanchi with his mother's and uncle's blessings. Sivanesan's final advice to him was, "My boy, you need your spear on your long journey. But once you reach Kanchi, throw it away. Focus only on your studies."

The Mysterious Rope

LYING IN THE DARK prison cell, Paranjothi smiled. *I followed my uncle's advice and threw my spear—but the wicked spear pierced an elephant, and now I am in prison.* What would his mother and uncle think if they knew that he was spending his first night in Kanchi in prison? And what about Umayaal, standing alone behind the wall of the house, her eyes filled with tenderness and tears as she said goodbye to him? *If someone predicted these events this afternoon, I would not have believed him.* Suddenly, Paranjothi recalled Naganandhi's words: 'You will get into trouble tonight.' *Can that monk really predict the past, present and future?*

Paranjothi laughed as he thought of his meeting with the monk. After walking all morning, he was about seven miles from Kanchi. Deciding to rest for a while, he lay down under a roadside tree with his bundle at his head and his spear by his side. He saw a Buddhist monk coming towards him. As Paranjothi's mother and uncle had warned him to have nothing to do with Buddhist and Jain monks, Paranjothi closed his eyes, pretending to be asleep.

Soon he felt someone staring at him and slowly opened his eyes. Even the fearless Paranjothi was terrified at what he saw. The monk was staring at him. The man's face was frightening. Even more frightening was the five-foot long cobra he held by the tail! Paranjothi jumped up in fright. *But wait: the snake is dead … its body is oozing blood.* "Sir, what kind of a joke is this? Why are you holding a dead snake over me? Throw it away."

"My child, how can you sleep like this in forest land? By now this cobra would have bitten you. Luckily, I came and killed it and saved you."

Paranjothi controlled his laughter at this lie. "Really, sir? I am my mother's only child. She will be grateful to you for saving me. What is your name? If I have to tell my mother about you …"

"They call me Naganandhi. Where are you going?"

"To Kanchi."

"I am also going there. I now have a travelling companion. Come, let us go."

What a suitable name for the monk! His face reminds me of a cobra. Whether by Naganandhi's true insight or by chance, the first part of his prediction has come true. I am certainly in trouble. Will the other half of his prediction—that I will be saved by Buddha's grace—also come true?

Paranjothi was not worried. He was confident of being released once it was known that he had been wrongly arrested. *It is best to have a good night's sleep. Ah! My stomach is growling in hunger. Fine city this is … starving a guest who has travelled all day to get here! Didn't I bump into that Digambara Jain? It must be the sight of his starving face which has brought me to this.*

Paranjothi became aware of a glimmer of light in the dark cell. He looked up in surprise and saw the moonlight shining through a small opening in the thatch. *How is it that I can suddenly see the moonlight? No, no. The opening must have been there: it is just that the moon has now moved into position over it. The opening is widening ... it is now wide enough for a man to pass. Emperor Mahendran's capital is a city of magic.* Paranjothi's heart almost stopped. *Aiyo, what horror is this!* A long snake slithered down from the opening in the roof. *No, no! It is not a snake: it is just a rope. Chi! That monk startled me with a dead snake this afternoon—now even a rope looks like a snake to me.*

Someone had deliberately made an opening in the roof and passed a rope through it. *Someone is helping me escape. But who cares about me in this city of strangers? And how does he know I am in this prison cell?* The rope touched the ground and wobbled around. *The person above is shaking the rope. Is he telling me to pull myself up with it?*

Paranjothi considered this unexpected offer of help. *It might get me into more trouble.* On the other hand, he was burning with curiosity to know who was taking such risks to save him. And there was yet another factor—he was starving. Paranjothi held the rope and gave a tug: it was tied tightly above. It would certainly bear his weight. He started to climb up.

The Front Courtyard

AFTER LEAVING AAYANAR and Sivagami, Emperor Mahendran and Prince Mamallan galloped to the palace. The guards at the gate shouted, 'Long live the emperor! Long live the brave Mamallan!' and made way for them. The ranks of soldiers assembled in the palace's front courtyard broke into a triumphant roar. A man standing alone in front of the others stepped forward respectfully.

"General," the emperor said. "Have the messengers been briefed? Are they ready to go?"

"Yes, my lord. They wait for your orders to leave."

The emperor turned to Mamallan. "My child, your mother must be worried. Have your dinner and explain matters to her. I will join you on the terrace after I see off the messengers." Having been a Jain for many years, the emperor continued his habit of skipping dinner even after converting to Shaivism.

"Alright, *appa*. But must we wait for all our troops to assemble? Can't we go to war with the divisions which are ready?"

Mahendran smiled. "We will discuss this later. Now go to your mother." After Mamallan left, he turned to the general. "Kalipahai, this is the message our men must carry: every town in Thondaimandalam and Chola Nadu must gather a division of thousand soldiers. They must be ready to march as soon as they receive orders. Is this clear?"

"Yes, lord."

"Have you made arrangements for the fort's security?"

"Except ascetics, no one is to enter the fort without interrogation. I have commanded the guards to search anyone leaving. Any suspicious person in the city is to be arrested."

"General, the Pallava dynasty's survival depends on the security of Kanchi Fort."

"Lord, lakhs of warriors from the Kaveri to the Krishna are ready to guard the Pallava dynasty."

"But where are their spears and swords?" Kalipahai was silent. "It seems that they make good spears in Chola Nadu. Did you see the spear hurled at the elephant? It has, 'Mamathirar,' written on it. Mamathirars are from eastern Chola Nadu, right?"

"Yes, my king."

"The man who threw that spear must be from there. He is one in a million. We must find him." The general was silent. "Another thing: change the orders regarding ascetics. On my way back after meeting Aayanar, I saw a Buddhist monk standing at a street corner. He disappeared into the shadows."

"What are your orders, lord?"

"Keep a watch on the Royal Monastery and see who this newcomer is."

"I will make arrangements at once."

General Kalipahai summoned each messenger in turn. He told the emperor the man's name and the town allotted to him. Each man saluted the king, mounted his horse and galloped away.

Bhuvanamahadevi

THE TORCHBEARERS STRUGGLED to keep up with Mamallan as he hurried to the women's quarters through the vast, beautiful palace. The Pallava dynasty's reigning queen, Bhuvanamahadevi, came to the entrance. Her dignity and mature beauty made her worthy of the title, 'Empress of the Three Worlds.'

She embraced Mamallan. The prince removed his crown and ornaments and washed his hands and feet. They worshiped the idol of Lord Nataraja in the puja room and went to the dining room.

As soon as they were seated, the queen said, "My child, the palace is in an uproar. The fort's gates have been shut. Won't you tell me what is happening?"

Mamallan looked at the servants. "*Amma*, let us go to the terrace after dinner. I will tell you everything then. But I beg you, stop waiting to have your dinner with me."

The empress smiled lovingly but did not reply. The emperor and the prince were busy with matters of state during the day. Lunch at the Kanchi palace was a grand, public affair, shared with powerful officials, visiting celebrities, famous artists and poets, ascetics and Vedic scholars. And so the emperor arranged for mother and son to dine together. The three of them usually gathered on the palace's terrace after that.

The empress and the prince sat on a marble platform on the terrace. Kanchi city, bathed in white moonlight, was unusually quiet. Mamallan's heart reached out to the fort's southern entrance. *Aayanar and Sivagami will be crossing the gate now. What a narrow escape they had! Who is the young man who threw his spear at the elephant and saved them?*

When her son remained deep in thought, Bhuvanamahadevi said, "My child ..."

Mamallan was startled from his dreams. "*Amma*, am I still a child?

I have defeated the bravest Pallava warriors and earned the title, 'Mamallan.' *Appa* too treats me like a child in the cradle!"

"To his parents, their son is always a child." The emperor had come to the terrace, unnoticed. Mother and son stood in respect. Once he sat on the platform, they joined him. "*Devi*," Mahendran asked. "Has the child told you everything?"

"No. All he does is complain about you and me."

"How can I not complain, *appa*? Must I look on helplessly as the enemy invades our kingdom? It looks like this *kaliyuga* will end by the time General Kalipahai gathers our forces! Why did you order me to be silent at the council? Everyone else gave their opinions ..."

Bhuvanamahadevi was incredulous: "An enemy invasion?"

"Yes." The emperor paused. "*Devi*, Narasimhan is still a child. He does not understand the coming war. Pulikesi, the king of Vatapi, has crossed the Tungabhadra River with lakhs of soldiers and thousands of elephants and cavalry. Pulikesi has prepared for this war for many years. Our spies were fooled. His army has destroyed our border patrols and is advancing rapidly. At present, we do not have the strength to stop this army. Our scattered forces are retreating. The Pallava kingdom is in peril. But, by the grace of Lord Shiva, we will ultimately triumph."

Mamallan waited patiently for his father to finish. "*Appa,* is the Pallava army retreating? What a shame! Let me march at once with the divisions which are ready."

"Patience, Narasimhan. The time will come when you march at the head of the Pallava army. Until then, obey me. I have an important task tonight: will you come with me?"

"Of course, *appa*."

"*Devi*, from today, I will treat Narasimhan as a friend. I give him the right to take part in the council of ministers. You too must stop calling him, 'My child.'"

Telling Bhuvanamahadevi to go to bed, Mahendran and Mamallan left the palace.

Freedom

WHEN PARANJOTHI CLIMBED up the rope to the thatch, two iron hands lifted him onto the roof. Naganandhi stood there with a warning finger on his lips. A young monk was with him. At a signal from his senior, he coiled the rope and bundled it into a piece of saffron cloth. Paranjothi saw Kanchi's mansions and terraces gleaming in the moonlight as far as the eye could see.

Naganandhi closed the opening in the roof and gestured to Paranjothi to follow him. Paranjothi and the young monk walked softly behind him over thatched roofs, terraces and pavilions. At the least stir in the street, Naganandhi signalled to the two men behind him and quickly sat down. After crossing seven or eight buildings, they came to a house in a corner with *paneer* trees. Clusters of flowers glowed like silver in the moonlight. The fragrance wafted everywhere with the gentle breeze. Naganandhi carefully scanned the street and then climbed down one of the trees. Paranjothi and the young monk followed him.

After a short walk, they came to the Royal Monastery–the biggest monastery in Kanchi. The sanctum of the monastery held one of Buddha's teeth. Whatever be their personal faith, the Pallava kings gave generous grants to all religions. The Royal Monastery had received such a grant. And some of Kanchi's wealthiest men were Buddhists. One of them, Dhanadasan, had renovated the monastery at great expense in gratitude for his only son's recovery from a severe illness. Coated in pearl-white cement, the Royal Monastery was beautiful in the moonlight.

"Ah, what an exquisite temple!" Paranjothi exclaimed.

Naganandhi stopped abruptly and covered his mouth. They were in the open space between the trees and the monastery entrance. Two white horses charged towards them from the shadows. The riders were warriors, one middle-aged and the other, young. Both wore large turbans.

The older soldier said, "*Buddham saranam gacchami.* Don't you know that it is forbidden to walk in the streets after the night's second watch?" He paused. "Where are you going in the middle of the night?"

Naganandhi said, "This boy is my disciple. We came to Kanchi only today. He is new to the city and got lost. I found him and brought him here."

"Where is this young man from?"

"Sengathankudi in Chola Nadu."

"What is your name?"

"They call me Naganandhi."

"Do not walk in the streets at night again, swami. Tell your disciple this."

Once the soldiers left, they went into the monastery. The doors quickly closed behind them. Paranjothi was mesmerised by the rows of lamps which adorned the sanctum. The scent of incense made him giddy.

Naganandhi placed a hand on his head. "My child, you made it through danger by Buddha's grace. Do you know who those two riders were? They were Emperor Mahendran and Prince Mamallan."

"Really?" Paranjothi was astounded.

"Yes. They are in disguise: no one in Bharat can match the emperor's skill in disguise."

Recovering from his surprise, Paranjothi asked, "But why was I in danger from them?"

Naganandhi laughed mockingly. "If they know that you are the one who threw the spear at the elephant, you will die. Do you know what kind of a man the prince is? No man must be braver or stronger than him. Brave men must wrestle with him and lose, or they will be sent to *Yamaloka*."

"If it comes to a fight, I will not give in to anyone," Paranjothi declared. "Prince or otherwise."

"I know, my boy. It is your courage which gets you into trouble. They will accuse you of driving the elephant mad by throwing your spear at it and they will punish you."

Paranjothi remembered overhearing such talk on the road. He began to believe Naganandhi's words. "Can they be so unfair?"

"It is in the Pallavas' genes. A hundred and fifty years ago, Mayurasanman, a young man like you, came to study in Kanchi. Jealous of his courage, the Pallavas falsely accused and jailed him."

"And then?"

"Mayurasanman escaped, founded a new kingdom on the banks of the Krishna and took revenge on the Pallavas. Like Mayurasanman, you too escaped from danger ..."

Paranjothi interrupted him: "Swami, right now, dying of hunger is my greatest danger!"

Naganandhi gave him food and took him to a verandah. "Lie here. I will give you forty-five minutes to sleep. You are not yet out of danger. We must leave the fort before dawn."

Paranjothi lay down and fell asleep at once.

The Magic Blindfold

PARANJOTHI WAS TROUBLED by horrible nightmares. In one, five Buddhist monks stood around him. One held a lamp above Paranjothi's face. He heard someone say, 'Naganandhi is right—there is an extraordinary light in his face. He will be a great warrior or a great soul.'

In another, an elephant chased him. Paranjothi quickly climbed a *paneer* tree. He broke a branch and dropped it on the elephant. Two horsemen came and shouted, 'You wretch, you killed the temple elephant!' They threw their spears at him.

Naganandhi stared into his face ... the monk's face changed into that of a cobra with its hood spread. The snake extended its forked tongue. Paranjothi screamed and jerked awake.

Naganandhi was really bending over him. "My boy, why are you afraid? Is it a nightmare?"

"It is nothing," Paranjothi replied. "I was startled when you suddenly touched me."

"Let us go. We must leave the fort before sunrise, by Lord Buddha's command."

"To whom?"

"To me: it is a command to save you from danger. Don't you trust me?" Naganandhi asked affectionately. Paranjothi was silent. "Let it be.

Just obey me until daybreak. I will carry out Lord Buddha's command and leave you outside the fort. You can do as you like after that."

Paranjothi could not refuse a request made in such a tender voice. "Alright, swami."

"Will you trust me for the next forty-five minutes? I must blindfold you."

Paranjothi hesitated for a second and then said, "Alright."

Naganandhi tied a small piece of cloth around Paranjothi's eyes. "My boy, hold my hand and come with me. You must not remove the blindfold until I tell you."

Naganandhi took Paranjothi's hand and led him. Paranjothi sensed that they had crossed the monastery's entrance and were walking along the streets. He guessed from the fragrance of *paneer* flowers that they were passing the house from which they had climbed down. Their direction changed. Again, he smelt *paneer* flowers. *Are we backtracking? This wicked monk is confusing me so that I cannot find my way.* They entered a building: from the scent of oil lamps, Paranjothi guessed that it was the Royal Monastery again. Then it seemed as if they walked endlessly in circles in dark caves.

"*Adigal*, how long must we play this game of blindfolds?"

"My boy, we are almost there. Be patient with me for a little while."

Suddenly, Paranjothi sensed that they had emerged from darkness into light.

"We have reached our objective." Naganandhi untied the cloth.

Paranjothi saw the moat as a stream of molten silver under the rising sun. Sunbeams played on the treetops of the dense forest on the other side. *I have reached paradise!*

A boat floated on the moat—the young monk who had helped Paranjothi escape from his cell stood in it, oar in hand. Naganandhi and Paranjothi climbed into the boat.

"Why do we need a boat to cross the moat?" Paranjothi asked. "We could swim across."

"Look," Naganandhi pointed. A short distance away, there was a crocodile with yawning jaws.

"Aiyo!" exclaimed Paranjothi.

"There are hundreds of crocodiles in this moat. These beasts are kept in iron cages and let out in times of war. They were uncaged last night."

"Is war coming?"

"What do you think all this commotion is about?" Naganandhi asked.

Paranjothi was silent. The boat reached the opposite bank.

Sculptor Aayanar

IT WAS A lovely spring morning, about three hours after sunrise. A beautiful house stood in the middle of a forest. Apprentice sculptors worked on granite blocks scattered under the trees. The clink of their chisels merged with the birdsong and the rustling of leaves.

Suddenly, the young sculptors paused, and their faces lit up: they heard the sweet tinkling of anklets from the house. Sivagami, their master's daughter, was back to dancing. For some reason, she had been sad for three days. The apprentices exchanged meaningful looks and went back to work.

Under Emperor Mahendran Pallava, there was an artistic revival in ancient Tamil Nadu. Buddhists, Jains, Shaivas and Vaishnavas fiercely competed to carve temples out of hills and employ skilled painters and sculptors.

Sculptor Aayanar was one of the artists in great demand. Born and raised in Kanchi, Aayanar earned the title, 'Master Sculptor,' when young. From the emperor to the common man, people came to marvel at his work. Entertaining visitors took up a large chunk of his working hours. Aayanar was a Shiva devotee and most of his work reflected Shaivism. Buddhists and Jains tried to convert Aayanar to their faith. Tired of all this, Aayanar decided to leave Kanchi.

Aayanar was also a master of Bharatanatyam. Even as a child, his only daughter, Sivagami, showed signs of being a gifted dancer. Aayanar had a desire: *I will teach Sivagami Bharatanatyam and carve statues of her dance poses. I can do this only if I leave the city.*

Emperor Mahendran, used to eccentric artists, made all the arrangements for Aayanar. The sculptor built a house in an isolated clearing in a dense forest about seven miles from Kanchi. He moved there with Sivagami and his widowed sister. As Aayanar wished, Sivagami's dancing skills grew by the day, and he carved remarkable, lifelike stone statues from her poses.

Even after Aayanar moved to his remote house, artists and art lovers took the forest track to visit him—these included the emperor and the prince.

Inspired by the rocks and hills on the seashore at Kadalmallai harbour, Mahendran Pallava and Mamallan wanted to create a sculptural paradise there. Thousands of sculptors gathered from all over Tamil Nadu and began work. The emperor and the prince often visited Aayanar to discuss the work and take him to Kadalmallai. On every visit, they marvelled at Aayanar's statues of dancers and enjoyed Sivagami's small recitals. The emperor commanded that Sivagami's debut dance recital be held at his court. It was this performance which had been interrupted halfway.

Divine Art

AAYANAR'S FOREST HOME was amazing. There was a huge courtyard in the center with wide halls on four sides. An attractive pavilion stood above the courtyard, supported by sculpted pillars. Granite blocks, broken stones and half-finished sculpture filled the courtyard. The walls were covered with brilliantly coloured paintings of Lord Shiva's various dance postures. A beautiful young girl's dance poses were also shown. One hall held rows of completed, lifelike statues which showed the same girl's intoxicatingly beautiful form. These statues depicted each one of the hundred and eight *abhinaya* codified in Bharatanatyam.

Sivagami, the subject of these paintings and statues, was dancing in the flesh, her anklets jingling. Aayanar sat watching her eagerly. Suddenly, he said, "Stop." Sivagami froze, holding her pose. An almost finished statue lay in front of Aayanar. He picked up his chisel and tapped a spot near one of the statue's eyebrows. "That is enough, my child. Come and sit with me."

Aayanar wiped the pearls of perspiration on her face. "My dear, Bharata, the author of the *Natya Shastra*, would be forced to learn the finer nuances of *abhinaya* from you. How well you express feeling through your glances and the arching of your eyebrows! You were born to dance."

Sivagami said in a tired voice, "*Appa,* I hate everything. I wish I had not been born a girl."

"What! Are you angry with me, Sivagami?" Aayanar asked affectionately.

Sivagami sighed. "Why would I be angry with you, *appa*? It is the sage who wrote the *Natya Shastra* whom I am angry with. I wish I had never learned dance."

"How can you say that! Dance is a divine art and the foundation of all the other arts. Rudracharya himself agreed …"

"Who is Rudracharya? Is it the man with the long, white beard who sat by the emperor?"

"Yes, he is Emperor Mahendran's music teacher. Although he is very old, he came to your recital. He was stunned by your performance. He told me, 'Blessings on your daughter. She showed me that my treatise on music is completely wrong. I should not have written about music without studying dance.' When Rudracharya himself said …"

"*Appa*, I do not care who said what! I hate everything. What is the use of the arts?"

"Tell me, what is the use of the trees bursting into flower in spring? What is the use of the peacock's dance and the nightingale's song? The arts are the same. True happiness lies in the pursuit of art. Why are you talking like this today, my dear?"

Sivagami was silent. Two teardrops shimmered like pearls at the corners of her large black eyes.

Aayanar was thoughtful as he tenderly stroked her hair. "My dear, I must not go on treating you like a child. Girls of your age are married and have children. If your mother was alive, she would have nagged me to get you married. But I have not forgotten my duty. Of the hundred and eight *abhinaya* listed in the *Natya Shastra*, I have carved statues showing forty-eight. Once I have done the other sixty, my first priority will be to find you a good husband."

Sivagami wiped her tears. "How many times have I told you not to talk about me getting married! Would I go anywhere, leaving you alone? Am I so cruel?"

Deep in his heart, Aayanar did not want Sivagami to get married. He had raised his precious daughter from childhood, educated her and taught her dance. *I cannot live for a minute without her!* But his conscience pricked him. *One day or the other, I must give her away in marriage.* "This war is a nuisance: even the prince's marriage is delayed. The queen wants Mamallan to get married soon, but the emperor insists that the marriage can take place only after the war. I heard that Bhuvanamahadevi is very upset over this."

Sivagami was furious. "*Appa*, let anyone marry or not marry. I am not getting married."

"How is that possible for a *Shaiva* girl, Sivagami? Tongues will wag!"

"I will convert to Buddhism and become a nun. Then nobody can criticise you."

Just as she closed her mouth, they heard a voice say, "*Buddham saranam gacchami.*"

Naganandhi was at the door. Paranjothi stood behind him, gaping in wonder at the house.

Immortal Creation

AAYANAR JUMPED UP and went to the door. "Welcome, welcome, swami."

Naganandhi looked around at the statues and then at Sivagami who stood leaning against a pillar. A vulgar smile flashed across the monk's evil face. "Is that also a statue?"

Aayanar laughed. "No, swami. That is my daughter, Sivagami. My child, look: Naganandhi swami is here. Pay your respects to him."

Sivagami, who had been looking at Paranjothi from the corner of her eye, turned to Naganandhi and greeted him with folded hands.

Paranjothi stood frozen by the door, staring at the marvels around him. He had never before seen such extraordinary paintings and sculpture. He looked at Aayanar and Sivagami. *These were the people in the palanquin!*

Aayanar, talking eagerly to Naganandhi, did not notice Paranjothi. But Paranjothi was aware of Sivagami's sidelong glances. In her Bharatanatyam costume and ornaments, Sivagami's youthful beauty was dazzling. Born and raised in a village, Paranjothi was naturally shy and unused to any woman except his mother. Turning away, he stared at the statues. *Ah, these statues show her in different dance poses!* A deep respect for Sivagami was born in his heart.

As Sivagami greeted him, Naganandhi's eyes gleamed with passion. "My dear, may Lord Buddha make your wish come true. You wished to become a Buddhist nun, right?"

Sivagami was disgusted at this blessing.

Aayanar expressed his own displeasure: "Swami, the child was joking. Sivagami's debut dance recital was held in Kanchi four days back. Pity you missed it."

"I heard all about the recital and your narrow escape from a mad elephant."

"We escaped by God's grace." Aayanar paused. "Will you have your *bhiksha* here?"

"If it is not too much trouble for you ...."

"Trouble!" exclaimed Aayanar. "It is a blessing."

Aayanar and Naganandhi sat on two stones in the courtyard. Sivagami stood by the pillar, listening to them talk.

Aayanar lowered his voice and turned eagerly to the monk. "Swami, have you heard anything about the Ajanta paintings?"

Without answering Aayanar's question, Naganandhi said, "Aayanar, your statues are superior even to God's creation. The human body lives for about a hundred years and suffers gray hair, wrinkles and disease. But your extraordinary statues are untouched by sorrow: they are immortal. Their soul will shine for thousands of years."

Aayanar glowed with pride. "Swami, all the credit goes to Sivagami. If she was not such a skilled dancer, how could I carve these statues? What a pity you missed the child's dance recital! Rudracharya was stunned. My only regret is that you and Navukkarasar were absent ..."

"Yes, Navukkarasar would have enjoyed Sivagami's *abhinaya* from the emperor's *Mattavilasa Prahasana*. The fight between the drunken Buddhist monk and the Kapalika must have been especially delightful."

Emperor Mahendran, accomplished artist and patron of art, had written the satirical play, *Mattavilasa Prahasana*, which poked fun at Buddhist monks and Kapalikas.

Aayanar's face fell. "Swami, Sivagami chose that piece to highlight the beauty of laughter. She did not mean to mock Buddhist saints."

"True," Naganandhi said. "It is the height of humour. But I heard that the emperor left before the court could laugh over it. And the court was dismissed …"

"Yes, I was a little upset. Sivagami was also sad for four days. She wore her anklets again only today. Swami, what is the reason for this war? Why must men kill one another?"

"Aayanar, you should ask emperors that. Lord Buddha spread his religion of love in this cruel world, but this is the age in which Buddhist monks are laughed at in royal courts."

Sivagami's eyes blazed in anger as her father struggled to argue with the wicked monk. "*Appa*, it is true that Lord Buddha spread the message of love. But this is the age in which false monks cheat and fool people in Lord Buddha's name. That is the reason for disasters like war."

What is this quarrel about? Let me send Sivagami from here. Aayanar said tenderly, "Sivagami, why don't you go to your aunt and …"

Naganandhi cut in: "Aayanar, I admit defeat. Sivagami is brilliant. There is truth in what she says." A strange smile again flitted across his cruel face.

Determined to change the topic, Aayanar looked around. He saw Paranjothi admiring the paintings and statues on the other side. "Swami, who is this boy? Is he your disciple?"

The Lotus Pond

"HE IS NOT my disciple, Aayanar—he is going to become yours. Paranjothi, come here."

Paranjothi turned to them. Aayanar exclaimed, "Who is this boy?

He looks familiar …"

Sivagami eagerly interrupted: "*Appa*, he is the one who threw the spear at the elephant."

Aayanar was pleasantly surprised. "Is this that brave young man? How effortlessly he threw the spear! Where is he from? Where has he been all these days? When did he meet you …?" Aayanar usually showed such interest only in his art.

"I met this boy on the road while coming back from Sittanavasal …" Naganandhi began.

Aayanar lost all interest in Paranjothi. "Ah, swami! Did you see the wonderful paintings there?"

"Yes, Aayanar. I will tell you about them later. I saw this boy sleeping by the roadside. A huge cobra was about to bite him. I gave up my oath of non-violence to kill the snake and save him ... he has a letter for you from the Thiruvenkadu doctor, Sivanesan. This boy is his nephew."

Aayanar embraced Paranjothi. "Are you my dear friend's nephew, boy? Where is the letter?"

Naganandhi said, "Aayanar, his uncle gave him letters for you and Navukkarasar. He kept them in his bundle. He lost the bundle on the night he threw his spear …"

"I picked up a bundle from the spot, but the fort commander sent men for it the next day. Why do I need a letter? Isn't it enough that he is my dear friend's nephew? Sivagami, this is the brave boy who saved us from the elephant. Thank him."

Sivagami said, "I will not thank him. Why could he not just mind his own business?"

Her three listeners were shocked at Sivagami's harsh words.

Naganandhi asked Aayanar, "What is wrong with your daughter? Is she ill?"

"No, swami. She is just a little upset because her dance recital was interrupted. She thinks it is a bad omen …. Sivagami, my dear, go to your aunt and tell her that we have guests."

"Okay, *appa*."

As Sivagami walked away, she heard Naganandhi whisper, "Aayanar, watch your daughter carefully. When a young girl is tired of life, it usually means a love affair."

This Buddhist monk is evil. He has poison in his heart and on his tongue. Why must father be his friend? Sivagami entered the middle section of the house. Doves, parrots and mynahs fluttered and shrieked. A peacock swished down to her from the roof. Only the fawn was silent as it looked up at her. Aayanar kept these creatures as pets for Sivagami and as subjects for his art.

Sivagami scolded them: "Quiet! What a headache!" At once, there was a miraculous silence. "I will take only Rathi with me ... she will be quiet. Come, Rathi." Sivagami walked on, followed by the fawn. The other birds silently cocked their heads and followed Rathi with jealous eyes.

The back part of the house was the kitchen, filled with smoke and the pleasant aroma of food.

Sivagami stood in the courtyard and called, "*Athai*."

An old lady came to the kitchen door. "Yes, my child?"

"We have two guests—the Buddhist monk with a face like a tomcat is here again."

"Darling, you must not talk about your elders like this. And where are you off to with Rathi?"

"*Appa* and the monk are having an argument. I will stay at the lotus pond until it is over."

Sivagami crossed the backyard and walked into a dense forest. "Rathi, can anyone be as wicked as men? The man for whom I worked night and day to master dance—he missed my recital."

Poor Rathi followed, nibbling at the *arugam* grass. After about ten minutes, they came to a clearing in the forest with a beautiful pond, covered with lotuses and water lilies.

Sivagami stood by the pond and looked at her reflection. "Rathi, if he comes again, I will say, 'Enough of your friendship. Go away.'" Sivagami held the *abhinaya* for her words of rejection.

A thoroughbred horse stopped a short distance away in the forest. The warrior riding it dismounted noiselessly and came to the lake.

Rathi as Messenger

SIVAGAMI HEARD THE horse and sensed the rider coming towards her. Her heart told her who it was. Controlling her urge to turn, she stood as still as a statue.

Mamallan, spear in hand, came and stood by Sivagami. His reflection appeared in the water beside hers. Sivagami did not turn to him. A slight smile lit up the prince's handsome face. He too did not look at Sivagami but at her face's reflection in the water.

Sivagami turned towards the fawn on her other side. "Rathi, who is this? Ask him why he is here."

Mamallan frowned. He too turned to the fawn. "Rathi, your mistress has become the queen of Bharatanatyam in Bharat. How will she remember her old friends?"

Sivagami replied angrily, "Rathi, tell him—he is the emperor's son. How can he be friends with a poor sculptor's daughter? I am a fool to want fruit which is out of my reach."

Mamallan said lovingly, "Rathi, Sivagami Devi, master of Bharatanatyam, is not holding an *abhinaya* on the stage. Tell her to stop her dance and talk to me honestly."

Sivagami's eyes flamed like the *kovai* fruit. "Yes, Rathi, hundreds of princesses do penance for Mamallan's favour. How will he remember this poor stage dancer?" Her voice faltered and tears fell from her eyes.

Mamallan's heart melted, and his voice brimmed with affection. "Sivagami, when I am crowned, I will offer my emperorship to your beautiful, dancing feet. Don't you know my heart?"

Sivagami refused to yield. "Rathi, I have learnt about men's hypocrisy through stories and poems, but not one of them can rival the Kanchi prince."

The prince was now truly angry. "Sivagami, what is wrong with you? I came eagerly searching for you, but it seems you are sorry to see me. I will go." He took a step.

Sivagami sobbed, "Rathi, let him go if he wants, but tell him not to blame me for it."

Mamallan stopped. "How is it my fault? Let her explain before throwing a tantrum."

Sivagami turned to him with flashing eyes. "How you praised my dance! How you flattered me! After all that, why didn't you come for my dance recital?"

Mamallan burst out laughing. "Who said I was not at your recital? I sat in the upper gallery with my mother. I was afraid that if I sat openly in the hall, you might be distracted. All this fuss was about that!"

Sivagami's face glowed with happiness. "Why didn't you tell me this earlier?"

"You did not give me a chance to tell you. There is much more to say. Come, let us sit on your throne."

Looking at a log under a tree, Mamallan took Sivagami's hand to help her up. But Sivagami pulled away her hand and leaped to the bank like a deer. Rathi looked at the two of them seated on the log. Deciding that they no longer needed her services as a messenger, the fawn began crunching the green grass on the shore.

The Wedding

SIVAGAMI SAT WITH her face turned away.

Mamallan asked, "What are you angry about now? I will think you do not love me."

Sivagami turned to him. "If you loved me, would you have forgotten me for three days?"

"I have been longing to see you, but important matters of state came up. Do you know why your recital was stopped halfway? After decades, the Pallava kingdom is going to war …"

Sivagami interrupted him: "Yes, I heard. Are you upset?"

"Upset? Never! Anyone born into the Pallava dynasty will only be excited. There has been no war since the days of my grandfather, King Simhavishnu. Our soldiers' weapons have rusted. Now the time has come to use them. I do not fear the flash of thousands of spears and swords on the battlefield—but I fear the spears and swords which flash from your eyes."

Sivagami murmured, "All men are the same. They try to hide the truth with sweet talk."

Mamallan heard her. "You keep piling up my faults. What truth am I trying to hide?"

Anger warred with shyness on Sivagami's face. "The war has delayed the wedding. I asked whether you were upset about that."

Mamallan was surprised. "The wedding has been delayed? Whose wedding?"

"Oh, you do not know, do you? Shall I tell you? The Emperor of Emperors, Mahendravarman Pallava of Kanchi, has a famous son, Mamallan. Messengers were to be sent to Madurai, Vanji and the north to discuss marriage alliances. An evil king chose this time to invade the Pallava kingdom and made it necessary to postpone the wedding. All this is news to you, right?"

Mamallan laughed heartily. "Is this why you are giving me a hard time? I was afraid that Aayanar had arranged your wedding. Nothing like that has happened, I hope."

Sivagami looked mischievously at him. "Why not? My father often talks about my marriage. He plans to choose one of his clever apprentices as my husband."

"Good. Did your father really say that? I must thank him."

Sivagami was serious. "I said, 'I do not want to get married. I would rather become a Buddhist nun.'"

"What harm have Lord Shiva and Vishnu done to you?"

"I have nothing against Shiva and Vishnu. I am only against marriage. I will become a Buddhist nun and go on a pilgrimage."

Mamallan was stern. "Can you disobey your father? You must marry the cleverest of his apprentices."

Sivagami's eyes filled with tears. "Why are you so eager to palm me off on some foolish boy? I am not standing in the way of you marrying some princess."

Happy mischief danced on the prince's face. "Who are you calling a foolish boy? How many times has your father said, 'The prince has the greatest gift for sculpture?' If you must marry the cleverest of Aayanar's apprentices, you must marry me. Must I not thank your father for this?"

Sivagami jumped up and burst into sobs. "Lord, why do you tease me with empty promises?"

Mamallan pulled her back to his side. "Sivagami, don't you know me yet …?"

Sivagami interrupted him: "These are tears of joy, lord, not sorrow."

I Swear Upon My Spear

MAMALLAN WIPED SIVAGAMI'S tears with his stole. His eyes devoured her face. "Do you remember, Sivagami? When the emperor and I visited your house those days, you were never shy—you ran to me and dragged me with you. We played while our fathers chatted. I asked you to teach me Bharatanatyam and you laughed at my clumsy efforts. I was charmed by your sparkling teeth. We played catch. Sometimes, you stood still among Aayanar's statues. I passed by, pretending not to see you and turned back to catch you when you laughed. It seems just a happy dream now … when I was sixteen, my father took me on a three-year journey across the land."

"Those three years were three ages to me."

"When I came back, you had changed. You looked like a divine nymph. You did not come running to welcome me; you did not chat. You hid behind a pillar. You turned away when I looked at you and gave me sidelong glances when I turned away. Sometimes, I saw your eyes fill with tears. I heard you sigh for no reason. To my surprise, I sometimes caught myself sighing!"

Sivagami burst out laughing.

Mamallan continued, "I had changed too. Day and night, even when I was busy with state affairs, my heart was filled with thoughts of you. We met by this lily pond. You quarrelled with me for not coming to see you for three years. You asked me to swear that I had not forgotten you. I knew the pain of not being able to forget you even for a second. Still, to please you, I promised. This is the first time we are meeting here after that. I hoped to find you here—and here you are!"

"But you have not answered my question about the messengers sent to Madurai and Vanji."

Mamallan chuckled. “It is my mother’s work: every mother wants to see her son married. I was waiting for a chance to tell the emperor what is in my heart. The war has made it pointless.”

Sivagami was troubled. “Lord, will you really go to war?”

“I have been arguing with my father about this for the past three days. The Pallava soil has been invaded by the Chalukyas—mustn’t I destroy them and teach them a lesson?”

“Lord, the Pallava army and its commanders will do that. Must you go?”

“And what am I supposed to do while the Pallava army fights the Chalukyas? Eat and drink and play draughts with the women in the palace? Will I be worthy of your love?”

“Lord, go defeat the enemy and come back wearing the garland of victory. But swear an oath to me on your spear: you will not forget me even on the battlefield.”

Mamallan smiled. “Is that all? Here …” He raised the spear but suddenly hesitated. “This spear is not mine. I am not sure whether I can swear an oath on someone else’s weapon.”

“Whose spear is it?”

“It belongs to the brave young man who saved you and your father. I am keeping it so that I can give it to him personally. We searched for him for three days but could not find him.”

“Lord, what will you give me if I take you to him?”

“You know where he is? Tell me at once. I have given myself to you. What more do you want?”

“That young man is now in our house.”

Mamallan jumped up in surprise. “What! How did he get there?”

“Haven’t I told you about the Buddhist monk who comes here often and urges us to go north with him? That Naganandhi brought him here.”

“Ahah, what the emperor said was right. Listen …”

They heard drums and conches and the galloping of horses in the distance.

“It is the emperor. I will go and join him. You will go home quickly, won’t you?”

“I will take a shortcut. Lord, will you come here again before you go to war?”

"I promise on the spears which blaze from your dark eyes: I will come."

Mamallan kept looking back as he walked quickly to his horse. Sivagami gazed after him with a radiant face until the horse disappeared into the forest. She then hurried home with a happy new spring to her steps. Rathi, forgotten by her mistress, skipped after her.

The Pearl Garland

AT THE SOUND of the drums, Aayanar hurried to the door and waited eagerly for the emperor.

Emperor Mahendran was of extraordinary physical build. His majestic face radiated the courage, wisdom and artistry inherited from generations of kings. He wore an exquisitely beautiful crown, earrings, armbands and warrior's anklets, crafted by Kanchi's skilled goldsmiths. Rows of gem-studded gold garlands adorned his broad chest. The weavers of Kanchi proudly declared that when the emperor wore their famous cloth of gold, the silk shone brighter.

Mahendran was a master of Tamil, Sanskrit and Prakrit. Poets from Taxila to Kanyakumari came to his court for his patronage. He was also an accomplished artist himself. A highly skilled sculptor, painter, musician and playwright, he had earned many titles in these arts. He was also known for his virtue. Even after converting to Shaivism, he treated all religions fairly.

Mahendran dismounted from his horse. "Aayanar, did you have a comfortable journey that night? How is Sivagami?"

Aayanar folded his hands in respect. "We had a comfortable journey. The child was not well for three days …"

The emperor was worried: "Is that so? How is she now?"

"She is better today," Aayanar replied.

The emperor sat on a beautiful granite throne carved specially for him by Aayanar. At a signal from Aayanar, Sivagami greeted Mahendran.

Aayanar said, "Lord, the child is sad because her dance recital was interrupted. You must bless and encourage her."

"Aayanar, dance itself took an avatar as your daughter and performed for us. How I regret having to leave in the middle of the recital! But it was urgent."

Aayanar was furious: "I heard, lord. Foreigners have invaded our land. How dare they!"

"They will be punished. Enemies have not invaded the Pallava kingdom for years. My father sent me to Sri Lanka to gain first-hand knowledge of war. But Narasimhan is lucky—he will fight here itself. Pulikesi, the king of Vatapi, is marching here with a huge army. We must gather our forces and go to war. I am angry about the invasion, but I am angrier that it interrupted Sivagami's recital. The Chalukyas must be punished for this."

Aayanar flushed with pride and looked affectionately at Sivagami, standing with bowed head.

The emperor took a beautiful, two-stranded pearl garland from a carpetbag. "All my plans for the day of the recital were upset. I will honour Sivagami here instead."

"Lord, what does the place matter? Sivagami, you are lucky—you are being honoured by the most virtuous and accomplished artist in Bharat!"

Sivagami respectfully held out her hands. Just as Mahendran put the pearl garland in her palms, it slipped to the ground. Sivagami was startled: another bad omen! Aayanar's face fell. Even the steadfast Mahendran faltered. The very next second, Mamallan picked up the garland and put it in Sivagami's hands. She took it eagerly, touched it reverentially to her eyes and wore it around her neck. Her face glowed with pleasure at receiving the pearls from the prince.

The Buddha Statue

THE EMPEROR WATCHED discreetly and then said, "Aayanar, your daughter will bring glory to the Pallava kingdom. Nothing must stand in the way of her dance."

"My king, with you and the prince to encourage her, why should I worry?"

"Due to the war, we may not be able to visit you for some time, but your work must not be affected." He paused. "Sivagami is no ordinary woman. She was not born to get married and waste her life in small pleasures. Only one woman in a million is gifted with such understanding of dance. It will be best if Sivagami considers herself a nun: she should dedicate herself completely to dance." Mahendran's motive was unclear.

Aayanar was frank: "Lord, you have said what is in my heart. There are millions who can marry and raise children, but only a few can pass on this extraordinary, divine art to posterity." He turned to Sivagami. "Did you hear the emperor's golden words, my child?"

Sivagami, who could express countless emotions with her face and eyes and a curl of her lips, now controlled herself with great effort. Her face was as blank as a stone statue.

But Mamallan flushed and his lips quivered. He turned aside and moved away, as if studying some paintings and statues.

The emperor rose from his throne. "Aayanar, I have many urgent matters to attend to, but I forget everything when I come here. I must see your new statues and leave quickly."

He walked ahead, followed by Aayanar and Sivagami. He identified the new statues and their various hand gestures. He stopped before the last statue. "Aayanar, even you have never before carved a statue as lifelike as this one. The face and the curves of the body beautifully express the heartache caused by a lover's absence. The eyes, the eyelids—even the eyebrows, speak to us. You completed this statue after Sivagami's dance recital, right?"

"Yes, lord. I finished it only this morning. Sivagami danced for me and held this *abhinaya*."

Mahendran smiled at Sivagami. "Aayanar, Sage Bharata lists only seven types of *abhinaya* that the eyebrows can express. If he sees Sivagami dance, he will change that to seven hundred."

As the emperor casually walked on, he saw a magnificent Buddha statue some distance away. He stopped. "Ah, the compassionate Buddha tried to end war on earth. Only the good Emperor Ashoka Maurya took his advice and became the symbol of nonviolence."

The emperor went to the door, followed by the others. Mahendran turned back at the threshold. "Aayanar, I do not know when I will return, but this I must say: many dynasties have come and gone. Hastinapura, Pataliputra, Ujjain—all vanished without a trace. The Pallava dynasty may also die, but your sculpture will live as long as divine Tamil and Tamil Nadu endure."

Aayanar's voice shook with emotion. "Lord, thousands of sculptors like me will be born and will die. But as long as art lives, your name, and that of the prince, will be immortal."

How true his words proved to be! The great Tamil sculptors who created Mamallapuram have been forgotten. But the names, Mahendran Pallava and Mamallan Pallava, remain immortal.

The emperor and the prince mounted their horses.

Mahendran said, "Aayanar, before I leave for the north, we must finalise the work to be done in Mamallapuram. Come to Kanchi tomorrow."

"I will be there, lord," Aayanar said.

Aayanar and Sivagami watched the departing horses. Mamallan said goodbye to Sivagami with his eyes. After riding a short distance, he turned back and saw Sivagami looking after him. He smiled and raised his spear before slapping his horse and galloping away. Sivagami's eyes lit up with joy at the prince's gesture. She stared at the horses until they disappeared into the forest.

Sivagami remembered Paranjothi. *Where is that young man?* Just as she was about to question her father, she saw Aayanar walk towards the Buddha statue. To her surprise and fright, Naganandhi and Paranjothi suddenly stood up from behind the statue.

The Secret of Ajanta

AAYANAR WAS ANNOYED with Naganandhi for criticizing his beloved daughter. So, when Sivagami left the hall, he had turned away from him to Paranjothi. "My boy, how can I help you?"

"Sir, I came to Kanchi to study under Navukkarasar and to learn sculpture."

"My boy, I am obliged to do anything for my friend. Navukkarasar is not in Kanchi now: he is on a pilgrimage. Never mind, I will take you to his *matham*. I will also present you to the emperor. He will be delighted to meet the brave man who saved us ..."

"If you love this young man, do not do that," Naganandhi warned. "He will be sentenced to death for escaping from the emperor's prison."

"Shiva! What do you mean? Was this boy in prison? When? Why?"

"After saving you, he lost his way. The city guards, suspecting him of being a spy, put him in prison. He climbed out through the thatch that night ..."

Aayanar looked at Paranjothi in amazement. "Ah, it looks like my friend's nephew is no ordinary boy! Never mind, swami. Once the emperor knows that he saved us, he will pardon him."

"The emperor will pardon him for your sake, but he will be drafted into the army at once. Don't you know that army recruitment is going on everywhere in the Pallava kingdom?" Naganandhi paused. "He is his mother's only child. If anything happens to him, the poor woman will curse you. Not only that: a girl will be forced to remain a virgin all her life."

Aayanar stared at Paranjothi. *Has Sivagami fallen in love with this boy? Is that why she was in a strange mood for the past three days? In a way, it is good. If Sivagami must get married, I can give her to my dear friend's nephew and make him my apprentice.*

Naganandhi guessed what was running in Aayanar's mind. "No, Aayanar, you are wrong—his uncle's daughter waits for him in Thiruvenkadu."

Aayanar asked Paranjothi, "Is that right, my boy? Are you to marry my friend's daughter?"

"Yes, sir," Paranjothi said shyly.

The monk went on, "And it is not a good idea to send him to Navukkarasar's *matham*. Kanchi Fort is preparing for a siege. The emperor has sent Navukkarasar on a pilgrimage to Chola Nadu."

Aayanar said, "My boy, what confusion! What do you want to do?"

Paranjothi replied, "Sir, I want to become a scholar. And I do not want to go back without learning sculpture. Please make me your apprentice."

Aayanar was delighted with his humility. "Alright. Stay here and learn sculpture from me."

"What about the *guru dakshina*?" Naganandhi asked. "It must be paid in advance."

Aayanar laughed.

"I am not joking. Paranjothi's *guru daskhina* is the secret of Ajanta's paintings," the monk said.

Aayanar's face flushed with excitement. He was a new man. "Swami, what is the connection between this boy and Ajanta's secret? What can he do?"

"The secret has reached the Buddhist *sangha* at the Nagarjuna Hills. Someone must go and bring it here: your new apprentice is the best person for this."

"Nagarjuna Hills? That is on the bank of the Krishna. There will be many dangers on the way."

"Paranjothi is brave enough to face them. You saw how he threw his spear at the elephant."

"But it is a long distance away. Can he walk there and back?"

"He must have a good horse. If he rides, he can accomplish his task and be back in a month."

Aayanar looked eagerly at Paranjothi. "My boy, can you do this? Will you go?"

Paranjothi was wide-eyed. "I am ready to obey you, but I have no idea where to go and why!"

Naganandhi said, "Listen, my boy. A long way to the north, beyond the Godavari River, lies the Ajanta Hill. Ages ago, the hill was carved into Buddhist shrines with extraordinary paintings of Buddha's avatars and miracles. These five-hundred-year-old paintings are as bright as if newly painted. The descendants of those master artists still live there, painting new scenes. They know the secret of mixing colours which do not fade even after thousands of years. For a long time, Aayanar has been asking me to find this secret formula for him. I have tried. I know one of the painters in the Ajanta caves. I hear that he is now in the Buddhist *sangha* at the Nagarjuna Hills. If you go there, you can get the secret formula from him."

Aayanar said, "Young man, if you bring me the secret formula, you will fulfill one of my heart's deepest desires. But I will not force you …"

Paranjothi preferred action to study. He was excited about riding a thoroughbred horse and proud of being chosen for an important assignment. "Sir, my uncle asked me to obey you. If you order me, I will go."

"There is no time to waste, Aayanar," Naganandhi said. "It will be best if he comes back before the Vatapi army's invasion. How can we arrange the horse?"

"That is easy: I will ask the emperor for a horse. Emperor Mahendran is as eager as I am to find the secret formula behind the Ajanta paintings."

"Ask the emperor for a signet ring as a travel pass. Paranjothi may need it in these times of war." Naganandhi added, "Do not mention my name. You know the emperor's views on Buddhism."

They heard drums and conches.

"Swami, we are in luck—it is Emperor Mahendran himself!"

A smile flashed across Naganandhi's bitter face. "Aayanar, the emperor's arrival is a good omen. But, if he sees Paranjothi and me now, all our plans will be ruined. We will surrender ourselves to Lord Buddha!" The monk pulled Paranjothi and disappeared behind the Buddha statue.

Aayanar hesitated: "But what if he knows ..." The close sound of horses' hooves gave him no time to argue. "Be careful, swami," he said and hurried to the door.

Now, Sivagami was startled to see Naganandhi and Paranjothi coming from behind the Buddha.

Aayanar was agitated: "Swami, what a narrow escape!"

"Anyone who surrenders to Lord Buddha is not in danger," the monk replied. "But you forgot the most important thing: the horse."

"I did not forget, swami. I was shaken up ... my tongue could not talk about horses."

"Yes, even I was shocked for a second," Naganandhi said. "Aayanar, you must tell Sivagami our plans. She is looking at us as if we are ghosts."

The Siddha Hills Paintings

SIVAGAMI LOOKED AT the monk with suspicion and disgust before turning to her father. "*Appa*, why were they hiding?"

"My child, Naganandhi has taken a vow to never meet a member of the royal family. Since this young man came with him …"

"*Appa*, how happy the emperor and the prince would have been to meet him! Did you see the spear in Mamallan's hand? It belongs to this young man."

Naganandhi interrupted, "What is so strange about that, Sivagami? The Pallava dynasty now needs weapons. Aren't they collecting every broken spear, sword and lance in the country?"

Sivagami looked at him fiercely. "*Appa*, Mamallan admires courage. He may have wanted to return the spear to this young man. You must take him to the emperor's camp at once."

Aayanar stammered, "My child, it is what I wanted to do. I will take him to the emperor."

Ashamed at being caught hiding, and shy before Sivagami, Paranjothi had stayed silent. Sivagami's words now freed his spirit and tongue. "Sir, I too thought that the prince had my spear. Please get it for me. A good weapon is essential on a long voyage, right?"

"What is the hurry over weapons?" Naganandhi objected. "I can get you any number of spears and lances. What is important is the horse and the signet ring: you slipped up there, Aayanar."

"Leave that to me," Aayanar said. "The emperor has ordered me to meet him in Mamallapuram tomorrow. I will get them from him. Take care of the other travel arrangements."

"*Appa,* is this *anna* going on a long voyage? Where is he going? Why?"

Aayanar's voice shook with excitement. "I am sending him on a very important matter, my child. My dream of the past nine years will soon come true with this good Buddhist monk's help."

"What dream is this?" Sivagami asked. "I am confused."

"Haven't I often told you about the wonderful paintings in the Ajanta caves? I am sending this boy to bring me the secret formula of mixing colours so that the paintings remain fresh even after five hundred years."

"Colours that do not fade after five hundred years? I do not believe this, *appa*." The look Sivagami gave Naganandhi openly expressed her doubts and suspicions.

Aayanar said, "I too was skeptical at first. I believed it only after seeing it with my own eyes."

Sivagami and Naganandhi exclaimed together in surprise: "You saw it with your own eyes? When?" "You went to Ajanta? Why didn't you tell me?"

"I have not been to Ajanta, but I have seen the paintings at the Siddha Hills. Swami, you have been to the Siddha Hills. What did you see there?"

"Ah, I understand. At the cave entrance, there are two apsaras showing *abhinaya* from the *Natya Shastra*. I wondered, *Who is the master painter who has drawn such exquisite forms?* Now I know—only Aayanar could have drawn such great, lifelike figures."

"Yes, swami, I am the one who drew those figures. And did you notice anything else?"

"The top half of the apsaras glowed as if freshly painted; the colours of the lower half were dim."

Aayanar then told them the story of those paintings.

Twelve years ago, when Emperor Mahendran was still a Jain, Aayanar had accompanied him on a visit to the famous Jain temple in the Siddha Hills. They marvelled at the lovely paintings on the cave walls. The artist was a monk who lived there at that time. Mahendran and Aayanar did not believe his claim that those paintings would live for a thousand years. The Jain monk challenged them. Let Aayanar paint two apsaras at the cave entrance; let him paint the upper part of the figures with the colours mixed by the monk, and the lower part with Aayanar's own paint mix. They would examine the paintings after three years: if the monk's claim was proven to be true, Aayanar must admit defeat and become a Jain. If Aayanar converted to Jainism, the monk would teach him the secret formula for this paint.

Aayanar accepted the challenge and painted the two parts of the apsaras as specified. After three years, the upper half of the paintings glowed in fresh colours while the lower half had faded. The amazed

Aayanar was ready to convert to Jainism and learn the secret formula, but the Jain monk was missing. Furious at the emperor's conversion to Shaivism, he had left the Pallava kingdom. Aayanar's eagerness to learn the secret formula grew over the years.

Naganandhi said, "Aayanar, your longing will be satisfied soon: just get the horse and permit for Paranjothi's travel."

Sivagami sympathised with her father. At the same time, she suspected Naganandhi of weaving some deceitful plot. *I must warn Paranjothi.*

Shatrughan

THE EMPEROR GALLOPED from Aayanar's house and joined his escort. He looked meaningfully at a man, who came up to him at once. "Shatrughan, do you know sculpture?"

Shatrughan's face was expressionless. "No, my lord."

"It is time you learnt this art. This is the best place for it. Just watch Aayanar's apprentices. You must also watch any stranger who comes here to study. There is no need for him to see you."

Shatrughan's eyebrows rose slightly. "As you wish, my lord. I will start at once."

"Good. Report to me at once if you learn anything new about sculpture." Saying this, Mahendran nudged his horse into a gallop along the forest trail. Knowing that this was a sign of his father being in deep thought, Mamallan urged his own horse to go faster. Their escort fell behind them.

The prince had heard bits of the emperor's conversation with Shatrughan. *Father has assigned the Pallava kingdom's best spy to Aayanar's school. I must ask him about this.*

The forest track met the highway which led from Kanchipuram to Mamallapuram. A wide canal flowed along one side. A line of barges sailed to Kanchi, loaded with sacks of rice. The scene was a feast for the eyes: the highway edged with thick trees, the clear canal shadowed by branches, the distant green plains. The sweet notes of the flute played by one of the boatmen drifted on the breeze. As if warning that this peace was an illusion which would soon be shattered, a boat filled with spears, lances, swords, daggers and shields came down the canal.

The emperor said bitterly, "Ah, preparations for war have begun in the Pallava kingdom!" He turned to his son. "Narasimhan, there is something you want to ask me."

"How did you know, *appa*?"

"By your face: didn't we just discuss *abhinaya* and facial expression?"

"Why have you sent Shatrughan to Aayanar's house?"

"Why does one send a spy? To spy, of course. One must be careful in times of war. A spy may hide under a monk's saffron robes; conspiracies may be hatched in sculpture ..."

Mamallan was shocked: "What? Aayanar is conspiring against you? I cannot believe it!"

"That good man would give his life for us. Unknown to him, there may be spies in his house."

The prince calmed down. "How did you know? I saw only the paintings and sculpture."

"Narasimhan, those involved in affairs of state must always have their ears and eyes open. What were your eyes doing while we were at Aayanar's house?" The emperor looked at the prince.

Recalling that his eyes had been busy talking secrets with Sivagami, the prince blushed in embarrassment. The boatman's sweet music followed him from a distance.

The Royal Swan

MAHENDRAN IGNORED HIS son's embarrassment. "Didn't Aayanar's behavior make you suspicious? Didn't you notice him often looking anxiously at the Buddha statue? Didn't you see him hesitate and fumble when we went near it?"

Mamallan's eyes widened in surprise. "Maybe someone was hiding behind the statue!"

"Yes, there were two men there—the Buddhist monk and the young man we saw outside the Royal Monastery that night. They did not do a very good job of hiding themselves."

"That is why you spent so much time at Aayanar's house!" Mamallan paused. "*Appa*, I wanted to give this spear to that young man."

"He no longer needs that spear. Paranjothi is going to learn sculpture from Aayanar."

"Paranjothi … what a unique name! I had so many dreams about that brave young man. I wanted to make him my dearest friend. But how can I be friends with an enemy spy!"

"The boy is innocent. I think that false monk is using him for some evil purpose. I suspect the monk of being Vatapi's spymaster."

"*Appa*, you were suspicious about the monk that night. Why didn't you arrest him then?"

"If I had arrested him that night, I would not have found a serious gap in our security." He went on. "We saw the monk and the boy that night. The next morning, they were not in the monastery. But they had not left the fort through any of the entrances. So, I suspected there was a hidden entrance to the fort. Now I know where it is."

"Was that why you were galloping? Where is this secret entrance, *appa*?"

"Behind Buddha's statue in the Royal Monastery, Narasimhan." He paused. "Look, the Royal Swan."

Mamallan saw three barges sailing down the canal from Kanchipuram. The one in the center was a shell-white, swan-shaped boat. A white, silk canopy stood over the golden throne in its bow. The Pallavas' nandi flag fluttered majestically above. The Royal Swan and the barge ahead of it were empty; the third boat was occupied.

"Ah, the council of ministers is here. Did you ask them to come, *appa*?"

"The council is meeting at the port. I have a few things to tell you. I also need a promise from you."

Mamallan was stunned. *I just made a promise to the love of my life, Sivagami. And now, my father, whom I love and respect above everyone, is asking for another promise!*

The Promise

THE BARGES REACHED them. There were shouts of "Long live the Emperor of Emperors, Mahendran Pallava!" and "Long live the crown prince, Mamallan!" from the boats and the shore. Conches and trumpets blared and drumbeats shook the earth.

The emperor's escort got into the first barge. Mahendran and Mamallan sat on the golden throne in the Royal Swan. The three boats sailed towards the port.

When the blare of music died, the emperor said, "Narasimhan, kings must be careful not to make promises without knowing the details."

The prince's voice shook: "*Appa*, you only have to command me: have I ever disobeyed you?"

Mahendran controlled his own emotions. "Lion of the Pallavas, I know that you will obey my command, however bitter it may be, but this matter is crucial. There are some things you must know. On the day after tomorrow, I go north to the battlefield. I do not know when I will return ..."

"*Appa*," Mamallan said passionately. "Are you leaving me here?"

"Narasimhan, let me finish. I have ruled this ancient Pallava kingdom for twenty-five years. We have had no major wars in my time or in my father's. This is my first war. I will ask the council of ministers to let me fight it my own way. You, too, must agree. Victory or defeat: let it be on my head. You need not have any part in it ..."

"*Appa*, there is no defeat—we either win or die bravely. And how can I have no part in it?"

"Spoken like a man of the brave Pallava clan, Narasimhan! But there is no need for both of us to die at the same time. Mustn't one of us stay alive to take revenge for the other's death?"

"*Appa*, it is clear that there is bad news from the battlefield. That is why you are talking like this."

"Yes, my boy, there is bad news. The Kangapadi army has surrendered to Pulikesi. The Chalukyas are advancing rapidly towards the North Pennai."

"What else can we expect from that coward, Dhurvineedhan! So what? Isn't our northern force waiting at the North Pennai? Isn't my uncle coming with his army from Vengi?"

"Pulikesi's brother, Vishnuvardhanan, is marching on Vengi with a large force."

"Ah, is the Chalukyan army so large? Why is it that we alone are …" the prince stopped.

"It is my fault," Mahendran said. "I did not expect war in my lifetime. Instead of preparing for war, I wasted my time on dance, painting and sculpture."

"So what, *appa*? Didn't Aayanar say that countless emperors have come and gone and been forgotten? But your name will live on."

"If we lose this war, Mamallapuram will just be a symbol of our disgrace."

"The world laughs only at those who run away from the battlefield. When we are ready to die, why should we fear disgrace?"

"A brave death is our last recourse. We must first try to destroy our enemy. That will not be easy—the king of Vatapi is skilled in war strategy. But we will finally win. For that, I need your cooperation. Whether you like it or not, you must do as I say …"

Mamallan's voice shook with emotion: "*Appa*, you are not just my beloved father; you are also the king who owns my body, mind and spirit; you are the supreme commander of the Pallava forces. You are entitled to command me—however bitter it may be, I will obey."

The harbour was visible at a distance. The majestic nandi flag fluttered from the mastheads of the ships and hid the sky. Mamallapuram's hillocks spread a little to the south.

The emperor turned to Mamallan. "My son, I am confident that I will return from the war to finish the work we have begun. But, if I do not return, you must complete it." He paused. "You must take revenge: you must erase the Pallava kingdom's disgrace."

"That is my duty. I do not need to promise to do my duty."

"My son, to take revenge, you must guard your life. The Pallava dynasty has thrived for five hundred years. Its survival is now in your hands. This is the promise I want from you: you must remain in Kanchi Fort until I return or until you are sure that I will never return. Promise me this." Mahendran held out his right hand.

Mamallan took his hand. "As you wish, *appa*. I will not leave Kanchi Fort until you return."

A sudden roar came from the distant ocean. Emotions crashed like waves in the prince's heart.

The Ocean's Child

THOUSANDS OF YEARS ago, Kanchipuram's royal dynasty had ended without heirs. The elders lamented, 'A kingdom without a king will be ruined. Its subjects will suffer.'

A great saint comforted the people with a prophecy. "Do not fear. I saw this in my dream: the ocean will give Kanchipuram a king."

From that day, a watch was kept on the seashore.

One day, an unknown ship sailed near the coast. There was a sudden storm, and the ship was tossed about. Its mastheads shattered and it overturned. The passengers' cries mingled with the sea's roar.

The wind calmed as soon as the ship sank. The men watching helplessly from the shore quickly launched boats to rescue anyone who might have miraculously survived the shipwreck. A boatman saw a speck of gold floating on the blue waves. *Is it the sun? No, it is a child!* The baby was tied to a plank with a cloth of gold. When the gentle spray of the waves fell on its radiant face, the child laughed.

The boatman picked up the child, untied it and embraced it. He made a bed for the child from the *thondai* creepers he had on board to tie his loads and sprinkled tender buds on top.

The saint who had made the prophecy said, "This is the king I saw in my dream. His dynasty will rule Kanchi for a thousand years." The crowd cheered. The saint named the child Ilanthiraiyan and blessed him. "As he lay on a bed of *thondai* creepers, he will also be known as Thondaiman. The kingdom of Kanchipuram will be called Thondaimandalam after him."

A Tamil poet called the child Pallavarayan as he lay on a bed of *pallavam* or tender buds. Later poets wrote that the child was the descendent of a Chola prince who was shipwrecked on his way home from the island of Mani Pallavam. Other poets wrote that the Pallavas were descendants of Dronacharya's son, Ashwatthama. Whatever be their lineage, one truth stood out: the Pallavas' deep love for the sea was in their very blood. Their ancient nandi flag flew majestically over many islands in the southern seas and ocean trade flourished under them.

Kadalmallai was the greatest of the many harbours which stood along the southern coast. The sea curved from the north to the south, making Kadalmallai almost an island. It was a natural harbour near Kanchipuram, where hundreds of ships stopped to load and unload cargo. The port was filled with warehouses and toll booths and was home to boatmen and fishermen. Mahendran Pallava moved government officials and sculptors there. He built a beautiful royal palace and named the port Mamallapuram after his beloved son.

The Stone Temples

FIVE HILLOCKS STOOD on the southern side of the port. Hundreds of sculptors were carving temples out of them. Mahendran and Mamallan stood by a majestic stone elephant.

Seven years ago, the emperor and his son had stood on this very same spot, looking at the bare hillocks and rocks.

Mamallan exclaimed, "*Appa*, doesn't the shadow of that rock look like an elephant?"

The emperor was thoughtful. "My child, you do not realise the significance of your words ..."

The sixteen-year-old prince went on, "Look: doesn't the shadow of that hill look like a temple?"

"Yes, Narasimhan, it does. We will carve temples out of these hillocks. And we will carve these rocks into elephants and lions and bulls. Even after thousands of years, men will marvel at our work."

Soon the silence was broken by the clink of chisels, as sculptors began work on the stone.

Now the emperor and the prince stood among rocks transformed into elephants, lions and bulls.

Mahendran said, "In many ways, I am glad that war is coming. My only fear is that it may stop this work and I may not live to see it finished. Have you heard about the annual festival held by Emperor Harshavardhan at Kannauj?"

"He has built temples to Shiva, Suryanarayana and Buddha. People come and pay homage to all three gods at the annual festival."

"Harsha's empire is much larger than ours. If my dream comes true, not only Harsha, but no other king will be as famous as the Pallavas. Harsha's temples are made of brick and wood: they will disappear in a hundred years. But these stone temples will be immortal ..."

"Which deities will you enshrine in these five temples, *appa*?"

"My son, I will dedicate four temples to Tamil Nadu's four faiths: one to Shiva and Parvathi, one to Vishnu and Lakshmi, one to Buddha and one to Mahavira." He went on, "Narasimhan, I converted to Shaivism to bring about religious harmony. Shaivism is the only religion which accepts other religions as its equal. I was waiting for the Jains' anger to cool—but the monks rushed to spoil everything."

"What have they done?"

"The Jain monks are the cause of this war. They have turned our allies into our enemies. Do you know who crowned Dhurvineedhan's father? It was your grandfather, King Simhavishnu. Now, Dhurvineedhan has joined forces with his longtime enemy, the Chalukyas. Pujyapadhar, Dhurvineedhan's guru, is marching with Pulikesi's army. If monks, who have renounced the world and violence, march with an army, think how much they hate me!"

"Why do we care, *appa*? Let all the Jain and Buddhist monks join our enemies. By the grace of Lord Shiva and Vishnu, we will win."

The emperor said sadly, "I am not worried about victory or defeat. I regret that my plans have been upset."

"And to whom do you plan to dedicate the fifth temple, *appa*?"

"I believe a new faith has taken root abroad. The great soul who founded it is called Jesus Christ. Once I know more details about this faith, the god of that religion will stand in the fifth temple. But now, it looks like all this will remain just a dream!"

"Why should the war stop this work?"

"I hope it does not. That is why I asked Aayanar to come here. The work goes slowly because he lives in the forest. I will ask him to stay here and supervise the work … ah, here he is!"

Mamallan turned back expectantly and was not disappointed. Aayanar looked out from one side of the palanquin … on the other, Sivagami's face shone like the full moon in broad daylight.

A Horse

AAYANAR AND SIVAGAMI paid their respects to the emperor who welcomed the sculptor and blessed his daughter: "May good fortune be yours. May Bharatanatyam achieve greatness through you."

Mahendran turned to Aayanar. "There will be increased movement of armies on the roads until this war ends. So it will be best if you move here …"

The unfinished statues in his forest home flashed before Aayanar's eyes. "My king …"

Mahendran was stern. "Enough! You will move here tomorrow. This is my wish."

Aayanar trembled. "As you wish, my king."

"Aayanar, these temples must be completed as soon as possible. You will not take up any other work. I have ordered the chancellor to give you funds and arranged for you to have all the men and supplies you need. If anything interrupts your work, you can speak to the prince." Mahendran paused. "I will be leading the army north tomorrow. Until I return, the prince will deal with all affairs of the kingdom. From tomorrow, Mamallan will be the emperor."

Sivagami was overjoyed. *The emperor is leaving. The prince is not going to war—we can meet easily.* She smiled and dreamt of meeting Mamallan by the lotus pond. She looked at the prince out of the corner of her eye. Mamallan did not turn towards her at all. *Aiyo! Why is he angry? Doesn't he like me being here? Yesterday, his eyes devoured me and spoke secrets. Why doesn't he look at me now?* Her eyes filled with tears, and she quickly moved behind a rock.

Mamallan's heart overflowed with love for Sivagami. When he saw her in the palanquin, he wanted to run, take her hand and help her down. Unable to do this, he was angry with everything and everyone. *Why am I a prince? Why can't I be a poor sculptor's son?* His anger grew when Sivagami smiled. *Doesn't she realise that it is a shame to stay away from the battlefield? As if I can see her often! I have promised my father that I will not leave Kanchi Fort.*

Noticing Aayanar looking up at him and the prince in turn, the emperor asked, "Aayanar, is there something you need from me or the prince?"

Aayanar stumbled over his words. "Yes, my lord. I need a good horse."

The emperor exploded. "A horse? Aayanar, do you know that a war is coming? Do you know how many messengers must ride from Kanchi every day? Ask me for anything except a horse."

Having never heard the emperor talk like this, Aayanar was speechless in fear.

"Oh," Mahendran went on. "It looks like you insist on a horse! Let it not be said that the Master Sculptor of the Pallava kingdom begged for a horse but was refused. I will give you a horse: but tell me why you need it. You and Sivagami have a palanquin and bearers."

Aayanar picked up courage. "Lord, we have often talked about finding the secret of Ajanta's paintings. A man who knows the formula for the pigment is now at the Buddhist *sangha* in the Nagarjuna Hills."

"Why didn't you tell me this earlier, Aayanar? I would not have objected. I will give you a horse. Do you need anything else?"

"It is war time. I need a travel pass stamped with the nandi ensign."

"I wll give you that too. Are you planning to go on this important mission yourself?"

"I do not even know how to climb on a horse, lord! I plan to send one of my apprentices."

"He will have to use roads on which the enemy advances. He will need a good weapon. Give him this." The emperor held out the spear he had taken from Mamallan. "This spear belongs to him. This is the weapon which saved you and Sivagami from the elephant. Paranjothi will be glad."

Aayanar was shocked. He stammered, "My king … how … how did you know this?"

"Lord Buddha told me in a dream. He also told me about the men hiding behind his statue. Aayanar, nothing escapes the eyes and ears of the Pallava emperor in this kingdom."

Aayanar clasped his hands and choked out, "My king, forgive me if I have done wrong. My passion for painting made me do this."

"Sculptor, I too long to discover Ajanta's secret. Send the good Paranjothi, but do not tell that Buddhist monk that I know everything. For some reason, Buddhists are suspicious of me. They know nothing about my devotion to Lord Buddha. Aayanar, I plan to install a statue of Lord Buddha in one of these temples. I was discussing this with Mamallan when you arrived."

Sivagami listened to this dialogue with mixed emotions. *How clever the emperor is! It looks like nothing can be hidden from him. Does he know my secret too? Is that why the prince refuses to look at me? I must meet the prince soon and find out why he is angry.*

Sivagami picked up a piece of red chalk from the ground and drew on the rock. She showed waves with two lotus buds on them; a fawn stood by the water. From the corner of her eye, she saw Mamallan watching her. *He will understand my message. Others will see just a scribble. If he truly loves me, he will meet me at the lotus pond.*

The emperor and the prince rode back to Kanchi that evening. As they passed the rocks by which they had stood that afternoon, Mamallan fell back a little and stopped. He picked up the piece of chalk and drew a spear between the lotus and the fawn which Sivagami had drawn.

The Mountain Track

FOUR DAYS LATER, Paranjothi, dressed as a warrior, spear in hand, rode a thoroughbred horse along a mountain track. He was exhausted by the day's journey in the burning sun: so was his horse. He let the animal trot slowly up the mountain and looked back on the last week. *Eleven days ago, I was a simple village boy who walked from Sengathankudi. Am I the same boy who is now riding this handsome horse?*

Wiping away his sweat, Paranjothi longed for the beautiful roads in

Thondaimandalam and Chola Nadu. Those roads were shaded by huge banyan and neem trees. Green rice fields rippled in the breeze. Coconut and mango groves, and fields of bananas and sugarcane, cooled the eyes. Pools of lotuses and water lilies lay scattered everywhere. The birds sang the glory of the God who had created such beauty. This bare mountain was nothing like those roads.

As the sun set behind the western hills, Paranjothi turned a corner. After a long day in which he had seen only thorny thickets and cacti, he now saw thousands of *purasu* trees stretching away into the distance, their thick bunches of flowers glowing blood-red in the setting sun. Paranjothi associated *purasu* trees with funeral pyres because of the *purasu* trees that stood in Sengathankudi's cremation ground, bursting into bloom at this time of the year. Now, alone on a forest track, far away from home, the sight of these trees filled him with fearful thoughts of ghosts. The otherwise courageous Paranjothi was terrified of ghosts. *The inn where I must spend the night is at the junction of those two hills. It will be hours after dark before I get there. It will be pitch dark with no moonlight. Oh, why did I delay so much on the way!*

He urged his horse into a gallop, but the tired animal refused to go any faster. The bare mountains were frightening: not even a bird or animal was in sight.

Ah! I hear horses' hooves behind me. I will have company in the dark. Paranjothi stopped and listened. The sound stopped. *Was it my imagination? It must be because I am longing for company.*

Paranjothi rode on. Again, he heard horses' hooves behind him. He turned back but saw nothing on the curving mountain track. The sun set and darkness spread. When he came to a straight stretch, Paranjothi urged his horse into a gallop, stopped abruptly and turned back. He saw a horse and rider some distance away. The rider stopped his horse as soon as Paranjothi stopped. The furious Paranjothi turned his horse, held his spear ready and galloped towards the rider.

The Travel Companion

THE RIDER, A huge man with a large mustache and turban, shrieked, "Aiyo! Ghost!" and slipped off his horse, falling flat on the ground.

Paranjothi burst out laughing. *I am not the only one afraid of ghosts.*

The fallen man shrieked again. "Aiyo! The ghost is laughing! I am terrified!"

Enjoying himself, Paranjothi leaned down over the man, prodded his hand with his spear and said in a deep, 'ghostly' voice, "You! I will not let you go: I will swallow you!"

Suddenly, the stranger gripped the spear and pulled Paranjothi head first onto the ground. The man jumped on him and shook him, shouting, "Ha, ha, ha! You are a man. You tried to frighten me. What a joke!" He got off Paranjothi's chest and pulled him up. He put his arm over Paranjothi's shoulders and said pleasantly, "My boy, I was afraid that I would have to cross this cremation ground alone. Thank goodness you are here for company. Where are you going?"

The stunned Paranjothi was angry and ashamed. He pushed the man's arm from his shoulder and said heatedly, "What is it to you where I am going?"

"It is nothing to me, my boy. It is enough that I have a travelling companion for the night. You must be on some secret mission but …" he stopped and stared at Paranjothi. Before Paranjothi could react, the stranger again knocked him down, sat by him and held his throat in a stranglehold. "Are you a Vatapi spy? Tell me the truth," he barked.

Paranjothi teared up in rage and shame. "If you are a true warrior, fight me face-to-face."

"If you are a Vatapi spy, I will send you to *Yamaloka* now. If you are not a spy, why must I fight you? Let us be friends. Just prove you are not a spy. Look, do you have a bull ensign like this?" The stranger took a round, copper plate from his lap with his left hand. It was the nandi seal carried by the Pallava kingdom's royal messengers.

Paranjothi reluctantly showed the man his own seal. The stranger released his throat, pulled him up and hugged him. "My boy, forgive me. But it is better not to trust anyone in wartime. Get on your horse.

We can chat on our way." The warrior sprang easily on his own horse.

Paranjothi mounted his horse. *Chat with him? Once this trail ends, I will teach him a lesson.*

Dusk fell. The two horses fell into step in the dim light of the stars which sparkled like diamonds in the sky.

Mayurasanman

FOR SOME TIME, the only sound on that forested mountain track was the soft tread of the horses.

Paranjothi was angry that the stranger had dragged him off his horse, sat like a mountain on his chest, knocked him down and caught his neck in an iron chokehold. At the same time, he respected the man's skill, courage and intelligence. *Who is this man? His fighting skills prove that he is a great warrior. He defeated me in the blink of an eye. How I would love to have such a brave warrior as a friend! What a difference between this man and the Buddhist monk! Naganandhi was kind and helped me, but I disliked him. This man pushed me down and sat on my chest, but I respect and love him.*

Paranjothi remembered Naganandhi's warning: 'Do not trust anyone. Do not tell anyone where you are going or show him the message you carry. Many people are plotting to discover Ajanta's secret formula. They will kill for it; they will try to trick you. Do not be fooled ...' *Maybe this man is one of them. Did he drag me off my horse to find the monk's message?* Paranjothi calmed down when he felt the manuscript securely tied to his belt. *It will not be easy to take it from me.*

They heard a fox's forlorn, terrifying howl. Paranjothi's hair stood on end; he broke into a sweat.

The soldier said, "My boy, how brave you are to take this forest trail alone at dusk! I have travelled alone many times in my life, but even I was scared out of my wits some time back."

Paranjothi said, "Sir, you shouted, 'ghost!' and fell off your horse. Were you really scared, or did you pretend so that you could pull me down? You do not look the least frightened now."

"That is because two men together can defeat hundreds of ghosts. I believe thousands of ghosts haunt these hills at night. My boy, do you know the story of this land?"

"No, tell me."

"About two hundred and fifty years ago, Veerasanman, a Brahmin from the north, came to Kanchi with his young disciple, Mayurasanman. They were Vedic scholars whose credentials had to be approved by Kanchi's Sanskrit pundits. One day, as the two men walked down the street, they met some Pallava soldiers. Deep in discussion, they did not give way to the riders. An angry soldier leaned down from his horse and kicked Veerasanman. Mayurasanman was furious at this insult to his guru. He grabbed the man's sword and threw it: the soldier fell down, wounded. The other riders chased Mayurasanman. To save his life, Mayurasanman picked up the fallen soldier's sword, jumped on the man's horse, cut down his pursuers and fled from Kanchi.

"A company of Pallava soldiers set out to catch Mayurasanman, but he escaped to the Sri Mountains on the banks of the Krishna and hid in the dense forests. He built a huge army with the hill tribes living there. He founded an independent kingdom and marched on Kanchi to avenge his guru. The two armies met in this mountain region. The war raged for seven days. Thousands of soldiers died. A river of blood spread across the hills. This *purasu* forest sprang up after a few years. Every year, in the month of the battle, the trees shed their leaves and are covered in blood-red flowers. The villagers here believe that the ghosts of the thousands who died haunt the hills. Armed with spears and swords, these ghosts ride over these deserted hills shouting, 'Ha, ha!' They kill any solitary traveller and slake their thirst with his blood."

Paranjothi's fear vanished. *This story of wandering ghosts is pure superstition.* He mocked his companion: "Did you think that I was one of those two-hundred-and-fifty-year-old ghosts?"

The man replied in a hurt voice, "I am ready to fight any flesh-and-blood man with sword, spear, bow or hands. But who can fight with ghosts?"

Paranjothi changed the topic. "Tell me the result of the war. Who won?"

"The Pallava army, which was thrice as large as Mayurasanman's, won the battle. They brought Mayurasanman, with thirty-six wounds, before the Pallava king."

"What happened then?" Paranjothi asked eagerly.

His companion provoked Paranjothi's curiosity: "Why don't you tell me what happened?"

Vijayanthi

PARANJOTHI SAID BITTERLY, "A hero like Mayurasanman would never surrender. As was the custom, I suppose the Pallava king had him buried alive and crushed by an elephant."

"No, my boy, no. That is what other kings would do, but the Pallava kings have a unique style … the king forgave Mayurasanman, praised his courage and returned his kingdom to him."

"What?" Paranjothi was astounded. "And did Mayurasanman thank him?"

"Not only Mayurasanman: for two hundred years, every king belonging to the Kadamba dynasty which Mayurasanman founded, has paid levies and remained grateful to the Pallavas. Their kingdom flourished along the Krishna–Tungabhadra shores, with its capital at Vijayanthi. Whenever they faced threats, the Pallavas helped them. Did you know that Pulikesi's uncle, Mangalesan, attacked Kadamba twenty years ago?"

"No," Paranjothi said interestedly. "What happened?"

"The Pulikesi who is now marching on the Pallava kingdom was a child then. Mangalesan ruled Vatapi. He dreamt of expanding his realm and becoming an emperor. He invaded Kadamba and laid siege to Vijayanthi. The Pallavas' northern army went to help the Kadamba king. A great battle was fought near Vijayanthi …"

"And?"

"What else? The brave Pallava army won and the defeated Chalukyas fled. If only the Pallava army had chased and destroyed the Chalukyan forces, we would not be facing war now."

Paranjothi was eager to learn about wars, victories, defeats and strategies. He forgot his exhaustion. "Why didn't the Pallava army chase the defeated Chalukyan army?"

"Mainly because the Pallava army suffered a heavy loss at Vijayanthi—their general died there. It was General Kalipahai: the present Kalipahai's uncle."

"I have heard of him—and of Thilagavathi who was to marry that brave man. All my relatives are staunch Shaivas. I came to Kanchi to see Navukkarasar…" Paranjothi stopped.

"Is that so? I am also a Shaiva. Did you meet Navukkarasar?"

"No. Before that, this mission came up."

"What mission?"

Paranjothi was careful: "Sir, ask me no questions and I will tell you no lies."

"Ah, you clever boy!" The man continued. "I have a son like you—he is your age. He insisted on coming with me on this voyage. I refused and he is angry with me."

Paranjothi felt a pang of jealousy. *How lucky that boy is to have such a brave father!* "Sir, you stopped halfway through your story of the battle at Vijayanthi. General Kalipahai died, but surely the Pallavas had other commanders? Why didn't they chase the retreating Chalukyan army?"

"Have you seen Emperor Mahendran of Kanchi, my boy?"

The question seemed out of place. Paranjothi remained silent.

"Mahendran had strange ideas. There should be no war, no enmity. All men should spend their lives happily on sculpture, music and dance. He did not hunger to expand his kingdom. When Pulikesi asked him for a truce, he agreed."

"When did Pulikesi become king?"

"His greedy uncle, Mangalesan, imprisoned Pulikesi and his brothers and became king. When Mangalesan marched on Vijayanthi, the boys escaped. Pulikesi killed the defeated Mangalesan on his return to Vatapi and crowned himself king. He sent a messenger to Kanchi asking for a truce. Like making peace with a cobra, Emperor Mahendran made peace with that despicable man. Mahendran is now suffering for that."

"How?"

"Pulikesi's army has captured Vijayanthi and is advancing. I heard that Pulikesi looted Vijayanthi and ordered it to be burnt. If it is true, all I can say is that Mahendran deserves this and more."

Paranjothi was silent. He was troubled by the burning of Vijayanthi.

After a while, the soldier said, "My boy, I will not ask where you are going and why. But I am sure you will not mind telling me where you plan to spend the night."

"I heard that there is a Mahendran guest house over this hill. I planned to stay there tonight."

"Look, there is a light: that is the Mahendran guest house. I too will spend the night there."

Kumbakarnan

WHEN THE TRAVELLERS reached the guest house, the four guards there drew their swords and shouted, "Stop!" Another guard stood at the entrance with a bright torch.

The stranger took out some identification from under his tunic. At once, the guards respectfully made way for him and went to Paranjothi. When the stranger said, "He is with me," the guards made way for Paranjothi too. The man showed his identification to the guest house's commander and said, "We will be spending the night here. The horses must be fed."

The commander respectfully said, "As you wish, sir."

Paranjothi was amazed. *He must be on urgent government business. Maybe he is an important Pallava general. Once my task is done, I will search him out and be his friend.*

As they had their dinner, the soldier said, "My boy, I was your age at the time of the Battle of Vijayanthi. I stayed here then. That night, I had a strange experience ..."

"What was it?" Paranjothi asked eagerly.

"*Thambi,* we have been talking all this while without knowing each other's name. I do not mind telling you mine: my parents named me Vajrabahu. But my friends call me Kumbakarnan—nobody can sleep like me! The last time I came here, I was exhausted by my day's travel. I slept like a log. Do you know what happened?"

"Did you dream of a ghost and wake up shrieking?" Paranjothi asked mischievously.

Vajrabahu laughed. "No, I dreamt that the house collapsed on me. I woke up to find five or six thugs sitting on me and holding me down: they were trying to steal the message I was carrying for General Kalipahai. Those ruffians thought I had the palm leaf in my waist belt."

Vajrabahu's eagle eyes noted Paranjothi's right hand instinctively touching his own waist. "What happened, sir? Did those thugs get the palm leaf?"

"They got blows on their heads from my fist. They were happy to escape with their lives!"

Paranjothi laughed. "Those fools deserved it. They disturbed your Kumbakarnan-like sleep. One of them should have come in quietly and felt your waist—he would have got the palm leaf."

"Even then, he would not have found it. I gave the palm leaf to Lord Agni."

"What? Fine messenger you are! Why travel after burning the message?"

"Before throwing it into the fire, I memorised the message." Vajrabahu paused. "*Thambi*, I will be leaving early in the morning. I like you very much. If you ever need my help, do not hesitate to come to me." He left for his room.

The worried Paranjothi went to his own room. *The monk warned me not to sleep in a room with other men in a guest house. Thank goodness I have been given a room to myself.* He settled down to sleep. *I must sleep lightly and wake up at the least noise.* But his youth, and the exhaustion of the day's travel, sent him into a deep sleep. He had nightmares. He was one of the ghost riders who wandered in the *purasu* forest. He was sleeping. A line of ghosts felt his waist. *Thank goodness the palm leaf is not at my waist—it is under my pillow.* He saw a black ghost and a flesh-eating, fire-spewing demon coming towards him. His closed eyes were dazzled by the fire in the demon's mouth. Unable to bear the light, he opened his eyes.

There was no flesh-eating demon or black ghost. Instead, he saw Vajrabahu and the guard commander with a lighted torch in his hand. Paranjothi sat up with a start and gripped his spear.

The Theft of the Palm Leaf

VAJRABAHU SAID CALMLY, "My boy, we are not ghosts. You teased me about dreaming of ghosts ... your shrieks woke everyone in the guest house."

Paranjothi gave an embarrassed laugh and stood up. "Is it dawn? Shall we go?"

"Nonsense! It is midnight. You screamed in fright when you were safely in bed: how will you travel alone in the middle of the night?"

Paranjothi's self-esteem was hurt. He accused Vajrabahu: "The frightful stories you told me last evening must have given me nightmares."

"Leave it. Sleep peacefully now. Keep this torch."

Vajrabahu and the commander left.

Paranjothi closed his eyes but could not sleep. He tossed and turned. The torchlight troubled his eyes. *Shall I put out the torch?* Suddenly, a thought struck him. He sat up and took out a slim bamboo cylinder. He took a palm leaf bundle from it and went to sit by the light of the torch.

To his disappointment, he could not make out the closely written words. *It is not Tamil. Is it Sanskrit or Pali or Brahmi? One must learn all the languages spoken in the land. How I regret wasting all these years! And why did this war come just when I finally reached Kanchi to study? Why did this dangerous mission land on my head?* Paranjothi's eyes grew heavy and closed. Before he could get back to the bed, he lost consciousness. He lay on the ground and the scroll slipped from his fingers.

The door opened quietly, and Vajrabahu noiselessly came in. He picked up the scroll, went out and closed the door. He walked to a large room in a corner of the guest house. He carefully read the scroll in the light of a lamp. He frowned and looked up thoughtfully at the roof. He clasped his hands and stared at the floor. He stared into the flame. Finally, his face cleared.

He took four blank palm leaves, cut them to the size of the leaves in front of him and began to write. He finished quickly and compared them to the scroll he had taken from Paranjothi. He carefully put away

Paranjothi's scroll and went to the boy's room with his own scroll. Paranjothi was still unconscious. Tendrils of smoke wafted in the air, spreading a strange fragrance. Vajrabahu covered his nose with a cloth, placed his scroll by Paranjothi's hand and snuffed out the torch. In an instant, he was gone.

Back in his room, Vajrabahu once again intently studied the scroll he had stolen from Paranjothi. Deep in thought, he then held the leaves one by one to the lamp's flame. Once they were reduced to ashes, he took four fresh leaves and began to write on them. He paused often to think. As he finished writing and placed the scroll in a cylinder, the eastern sky lightened.

Paranjothi woke to find dawn's soft light shining through his window. He pounced on the scroll lying beside him, rolled it into the cylinder and secured it to his waist. He recalled the events of the night: his dreams, Vajrabahu and the guard's visit, examining the scroll in the torchlight and his heavy sleep. He felt slightly giddy and his stomach was uneasy. There was a strange smell in his room. He was ashamed. *How foolish of me to drop the scroll and sleep!* He heard horses' hooves and rushed to the entrance. He found the guards looking after a rider in the distance. *Oh, Vajrabahu has left.* Paranjothi asked the guards. "Sir, who is Vajrabahu? Do you know him?"

"No. But didn't you see the signet ring with the lion seal which he carried? Only those involved in the most urgent official matters carry that ring," the guard said.

Paranjothi said, "Sir, where is my horse? I must go to the Buddhist *matham* on the bank of the North Pennai. How much further is it?"

They pointed in the direction taken by Vajrabahu. "You will reach the North Pennai by noon. From there, go west along the shore. The *matham* is at the confluence of the Papagni and Pennai rivers."

Paranjothi mounted his horse. *Vajrabahu is headed in the same direction. I should have got up earlier and gone with him. I could have passed the time listening happily to his stories.*

The *Matham*

ON THE NIGHT of their return from Mamallapuram, Emperor Mahendran and the prince left Kanchi Fort in disguise. Leaving their horses in a hidden spot, they walked along the moat in the dim starlight. The prince was surprised at the sudden sound of oars. Mahendran gestured to him to remain silent. They hid behind a bush and watched.

A boat silently stopped by the fort. Two men climbed out, dragged the boat to the shore and hid it in a thicket. The men stood by the fort's wall for a second: the next second, they vanished! Like a spider which swallows two mosquitoes in an instant and goes back to being motionless, Kanchi Fort swallowed those two men in the blink of an eye and was still. Before the prince could recover from his shock, a man came out of another thicket and saluted the emperor.

Without a flicker of surprise, Mahendran said, "Shatrughan, what is your guess? Where does this door in the fort's wall open?"

"Behind the Buddha statue in the Royal Monastery, lord."

"The man who made this door must be extremely clever, right?"

"The man who painted it is even cleverer, lord. I examined this place in broad daylight but saw no door."

"Alright, Shatrughan. I am leaving for the north tomorrow."

"Lord, I will be ready."

"No. Until you receive further orders from me, follow Naganandhi. And if the Buddhist monk passes any messages to anyone ..."

"I know what to do, lord. But what about the message he sent through the Sengathankudi boy?"

"I will see to that. On no account must you lose Naganandhi. If there is news, send word to me."

The emperor and the prince rode back to the palace.

Mamallan asked, "Mustn't we seal the Royal Monastery and the opening in the fort's wall?"

"No, my son. For now, the door will show us our enemies' plots."

Mamallan's respect for his father grew. *He saw the men hiding behind Buddha's statue and guessed the location of the secret door in the fort's wall.*

After the emperor left, time was heavy on the prince's hands. He never thought of disobeying his father, but he was upset at being forced to stay in the fort while a great war loomed over the kingdom. He often thought of Sivagami. *Did she get the meaning of the spear I drew between the lotus and the fawn? Is she angry? She does not know about my promise to father. Maybe she can come here ... no, after father's strict instructions, Aayanar cannot take a break from his work.*

When he heard that Navukkarasar was back in Kanchi, Mamallan went to visit the saint. *I have a message for him from father.*

Navukkarasar, then about fifty-five years old, often went on pilgrimages. He weeded temple courtyards with his hoe and composed exquisite Tamil verses filled with Shiva bhakti. His golden body was covered with holy ash and adorned with chains of rudraksha beads. He wore a pure white waist cloth. His face radiated wisdom and grace. The saint warmly welcomed the prince and asked about the emperor and the coming war.

Mamallan said respectfully, "Swami, the emperor thinks that Kanchi may come under siege. He advises you to close the *matham* and go on a pilgrimage until the war ends."

Navukkarasar thought it over: "I agree with the emperor."

Just then, a disciple came hurrying to say, "Aayanar is here."

The Second Dance Recital

MAMALLAN SAW AAYANAR at the entrance. *Ah, I hear the sound of anklets—it is Sivagami!*

Sivagami met the prince's yearning eyes and her face glowed. Then, it darkened in anger. She bowed her head and followed her father. In all the excitement, no one noticed this exchange of glances. Aayanar hurried to Navukkarasar and fell at his feet. Sivagami stood behind her father even after everyone was seated.

Navukkarasar asked, "Aayanar, is this your daughter, Sivagami? I heard about her remarkable dancing skills. She had her debut dance recital recently, right? I am sorry I missed it."

"I too missed you, swami. Rudracharya was stunned by her dance. He admitted that dance was the foundation of art." Aayanar's voice glowed with pride.

"Aayanar, dance is truly the foundation of art. Doesn't the God who creates, guards and destroys millions of universes perform his *ananda tandavam* at Chidambaram?" Navukkarasar asked.

Aayanar sadly said, "Sivagami was to perform the *abhinaya* for three of your compositions, swami ... but her recital was interrupted."

"I heard, Aayanar. This war will ruin many plans. I sent for you because I wanted to shift my *matham* from this busy Ekambar Temple street to peaceful Metrali which is surrounded by gardens."

Aayanar said, "Swami, I am ready to start work on the new *matham*—but the emperor has ordered me to complete the harbour work at the earliest."

Navukkarasar said, "You can postpone my work. The emperor advises me to go on a pilgrimage until the war ends. If Kanchi Fort is besieged, ascetics like me should not get involved."

Mamallan said, "If only Jain and Buddhist monks too stopped interfering in affairs of state!"

At this mention of Buddhist monks, Aayanar remembered Paranjothi. "Swami, a boy from Sengathankudi came to study at your *matham*. He brought letters from Thiruvenkadu's Doctor Sivanesan. I sent him to the Nagarjuna Hills to learn a great secret behind painting."

Navukkarasar was worried. "That is so far! Isn't that where the war is raging? Didn't you say he was a young boy?"

"He is young but very courageous." Aayanar narrated the incident of the elephant. "I will send him to you as soon as he returns, swami."

"Aayanar, I have no idea where I may be when he returns. Let him continue as your apprentice. Let me see one of Sivagami's dances now."

"Swami, Sivagami is blessed to dance for you." Aayanar turned to his daughter and was surprised at her unhappy expression.

Noticing this, Mamallan said, "Maybe she is reluctant to dance before me. Swami, let me go."

At once, Sivagami jumped up. "*Appa*, which song do you want me to perform?"

Aayanar proudly chose one of Navukkarasar's verses praising Lord

Shiva: *Vadiveru thirisulam thondrum.* Sivagami danced as she sang. Her voice was as sweet as the hum of the honeybee floating on a soft breeze. She used her body and face to portray every sentiment of the beautiful song through her *abhinaya*. Her audience saw Lord Shiva himself standing before them with his sharp trident, the crescent moon and *kondrai* flowers on his matted hair. They were carried to Kailash and came back to earth only when the dance ended.

Navukkarasar wept, "Aayanar, your daughter brought Lord Shiva himself before us."

Aayanar too shed tears of joy and said, "My dear, will you do one more dance? Let it be one of swami's verses from Thiruvarur."

Navukkarasar's Blessing

SIVAGAMI CHOSE *MUNNAM avanudaya namam kettal.* In this exquisite composition, Navukkarasar describes a woman's love for Lord Shiva. As Sivagami danced, it was as if all the love felt by women from the beginning of time took form in her. *This is no ordinary love—it is divine.* They saw the first flush of love bloom in a shy young girl's heart; they saw her delight at hearing her lover's name; they saw her mesmerised by his captivating appearance; they saw her lose her heart and mind to him; they saw her renounce everything that stood in the way of her love—her parents, society and tradition; they saw her forget the world and herself; they saw her surrender at the feet of her beloved.

After portraying every nuance of this love, Sivagami came to the final line, *Thalaipataal nangai thalaivan thaale*—'she fell at her beloved's feet in surrender'. Sivagami clasped her hands and fell like an uprooted tree. There were alarmed cries. Aayanar hurried to his daughter and sat beside her, trembling. The agitated Mamallan gently picked her up and placed her on her father's lap.

A crowd gathered around them with cries of, 'Water! A fan!'

"Make way," said Navukkarasar in ringing tones. He looked down compassionately at the unconscious girl and smeared holy ash on her forehead. There was pin drop silence in the hall.

Sivagami's eyes flickered open like the blue water lily blooming at dawn. She saw Navukkarasar and folded her hands in worship.

"May you be a queen, my child," the holy man blessed her.

There was a tremulous smile on Sivagami's lips. Her eyes searched the room and rested on Mamallan's face. They showed her forgiveness and asked, *Did you hear his blessing?*

Navukkarasar said, "Aayanar, I have now seen Bharatanatyam's full glory. Sivagami will make the *Natya Shastra* famous. Her dance deserves to be dedicated to Lord Shiva at Chidambaram."

They heard a horse at the entrance. Mamallan went to the door and came back. He folded his hands in respect to Navukkarasar. "Swami, there are urgent messages from Madurai. I must go." The prince turned to Aayanar. "When you are back at the port, send me news of Sivagami's health. For certain reasons, I cannot leave Kanchi for some time."

Mamallan tried to speak to Sivagami with his eyes, but she kept her head bowed. The loud thud of his feet as he walked away showed his annoyance.

Sivagami heard horses' hooves and the rumble of chariot wheels. *My very life is leaving on that chariot.*

Aayanar and Sivagami said goodbye to Navukkarasar.

The saint held back the sculptor until Sivagami was out of earshot. "Aayanar, I am worried about your daughter. When God makes a person exceptionally gifted, he also makes her suffer..."

Aayanar felt a thunderbolt fall on his head. "Swami, why should my innocent daughter suffer?"

Navukkarasar's eyes brimmed with tears. "Ah, why did God give me the power to see into the future! I have a premonition that sorrow looms over your beloved daughter. Do not lose heart, whatever happens. God may test those he loves, but he will finally gather them close to him."

Navukkarasar went into the *matham*. Aayanar walked away with a heavy heart.

Kannapiran

HIDING HIS SORROW, Aayanar asked Sivagami, "My child, shall we leave for the port?"

"Let us see Kamali and leave in the morning, *appa*," she replied.

A two-horse chariot rumbled to a stop at the entrance. The charioteer, a strong, twenty-five-year-old man, jumped off its deck and came to them. "Sir, have you seen Sculptor Aayanar and his daughter, Sivagami, who have come from Mamallapuram?"

"Ah, it is you, Kannapiran." Aayanar said. "Don't you recognise us?"

"I do not know … where have I seen this flat nose and flapping ears? I cannot remember …" Kannapiran knocked himself on the head in thought.

"My dear fellow, do not break your head and blame us for it! We are the Aayanar and Sivagami you are looking for."

The witty charioteer examined their faces. "Now, now, why didn't you tell me this earlier? I thought so, too. But which one of you is the sculptor? And who is his daughter?"

Sivagami burst out laughing. "*Anna*, I am Sivagami; this is my father. We are standing on the earth; above us is the sky. You are Kannapiran; my sister is Kamali. Now do you remember everything? We are planning to spend the night in your house. Can we or can we not come?"

"My dear, you must come. Do you know what Kamali said? 'Look here, Sculptor Aayanar is visiting Navukkarasar today. My friend, Sivagami, may come with him. You can come home tonight only if you bring them with you.' I said, 'Kamali, they are important people. Will they come to our poor home?' Kamali said, 'Tell them I am dying.'"

"My goodness, is Kamali ill?" Aayanar asked anxiously.

"Yes, sir. Without seeing her friend for a year, Kamali is slowly dying of worry... "

"In that case, let us go at once," Sivagami said.

The gathered crowd watched as Kannapiran, the Pallava kingdom's greatest charioteer, helped Aayanar and Sivagami on to the chariot which sped down the wide street.

Sivagami remembered the messengers sent regarding the prince's marriage. "*Anna,*" she asked anxiously. "Why did the prince hurry to the palace? What was the message from Madurai?"

"I never pay attention to matters of state, *thangachi,*" Kannapiran replied.

"Excellent, boy!" Aayanar approved. "One must be very careful when working in the palace."

The chariot passed the palace. Sivagami looked at its many stories, the long wall, the tower above the entrance gate with its guards and the strong inner walls. She sighed. *How many fort walls and palace halls separate me from the handsome prince who has stolen my heart!*

Kamali

THERE WAS A spacious garden behind the emperor's palace. Horse stables, chariot stalls and houses for the charioteers and gardeners stood against the wall behind this garden.

Kannapiran stopped before a house and jumped down. "Kamali, *appa*—look who I have brought."

Kamali ran out excitedly and hugged Sivagami.

An old man followed her from the house, went to Aayanar and said, "Welcome, sir."

When Aayanar lived in Kanchi, Kamali's parents were his neighbors. The girls were childhood friends whose bond grew stronger with the years. When Aayanar moved to the forest, Kamali spent months with them. After Aayanar, it was Kamali who encouraged Sivagami to dance. She said, "There is no one in the universe who dances as well as my sister!"

Kamali's father was a famous horse trader who imported steeds from Arabia and other lands. The horses arrived by ship at Mamallapuram. The commander of the Pallava cavalry and the palace's stable keeper, Asuvabalan, first inspected the horses and chose any which suited them. Only after that were the horses sold to the public.

Asuvabalan often visited Kamali's father. His son, Kannapiran, sometimes came with him. While the fathers conducted business, the son and daughter conducted romance. Kannapiran and Kamali were married a year-and-a-half back. Sivagami and Kamali had not met since then.

After dinner, Aayanar and Asuvabalan sat on the airy verandah, discussing the coming war. Sivagami and Kamali lay in a room adjoining the palace garden, talking about Kamali's married life. Their happy laughter often rang out.

About four hours into the night, Aayanar called, "Sivagami, my dear, we must leave at dawn. Enough talking—sleep."

The girls closed their eyes. A little later, thinking that Sivagami was asleep, Kamali got up quietly, opened the door and went out.

But Sivagami was awake. Waves of emotion crashed in her heart. *From the day Kamali fell in love with Kannapiran, her love is pure joy. Why is my love different? How much pain and anger it has! It is because he is a prince and I am just a poor sculptor's daughter. But he is the one who came in search of me and lit the fire of love in me. How that fire burns my body and heart!*

After tossing and turning for a while, Sivagami sat on the window ledge. A tender breeze caressed her, carrying the fragrance of *shenbagam* and jasmine along with vague memories and fears. *Thousands of years ago, in another lifetime, I smelt this fragrance ... I felt the same sweet pain. My love is near, but I cannot reach him. Mysterious shadows stand between us.*

Kamali's Wish

UNABLE TO BEAR the sweet pain of her thoughts, Sivagami quietly opened the door and went out. Bathed in the soft light of the crescent moon, the garden was a dream world. Kannapiran and Kamali's voices came through their open window. Sivagami turned away, but when she heard the word, 'Mamallan,' her feet refused to budge. She stood by the wall and listened.

"What is so strange about the Pandyan king wanting his daughter to marry Mamallan? As if all the kings will not vie with each other to make Mamallan their son-in-law!" Kamali said.

"The queen wanted Mamallan to get married, but the war spoiled her plans. Now she is delighted that the Pandyan king has come forward himself. Mother and son began to quarrel."

"Quarrel? Why?"

"If anyone mentions the word, 'marriage,' the prince becomes furious. Kamali, shall I tell you a secret? Everyone thinks that the prince does not want to get married because of the war. But there is another reason—and it involves your sister, Sivagami." He paused. "Prince Mamallan Narasimhan, as brave as Arjuna, as handsome as Manmatha, as skilled a charioteer as Kannapiran—he loves your sister."

The shocked Kamali could only manage an, "Ah!" She recovered quickly and said smugly, "Haven't I always said that our prince is clever? That is why he loves my sister."

"It looks like you girls planned this. You caught me—now, your sister has caught Mamallan."

Kamali was furious. "Am I the one who chased and caught you? Am I the one who followed you into every nook and corner of the house, held your hand and begged you to marry me?"

"No, you were only joking when you used your eyes as a trap—I fell into it by myself."

"Leave our story aside. How do you know about Mamallan and my sister? Tell me that."

"It takes one thief to know another. Do you remember how I looked at you in your father's house those days? The prince looks at your sister with the same passion."

"Is that all?"

"What more do you want? Didn't I tell you how your sister fainted while dancing? The prince ran to pick her up. How his hands shook! I had my doubts before that ... now I am sure."

Sivagami broke into goosebumps and controlled her urge to burst into tears.

"What a keen observer you are! You clever man! And Mamallan is lucky," Kamali said.

"Lucky? When I think of all the trouble this will cause ..."

"Kanna, my sister is equal to a thousand princesses. Wait and see: my wish will come true."

"What wish is that?"

"The war is over, and the prince is to be crowned. He rides through Kanchi's streets in a golden chariot, seated on a gem-studded throne. Sivagami sits beside him. You are on the chariot's deck. I am standing on the terrace above the palace gates. When the chariot reaches the gate, I shower them with *shenbagam* and jasmine. I also throw a basket of flowers on your head ..."

Sivagami returned to her room, went to bed and sobbed. As she hovered between sleep and wakefulness, the shadowy figures she had seen earlier took form. A stag and a spotted deer frolicked in a field of jasmine. The spotted deer playfully hid in a jasmine bush, her spots blending with the flowers. The stag walked on, not seeing her. The spotted deer laughed. Then, she saw two sparks in a jasmine thicket: they were the glowing eyes of a huge tiger. The spotted deer trembled. She tried to call out to the stag, but no sound came from her throat.

Sivagami shuddered. *I am the spotted deer ... will I escape?... will he come to me?*

The Forced March

PARANJOTHI TRAVELLED ALL day. At sunset, he reached the Buddhist *matham* at the confluence of the Pennai and the Papagni. A monk stood at the monastery entrance, his saffron robes glowing in the light of the setting sun. He questioned Paranjothi who could not understand the language.

Making a guess, Paranjothi replied in Tamil: "I am on my way to the Nagarjuna Hills. Naganandhi swami asked me to stop here and go on after getting directions."

The monk's face changed on hearing Naganandhi's name. He signalled to Paranjothi to wait and went in. He soon came back and took Paranjothi into the monastery. This building was carved out of rock and was smaller than Kanchi's Royal Monastery, but the plan was the same. In the center was a shrine where the monks could pray and meditate. A huge Buddha was carved on the rock face with a Bodhi tree spread above him and *gandharvas* showering flowers on him. Rows of lighted lamps glowed in the dark. The fragrance of flowers and incense helped the mind focus. On either side of the shrine, there were rock-cut cells where the monks studied and slept.

The monk took Paranjothi up a flight of steps. There were rock-cut cells on this upper floor too. The monk left Paranjothi in a spacious cell where a big monk was seated in *padmasana*.

Paranjothi folded his hands in respect. *This must be the abbot.*

The monk bowed thrice to Lord Buddha, turned to Paranjothi and spoke in Tamil: "My child, who are you? Why are you here? Who sent you?"

Paranjothi gave him the details of Naganandhi sending him on this mission.

"Where is the scroll Naganandhi gave you? Can I see it?"

"Forgive me. Naganandhi commanded me to give it only to Satyashraya." Paranjothi could not figure out the meaning of the mysterious smile on the monk's face at the mention of Satyashraya.

"Do as Naganandhi commanded. Stay here tonight. The road to the Nagarjuna Hills is dangerous. I will send you with some soldiers who are going there. They will escort you safely."

The abbot gestured to a monk, who gave Paranjothi his dinner and showed him to a cell for the night. After his sleepless night and long day's travel, Paranjothi sank into a deep, peaceful sleep.

Somebody shook him awake. It was the monk who was at the gate the previous day. The abbot was with him. "My boy, the men going to the Nagarjuna Hills are leaving. You must go."

Paranjothi quickly rose, took the cylinder which was by his head and secured it to his waist. He followed the monks to the monastery's entrance. In the dim light of the crescent moon low on the horizon, he saw his horse and six other horses. By each horse stood a strapping soldier.

"These soldiers will take you to the Nagarjuna Hills by a shortcut," said the abbot.

Paranjothi climbed on his horse with a vague sense of foreboding. The horses galloped westwards along the banks of the North Pennai.

The War Camp

THE SOLDIERS RODE before and behind Paranjothi. Once it was light, Paranjothi got a good look at the solidly built, large men. He was confused. *These are army men on an important war mission. Why has the abbot sent me with them?* Each time he tried to go ahead or fall back, the soldiers blocked him. *Am I being escorted, or have I been arrested? The Nagarjuna Hills are to the north, but these men are heading west.* At noon, Paranjothi decided to test the soldiers. He turned his horse northwards—in the blink of an eye, the six soldiers surrounded him with pointed spears.

Paranjothi's blood boiled. He aimed his spear at the soldier near him. His spear flew somewhere, and he fell flat on the ground: one of the men had lassoed him and dragged him down. His horse galloped away. There was no way to escape. *It is no use fighting. Let whatever happens, happen.*

The soldiers tied Paranjothi's hands behind his back and put him on the sturdiest horse with a soldier sitting behind him. They again rode west. About two hours before sunset, they reached the summit of a hill.

Paranjothi saw an amazing sight. An army camp stretched away into the distance on the broad plain. Thousands of war elephants stood in rows like black hills, with tents pitched in between them. Horses, bulls, camels, chariots and carts were everywhere. Lakhs of soldiers were clustered like ants around spilt sugar. Rows of flags fluttered above the tents. In the center, a majestic flag reached out to the sky. A wave of sound roared from the camp.

Forgetting his bonds, Paranjothi gasped in wonder. *It is the Pallava army camp. How I wish I could become a soldier in this magnificent force which is raring to fight!*

Paranjothi was like a traveller lost in the dark night who finds his way in a sudden flash of lightning. In that instant, he realised his life's purpose—it was not to be a scholar or a sculptor. *I am born to be a warrior. I will behead my enemies, plunge my spear into their hearts, swim in a river of blood, blow the conch of victory and be hailed as the King of Warriors.*

He imagined Emperor Mahendran's majestic form, as seen by him from his hiding place behind the Buddha statue in Aayanar's house. *The emperor will be seated on his throne under that high flag. I will fall at his feet and say, "Lord, let this ignorant village boy join your army." Who cares about sculpture and art! To hell with Aayanar and Naganandhi!*

As they neared the camp, Paranjothi had doubts. *The Pallava flag has the nandi, but these flags show the ferocious varaha. Is this the Vatapi army? My goodness! What a mighty enemy force!*

The soldiers dismounted at the entrance and took Paranjothi inside. His doubts were confirmed. *This is the enemy camp. They have trapped me.* His heart sank. The pain from his bonds was unbearable. Broken in body and spirit, he stumbled and was dragged along by his captors.

Then he saw a familiar face: it was Vajrabahu. Paranjothi felt a flash of joy which soon died. *This man is the cause of my trouble.*

Vajrabahu seemed astonished to see Paranjothi. "My boy, what is the meaning of this?" He questioned Paranjothi's escort. "Do not worry, my boy. Tell King Satyashraya Pulikesi the truth, and no harm will come to you."

More than Vajrabahu's words, Paranjothi was encouraged by the signal which flashed like lightning from his bright eyes.

Satyashraya

PULIKESI RULED A kingdom which extended from the Tungabhadra in the south to the Narmada in the north, with Vatapi as his capital. When Pulikesi and his brothers were children, they were imprisoned by their uncle, Mangalesan. They escaped and lived in hiding in the dense jungle for many years. The hardships they faced hardened their bodies and sharpened their minds, making them matchless warriors and brutal fanatics. When the opportunity came, Pulikesi defeated Mangalesan, imprisoned him and ascended the Vatapi throne. With his brothers' help, he expanded his empire. He locked horns with the powerful Emperor Harshavardhan. The battle raged for years. When Pulikesi realised that victory was impossible, he negotiated for peace.

Harsha praised Pulikesi's courage and made him emperor of the lands south of the Narmada.

When Mahendran Pallava converted from Jainism to Hinduism, the Jain monks were furious. They could not bear to see Hinduism rise in Kanchi which had long been the center of Jainism. Using their great influence in Vatapi, they arranged a marriage between Pulikesi's brother, Vishnuvardhan, and the daughter of the Kanga king, Dhurvineedhan. Instigated by the monks, Pulikesi's own expansionist dreams made him march south with a huge army.

The monks came with the army, dreaming of humbling Mahendran Pallava and entering Kanchi victoriously. They soon realised that the army camp was not Vatapi, and Commander Pulikesi was not Emperor Pulikesi. In Vatapi, Jain gurus like Pujyapadhar were more respected than the emperor himself. On the battlefield, no one even looked at them. After Pulikesi overruled their objection to burning Vijayanthi, the monks left the army.

Pulikesi sat on a golden throne in a spacious tent under the high-flying varaha flag. A group of army commanders sat on a carpet before him. The men spoke a mix of Tamil and Brahmi.

Pulikesi grumbled, "What were these Jain monks thinking when they marched with our army?"

"Good riddance to them," a commander said. "If they had stayed, we would be building temples and *mathams* and stupas: not waging a war." His listeners laughed.

"We have got rid of the Jains, but it looks like we are waging the war according to the Buddhist monk's plans," another commander pointed out.

Pulikesi said, "That is different. We have always profited by the Buddhist monk's advice." His stern eyes bored into a man in the group as he said sarcastically, "Our spies are doing an excellent job: instead of our men finding the monk's messenger, the messenger has found us."

Maitraiyan, the Chalukyan spymaster, bowed his head. "There has been a mistake. The men I sent are still not here …" There was a disturbance at the tent's entrance. "Ah, here they are!"

The soldiers who had arrested Paranjothi dragged him into the tent. "What is this? Who is this boy?" Pulikesi thundered.

The Mysterious Scroll

EMPEROR PULIKESI WAS tall and emaciated, with a hard, ruthless face. His bloodshot eyes had the eagle's predatory stare. Paranjothi saw his majesty, cruelty, intelligence and anger. *He is Yama!*

The captain of Paranjothi's escort saluted Pulikesi and started his report.

Pulikesi interrupted with an angry roar: "Enough! Who is this? Why have you brought him here?"

The captain's voice shook in fear. "The young man says he brings a message from the monk, Naganandhi, for Satyashraya. Here is the scroll."

Pulikesi snatched the scroll. He was surprised and confused even after reading it twice.

Paranjothi was also confused. *I never thought I would end up before the enemy king! What did Vajrabahu mean by telling me to tell Pulikesi the truth?* He remembered Naganandhi's words: 'You must give this scroll to Satyashraya himself and to no one else. One never knows where he will be and what disguise he will be in.' *Is Pulikesi the 'Satyashraya' Naganandhi referred to? Is the scroll about Ajanta's secret formula? Am I caught in a conspiracy?*

Pulikesi burst out laughing. His eagle eyes seemed to penetrate Paranjothi's heart. His voice was stern. "Boy, tell me the truth. Who are you? Where have you come from? Who gave you this scroll? Do you know what is written in it?"

Not understanding a word, Paranjothi remained silent. Pulikesi's temper rose. The men said in turn, "He is deaf." "No, he is dumb." "No, he does not understand our language."

Pulikesi agreed, "Yes, that must be it. It is the only disadvantage of the Jain monks leaving in a huff: they could translate any language. Never mind, throw him in prison. We will deal with him later … no, let him stay here. Bring Vajrabahu, the warrior who was here earlier." Pulikesi went on. "Do you know what is written on this scroll? Listen. 'Please give Ajanta's secret formula to the boy who carries this scroll. Even after living in the Ajanta caves for two years, I have not been able to learn the secret—so carefully do the Buddhist monks guard it.' The writing seems to be Naganandhi's." Pulikesi gave the scroll to his spymaster. "What do you think, Maitraiyan?"

Maitraiyan examined the scroll carefully. "Satyashraya, there is a mystery here. We can solve it if we question this boy in the right way."

"And what is the use of that? We will not understand anything the boy says," Pulikesi pointed out. "That is why we are waiting for Vajrabahu."

Vajrabahu entered the tent and paid his respects to Pulikesi. "Emperor, what can I do for you?"

"Vajrabahu, like you, this boy has brought me a scroll. But the contents are a mystery. I sent for you to question the boy. Ask him who gave him this scroll and whom he was asked to give it to."

Vajrabahu stared at Paranjothi. "Oh, it is this boy. I met him at the Mahendran guest house the other day. He looked suspicious and I questioned him. He is secretive: he did not say a word."

"Question him now," Pulikesi commanded. "If he refuses to reply, we will make him talk."

"My king, he looks brave: we will not get anything out of him with threats. Let me question him." He turned to Paranjothi. "My boy, as I told you earlier, tell Satyashraya the truth. Do not be afraid—I will see that you escape."

Paranjothi said, "Sir, why should I be afraid? What have I to lose but my life? Naganandhi asked me to take that scroll to the Nagarjuna Hills and give it to Satyashraya. If, as you say, the scroll is meant for this man, let him give me his reply. I will go back with it. Or, if the scroll is not for him, ask him to give it back to me. What else can I say?"

"King, the boy says that Naganandhi gave him the scroll. He says it has a message about some secret formula for mixing pigments in the Ajanta caves. May I have a look at the scroll?"

Pulikesi gave him the scroll. "There is nothing to be learned from it. Have a look."

Vajrabahu examined the scroll. "Lord, this reminds me of something Naganandhi said. He said that he had to send a message to your brother. Maybe this message is for King Vishnuvardhan?"

Pulikesi's face cleared. "Vajrabahu, you are a genius! Why don't you stay with me? You would be useful in many ways." Pulikesi consulted his commanders. "I too must send a message to Vishnuvardhan. Let nine soldiers go with my message and let this boy go with them. If my brother also cannot understand the meaning of this scroll, order him to behead this boy!" He turned to Vajrabahu. "Explain this to the boy," he commanded.

Vajrabahu told Paranjothi, "My boy, nine of the king's soldiers are leaving for the Nagarjuna Hills tomorrow morning. Go with them. Do not worry: I will meet you tomorrow night."

Paranjothi beamed. "Sir, I am ready to travel to hell with you. I am that eager to hear your stories!"

"What is the boy saying?" Pulikesi asked.

Vajrabahu replied, "The boy is very clever. He says that if the scroll is not meant for you, you must return it to him. There is a saying in Tamil—the young cub knows no fear."

Pulikesi laughed. "Is that so? Alright, let us give the scroll to the boy. Untie his bonds."

The men untied Paranjothi's bonds, gave him the scroll and took him outside the tent.

The next day, at twilight, Paranjothi and his nine-man escort crossed a narrow stream on a mountainous forest track and reached an old, ruined house. An old man sat on the verandah. With a gray beard and head, the man fingered his prayer beads and ignored the ten riders who stopped before the house. When questioned by the captain, he replied shortly and went back to his prayer beads. The soldiers decided to spend the night in that ruined house and posted a guard in each direction.

The exhausted Paranjothi went to sleep as soon as he lay down. *Vajrabahu said that he would meet me tonight. Now it is too late ...*

Paranjothi had a dream. Pulikesi's eagle eyes stared at him. "Let him be crushed by an elephant," he ordered. Paranjothi threw his spear at the elephant and ran. The elephant chased him. He turned back with a start when its trunk touched his shoulder. The elephant's face changed into that of the old man with the prayer beads and its trunk became the man's hand. Paranjothi sat up abruptly. *It is not a dream! The old man is waking me up!*

The Mysterious Old Man

IN THE DIM moonlight, Paranjothi saw the old man signalling him to take the spear he held out and follow him. When Paranjothi hesitated, the old man gripped his hand tightly in his own left hand. At once, Paranjothi had a flash of memory; he jumped up and took the spear from the old man. They left the house by the back door. Paranjothi saw his horse saddled and ready, along with another horse. They jumped on the horses.

The old man asked, "My boy, don't you know me?"

"Your beard fooled me, but I recognised your grip: you are Vajrabahu, the braveheart who does not fear ghosts."

The old man laughed loudly and removed his gray beard: it was indeed Vajrabahu. "My dear boy, think well. Are you willing to come with me?"

"I am ready. It looks like you are the one who has no plans of leaving this place. If you insist on talking so loudly, won't they wake up and catch us?"

"I want to wake them. I do not want it said that the brave Vajrabahu, descendent of Achyuta Vikranta, cheated his sleeping guards and escaped." He roared with laughter at some thought.

The guard at the house's entrance was alerted by the sound of horses and voices. He came to the back, saw the two riders, shouted in alarm and ran into the house.

Confused cries filled the air: "What?" "Disaster!" "They are making their escape!"

Vajrabahu deliberately reined in his horse to a slow trot and started on the road they had travelled the previous day. He stopped now and then. To Paranjothi's questions, he said, "Mustn't we give the Chalukyas a chance to catch us? What if they go some other way?" He paused. "Did you notice the Durga temple at the mountain pass a short distance from here?"

"No."

"Why would you notice anything? Maybe your thoughts were in Thiruvenkadu village ..."

Paranjothi was surprised. *My mind keeps going back to Thiruvenkadu ... but how does this imposter, Vajrabahu, know that?*

Vajrabahu went on: "When we rode past the Durga temple yesterday, I swore to sacrifice nine men to her before sunrise. If those men take another route, I will not be able to fulfill my oath."

As the bright day broke, Paranjothi and Vajrabahu reached the mountain pass. They took the narrow track between high rock walls. Once they crossed the pass, the high rock wall stood on one side and a deep valley on the other. Vajrabahu stopped his horse. The cool morning breeze blew down the pass. They heard horses' hooves above the birdsong.

"My boy, I am asking you once more—you must decide before the Chalukyan soldiers are here. Do you want to come with me?"

"I am with you. How can I go back?"

"You can still go back and join them." He went on. "They think that they are going to the Nagarjuna Hills, but they are actually going to *Yamaloka*."

"Who is sending them there?"

"If you want, you and I will send them. If not, I will send them there on my own."

Paranjothi was thoughtful. "Where are you going?"

"To the Pallava army camp."

"Ah, just as I thought! You are a spy for the Kanchi emperor." He paused. "Sir, if I come with you, can I join the Pallava army?"

"Of course: the Pallava army will be lucky to have a brave warrior like you."

Paranjothi said, "Sir, forgive me. I will go to the Nagarjuna Hills, hand over Naganandhi's scroll and then come to the Pallava army camp. Or Aayanar and Naganandhi will be disappointed."

"That is a waste of time, my dear boy. Naganandhi's scroll has been burnt."

"What are you saying? Here it is."

"That is the scroll written by me, my boy."

"My suspicions were right," Paranjothi said and hurled the scroll into the valley. "You added a drug to the torch which made me faint—you then stole the scroll from me."

"Your mind is as sharp as the tip of your spear."

Paranjothi looked at Vajrabahu in awe. "Sir, what was written in Naganandhi's scroll?"

"He asked Pulikesi to march to Kanchi at once and crown himself emperor of the south."

"Oh, how foolish I am! Was that the treasonous message I was carrying?" Paranjothi lamented.

"You can cry over the past later. The Chalukyan soldiers are galloping here on their way to *Yamaloka*. What are you going to do?"

"I am with you."

"Right. We will position ourselves on either side of this pass. Hurl your spear on the first soldier's chest. Then do your best with this sword." Vajrabahu gave him one of the two swords he carried.

Paranjothi eagerly took the sword and prepared himself for his first battle.

The Mountain Pass

AN HOUR LATER, the sun's crimson rays fell on blood-spattered rocks. The mountain pass was littered with nine corpses with missing limbs, split heads and wounded bodies. Vajrabahu agitatedly turned them over and examined their clothes, clearly looking for something important.

Paranjothi sat on a rock some distance away, exhausted. His hand rested on a sword; a bloody spear lay by his side. Vajrabahu had killed five Chalukyan soldiers and Paranjothi, three. Paranjothi had admired Vajrabahu's fighting skills. The ninth soldier had turned back his horse and tried to flee. Vajrabahu had hurled his spear at the man's back and killed him. Paranjothi was now disgusted: *Only a coward throws a spear at a man's back.*

Vajrabahu exclaimed as he picked up and examined a scroll. He then hurried to his horse and climbed on it. Seeing Paranjothi on the rock, he asked, "My boy, aren't you coming?"

Paranjothi gave Vajrabahu a look of loathing and bowed his head.

Vajrabahu rode to Paranjothi. "My dear boy, you fought like a seasoned warrior and killed three Chalukyan soldiers. I plan to ask the general of the Pallava army to make you its cavalry commander. Why are you now so exhausted and sad?"

Paranjothi was silent. He avoided Vajrabahu's face and looked at the glowing eastern hills.

"My boy, when the two armies faced each other at Kurukshetra, Arjuna threw down his bow and said sadly, 'I do not want the kingdom. I cannot fight!' You remind me of Arjuna."

Paranjothi's exhausted eyes glowed. "What happened then?" he asked eagerly.

"Luckily for Arjuna, Lord Krishna was his charioteer. The Lord said, 'Arjuna, rise! You are a man, a kshatriya. War is your dharma—pick up your bow.' With that, Arjuna's weariness disappeared and he regained his spirit ..."

"And then?"

"And then Arjuna picked up *Gandiva*, nocked his arrows and let fly. Lord Krishna blew his *Panchajanya* and the Mahabharata war began."

"How did the war happen?"

"Goodness! If I sit here telling you the story of the Mahabharata, what will happen to us in this war?" Vajrabahu turned his horse and rode up the mountain track.

Paranjothi grabbed his spear and sword and jumped on his horse. He quickly joined Vajrabahu.

Vajrabahu turned to him. "My boy, you look like you want to fight with me ..."

Paranjothi said bitterly, "I will not stab you in the back. I will fight you face-to-face. I do not have the courage to hurl my spear at an enemy who is running from the battlefield."

"Do you know what would have happened if I had not thrown my spear at that last soldier? The Vatapi army would be in Kanchi within a month. And you know what happened to Vijayanthi."

"How can that be? What is the Pallava army doing? What is Mahendran Pallava doing?"

"That is a mystery, my boy. Mahendran Pallava left Kanchi, and nobody knows where he is."

Paranjothi was silent. "Sir, tell me what Arjuna did next."

Pulikesi's Love

PARANJOTHI AND VAJRABAHU rode non-stop through mountain terrain, dense jungles, dry, wide riverbeds and beautiful villages nestled in mango groves. Vajrabahu told Paranjothi brave tales about Arjuna, Bheema and Abhimanyu. Paranjothi saw himself fighting bravely along with the Pandavas at Kurukshetra. He mimed stringing his bow, hurling his spear and whirling his sword at his enemies.

Sometimes, Vajrabahu was deaf to Paranjothi's questions. Deep in thought, he galloped across forests and rivers. Paranjothi had difficulty keeping up with him. Vajrabahu sighed deeply when they crossed green coconut groves and spreading banyan trees and said, "My dear boy, when I think of the Chalukyas' huge elephant brigade and see these green groves, I could weep. Do you know how much food an elephant needs in a day?"

"No, sir."

"It will not be satisfied even after eating six measures of rice, nine bunches of bananas, twenty-five coconuts and half a banyan tree."

"Oh my!" exclaimed Paranjothi.

"And it will still have room in its stomach for the mahout. Luckily, elephants are vegetarian!"

Paranjothi laughed. "How many elephants are there in the Chalukyan army?"

"Fifteen thousand, my dear boy. If these elephants march to and from Kanchi just once, these green fields and groves will become deserts."

"Why do you keep saying that the Chalukyan army will come to Kanchi?"

"My boy, only God can stop fifteen thousand elephants and five lakh infantry soldiers." He paused. "I once thought that Kanchi Fort was secure, but now I know how wrong I was."

Paranjothi remembered Naganandhi and the secret passage. "Isn't the fort secure?"

"Elephants cannot be forced to eat flesh, but they can be forced to drink arrack. The Chalukyan army carried huge vats of arrack. They plan to make drunken elephants smash the fort gates."

"What barbaric warfare!"

"All warfare is barbaric, my boy."

"How can we call the war that Emperor Mahendran is waging to save the country barbaric?"

"Do not let me hear the words, 'Emperor Mahendran.' My blood boils when I think of how he ignored the country's security and wasted his time on song and dance!"

Paranjothi stared at Vajrabahu. "Do you think that it is impossible to defend Kanchi Fort?"

"If the Vatapi forces reach Kanchi, even God cannot save the fort. That is why I killed the man who tried to escape. I gave Pulikesi a scroll which is supposed to be from Naganandhi. If Pulikesi believes it, Kanchi will be safe."

"Sir, what is written on that scroll?"

Vajrabahu echoed Paranjothi's earlier words: "Ask me no questions and I will tell you no lies."

"Sir, will your scroll make the Chalukyan army go back to Vatapi?"

"My dear boy, only God can save Kanchi from Pulikesi's disastrous love. 'Have you seen Kanchi?' Pulikesi asked me. 'Yes,' I replied. As I described Kanchi, his eyes blazed like that of a greedy cat looking at a mouse!"

Journey's End

AS THE SUN set, they saw the Pallava army camp. Paranjothi realised that Vajrabahu was right to be worried. *The Chalukyan army is a mountain—the Pallava army is a molehill!*

"Do you see, my boy? Do you still believe that the Pallava army can win?"

"Certainly, sir. The Pallava army has the might of dharma—and it has Emperor Mahendran."

"What! You seem to have extraordinary faith in Emperor Mahendran. Have you seen him?"

"Yes. Once in Sculptor Aayanar's house when I was hiding behind the Buddha statue. And then in disguise one night in Kanchi. He looked a lot like you. He had the same big mustache."

"Yes, I have heard that Emperor Mahendran sometimes wanders about in disguise. Some people have even suspected me of being the emperor."

"I have no such doubts, sir."

"Let that be. You have seen the Chalukyan and Pallava armies. Do you still want to join the Pallava army?"

"I burn with eagerness to join it. Why are we wasting time talking here?"

"In that case, let me go."

"What! Are you going to leave me here?"

"Yes. I will go first and tell the Pallava emperor about you. If it pleases him, he will send for you. Until then, you must wait outside the camp."

"Sir, you must help me to meet the emperor. I want to ask him to let me be in charge of Kanchi Fort's security."

"Oh! It looks like you want to save Kanchi from Pulikesi just as you saved Sivagami from the elephant. And your uncle sent a brave warrior like you to sing hymns and carve rocks—what a mistake!" He paused. "I too have a request for the emperor. 'Stop sculpting rocks. Ask the sculptors to build a Bharata pavilion in every town. Arrange for the Mahabharata to be read daily to the people.'"

"What is the purpose of that?"

"This war cannot be won just by Emperor Mahendran and the army. Every person in the Pallava kingdom must be brave and strong and know how precious life is." Vajrabahu affectionately hugged Paranjothi. "My boy, I have a son your age. If the two of you get together, what wonders you will accomplish!"

Paranjothi's voice shook. "Sir, I lost my father when I was a child. Accept me as your son."

After Vajrabahu left, every second seemed an age to Paranjothi. He waited eagerly for a sign from the emperor. Suddenly, there was great excitement in the Pallava camp. A mighty roar filled the air and echoed from the hills. The sound of trumpets, conches and war drums split the sky. Paranjothi went to the guards outside the camp and asked the reason for the celebration.

"Emperor Mahendran Pallava has reached the camp!" they said excitedly.

PART 2

KANCHI UNDER SIEGE

The Northern Gate

ONE MONSOON EVENING, the crimson sun set behind the ramparts of Kanchi Fort. The gold-edged clouds above the northern horizon dimmed and became dark blue, reminding one of Lord Vishnu's hue. Even the trees and bushes seemed to shiver in the cold wind. Kanchi Fort's wide northern gate was quiet at this beautiful twilight hour. These gates had remained locked and bolted from the inside since Emperor Mahendran left Kanchi eight months ago.

Two soldiers stood guard outside, armed with spears and swords. They stared at the deserted highway snaking away into the distance, as if expecting someone.

A cloud of dust rose in the distance and horses' hooves were heard. The war drums on the terrace above the gates beat a warning as the vague outline of horses was seen. The two riders in front held nandi flags. Behind them came a majestic man in battle gear, riding a black, thoroughbred horse. More riders followed. All the horses stopped at the moat.

A flag bearer cried, "Open the gates for Paranjothi, the brave commander of Kanchi Fort!"

The guards folded their hands in respect to the man on the black horse. Paranjothi proudly showed them the lion-etched signet ring in his hand. Eight months back, he had come to Kanchi as an innocent boy—his mature face was now battle-scarred. The guards saluted him and blew their horns. The massive gates clanked open, making way for the travellers.

Paranjothi crossed the moat. Ranks of armed soldiers stood in the stone-paved, circular courtyard beyond the gate. In the middle was Mamallan in a two-horse, ornamental chariot. Kannapiran stood by it, holding the horses' reins tightly. A massive nandi flag rustled loudly in the northern wind, as if crying, 'welcome,' to the new commander.

Mamallan jumped down. At a signal from him, a soldier roared,

"Welcome to Commander Paranjothi, the brave warrior who defeated Pulikesi's demonic Chalukyan forces!" The sound of drums, trumpets, conches and cymbals mixed with the soldiers' enthusiastic cheers.

Surprised at this grand welcome, Paranjothi quickly jumped off his horse. Before he could fall at the prince's feet, Mamallan stopped him and hugged him.

"Brave warrior, I have been eagerly waiting to see you for the last eight months!" The prince seated Paranjothi beside him in the chariot and Kannapiran climbed to the deck.

Mamallan asked, "Commander, shall we go straight to the palace? What do you want to do?"

"Lord, I would like to inspect Kanchi. There is no time to lose."

At the prince's command, Kannapiran drove the chariot forward. The fort gates closed. Silence once again descended on the northern entrance.

Old Friends

THE CHARIOT MOVED down Kanchi's wide, beautiful streets. Paranjothi remembered entering the northern gate eight months ago. *How different today's entrance was!*

Mamallan said, "Commander, you are very thoughtful."

Paranjothi came back to the present. "Forgive me, lord. I can hardly believe that I am seated as an equal beside the prince who defeated all the southern kings and earned the title, 'Mamallan.'"

"Nonsense! It is my privilege to sit beside you. Aren't you the great warrior who whipped Pulikesi's army? Aren't you the whirlwind which scattered his elephant brigade? The emperor's messages described the cavalry's bravery under your command ..."

"Ah, lost in the warmth of your welcome, I forgot to give you the scroll which the emperor sent."

Mamallan laughed. "Commander, are you sure that this is the emperor's scroll? It has not been changed somewhere on the way?"

Paranjothi smiled in embarrassment. "You know that story!"

"I know everything—including how you became friends with Vajrabahu." The two men laughed together. "I insisted that the emperor send me a detailed report of the battle every week. Commander, I am seeing you for the first time, but I have known you through my father's letters. Today, I see you as an old friend."

"Lord, I feel the same—not a day passed without the emperor saying something about you."

The prince held Paranjothi's hands. "Commander, we are lucky. We are kindred spirits. As Thiruvalluvar said, friendship grows between kindred spirits even without personal interaction."

"My prince, I do not know Thiruvalluvar or his works. The emperor has made you responsible for educating me—read his scroll."

A little embarrassed, Mamallan replied, "I am obliged to obey the emperor's every command …"

Paranjothi interrupted: "But this command is not for my benefit—it is for yours. I believe you have every virtue … except patience. Once you start teaching me, you will learn patience. How much confidence the emperor has in my intelligence!"

Mamallan burst out laughing and Paranjothi joined him. Seeing them laugh, Kannapiran could not control his own laughter. Hearing them, the horses neighed. This made the men laugh more.

An Oath of Friendship

PARANJOTHI STARED EAGERLY at Kanchi's mansions, crowded markets, lamp-lit temples, schools and art pavilions. The city bustled with activity. *The people have regained confidence and go about their routine. But very soon, this beautiful city will become dark and deserted.*

They reached the Ekambar Temple. Paranjothi said, "The last time I was in Kanchi, I searched for this temple but did not get to it. Please stop the chariot. Let me have a good look at Kanchi's heart." He gazed at the endless rows of lighted lamps inside, the magnificent temple car standing at the junction of four wide streets, the stalls with mountains of flowers, bananas and coconuts and the exquisitely sculpted hundred-pillared halls. "Ah, Pulikesi's love is easy to understand!"

"Pulikesi's love? What do you mean, commander?"

"Vajrabahu told me about Pulikesi's love for beautiful Kanchi. Like a man's face changes when he hears his lover's name, Pulikesi's face changes when he hears the word, 'Kanchi.'"

"Commander, Vajrabahu is clever—but wasn't it taking too much of a risk to meet Pulikesi in person?"

Ignoring the question, Paranjothi asked, "Sir, are Aayanar and Sivagami well?" Paranjothi noted the change that came over the prince's face at the word, 'Sivagami.' *Ahah, Mamallan is an example for Vajrabahu's words on love!*

The prince spoke with a new fervour: "I know that they are well, although I have not seen them for months." Mamallan's voice shook. "Commander, you have served the Pallavas well—but your greatest service was saving Aayanar and Sivagami. Take this as a symbol of my appreciation ..." He held out the spear which Paranjothi had thrown at the mad elephant.

Paranjothi's heart melted. Speechless, he grasped the spear's hilt.

Mamallan continued to hold the spear with one of his own hands. "I have often prayed at this temple to be blessed with a close friend ... you are the answer to my prayer. Commander, let us swear eternal friendship on this spear which saved Aayanar and Sivagami's lives."

The Ekambar Temple bell pealed in accompaniment to the *deeparadhana.*

That night, Kannapiran told Kamali, "Darling, I drove your friend's rival in my chariot today."

"What! Tell me at once who she is. I will go and poison her!"

"Not 'her.' It is 'him.' The man who saved your friend from the elephant has come back from the battlefield as the commander of Kanchi Fort. If you saw the prince enjoying his company, you would think that he had forgotten even Sivagami."

"Kanna, Mamallan is so fond of that boy only because he saved Sivagami."

"How clever you are! What a pity you married a mere charioteer. You should have married the chief minister of this kingdom."

"Don't you know, 'love is blind,'" replied Kamali.

Sivagami's Birthday

THE EXCITEMENT, THE disciples and the clink of chisels on stone were all missing from Aayanar's forest home. The fresh leaves of spring had given way to a mature, dark green. Dried leaves littered the ground, where the rainwater puddled. The forest birds' songs seemed sad.

Aayanar had returned to the forest with just one apprentice. He heard rumours that Paranjothi had joined the Pallava army and become a brave cavalry commander. Naganandhi too did not return. Aayanar's longing to know the secret of permanent paint pigment increased. He ignored his sculpture and devoted all his time to experimenting with formulas for paint pigments. He even lost his enthusiasm for Sivagami's dance.

This suited Sivagami. She spent her time thinking about her love, imagining the future and building castles in the air. *There has never been a love like mine in the whole world!*

Aayanar and his apprentice worked under a tree. They ground leaves and extracted the juice which bubbled in a pan on a stove beside them. They were surrounded by more pans with thick, coloured liquids. The sculptor's calm face had changed—a greedy hunger filled his eyes.

Sivagami sat on the throne in the hall, mimicking different voices in an imaginary conversation.

A palace messenger said, "Lady, we are only following the prince's orders."

Sivagami said angrily, "I care a fig for the prince's orders! Looks like Mamallan has no work today—he suddenly remembers the sculptor's daughter. What is in that ivory box? Open it."

"These are wonderful pearl garlands from Korkai port. Look, my dear lady: even Emperor Harshavardhan's queen does not wear such pearls."

"Who wants pearls? Tell your prince this: there is a *punnai* tree on the bank of the lotus pond. Its flowers outshine his Korkai pearls. If he wants, let him come to see those flowers. And what is in those baskets?"

"Jasmine and *shenbagam* from the palace garden …"

"No! Take everything away at once. Tell your Pallava prince, 'Flowers were once the breath of life to Sivagami, but now she cannot bear the sight of them.' And why has the prince sent all this?"

"My dear lady, today is your birthday."

"Is it? I am delighted that the prince remembers this poor sculptor's daughter's birthday. But his memory is weak. Take all this back to him and say, 'Today is not Sivagami's birthday.'"

Aayanar's loud voice said, "Sivagami, my child, what is wrong with you? Why are you chasing them away like this? When the prince has remembered your birthday and sent you gifts …"

"Keep quiet, *appa*. The prince wants to cheat us with pearls and flowers. Whoever you may trust, never trust Mamallan. Messengers, tell your Pallava prince this: the day on which Mamallan's heart melts and he comes to see the sculptor's daughter will be her birthday."

Sivagami was silent. Then she spoke in the messenger's voice again. "Lady, the prince sent these birthday gifts ahead. He will be here soon in his golden chariot."

"Ahah, did Mamallan say he is coming? In that case, today is indeed my birthday. *Appa*, don't you know today is my birthday? At least today, stop your experiments … I hear the chariot!"

Sivagami jumped up. The sound of chariot wheels really came from outside. With indescribable happiness on her face, she ran eagerly to the door. Yes, the prince's golden chariot was there with Kannapiran on the deck. *But who is the man in the chariot? It is not the prince.*

Sivagami held one of the stone pillars at the entrance and stood like a statue.

Love's Tempest

PARANJOTHI BOWED HIS head, unable to meet Sivagami's eyes. The previous night, Mamallan had confirmed Paranjothi's suspicions that the prince and Sivagami loved each other.

Paranjothi's love for Umayaal gave him joy and peace, but Mamallan's love made the prince's heart a volcano spitting fire and smoke. Paranjothi's own heart melted as he thought of all the obstacles to their love. *The biggest obstacle will be the emperor. Will this love ever be realised?*

Paranjothi was devoted to Mahendran as to a father. He had earned the emperor's love and trust and knew his thoughts. *I am sure the emperor knows of the prince's love. He is against it. If I do my duty to the emperor, I will betray my friend. If I do my duty as a friend, I will be going against the emperor's wishes. And can this star-crossed love be good for Sivagami?*

On his first visit here, Sivagami had seemed a divine being to Paranjothi. *Sivagami evokes a pure emotion in me: a sacred mix of devotion, respect, affection, honour, happiness and maternal love.* Paranjothi's love for Sivagami could be compared to Lakshmana's love for Sita.

Once she realised that Mamallan was not in the chariot, Sivagami ignored the passenger and turned to Kannapiran. "*Anna*, is everyone at home fine?" Her disappointment was clear.

"No, my dear girl, no. Kamali has a headache, my father's knee is acting up and I am ill … something is wrong with my stomach. Kamali says, 'A cat is the only medicine for you.'"

"Cat medicine? What kind of joke is this?"

"I am always hungry. Last night, I ate nine *appams*, seven *dosais* and twelve *kozlukattais* and asked, 'Is there anything else to eat?' Kamali said, 'There is a mouse in your stomach. Eat a cat—only then will your hunger be satisfied.'"

Sivagami burst out laughing. Paranjothi too could not control his mirth. Hearing him laugh, Sivagami turned to him. "Who is this?"

Paranjothi picked up courage. "My dear lady, don't you recognise me?"

"Who … the boy from Thiruvenkadu?"

"Yes, I am Paranjothi ..."

Kannapiran interrupted: "Sorry, I forgot the introductions. This is the commander of Kanchi Fort, sent by the emperor himself. Without his permission, Lord Yama himself cannot enter the fort."

Paranjothi knew that Kannapiran, an eccentric genius, had the privilege of talking like this even to the prince. Ignoring him, Paranjothi asked Sivagami, "Where is your father? Is he inside?"

Sivagami's face showed her dislike of Kannapiran's amusing speech. "There is father."

Aayanar hurried to hug Paranjothi. "It is Paranjothi." He lowered his voice. "My boy, did you succeed in your mission?"

Paranjothi's voice shook. "Not this time. But, one day, I will bring you the secret of Ajanta's paintings."

"My boy, I heard that you joined the Pallava army on your way—but it does not matter. I will soon discover the secret formula for everlasting pigments myself. I am conducting some experiments. Come, let me show you." Aayanar moved towards the tree under which he had been working.

Sivagami stopped him: "*Appa, anna* has come back after eight months. Let us hear all his news."

"Yes, yes. Come, my boy." Aayanar led Paranjothi into the house.

Art Frenzy

PARANJOTHI AND AAYANAR sat on the platform, while Sivagami leaned on a nearby pillar.

"Do you know, *appa*? He is the new commander of Kanchi Fort," Sivagami said.

"Is that so? Naganandhi predicted that he would rise to a great position ..." Aayanar recollected himself abruptly. "My boy, what did you do with the scroll?"

"Sir, Chalukyan soldiers caught me and took me to Pulikesi. They took the scroll from me ..."

Aayanar gasped in surprise. Paranjothi heard a snake-like hiss which the others missed.

Aayanar asked eagerly, "My boy, did you really meet Emperor Pulikesi? What did he say?"

"He spoke in an unknown language ... it looks like you are eager to meet the Vatapi emperor."

"Yes, my boy. I even wish that I had carried the scroll myself. I believe Emperor Pulikesi lived in the Ajanta caves for two years when he was a boy. So, he will know Ajanta's secret, right?"

Vajrabahu was right to criticise art. See how Aayanar's passion for art has made him mad! It makes him forget that Pulikesi is the enemy—he wants to meet him! Paranjothi said, "Sir, I have not yet told you why I am here. The emperor commanded me to tell you ..."

"Oh, Mahendran Pallava! Once, the sculptors in the Pallava kingdom gave him the title, 'The Prodigy.' We should have called him, 'The Fickle Minded,' instead. He asked me to move to Mamallapuram saying, 'The five rock temples must be completed in six months.' Within a month, he ordered, 'Stop work on the temples.' He has changed, my boy."

"He is the same. The war forces him to do certain things ..."

"Shall I tell you the real reason for stopping work in Mamallapuram? It was to save the rice and dhal given to the sculptors. All the grains in the warehouses have been moved to Kanchi."

"These are essential moves during a war, sir. Kanchi Fort must be prepared to face a siege for one or two years. If only you saw the huge Chalukyan army marching ..."

"I have been hearing, 'The Chalukyan army is coming!' for the past eight months."

"But do you know why that mighty army is not yet here? If Mahendran Pallava had not gone to the battlefield, Kanchi would have vanished. Sir, I have seen thousands of Chalukyan war elephants standing like mountains stretching into the distance. The Pallava army has fewer than a hundred elephants, but we stopped the Chalukyan army at the North Pennai."

"My boy, I am glad to see your devotion to the emperor. What message did he send me?"

"Pulikesi's forces have crossed the North Pennai. It is impossible to hold him off much longer. The emperor has sent me to prepare Kanchi Fort for a siege which may go on for a year or two. We are evacuating all citizens from the fort and surrounding villages. The emperor thinks that it is unsafe for you to be here when the enemy arrives ...."

"What do I care which king comes or goes? And what can anyone take from me? Let them take these stone statues and chisels. Let them scrape the paintings off the walls and take them ..."

"Sir, you are speaking in anger. The Pallava kingdom is in great danger ..."

"What does the emperor command us to do?"

"You and your daughter may come to Kanchi Fort. Or you may go to Thiruvenkadu with an escort and stay with your friend, Sivanesan. You can do as you want."

Aayanar turned to his daughter. "Sivagami, what do you say, my dear?"

Sivagami had disappeared from her place by the pillar.

Little Kannan

WHILE AAYANAR AND Paranjothi talked, Sivagami quietly went out in answer to Kannapiran's signal. "*Anna*, did you call me? Is there any news from Kamali *akka*?"

Kannan lowered his voice. "Kamali asked me to tell you to poison that young man at once. He is Mamallan's rival for the kingdom. It is the talk of the town: the emperor has adopted Paranjothi and made him the heir to the kingdom. Mamallan will not inherit the kingdom."

"If only it was true .... it is the kingdom which stands between us. It is enough to have each other—why do we need the kingdom?"

"Looks like all women are the same! Kamali says, 'Isn't it enough that we have each other? Why must you work in the palace? Come, let us go and live in peace in some village.'" He paused. "I would like to do that, but little Kannan is in the way."

"And who is this little Kannan?"

Kannapiran smiled and looked rather foolish. "Little Kannan is in Kamali's stomach."

"I am so happy for you!" Sivagami exclaimed. "Is there anything else?"

"Just a small matter. This morning, Mamallan took me aside and said, 'Kanna, I did not sleep well last night.' 'That is clear from your face. Why didn't you sleep?' I asked. 'I wrote a letter.' 'To whom?' I asked. 'My father.' 'Okay,' I said. Then, very softly, 'I also wrote another letter ...'"

Sivagami said in a choked voice, "*Anna*, give me the letter!"

"You must not run away like last time. I had to blink like a fool when

Mamallan asked, 'What did Sivagami do when she got the letter? How was her face? How were her eyes?'"

"Enough of your jokes, *anna*. Give me the letter."

Kannapiran deliberately delayed before giving the scroll to Sivagami. She ran to the lotus pond.

The Snake Hisses

SIVAGAMI SAT ON the wooden plank under the *magilam* tree and took out the scroll which she had kept close to her heart. She pressed the scroll to her eyes and to her red lips and threw away the blank upper leaf. Like a child fearing that the *paniyaram* in its hand will disappear if it is eaten, Sivagami delayed the pleasure of opening the scroll. She then began to read.

'To Sivagami: the queen of Mamallan Pallava's heart.

In my previous letter, I said I would meet you in person, but I could not do this.

Love of my life, I had a dream last night. I was asleep ... I floated on the wind ... It was darker than the black ink which underlines your eyes.

To my joy, I saw your figure shining in that darkness. I thought, *Brahma made her body from the softness of a swan's feathers, the fragrance of jasmine, the moonbeams, the music of ragas.*

Like dew on the water lily, there were two tear drops at the corners of your eyes. I felt your breath on my face. Every cell in my body longed to embrace you, but I was afraid that if I touched you, your body would dissolve. As I drowned in sweet intoxication, you smiled and came closer.

I heard a cobra hiss and turned quickly. Two birds were fondling each other on the branch of a tree. A black-and-yellow cobra was slithering towards them. I drew my sword … and woke up.

Queen of my heart, I do not believe in dreams, but I fear that you are in danger. You must be careful. As long as I have my sword in hand, no danger will come to you or your father.

It will soon dawn. Let me give you my second piece of news. I have a new friend. It is none other than the brave young man who saved you and your father from the elephant. The emperor has sent him here to guard the fort. We were talking all night: mostly about you.

He brings you a message from the emperor asking you to come to Kanchi Fort or to go to Chola Nadu. Wait until I come there and discuss things with you. There is one advantage to the coming war—I will soon be free to leave the fort and come to you.

My darling, how wonderful it would be if I was just your father's apprentice! There would be no barrier between us. I need not have stayed away from you for eight months.'

Sivagami came to the scroll's end and read it once again. She turned to the fawn. "Rathi, I cannot read the prince's letter to you—you will not understand." She took the scroll and climbed two steps up the *magilam* tree. She reached into a hollow in the trunk and took out seven or eight scrolls. She added the recent one, put them all back in the hollow and climbed down.

Talking to her fawn and parrot, Sivagami headed home. "Come, Rathi and Shuka Brahmarishi. *Appa* will be waiting to eat. Are you angry because I did not read Mamallan's letter to you..."

As Sivagami disappeared into the forest, Naganandhi came out of hiding from behind a big tree. He walked softly to the *magilam* tree, pulled out the letters from the hollow and quickly read them all. He sighed ... the sound was like the cobra's hiss.

Rathi's Happiness

SIVAGAMI TILTED THE fawn's head and Rathi's wide eyes looked up at her. "Rathi, I am the luckiest girl in this universe. Mamallan says, 'What do I care about the kingdom? Sivagami, you are enough for me.' Isn't it enough if we have each other, Rathi? Why do we need the kingdom?"

Rathi shook her head as if to say, 'Enough of this nonsense!' and bound away to graze.

Sivagami was startled and embarrassed to hear Aayanar calling, "Sivagami, my dear!" *Did he hear me talking to Rathi?*

Aayanar smiled and calmed her. "My child, were you talking to Rathi? You poor girl! You do not have anyone to talk to in this jungle. At least in Kanchi, you have your friend, Kamali ..."

Sivagami hugged him. "*Appa*, do you know ... Kamali ... Kamali ..."

Aayanar was alarmed. "My dear, is something the matter with her?"

Sivagami burst out laughing. "Yes, *appa*. Kamali has a little Kannan in her stomach."

Aayanar held Sivagami tenderly. "I am glad, my dear. I blessed Kamali at her wedding saying, 'May you soon be blessed with a son. And may he become my apprentice and study sculpture ...'"

Aayanar fell silent. *I thought of marrying Sivagami to Paranjothi. But he has now become a great warrior and fort commander. Will he agree to marry a sculptor's daughter?*

"*Appa*, what are you thinking?"

"Nothing, my dear. Where did you go suddenly while I was talking to Paranjothi? The emperor has sent an important message. Come, we will go home and discuss it. Your aunt will be wondering where we have gone without eating."

They walked back silently. Aayanar's mind was fixed on Sivagami's future. Sivagami's heart buzzed like a honeybee around Mamallan's letter in the hollow of the *magilam* tree.

Dance of Joy

SIVAGAMI AND AAYANAR sat under a tree. Stoves and pans and mortars were scattered around.

Aayanar remarked, "My child, how come you look so happy today?"

Sivagami hesitated. "It is Kamali's news. And you said that we had news from the emperor ..."

"The enemy is marching on Kanchi. The city may come under siege. The emperor asks us to go to Kanchi or to Chola Nadu. What do you say, my dear? I want to stay here. My heart is at peace only in this forest."

"It is the same for me, *appa*. Why don't we stay here?"

Sivagami said this because Mamallan's message had asked her to stay there. She longed to see Kamali, but she knew that the prince disliked her staying in Kannapiran's house. Mamallan had said in a letter, 'My heart aches to think that you are sleeping on a mat on the floor of my charioteer's house—you who should sleep in a palace's jasmine-strewn, golden bed.'

Sivagami's love for Mamallan won over her friendship with Kamali. *After daring to love the prince, I have done something which stains his honour. I will not go to Kanchi against his wishes.*

Aayanar was worried: "Mahendran Pallava is wise. It may be dangerous to ignore his orders. There is no one to advise us. Naganandhi has not been here for eight months. I wonder what has happened to him."

To cheer up her father, Sivagami said, "Would you like to see me dance today?"

"Can I too watch Sivagami dance?" asked another voice. Naganandhi was there. "*Buddham saranam gacchami. Dhammam saranam gacchami. Sangham saranam gacchami.*"

Aayanar was delighted. "Swami, welcome, welcome. I was just talking about you ...."

"Really? Do you remember me? Does Sivagami say my name? I am lucky. Aayanar, Sivagami is famous throughout the land. You are blessed to have her as your daughter. Will I now have the privilege of watching the dancer whom the entire south is praising?"

Sivagami's dislike of Naganandhi was softened by his praise. When Aayanar asked, "Will you dance, my dear?" she replied, "Yes, *appa*."

They went into the house and Sivagami quickly changed into her Bharatanatyam costume. Mamallan's words of love and Naganandhi's praise gave her new enthusiasm.

Her dance had no song or meaning or *abhinaya*. It was a dance of sheer happiness. In it was seen the elephant's dignity, the Panchakalyani horse's grace, the fawn's leap, the wild peacock's captivating walk, the swan's exquisite beauty. She lost herself in a flood of ecstasy.

The Coward

NAGANANDHI SAID, "STOP, Aayanar—Sivagami and the earth cannot bear any more of this!"

Aayanar stopped the beat and Sivagami stopped dancing.

"Aayanar, how can you hide such divine art in this forest? It is like a miser locking up a priceless gem in a box. Your daughter's precious gift belongs to the world. Come with me to Nagapattinam where the Buddhist Mahasangha is to meet. Master sculptors, musicians and dancers will come there from Kannauj, Kasi, Gaya, Java and China. Let your daughter's and your fame spread through the world. Let us go to Uraiyur. The Chola prince, Parthiben, is an accomplished artist. He will be delighted to see Sivagami dance. We will show Sivagami the wonderful paintings in the Siddha Hills and go on to Madurai. Sadayavarman Pandyan is a great admirer of art. If he sees Sivagami dance, he will not leave you in poverty in this jungle: he will arrange for you to live in the loftiest palace in Madurai."

Aayanar and Sivagami listened to Naganandhi like mesmerised cobras which sway to the snake charmer's pipe.

"Aayanar, what do you say?" Naganandhi asked.

Naganandhi's plan suits the emperor's command. But Aayanar felt a strange reluctance. "What can I say? It is up to Sivagami."

Sivagami imagined herself dancing to the applause of thousands of people. But there was a vague suspicion in her heart too. "What do I know, *appa*? I will do whatever you think is best."

"Okay, Aayanar, what have you been doing? I do not see any new statues," Naganandhi said.

"You are the cause, swami," Sivagami accused. "*Appa* wants to find the secret of Ajanta's pigments. For the past seven months, all he does is grind coloured leaves into paste."

"What a waste of time! Haven't I promised to find the secret for you?" Naganandhi asked.

Aayanar said heatedly, "You gave me your word, but there is no sign of you keeping it. It was no use sending that scroll. That boy is now a great army commander—do you know?"

"I heard. I believe he came to Kanchi only yesterday—is it true?"

"Yes, he was here this morning. The emperor has sent him to guard Kanchi Fort. How he has changed in eight months! The humble, shy Paranjothi who came with you has gone. He is Commander Paranjothi now. What pride!" Aayanar hated Paranjothi for returning without Ajanta's secret.

Sivagami interrupted him: "*Appa*, he was not conceited. How respectfully he treated you! He hesitated to tell you the emperor's command."

Naganandhi asked, "Aayanar, what was the emperor's command?"

Aayanar said sadly, "He commands us to leave this house. What do you think of that? At one time, Mahendran Pallava was devoted to sculpture. What a high opinion I had of him!"

"I too had an opinion of your emperor. Only now do I realise how clever he is. The Pallava army has less than fifty thousand soldiers. With this small force, he kept the mighty Chalukyan army pinned to the North Pennai for eight months. Mahendran Pallava is extremely clever, Aayanar. Let that be. What did Paranjothi have to say?"

"Poor boy! He was captured by Chalukyan soldiers. He somehow escaped and managed to throw the scroll into a waterfall in the valley. Clever boy!"

Naganandhi sighed. "Clever … and lucky too. What a blunder I made!"

Sivagami smiled. "*Appa*, did you hear this? Kannapiran said that the people say that Mahendran Pallava may disinherit Mamallan and give Paranjothi the kingdom."

"Kannapiran is mad. He blabbers nonsense," said Aayanar.

Naganandhi said, "It would be better if Mahendran Pallava gives Paranjothi the kingdom instead of crowning that cowardly Pallava."

Storm in the Mind

SIVAGAMI FELT AS if she had been struck by a bolt of lightning.

The startled Aayanar asked, "Cowardly Pallava? Who is that?"

"It is the talk of the kingdom. Ah, but you are isolated in this forest. How would you know!"

"Know what? Whom does the world talk about?" asked Aayanar.

"I am talking about Prince Narasimhan Pallava, titled, 'Mamallan.' It is well known that he is a coward. I believe he trembled and fainted when he first heard the news of the Chalukyan invasion. Aayanar, why do you think the emperor did not take him to the battlefield?"

Aayanar was furious. "You wicked monk! How dare you talk like this about the great warrior who, at the age of eighteen, defeated all the southern kings and earned the title, 'Mamallan!'"

"Let me tell you this: the title, 'Mamallan,' is a hoax. All the kings defeated by Narasimhan were commanded to quickly surrender to him. The emperor hoped that at least in this way his son would gain courage. But that did not happen. Narasimhan trembled at the thought of war ..."

"Swami, stop! I cannot bear to hear you talk like this about the prince," Aayanar protested.

"I do not know what you will say when you hear the rest of the truth. But I do not want to talk about that before Sivagami."

Sivagami was in agony over Naganandhi's words about Mamallan. She stood abruptly and, without a backward glance, walked into the rear section of the house.

Naganandhi saw Sivagami's feet in the gap between the door and the floor. He raised his voice. "Aayanar, the emperor has another great worry about his son. In the history of the Pallava dynasty, there has never been such a seducer of women. The emperor got hold of a love letter written by the prince to a woman. That is why he has ordered the prince not to leave Kanchi ..." The feet under the door disappeared.

Sivagami ran into the forest as if chased by a thousand demons. She ran until she was exhausted and sat on a tree root. Her parrot and deer followed her. Rathi gently put her face on Sivagami's hand. Sivagami pushed her away shouting, "Chi! You miserable, unlucky creature! Go away!"

The foolish Shuka, ignorant of time and place, cried, "Mamallan, Mamallan!"

"You dimwit! Bringer of misfortune!" Sivagami raised her hand, but the parrot escaped. She remembered the letters in the *magilam* tree. *I must burn them right now*. She ran to the pond, climbed the log and put her hand into the hollow. She jerked back in terror as though bitten by a snake. She again searched the hollow: it was empty. *Where are the scrolls?*

Naganandhi came out of the forest on the other side of the lotus pond. He saw Sivagami search the hollow and draw back empty handed. The monk was as shocked as Sivagami.

Shatrughan's Story

IN THE PALLAVA army camp on the banks of the Papagni, Emperor Mahendran sat in a tent above which the nandi flag flew majestically. Shatrughan stood before him, dripping with perspiration. He looked as if he had travelled a long way.

The emperor stared at him. "Is it you, Shatrughan? It looks like you bring very important news."

"Yes, lord. I could not trust anyone with it." Shatrughan gave the emperor his report.

After sending Paranjothi to the Nagarjuna Hills with the scroll, Naganandhi went south. He spent a few days in a Buddhist monastery hidden in a dense forest on the bank of the Kedilam. He gave the monks there some instructions. It looked like one of them went to Uraiyur and another to Talakadu, the Kanga capital. Naganandhi then continued south to Nagapattinam. From there he went to Madurai where Maravarman Pandyan was on his deathbed. His heir, the young Sadayavarman Pandyan, ordered all strangers to be arrested. Naganandhi and Shatrughan happened to be locked up in the same cell and Shatrughan cultivated the monk's friendship. When they were freed, Naganandhi negotiated with the new Pandyan king for several days. At the end of the negotiations, Sadayavarman gave orders for mustering an army.

Naganandhi went north, accompanied by Shatrughan. The monk was very thoughtful. They reached the monastery on the Kedilam. Shatrughan guessed that Naganandhi suspected him of being a spy. This was confirmed when a young monk, who had earlier been in Kanchi's

Royal Monastery, kept staring at Shatrughan. When this monk gave Shatrughan his food, Shatrughan threw a little into the river. The fish which ate it turned blue, died and floated on the surface. That night, Shatrughan secretly searched the monastery and the surrounding hillocks. He found caves filled with weapons. At one spot, he heard the blood-curdling hiss of a thousand snakes but could not discover where this sound came from. The next morning at sunrise, Naganandhi left the hidden monastery and went north along the shore of the Thiruparkadal lake. Shatrughan followed him secretly. Finally, Naganandhi reached Aayanar's forest home.

Shatrughan had left a man called Gundodharan to guard Aayanar. He acted like Aayanar's apprentice and lived there. Gundodharan had nothing important to report. The charioteer, Kannapiran, and his wife, Kamali, had sometimes come there.

In Kanchi, Shatrughan had assigned Kannapiran's father, Asuvabalan, to keep an eye on the prince. Mamallan had wholeheartedly obeyed the emperor's command and stayed in Kanchi for the past eight months. He had spent most of his time preparing Kanchi Fort for a siege.

"Excellent, Shatrughan! I can see by your face that you have something more to tell me."

"Yes, my lord. I have some scrolls for your eyes only. If I have made a mistake, forgive me."

The emperor shouted angrily, "You fool! Have you intercepted the message which Pulikesi sent Dhurvineedhan?"

"No, my king. These scrolls have nothing to do with the war."

"Thank goodness! I was worried that you had foolishly interfered and ruined my plans."

"My king, these are love letters." Shatrughan took eight scrolls from his turban and gave them hesitantly to the emperor.

Mahendran frowned. "Let me see … Shatrughan, for the good of the kingdom, I am forced to cruelly tear apart Narasimhan's tender heart."

Mahendran's Mistake

MAHENDRAN'S HANDS TREMBLED. He read a few letters carefully and skimmed quickly through the rest. He said sadly, "Shatrughan, you should not have brought these scrolls to me. I should not have read them."

"My king, forgive me."

"There is nothing to forgive. You only did your duty—how were you to know it would cause me pain?" Mahendran Pallava sighed. "Shatrughan, listen to this … 'Love of my life. My body and soul long to see you, but my father has commanded me not to leave Kanchi Fort. Sivagami, my father's command is the one thing I cannot defy in this world. Even if Lord Shiva appeared and asked me to defy my father, I would never do it. My father has stopped me from meeting the two lovers who are dearer to me than my life. One is Sivagami. Do you know who the other is? Will you be jealous? She is the Goddess of Victory, Jayalakshmi. I want to meet her on the battlefield and come to you wearing the garland of victory which she gives me.'"

Shatrughan bowed his head.

"Shatrughan, how lucky I am to have a son like this! Staying away from the battlefield to keep one's word to a father takes courage. And it takes even more courage to stay away from the girl one loves with a pure, young heart. My heart is full, but I have been defeated. I thought that if I parted Narasimhan and Sivagami, Narasimhan would be freed from Sivagami's clutches. But true love grows stronger with every day apart. All my well-laid plans have been ruined by Kamadeva's floral arrows."

The emperor laughed and went on: "Shatrughan, Mahendran Pallava will never be defeated by Kama's arrow! Fly like the wind to Kanchi with my message. Dhurvineedhan's army is on its way to Kanchi from Talakadu. Let Narasimhan go to battle and destroy it. Before he leaves, let him go and see Sivagami if he wants. I will not stand in his way."

Shatrughan's strange smile seemed to say, 'Do you expect me to fall for your tricks?'

Garuda and the Parrot

"KAMALI, I HATE everything … I want to go to war."

"What is stopping you?"

"Mamallan, of course. It is because I am his charioteer that I am stuck in this fort."

"Otherwise, you would have broken free, is it?"

"One day or the other, Mamallan has to go to war. Then you will see whether I go or not. If I die a brave death on the battlefield, will you tell little Kannan about me?"

"I will tell Kannamma that no one in the kingdom can beat you at brave talk while sitting at home."

"What did you say? Kannamma? I say no girls should be born on earth. Never!"

"True. God should not create women to suffer in a world full of foolish men."

"What nonsense, Kamali! How do we make you suffer?"

"You said that you were going to die on the battlefield—doesn't that make me suffer? Mamallan has not met Sivagami for eight months—doesn't that make her suffer? Why on earth did she fall in love with Mamallan? Can the parrot which lives on trees set its heart on the eagle in the sky?"

"You are the one who said that no woman in the universe is your sister's equal."

"I said that out of love for her. I now realise that no good will come out of this. I was wrong to encourage Sivagami, and you were wrong to give her Mamallan's messages."

"Kamali, what is stopping Mamallan from marrying Sivagami?"

"Kanna, can the son of a sculptor's daughter ascend the throne?" She continued. "Four or five days back, when you were out, a stranger came here. He and your father had a long talk. When I heard Sivagami's name, I stood at the corner of the wall and listened. Your father told the stranger that Mamallan sends messages to Sivagami through you."

"That old owl! That hypocrite! …"

They heard horse's hooves and looked out …. a man was galloping past the house. His face turned an instant towards them.

Kamali cried, "Kanna, it's him! That is the man who was talking to your father!"

"He is the spymaster, Shatrughan. He is bringing important news from the emperor. I will go and see what it is." Kannapiran hurried out.

Half an hour later, the chariot rumbled to a stop outside the house. Kannapiran jumped from the deck, ran into the house and banged into Kamali outside the kitchen.

"The emperor has given Mamallan permission to go to war. Mamallan is leaving now."

"Are you going too, Kanna?"

"What a question! How can I stay when Mamallan is going?"

"Mamallan is the heir to the throne. He must fight—but why should you?"

"What is this, Kamali? When our motherland is in danger, can I just shrug and stay at home? Pulikesi is marching here from the north. The emperor is holding him back. In the west, the king of Kanga, Dhurvineedhan, is hurrying to Kanchi with his army. The opportunity that I have been longing for has finally come. Send me away with a full heart."

"Kanna, I do not have the energy. When I think of Sivagami, I feel depressed."

"And Emperor Mahendran has asked Mamallan to go to the forest before leaving for the battlefield and send Aayanar and Sivagami to Kanchi. Isn't he a good man?"

Kamali's eyes filled. "Let everything work out for the best. Kanna, you must come back safely."

Siege Preparations

MAMALLAN, PARANJOTHI AND Bhuvanamahadevi sat talking in the pavilion near the women's quarters.

"Lady, the prince cannot complain about being cooped up in the fort for eight months. He has repaired the entire fort—what can Pulikesi and Dhurvineedhan do now?" Paranjothi said.

"You must tell me what Narasimhan has done, Paranjothi. He never tells me anything. He thinks a helpless woman, confined to the harem, knows nothing about war," the queen said.

"*Amma*, are you the helpless one?" Mamallan protested and his eyes flashed fire. "I am the wretch who is confined to this fort. Like a fox in the middle of a war between two lions, Dhurvineedhan is marching on Kanchi. Even after knowing this, I must stay put in this fort. My blood boils!"

Paranjothi was confident: "The emperor will definitely have a plan to punish Dhurvineedhan."

The prince's eyes filled. "The emperor will make plans and carry them out. But what am I doing with the titles, 'Heir Apparent,' and 'Mamallan?' What will history say about my courage?"

Unable to look him in the face, Paranjothi turned to the queen. "The war has not even started. Mamallan will have the opportunity to prove his courage."

Mamallan exclaimed angrily, "What is the use of any number of wars or opportunities? How do we know that my father will not keep me locked up in this fort?"

Trying to change the topic, Bhuvanamahadevi said, "Paranjothi, you have not yet told me how Narasimhan has secured the fort."

Paranjothi said, "Eight months ago, the moat was a small canal: now waves crash in it as if it is a sea. It is filled with crocodiles. I wonder how many Chalukyan soldiers will die in the moat!"

"But that is only if they step into the moat. What if they build bridges? Or bring boats?"

"Five thousand archers will hide on the fort walls to shoot those who reach the moat. And there are nasty surprises for those who manage to cross the water—they will fall into hidden pits and break their legs; they will be caught in traps. Those who reach the walls will be smashed by rolling rocks as they climb."

"What if they fill the moat and use their elephants to smash the fort's wooden gates?"

Paranjothi laughed. "That is exactly what they plan to do. They will use elephants, drunk on arrack. But when the beasts reach the wall, a rain of spears will fall on them. Think of them trumpeting in terror, stampeding back into the Chalukyan army and killing the soldiers! And if the elephants try to break the outer gates, their heads will be shattered by the spears embedded in the gates."

Mamallan joined in. "*Amma*, it was Commander Paranjothi who inspired these plans. When he first threw his spear at the elephant, the elephant turned and ran. This gave *appa* the idea of fighting the Chalukyan elephants with spears." Mamallan hugged Paranjothi affectionately.

Paranjothi continued: "Lady, yesterday I saw lakhs and lakhs of spears piled up here. Kanchi's clever smiths have copied the spear which I brought from Chola Nadu. Mamallan has strengthened the fort walls, prepared Kanchi for a siege and stockpiled a two-year supply of grain. He has sent many citizens away from the fort: most importantly, the Kapalikas. Yesterday, the clever prince ordered all the wine shops in Kanchi to be shut. Today, all the Kapalikas have left Kanchi, skulls and horns in hand."

A maid hurried in and whispered to Bhuvanamahadevi. The queen said excitedly, "Narasimhan, Shatrughan is here with messages from your father."

Liberty

THREE PAIRS OF eyes stared eagerly at the sweating, panting Shatrughan.

"Lady, Mahendran Pallava's first message is for you: eight months ago, you sent your husband to war with a smile. You must now send your son to the battlefield in the same way."

Brimming with emotion, shoulders held proudly, Mamallan asked Shatrughan, "What message do you have for me?"

"News to delight you, lord. Forgetting the debt of gratitude which the Kanga dynasty owes to the Pallava dynasty, Dhurvineedhan is marching on Kanchi. The emperor asks you to take command of our army at Kazhugukundram and defeat him before he reaches Kanchi. He has sent you the bull-and-spear." Shatrughan gave him a scroll.

Mamallan's face glowed as he read the scroll with the bull and spear emblem. He frowned at the end. "Shatrughan, he says that he has sent me a verbal message through you—what is it?"

"Even in the middle of a war, the emperor remembers his duty to art. He asked me to tell you to go to the forest, send Aayanar and his daughter here and then go to war."

Mamallan's happiness was complete. *Now I can say goodbye to Sivagami before leaving for the battlefield. Is my father doing this because he knows how I feel about Sivagami? But how? Ah, my dear friend, Paranjothi, must have sent word to him.*

The prince's affection for Paranjothi increased, and he gripped his hands tightly in gratitude.

The confused Paranjothi asked Shatrughan, "Sir, what is your message for me?"

"Like Lakshmana followed Rama, the emperor asks you to follow Mamallan. He says that he will soon return to Kanchi and take charge of its security."

Overjoyed, Mamallan hugged Paranjothi. "Ah, my dear friend is coming with me!" He fell at the queen's feet. "*Amma*, bless me."

Tears flowed down the queen's cheeks. "My child, may victory be yours. May you return safely."

Mamallan hesitated. "*Amma*, while Sivagami is in Kanchi, please treat her as your daughter-in-law."

"I will treat that motherless child as my daughter," the queen assured him.

Mamallan smiled. "No, *amma*—as a daughter-in-law is enough."

Bhuvanamahadevi frowned. "Why do you say that, son? Maybe ..." her eyes fell on Paranjothi and her face cleared. "Ah, I understand. Paranjothi, who came to learn sculpture from Aayanar, is trying to steal Aayanar's greatest work of art, is it?"

"Let it be, *amma,*" Mamallan said. "There is no time to lose. Give us permission to leave."

Within an hour of Shatrughan's arrival in Kanchi, the prince and Paranjothi set out for Kazhugukundram and ordered the army to be ready to march at dawn. That same evening, Mamallan and Paranjothi galloped to Aayanar's house with a small cavalry escort.

Mamallan built castles in the air about his meeting with Sivagami, but the walls came crashing down: a large padlock barred Aayanar's front door. Silence enveloped the house.

The Journey

ONE *KARTHIGAI* EVENING, an open bullock cart went along the road from Kanchi to Chidambaram. Sivagami and her aunt were seated in it. Rathi gamboled behind the cart, grazing the grass on the roadside. Shuka Brahamarishi happily perched on Rathi's back or Sivagami's shoulders or flew above the cart. Further back, Aayanar and Naganandhi talked as they walked together.

There had been fifteen days of continuous rainfall in *Aippasi.* The lakes and rivers overflowed with water. The paddy fields were at the start of the second season. Ragi and rye flourished in the drylands. The roadside trees and the coconut and banana groves were a feast for the eyes. Dark clouds skittered across the sky, sometimes scattering raindrops. The north wind crept over the lakes. The birds sang in hoarse tones as if the cold wind had made their throats sore.

They were now about ten miles from Kanchi. Sivagami had convinced her father to agree to Naganandhi's suggestion, and they had set out on this journey. But she could not stop her pain or extinguish the angry fire which raged in her.

When one hears something bad about a loved one, one instinctively rejects it and is ready to fight with the person who dares to criticise him. But if one believes that the loved one is at fault, one is angry not only with the loved one, but with the whole world. This is human nature.

Sivagami had built a temple in her heart for Mamallan. Naganandhi's poisonous words brought that temple crashing down. The monk's lies were so clever that Sivagami completely believed him. *With a great war raging in the kingdom, why else would Mamallan hide in the fort?*

Sivagami admired Paranjothi's courage. *A village boy who came to study Tamil and sculpture has become a great commander. Compared to him, people will surely call the prince a coward.*

Sivagami also believed that Mamallan was a womaniser. *Ah, he is an expert in seducing innocent girls with charming words. He even pretended that he would seat me on the Pallava throne.*

Her sweet dream world shattered. *My life will always be filled with sorrow.*

Every morning, when the rising sun made the dewdrops on the trees sparkle like diamonds, Sivagami's spirits lifted, and she tried to comfort herself. *Why must I ruin my life because Mamallan is a coward and a rogue? As Naganandhi said, the world is waiting to celebrate my dance.* She imagined herself dancing in great assemblies and countless people applauding her.

But when darkness fell, she drowned in an ocean of sorrow.

That evening, they heard a large army marching towards them. The sound of drums and trumpets, the stamp of feet and war cries grew louder. Soon they saw the army's front ranks.

Gundodharan Arrives

AAYANAR AND NAGANANDHI hurried up to the cart. Sivagami and her aunt got down and stood by the roadside. Only the aunt, deaf to the sound of the marching army, remained calm.

The monk hid behind a tree. His companions were not surprised, as they believed that he had taken an oath not to look upon royalty. But everyone was shaken. *What army is this? Since it is coming from the south, it cannot be the Chalukyan army. Then whose army is it?*

On their way, they had met an exodus of people going south, leaving Kanchi and its surrounding villages. Most of them were women, children, invalids, beggars, the old, the blind and Kapalikas. The Kapalikas cursed the Pallava dynasty and swore to burn Mamallan and Paranjothi alive and then smear their bodies with their ashes.

Naganandhi smiled at this, and his cruel face became fiercer. The monk stopped here and there and eagerly listened to the news. He reported, "The Kanga army stands on the western border. The Pandyan king is marching with a large force from the south. You know about the Chalukyan army in the north. There is only one direction for the Pallavas to escape … the east. If he wants, Mahendran Pallava can find refuge in the ocean."

"Are you saying they can drown in the ocean? How cruel!" Aayanar said angrily.

"Master sculptor, the Pallava dynasty comes from the ocean's child—won't the ocean help them? They do not have to drown—they can escape to Sri Lanka on ships. The present king of Sri Lanka is Mahendran Pallava's dear friend. But I believe he is fighting to stay on his throne. Poor man: the Pallavas' hard times are affecting their allies too." Naganandhi gave an evil laugh.

Naganandhi's wide knowledge of the world and appreciation of art evoked Sivagami's respect. He encouraged her to dream of performing on great stages and earning the title, 'Dancing Queen of Bharat.' *This dream will come true only with Naganandhi's help—appa is ignorant of the ways of the world. I must bury my hatred for the monk and be his friend.* But Naganandhi's criticism of the Pallava dynasty and Mamallan only fueled her hatred. *God, won't you stop Naganandhi's poisonous tongue?*

Aayanar was stubborn: "Why should Mahendran Pallava run to Sri Lanka? He has Kanchi Fort."

"Just as his cowardly son hid in it for eight months, Mahendran Pallava can hide there now. If only the Chalukyas had marched non-stop, the fort would have been reduced to dust in an instant. Now it has been strengthened, and he can stay safely inside for some time. I do not know what the Chalukyan army has been doing on the banks of the North Pennai for six months!"

Sivagami said heatedly, "Swami, it looks like you will go to the North Pennai and personally escort the Chalukyan army here! What do you have against the Pallava dynasty?"

Naganandhi was calm. "My dear, I have nothing against the Pallava dynasty. I only regret that we cannot travel as we planned under their rule. I wanted to take you to southern Chola Nadu. Now that the Pandyan army is marching from the south, I wonder whether it is wise to go in that direction."

"What do you think we should do then?" Aayanar asked.

"There is a peaceful place on the banks of the Kedilam with many hillocks and rocks. You can work on your sculpture there. I think that you should stay there until the war is over."

Aayanar was increasingly suspicious about the monk. "Let us decide later, swami."

Aayanar and Sivagami were afraid that the approaching army was the Pandyan force, but the nandi flag in the front ranks made it clear that it was the Pallavas. The soldiers marched majestically, roaring, "Death to Pulikesi!" "Death to Dhurvineedhan!" "Long live Mahendran Pallava!" "Victory to the brave Mamallan!" War drums and horns echoed everywhere.

Sivagami spirits rose. *If Mamallan is a coward, would the soldiers cheer him?*

No one saw the sparks fly from the concealed Naganandhi's bloodshot eyes.

It was a small force of about fifty horsemen and two thousand infantrymen. The army marched past the travellers in less than half an hour and the noisy road was silent again.

"Aayanar, shall we go on? Ashokapuram is about half an hour away," Naganandhi said.

"Let us go. Sivagami, get into the cart with your aunt," Aayanar replied.

Just then, they heard a horseman riding towards them from the direction of the marching army. Aayanar and Sivagami were surprised—the rider was none other than Gundodharan, who had suddenly disappeared on the day that Paranjothi had visited them.

Gundodharan cried, "Master, why did you abandon me?"

Gundodharan's Story

GUNDODHARAN FELL AT Aayanar's feet. "Bless me, master. By your grace, I have found you."

"I am delighted that you have found us, Gundodharan. But we did not abandon you. It was you who disappeared mysteriously that day," Aayanar said.

"Master, what could I do? Kannapiran said that my grandmother had found a girl for me to marry and had asked me to come at once. I had to rush to Kanchi to tell my grandmother that I did not want to marry. I could not find you in the house. I ran to the lotus pond, thinking that you might be there—but only this monk was standing by the pond …" Gundodharan stared at Naganandhi.

"Am I the only monk in the kingdom? You must have seen someone else," Naganandhi said.

"No, swami, it was you. You had seven or eight scrolls in your hand and were reading one of them. You were hissing like a snake …."

Sivagami felt a pang as she remembered the missing scrolls.

"Stop blabbering. I had nothing to do with a lotus pond or scrolls!" Naganandhi declared.

"It must have been someone else, Gundodharan. Let us hear your story later," Aayanar said.

"No, master, it was him. When I saw his face and heard him hiss, do you know what it reminded me of? Oh, I must not say anything—the monk will be angry. He may even bite me!"

Sparks flew from Naganandhi's eyes.

Realising that matters were getting out of hand, Aayanar said, "What can I do with such a foolish apprentice, swami? Leave it, Gundodharan. What happened to the girl your grandmother chose?"

"Master, I said, '*Paati*, Prince Mamallan is a bachelor; my guru's daughter, Sivagami, is not married. Why must I get married? If you want, you get married—I will make the arrangements.'"

Gundodharan's listeners burst out laughing.

"Master, when I rushed back after seeing my *paati*, I found the house locked. *My master has abandoned me. Only God can help me.* I fell asleep under a tree. And as if God heard me, the prince and Commander Paranjothi came there on horses."

"And then?" Aayanar asked impatiently.

"More soldiers came riding behind them. Kannapiran was driving the chariot …"

Sivagami's head whirled. Her heart burst with questions, but she was speechless.

"Master, you should have seen how quickly Mamallan turned his horse and galloped away! Goodness! Who would have thought that the prince has such a temper! The other soldiers had a tough time turning their horses at once. By the time I rubbed my eyes, got up and came from behind the tree, all the horses had flown like the wind and disappeared."

Sivagami's heart was a tempest of emotions: happiness that Mamallan had come in search of her; fear of his anger; anger at Naganandhi for making them leave; worry as to how to correct her mistakes. She gathered courage and asked, "*Appa*, how could the prince come to our house? Wasn't he hiding in the fort, afraid of the war?"

Gundodharan said, "Master, who is the wretch who told such a wicked lie? Mamallan stayed in the fort obeying the emperor's command. As soon as he got the emperor's permission, Mamallan left for the battlefield."

"Which battlefield?" Aayanar asked.

"Master, the whole country knows about it. Dhurvineedhan, the Kanga king, is marching on Kanchi. Mamallan is leading our forces in Kazhugukundram to stop and destroy him. Didn't you see the army marching past a little while ago? It was on guard duty at the North Pennai. It is going to join Mamallan on the battlefield. Don't you know all this?"

Aayanar was amazed to see the dull-witted Gundodharan become such an eloquent speaker.

Naganandhi's cruel face was hidden in the dark. He said agitatedly, "Aayanar, we must reach Ashokapuram before night falls. You can question Gundodharan later."

Aayanar said, "My child, get into the cart. We will question Gundodharan later."

Sivagami had many questions for Gundodharan but one above all else: *how did he get a horse? Did the prince get over his anger and send Gundodharan to bring us back?* She turned to Aayanar. "*Appa*, let *athai* ride in the cart. I will walk with you for some time."

The Origin of the Horse

THE CART ROLLED on with the aunt. Gundodharan held his horse's reins and walked with the others.

"*Appa*, ask Gundodharan how he got a horse," Sivagami said.

Gundodharan roared with laughter. "Master, monks who have renounced the world and wear saffron robes ride horses these days. I pushed a young monk into the lake and took his horse."

Aware that Gundodharan's words were provoking Naganandhi, Aayanar said, "What is this, Gundodharan? Can you call yourself my disciple and behave like this? It is wrong."

The agitated Naganandhi spoke quietly to Aayanar: "Ask him for the details."

Gundodharan related his story. "Thinking that you had abandoned me, I fell asleep sadly under a tree. I awoke at the sound of horses, hid behind the tree and watched. The riders all galloped away at once. *If only I had a horse! I could catch up with my master.* As I sat worriedly under the tree, a young Buddhist monk came out of hiding from behind another tree. He asked me whether Naganandhi had come to the house. I replied that I did not know the name but had seen a Buddhist monk at the lotus pond. The young monk walked away. Happy to have a travel companion, I went with him. But he soon cheated me. He climbed on this horse which was tied in a hidden bend of the forest and galloped away without a word to me. Never trust a Buddhist monk—except this monk who is travelling with us."

Aayanar said, "Gundodharan, do not slander respectable monks. Tell us what you did next."

"So what if I did not have a horse, master? I had my God-given legs. After two days of walking, my legs ached, and I sat down by the lake. And who should come riding by but the same young Buddhist monk! 'Swami, what is this? You left before me, but you are behind me,' I said. 'My dear fellow, I had to travel carefully. In this beggarly Pallava kingdom, any horse is immediately confiscated for the war.' We travelled together for some time, the monk riding and me walking. He kept mumbling, 'I am thirsty ...' I felt sorry for him. Saying, 'Swami, satisfy your thirst with the water of this sacred lake,' I pushed him into the lake. How happily he drank the water!"

Sivagami could not control her laughter. Aayanar scolded her and turned back to his apprentice. "You wretch! What did you do next?"

"I saw that the monk did not know how to swim. His stole lay on the shore. I tied one end to a tree, threw the other end to him and said, 'Monk, make your way carefully to the shore. I am off.' He screamed, 'Aiyo! The scroll!' 'What scroll?' I asked. 'The scroll I brought for Naganandhi. Look, it is there.' I saw a scroll on the shore. I showed it to him, saying, 'Do not worry, the scroll is safe.' That is all—I climbed on the horse and here I am."

Naganandhi's voice was filled with hate. "Aayanar, ask your apprentice to give me the scroll."

Aayanar was troubled. "Gundodharan, what have you done? Anyway, this is Naganandhi. Have you brought the scroll? Give it to me."

"So, this is Naganandhi. Swami, here is the scroll."

Naganandhi took the scroll and held it under the moonlight. He realised that he could not read it. He started walking faster. The road was silent except for the tramp of feet and horses' hooves.

Ashokapuram

ASHOKAPURAM WAS ON the road to Chidambaram, about seventy miles from Kanchi. In the center of the town stood a majestic stupa—one of those built by the great Emperor Ashoka. Thousands of Buddhist families and monks had once lived there. At dusk, the fragrance of incense had spread through the town, prayer bells had chimed, and lamps had sparkled in the sanctum.

Ashokapuram was now a deserted ruin. A small light glowed in the building which now housed the monastery. Darkness enveloped the other intact buildings. Only the Ashoka Pillar stood tall even after nine thousand years, proclaiming, 'Dharma is Immortal.'

Aayanar and his company reached Ashokapuram an hour after dark. Aayanar looked up at the tall stupa in the moonlight. "Ah, if only all the kings on earth were like Emperor Ashoka! Why can't all men practise non-violence and live happily?"

To his surprise, Gundodharan joined the discussion: "Master, like Ashoka Maurya, Mahendran Pallava tried to establish the creed of love in his kingdom. What can he do if Pulikesi wants to ruin this? As long as there are snakes on earth, men have to pick up sticks and kill them."

Naganandhi looked at Gundodharan with angry loathing.

"Gundodharan is right, *appa*," Sivagami said. "As long as there are evil men on this earth, we need good men who can keep them in check."

"Yes, Sivagami. And not only that—if love ruled the world, courage would disappear. What is a world without courage? What would happen to stories and poems and art itself?"

Gundodharan struck the pillar, and it gave a ringing sound. "Master, it is made of good metal. A smith should melt it in his forge and make thousands of swords and spears from it."

Naganandhi walked ahead to the monastery where an old monk came to the entrance with a lighted torch. Naganandhi read the scroll Gundodharan had brought. The old monk was frightened by the change which came over Naganandhi's face.

Aayanar's group reached the monastery just as Naganandhi finished reading the scroll. Naganandhi calmed himself and spoke to the old monk. "Swami, please arrange for these people to stay here." He turned to Aayanar. "Aayanar, I must leave at once. It may be a few days before I return. This monk will arrange for your comfortable stay … and Gundodharan is here to help you."

Naganandhi stared at Gundodharan as if tearing him apart. He then spoke tenderly to Sivagami. "Sivagami, I am going only because it is a very urgent matter. I will be back with you soon."

Aayanar and his family were given a room in one of the cells near the sanctum in the ruined monastery. Once they were inside, Naganandhi entered a dark cell nearby.

Who Was the Loser?

SIVAGAMI COULD NOT sleep. *How could I believe Naganandhi's wicked lies? How angry Mamallan must be with me for disobeying his instructions to wait for him! But he will forgive me …*

Sivagami finally closed her eyes, exhausted by her travel. When she was half-asleep, she was startled to hear horses' hooves and Gundodharan screaming. She woke the sleeping Aayanar and they hurried to the entrance.

Gundodharan stood there shouting, "Master, that monk has stolen my horse!"

Aayanar pacified him: "My dear boy, that horse does not belong to you."

"But why did he throw a snake at me?" Gundodharan protested. He explained that Naganandhi had quietly gone to the entrance, untied the horse and mounted it. Gundodharan, who happened to wake up then, ran and caught the horse. The monk took a cobra from his bag and threw it at Gundodharan. Gundodharan shrieked and ran while Naganandhi galloped away.

Aayanar found this hard to believe. *He is blabbering. Maybe he was dreaming.*

Gundodharan said, "Master, I must get my precious horse." He ran after the horse and disappeared.

For the first three days, Sivagami was bored. After hearing Gundodharan's news, she wanted to go back to Kanchi. Aayanar was even more restless. Having come this far at Naganandhi's suggestion, he did not know what to do.

At sunset on their fourth day at Ashokapuram, Aayanar and Sivagami heard thousands of running feet. They ran to the entrance. Some distance away, the road to Chidambaram was visible between the trees. They saw crowds running helter-skelter on the road. An elephant carrying a howdah rushed by, surrounded by seven or eight armed horsemen. A few men carried a tall flag post with a tattered flag. All through the night, they heard men running in groups.

Aayanar said, "My dear, there is a battle going on somewhere. It looks like these are the losers who are running away."

"*Appa*, these men do not look like Pallava soldiers—the enemy must have been defeated."

"We cannot see in the dark, but I too think Mamallan's force has won."

After sunrise, there was silence. Sivagami stood at the monastery entrance. *Why can't someone come this way? I can ask them about last night's commotion.*

The silence was shattered by the sound of galloping horses which soon came into view. *There must be thousands of horses! How happily the soldiers ride with their spears and swords.* Sivagami swelled with pride when she saw a man on a majestic black steed carrying the nandi flag. *Yes, the enemy soldiers were running for their lives. The Pallava army is chasing them.*

Sometime after the cavalry, two horses and a chariot came down the road. *They are taking the road leading to this monastery: they must be using it as a shortcut to catch up with the cavalry. Who is that on the first horse? Am I dreaming? Yes, it is Mamallan Narasimhan!*

Sivagami's eyes filled. Overcome with emotion, she shyly stepped back across the threshold. She turned back when she heard a shout and the thud of a horse being reined in. Mamallan's eyes bored into hers with an indescribable mix of surprise and joy, love and fury. In the next instant, his horse again flew like the wind. Commander Paranjothi, following Mamallan, saw Sivagami but did not stop even for an instant. Seeing Kannapiran in the chariot behind them, Sivagami signalled for him to stop. Kannapiran reined in the horses and the chariot clanked to a halt.

The Battle of Pullalur

KANNAPIRAN JUMPED DOWN, held the horses' reins in his hands and came to Sivagami. "*Thangachi*, when did you come here? What town is this?" he asked hurriedly.

"*Anna*, this is Ashokapuram. We stopped here on our way to Chidambaram. We thought the forest house was not safe. The prince has completely forgotten us …"

"As if Mamallan would ever forget you! As soon as the emperor gave him permission to go to war, we went to your house. How angry Mamallan was to find the house locked!"

"Oh, someone who did not bother to look our way for eight months was angry, is it? Never mind. Where are you all rushing off to?"

Kannapiran climbed back into the chariot. "Haven't you heard about the Battle of Pullalur? If you stay here, you will see me come back with the Kanga king, Dhurvineedhan, tied to my chariot."

"*Anna*, I will definitely stay here. Tell Mamallan." She hesitated. "Ask him to forgive me if I have done anything wrong."

Kannapiran bowed in acknowledgement. He cracked his whip, and the horses sprang forward. The next instant, the chariot disappeared as if by magic.

Aayanar came to the entrance. "Sivagami, who was in the chariot?"

"Kannapiran, *appa.* Mamallan and Paranjothi were riding ahead." She went on. "*Appa*, as soon as the emperor gave him permission to leave the fort, Mamallan came searching for us."

"In that case, Gundodharan told the truth."

"Yes. And it is also true that Mamallan is angry with us for not staying at home."

"That is why I said we should stay in place. You were the one who stubbornly insisted we go on a nation-wide pilgrimage. Now look at the consequences! But why couldn't they stop to say a few words to us? How fond of us Mamallan was once."

"As if he is any less fond of us now! Isn't a war on? Everyone is in a hurry. Kannapiran said that Mamallan would meet us on his way back."

About half an hour before sunset, Gundodharan suddenly appeared. Sivagami and Aayanar eagerly questioned him.

"I ran after that monk … and I ran straight into the battlefield. Oh my! I have never seen or heard of such a battle!" exclaimed Gundodharan.

"What battle? Where did it take place? Who won?" asked Sivagami excitedly.

Gundodharan gave them the details of the Battle of Pullalur.

A few days after Pulikesi invaded the Pallava kingdom, the Kanga king, Dhurvineedhan, gathered an army and marched on Kanchi. Emperor Mahendran ordered Mamallan and Paranjothi to intercept Dhurvineedhan's army. The two armies met at Pullalur, a village about forty miles south-west of Kanchi.

The Kanga army was three times larger than Mamallan's forces, but Mamallan and Paranjothi led from the front and ambushed the enemy. Their clever strategies and courage inspired the Pallava soldiers to fight bravely. At the height of the battle, a rumour spread that Pallava reinforcements had arrived. Hearing this, the Kanga soldiers panicked, broke ranks and ran for their lives.

Word came that Dhurvineedhan was riding south on his royal elephant. Determined to catch him, Mamallan and Paranjothi split the Pallava army into small groups and sent them after him on different roads. They too dashed southwards. Gundodharan caught a horse running away from the battlefield and followed them. Unfortunately, his horse broke a leg, and he was left behind. Gundodharan then walked back to Ashokapuram.

Parkadal

SIVAGAMI LONGED TO hear about Mamallan's courageous acts on the battlefield and Gundodharan obliged her: "What a sight it was to see Mamallan charge into the enemy ranks, whirling his sword! It flashed lightning! Each flash beheaded an enemy soldier ..." Gundodharan stopped suddenly. "Master, where is the old monk who was here?"

"My boy, I think he stays in the temple. Twice a day, he comes and asks us if we need anything."

"Master, I must see him at once. I will see him and come back."

When Gundodharan reached the ruined temple, he heard voices. Under cover of the darkness, he softly made his way inside and hid behind a pillar, holding his breath.

"Take them and leave at once. You must cross the Varaha River by sunrise."

"What if they refuse to come?"

"Say something to get them to leave. Tell them a great battle is going to take place here. If that does not work, tell them the Parkadal Lake has breached its banks." Naganandhi gave his deep, terrifying laugh. "If it rains tonight, the lake will certainly breach its banks. If they still refuse to leave and the flood reaches the monastery, there is one raft left in the monastery. Use it to take them to the hillock we saw last month. Whatever happens to the others, Sivagami must be saved—do you understand, swami?"

Gundodharan's heart beat fast. *Some disaster is coming tonight. It is my responsibility to stop it. Lord Muruga, help me!*

The two monks came out of the temple, followed by Gundodharan. It was now completely dark. A few stars glimmered in the cloudy sky. The old monk went towards the monastery while Naganandhi circled the temple and made his way south-west.

Gundodharan hesitated. *Shall I go to the monastery and warn Aayanar? Anyway, the monks have made it clear that they will be protected. My task is to follow Naganandhi.*

Gundodharan followed Naganandhi as the monk climbed on a horse tied behind a tree and rode away. *Ah, I am going to recover the stolen horse.* Gundodharan easily kept pace with the monk who was forced to ride slowly in the increasing wind and dark.

After about an hour, a vast bank stretched into the distance like a mountain range. Rain began to fall, accompanied by blinding flashes of lightning and deafening rolls of thunder. In the light of the flashes, Gundodharan saw Naganandhi tie his horse to a tree and climb the bank. He climbed after the monk. The wet clay was slippery. Finally, Gundodharan managed to pull himself up to the top of the bank with the help of a tree. A brilliant flash of lightning showed a terrifying sight.

The Parkadal Lake was seething in the storm. With the white crests of its crashing waves, it lived up to its name, 'Ocean of Milk.' Gundodharan's blood turned to ice: Naganandhi stood a short distance away, his arms raised above the boiling lake. His demonic laughter rose above the roar of the storm. By his side, the lake had breached its bank ... water was starting to run out through a small canal. A spade lay at Naganandhi's feet!

A Cry in the Dark

GUNDODHARAN STOOD FROZEN in horror. He recovered his courage and stumbled forward in the wet clay toward the spot where the lake had breached its bank. Another brilliant flash of lightning showed him that the canal was now wider, and the water was flowing faster. There was no sign of Naganandhi. The spade lay on the same spot. Gundodharan leaped across the canal, picked up the spade and quickly started throwing mud into the canal. *This is useless!*

Feeling a hand on his neck, Gundodharan dropped the spade and looked up. *It is Naganandhi. He has a stranglehold on my neck.* Gundodharan caught the monk's wrist with his strong hands. The monk's mad laughter echoed above his head.

The short Gundodharan and the massive Naganandhi wrestled stubbornly on the banks of the overflowing lake, in the pitch darkness, split at intervals by brilliant flashes of lightning. And then, above the roar of the waves and the rain and the banshee-shriek of the wind, a majestic voice shouted, "Gundodharan! Gundodharan!"

The wrestlers froze for an instant, but their grips did not waver.

Gundodharan wondered, *Who can it be? I heard horses' hooves behind me as I came here …*

"Gundodharan, stop fighting. Do not waste your time trying to dam the breach. Run and save Aayanar and Sivagami. Do you hear me?"

Gundodharan recognised the voice. "I hear you, lord. As you command."

There was a blinding flash of lightning, as bright as a thousand suns. *There will be a roll of thunder next.* Gundodharan grasped Naganandhi's wrist even more tightly. As he expected, there was an ear-splitting roll of thunder. At that instant, Naganandhi's grip loosened and Gundodharan pushed the monk with all his strength.

Gundodharan saw Naganandhi roll down the bank and fall face-down into the canal. *How is it that I can see in the dark?* Gundodharan looked around and saw that the branches of a palm tree were on fire. *Ah, the tree has been struck by lightning!*

In the light of the burning tree, he saw a horse galloping away. He also saw Naganandhi's horse. Gundodharan charged towards the horse, slipping and falling into the mud. Even as he untied the horse and jumped on it, the palm tree's light faded. The light drizzle became a heavy downpour. *I have never seen rain like this!* The skies opened and unleashed all their water. *Ah, Naganandhi chose a good time to split the bank: the lake needs the canal. Somehow, I must reach Ashokapuram before the flood waters.*

But long before Gundodharan could find his way back to Ashokapuram in the rain and the dark, a long stretch of the embankment collapsed. The flood reached Ashokapuram.

Where Is Mamallan?

THE HORSEMAN WHO had commanded Gundodharan was none other than Emperor Mahendran Pallava: doyen of the arts, expert war strategist, master of disguise. Mahendran guessed that the Buddhist monk, Naganandhi, was Pulikesi's personal spy in disguise. This was confirmed by the scroll Paranjothi carried. Mahendran forged Naganandhi's writing and sent a message to Dhurvineedhan asking him to march on Kanchi at once. The Kanga king obeyed.

When Naganandhi read the scroll which Gundodharan brought, he was amazed to hear Dhurvineedhan say that he was marching on Kanchi as instructed by the monk in his letter. As Naganandhi had not sent any such letter, he suspected a trick. He rushed to Pullalur on Gundodharan's horse, but before he reached the battlefield, the Kanga army was retreating. To save Dhurvineedhan's life, Naganandhi took the king with him and fled south.

Mahendran Pallava could not leave the inexperienced Mamallan to deal with Naganandhi's evil schemes. He arrived on the battlefield with a thousand hand-picked horsemen. The Kanga army panicked and ran for their lives.

Mamallan argued with his father: "Why couldn't you trust me to fight this battle on my own?" The prince asked the emperor's permission to chase and destroy the retreating enemy.

Mahendran agreed but with one condition: "You can chase the enemy up to the South Pennai, but you must not cross the river."

After alerting Gundodharan, Mahendran rode south-east in the wind and rain, and reached the South Pennai about half an hour before sunrise. The rain had stopped, and a few stars could be seen in the clear sky. The river roared past in a welter of foam.

Shatrughan rode out from a grove of fallen trees. "Lord, I have never in my life been so worried. I was foolish to send you on your own. How did you find your way in this storm?"

"Leave that aside, Shatrughan. Was Dhurvineedhan here? Did you see him?"

"Yes, my lord. They crossed the river here. Dhurvineedhan was on an elephant. The others went in boats. They managed to reach the opposite shore before the storm began."

"They must have gone to the place you mentioned. We do not have time to chase Dhurvineedhan now. We have more important things to do. Where are Mamallan and Paranjothi?"

"There are about five miles south. Who knows what troubles they faced in this storm!"

"We must go and warn them at once. They must cross the South Pennai before sunrise."

"What if the monk comes here?"

"He definitely will not come for a few days .... Gundodharan threw him into the Parkadal canal. Can't you hear the roar? Parkadal Lake has breached its banks. By tomorrow evening, there will be floods from the Varaha River to the South Pennai. Come, let us go."

"Swami, what about Gundodharan?"

"Gundodharan tried to plug the Parkadal breach. That is impossible. I ordered him to rush to save Aayanar and Sivagami. I wonder what he did."

"Did they too get trapped? Ah, what a terrifying night this is!"

"One good has come from it, Shatrughan. I have another weapon with which to defeat Pulikesi."

"Lord, you are truly a prodigy!" Shatrughan exclaimed in wonder.

It was difficult crossing the fallen trees in their path, but the two riders reached the Pallava army camp before daybreak. The camp was in great confusion. The soldiers cheered loudly when they realised that Mahendran Pallava was there.

On seeing Paranjothi, Mahendran said, "Commander, we must cross the South Pennai by daybreak. Let those who can, swim across; let the others hold on to logs or planks. Drive the horses and elephants into the water. Forget about weapons and food—it is enough to save lives. The Parkadal Lake has broken its banks. The flood will reach us within twenty minutes!"

Paranjothi was terrified. He stammered, "Lord … lord … Mamallan left for Ashokapuram last night. There …" again Paranjothi hesitated.

"I understand. Mamallan has gone to meet Aayanar at Ashokapuram. Very well. It is no longer our responsibility to save Mamallan: it is up to Lord Ekambar. Let us try to save the soldiers here."

At sunrise, Mamallan's horse struggled to swim against the flood near the monastery. Aayanar, Sivagami and the aunt, along with Rathi and Shuka, stood on the upper terrace, anxiously watching the prince. At the same time, Gundodharan made his way to the flood-encircled monastery on a raft. The water in the streets was rising by the minute.

Shuka's Welcome

AFTER MEETING NAGANANDHI in the temple, the old monk came to the monastery and urged Aayanar to leave at once. But Sivagami stubbornly refused. The monk's warning that a battle could be fought there, only increased her determination to stay. *I can see Mamallan's brave acts with my own eyes.* She imagined Mamallan single-handedly beheading his enemies.

Half an hour after dark, the old monk came running and shouted, "Danger! Leave at once—or you will die!"

Aayanar asked in disbelief, "Swami, what new danger threatens us?"

"Listen to that sound: the Parkadal Lake has breached its banks. We must leave at once. By daybreak, this monastery will be flooded."

Sivagami said, "*Appa*, I have never seen a flood. Let us stay and watch the fun. Let the monk go."

"Ignorant girl, this monastery and the temple will be submerged. What fun will you watch? Ten years ago, I saw the Parkadal breach its banks. Thousands of people died in this low-lying area. Ashokapuram fell into ruin after that."

Aayanar and Sivagami were troubled, but they could not make up their minds to leave at night. A strong wind started, along with rain. Sivagami was worried about Gundodharan being caught in the rain.

"Gundodharan is behaving very strangely," Aayanar remarked. He turned worriedly to the monk. "Swami, what do you suggest?"

"What can I say now? I said that we should leave in the evening itself, but you refused to listen. I will go to the neighboring village and bring a raft. Stay here until I come back. If we make it through the night, it will only be by Lord Buddha's grace. Ah, what a great responsibility Naganandhi has left me with!" Saying this, the old monk went out into the dark and rain.

Soon after he left, the flood reached Ashokapuram. The water seeped into the monastery through the gaps in the doors. Soon it knocked down the doors and poured inside. The rising water made Aayanar and his company move to the stairs.

Sivagami hugged Aayanar. "*Appa*, my foolishness has brought you to this! Oh, why did I bring this parrot and deer?" She fondled the creatures who sensed danger and stood close to her.

Aayanar tenderly patted Sivagami. "My child, if we are fated to go to Kailash like this, who can stop it? Listening to Naganandhi has brought us here."

"It is all Mamallan's fault," Sivagami cried. *He saw me at the entrance, but he did not take us with him. I hope we die just to make him suffer. That hard-hearted man deserves it! But why should appa and athai and Rathi and Shuka die because of my bad luck? Why can't only I die?*

The storm weakened. They went to the top storey and looked out. In the dim light of the coming sunrise, they saw water everywhere. Thatches, stacks of straw and trees floated on the water.

In her heart of hearts, Sivagami hoped that Mamallan would come to her rescue. *Useless wish! But what is this? Am I dreaming? Isn't that Mamallan on that horse which is swimming against the tide? Yes, yes! It is him! Goddess Parvathi, be merciful. Let him cover the distance safely.*

"*Appa*," Sivagami cried excitedly. "Look who is coming!

Shuka Brahmarishi tilted his head and cried out in welcome, "Mamallan! Mamallan!"

The Raft

MAMALLAN SMILED AT the parrot's welcome. He saw Gundodharan on a raft nearby and signalled to him. Gundodharan skillfully steered the raft around the monastery's pillars and stopped near Mamallan.

"Who are you, my fellow? Your face is familiar," Mamallan said.

Gundodharan showed him the signet ring hidden in his turban. "I am Shatrughan's man, lord. I have been with Sculptor Aayanar for eight months, as commanded by my master."

"How did you get this raft?"

"An old Buddhist monk was on it. If I counted you, there was no room for him on the raft—so I pushed him into the water and took it."

"How did you know that I was coming?"

"Lord, could I be Mahendran Pallava's spy without knowing even that?"

Mamallan leaped easily from the horse to the raft. He stroked the horse's face and said tenderly, "Dhananjaya, try to escape. God will save you." The horse began to swim swiftly towards the road where the tops of two rows of trees rose above the flood.

Gundodharan and Mamallan steered the raft carefully to the monastery. Aayanar and the aunt lowered Sivagami into Mamallan's arms. As the raft rocked, the terrified Sivagami screamed. Mamallan held her tightly and helped her sit. She screamed again when the raft rocked under Aayanar and her aunt. Shuka flew around in circles and alighted on a corner of the raft. The raft moved and Sivagami cried, "Aiyo, we are leaving Rathi behind!" But Rathi leaped into the boat.

Gundodharan said, "Lord, hold the raft in place for a while. I will be back." He jumped from the raft and swam into the monastery.

Sivagami's anxiety grew as they waited for Gundodharan. At last, he looked down from the terrace, carrying a sack. He handed the sack over first and then climbed into the raft.

The aunt felt the sack and said, "Beaten rice."

"You know me, lady ... I can bear anything, except hunger," Gundodharan agreed.

"What foresight!" the prince said approvingly. "Timely saviour: that is our Gundodharan."

Gundodharan and Mamallan had to navigate carefully among the trees and logs drifting in the fast-flowing water. Dark clouds still gathered in the sky. The light wind chilled them.

Sivagami soon got over her fright and began to laugh and play. She turned to Mamallan. "I have often dreamt of drifting endlessly in such a raft … is this a dream?"

Mamallan replied, "It seems like a dream to me too."

"But, in my dream, the boat had only me and one other person …."

"Who was that one person?"

"I will not say."

Towards evening, they were happy to see rocky, forested land a little distance away.

"Gundodharan, why don't we get down here?" Mamallan asked.

Gundodharan was worried. "Lord, the flood is strong and there are rocks on the shore."

The strong current carried the raft to the island. Gundodharan and Mamallan did their best to steer to the shore, but the raft sped straight towards the rocks, crashed, shattered and sank.

Mamallan's Thoughts

SIVAGAMI WAS THROWN into the water. Light flashed in her eyes and then there was only darkness. Her ears buzzed. There was sand under her toes. In a split second, she remembered the raft and realised that she was struggling to breathe underwater. *Ah, why couldn't Mamallan and I have held hands and died together?* A hand gripped hers. *It is Mamallan—are we both leaving behind this cruel world and going to paradise?*

The water level went down to Sivagami's hips. She was in agony as water flowed from her mouth and nose. Mamallan stood with her hand tightly in his. Gundodharan, Aayanar and her aunt stumbled against the current. Shuka screeched and flew in circles. Rathi had somehow made it to the shore and was now kicking her legs as she tried to clamber up a rock.

The raft had sunk at a spot where the current had plowed a deep hole. But just beyond that was a wide expanse of shallow, higher ground. This was the reason for their survival. They all stumbled onto the shore.

"Aiyo! It is gone!" cried Gundodharan. Everyone turned to him in alarm.

"The sack of rice is gone!" Gundodharan lamented.

They burst out laughing. The men and women went their separate ways to wring out the water from their clothes.

Mamallan said, "Gundodharan, the raft is gone. What shall we do?"

"Lord, I am glad the raft smashed against the rocks. Otherwise, we would have drifted out to sea." He paused. "We can get a raft at the village there, but it is best to stay here until the flood subsides."

"Nonsense, Gundodharan! Are you asking me to leave my army somewhere and stay here? I had planned to take these people to safety and then go back with you in the same raft."

"Lord, the army must have moved. The shores of the South Pennai must be completely flooded."

"That is why I must go back. What will Paranjothi and the others think of me?"

"Do not worry about them. The news of the breach would have reached them in good time."

As their clothes dried, Gundodharan told Mamallan about the emperor suspecting Naganandhi and Shatrughan assigning Gundodharan to watch Aayanar's house. He related the series of events which led to his fight with the monk on the shores of the lake the previous night. He ended with the commanding voice which made him grab the raft from the old monk.

Mamallan's respect for Mahendran Pallava grew, and he was amazed at Gundodharan's resourcefulness. "But why did you commit the sin of pushing the old monk into the water?"

"He is not a Buddhist monk, lord—he is an imposter. He was a guard at Kanchi Fort. He fell into Naganandhi's hands and became a traitor. I should have thrown a stone on his head!"

"In that case, why did you spare Naganandhi? He is the root cause of everything."

"Lord, I decided to kill that cobra, but I could not disobey the command, 'Stop fighting!' That is why I pushed him into the canal and left. Maybe that fraud of a monk drowned there."

"That evil man does not deserve an easy death. What danger he led Aayanar and Sivagami into!"

"Lord, let us not tell them about Naganandhi. They know nothing and will suffer unnecessarily."

Mamallan agreed. "Don't you know who commanded you on the lake's shore?"

"I guessed, lord. Forgive me, I did not dare to tell you."

Mamallan was pained. *My father followed me ... doesn't he have faith in me? What I have done now justifies his low opinion of me. I left the army by the river and got caught in the flood. How can I look him in the face when I next meet him? To hell with shame and disgrace! I will give anything for this one day's happiness. I can look back on it for the rest of my life.*

Gundodharan broke into the prince's thoughts: "Lord, let us first think about the night. We cannot stay in the open ... what if it rains? There is a village a little distance away. Let me go and make enquiries."

"Do that."

They heard Shuka crying, "Mamallan, Mamallan." The prince followed the sound and found Sivagami sitting by herself under a *magilam* tree on the shore. He sat beside her.

Under the *Magilam* Tree

MAMALLAN STARED AT Sivagami's face. Sivagami looked at the ground, the water, the sky. Her eyes sometimes hovered over Mamallan's face before quickly turning away.

Mamallan broke the silence: "What are you thinking, Sivagami?"

Her eyes brimmed with tears. "If only you knew how I suffered in the past year."

"Did anyone torment you?" Mamallan pretended ignorance to make her declare herself.

"No one tormented me. I am a simple girl who grew up in the forest.

I do not know how to express myself. Lord, I suffered because I could not forget you." Tears flowed from her eyes.

Mamallan's eyes blazed with passion. "I too suffered. Didn't you read my messages?"

"I memorised every word. I would be happy while reading the letter. Then I would be furious with you … why didn't you stop when you saw me at the monastery?"

"I was angry that you had disobeyed my advice to stay in the forest. But didn't I come back that night in spite of the storm? What important work I left behind! I am waiting for a smile from you, but you weep and make me sad."

"You are the cause of this change. Two or three years back, I was full of joy and laughter …"

"Sivagami, tell me about those happy days of your childhood."

"I was the apple of my father's eye. I knew no worry or pain. Everything in the world was a wonder and a joy. I delighted in the colourful flowers and the songs of the birds. I chased butterflies. At night, the stars seemed to wink at me. I imagined the moon to be a beautiful boat floating on the dark blue ocean of the sky. I gathered handfuls of stars into my lap.

"Dance became my passion. I danced as I played in the forest; my feet beat a rhythm when I went to bathe in the lotus pond.

"My life was a river of joy when you and your father came to our forest home one day …"

The Bud Unfurls

MAMALLAN CONTINUED: "WHEN we first came to your house, you were dancing. I clapped loudly at the end of the dance. There was not an atom of shyness in the happy look you gave me."

"Lord, I was an innocent, eleven-year-old girl. I did not know that the eyes which dared to look the sun in the face would soon be dazzled and forced to look down."

"Sivagami, you are a lighted lamp; I am the moth which flies around it."

Sivagami took up the thread: "Your father said, 'Play with Sivagami while I talk with Aayanar.' We held hands and skipped into the forest. After showing you my favourite places and trees, I took you home and showed you my birds. When you saw my father's statues of dancers, you said, 'I too want to learn to dance.' You held one of the statue's *abhinaya*, and I burst out laughing.

"I waited for your visits. My heart would leap at the sound of horses' hooves or chariot wheels. When I saw you, I felt the same joy which I felt when I saw the sun and the moon and the flowers and birds. I talked to you without stopping to take a breath ..."

Mamallan said, "Your words were like birdsong. Even if I did not understand, I would keep listening ..."

Sivagami continued, "You travelled with the emperor for three years. I grieved that I would never see you again. Then I decided to master dance and stun you with my performance when you came back. Finally, one day, you came .... you were a new man."

"You too had changed, Sivagami. You stood shyly behind a pillar, looked at me from the corner of your eye and smiled. That look and that smile captivated me."

"I was rooted to the spot. *Appa* said, 'Sivagami, why are you hiding behind that pillar? Come and pay your respects to the emperor. And look at the prince: see how big he has become.' I came forward. The emperor said, 'Aayanar, I did not recognise Sivagami at first—she has grown. I thought you had sculpted a statue in gold.' His words made me shy. I quietly went to the forest. I sat by the lotus pond and wondered what had come over me.

"I heard soft footsteps behind me. I did not turn back. You came and covered my eyes. Three years ago, when you did this, I would say your name, laugh and push away your hands. But now my body froze. Waves of emotion crashed in my heart.

"You sat by my side and held my hand. I was still. 'Sivagami, are you angry with me?' you asked. I was silent. You told me about your trip, but I heard nothing. My heart was filled with only one thought. *He is sitting beside me. He is holding my hand ...*"

Mamallan smiled. "What a fool I was! I thought you were listening with great interest to my tour experiences!"

Sivagami said, "When you were leaving, you said, 'I will be back soon.' I floated on a happy cloud. There was a fresh beauty in the sky and the earth and a new sweetness in the songs of the birds. When I sailed the night skies in my ivory boat, gathering the stars, you were by my side. I sang to myself. My father was amazed at my great progress in dancing …"

Mamallan interrupted her: "My father said that even the author of the *Natya Shastra* could not grasp the beauty of your dance. He insisted that your debut dance recital be held in the royal court at Kanchi."

"Lord, all my happiness disappeared after that unlucky recital. Thinking of you made me sad. I could not sleep and I forgot my love for dance. Rumours about your marriage arrangements pierced my grieving heart like a spear. I wanted you all to myself. I was the one who urged my father to visit Navukkarasar in Kanchi. You know what happened there …"

"I knew how you felt. That is why I sent you a letter through Kannapiran the very next day."

"That letter said that you did not approve of me coming to Kanchi. My pain grew day by day over the next eight months. Your letters cheered me for a while: then my heart would ache even more. I felt that I would never see you again. I began to think, 'Why can't I end my life? I will go mad if I continue like this.' Lord, do you now know why I did not stay in the forest house?"

They were startled by the distant sound of musical instruments and cheers.

The Welcome

AAYANAR AND THE aunt joined them as a crowd came towards them. Gundodharan walked ahead of it.

Mamallan was furious. *The fool, Gundodharan, has announced, 'The prince is here.' He has ruined my plans of spending what little time I have with Sivagami. What will the people think about me being here without the army?* The prince stepped back a little.

Gundodharan spoke softly to Aayanar and Sivagami. The crowd reached them, and Gundodharan pointed out Aayanar to the leaders.

The village head said, "Mandagapattu is blessed to welcome the King of Sculpture and the Queen of Dance. We will do our best to make you and your apprentices comfortable. Please be our guests for as long as you want."

Aayanar replied, "Good people, thank you for your help. We must stay with you until the flood waters ebb." Aayanar and his company went with the villagers.

Mamallan was amazed—except Sivagami, who glanced at him from the corner of her eye and smiled, nobody took any notice of him. *How clever Gundodharan is!*

Gundodharan said softly from behind the prince. "Lord, didn't you hear them say, 'Aayanar and his apprentices?' You and I are the apprentices."

"Are all Shatrughan's men as clever as you, Gundodharan? If so, even if a thousand Pulikesis march against us, we will be victorious."

The two men walked a little behind the crowd, but Mamallan stayed within sight of Sivagami.

The threshold of every house was decorated with colourful *kolams*. Young girls greeted Sivagami with *aartis*. Finally, they reached the small, beautiful Shiva temple at the end of the village. The air was filled with the fragrance of incense and sandalwood and flowers, smoke from ghee lamps and the smell of coconuts, ripe bananas and sugarcane. Aayanar and his company worshipped the deity. The *archakar* offered them holy ash, water, flowers and *kungumam*.

The village head said humbly, "Aayanar, we have heard much about Sivagami's skill as a dancer. Your daughter must please us with a dance recital in the sanctum tomorrow."

Sivagami looked at Mamallan. His smile and the glow in his eyes answered her question. She turned to Aayanar and said softly, "Alright, *appa*."

Aayanar said, "Sir, I am surprised that you know so much about Sivagami's dance. How is that?"

"Navukkarasar was here six months ago. After his disciples sang *Munnam avanudaya namam kettal*, Navukkarasar told us about

Sivagami dancing to this verse and fainting. We never dreamt that we would soon be privileged to see you in person." The headman continued. "After his visit, we built a hall in his name. You and your daughter will be the first to stay in it."

The Nandi Platform

MAMALLAN AND GUNDODHARAN stood at the Navukkarasar Hall's entrance.

Gundodharan said, "I cannot bear the thought of you sleeping like a poor orphan in this verandah."

"Gundodharan, my father did not bring me up to sleep only on a palace terrace. I have slept on the forest floor with tree roots as my pillow. And I have always wanted to wear a disguise and mix with the people."

"Lord, the villagers have heard of the Battle of Pullalur. I promised to describe the prince's heroic feats on the battlefield. They will be gathered at the temple tonight. Are you coming?"

"Yes, I am coming, but do not cause mischief and reveal my identity."

Mamallan and Gundodharan sat on the steps of the nandi platform. The villagers sat on the temple courtyard's clean floor.

Gundodharan described the Battle of Pullalur in all its violence and glory: "When Mamallan whirled his sword, the enemies died in thousands … Unable to face his fury, they ran from the battlefield. The one who ran fastest was the Kanga king, Dhurvineedhan."

"In which direction did Dhurvineedhan run?" a villager asked.

"I heard that he ran southwards. I also heard that Mamallan and Commander Paranjothi chased him up to the South Pennai." Gundodharan turned to the prince. "Sir, why are you pinching me?"

A villager asked, "You are just Aayanar's apprentice: how do you know all this, my dear fellow?"

Gundodharan said, "Looks like I must confess the truth." He rose and stood a little apart from Mamallan. "This man here … sir, why are you glaring at me? … he is Aayanar's apprentice. I am a Pallava soldier.

I was with Mamallan when he chased Dhurvineedhan. I fell back when my horse broke a leg. I got caught in the flood and climbed into these people's raft."

The villagers nudged each other and whispered. Many insisted that they had guessed that Gundodharan was not Aayanar's apprentice.

"Maybe Mamallan too will be washed ashore here by the flood," one man wondered.

"Maybe he will," Gundodharan said.

Sivagami's Dance

THE SHIVA TEMPLE was decorated with green banana plants and ivory-coloured tender coconut shoots and lotus buds. It blazed with the light of hundreds of oil lamps. The villagers gathered there at sunset, jostling for places in the front.

The full moon rose as if to watch Sivagami's dance. Silence fell when she stood on the platform. The audience was stunned by her dress and ornaments and the radiant glow on her face.

The villagers murmured, "Celestial nymphs like Rambha and Urvashi must be like this."

Sivagami danced to the beat of Aayanar's hands and his rhythmic music scale; she danced to the beat of a drum and the tinkle of her anklets. Sivagami danced on the earth; she danced on the moonbeams; she whirled among the stars. After dazzling her audience with various dances, she left the stage for a short break. There was a roar from the audience.

Forgetting himself in the excitement, Gundodharan turned to Mamallan and began, "Lord ..."

Mamallan shook Gundodharan out of his trance.

Gundodharan turned to the sanctum and prayed, "Lord, this dance is an offering to you!"

"Yes, it is an offering to God!" his neighbours agreed.

Sivagami returned to the stage and resumed her dance. Her audience clapped and exclaimed in wonder at her expressions, her body posture and hand *mudra*, but they were not satisfied. One of them whispered to Aayanar. Sivagami heard him. Reluctantly, she began to sing and dance to *Munnam avanudaya namam kettal.* At the end, her audience went into a frenzy.

Only Aayanar, Mamallan and Sivagami knew that her *abhinaya* fell short of the intense emotion seen during her performance for Navukkarasar. And she did not faint at the end of this recital.

Rebirth

ON THEIR THIRD evening at Mandagapattu, Mamallan, Aayanar and Sivagami went for a walk. They came to the spot where their raft had shattered. The flood had ebbed, exposing the submerged rocks. The bare rocks were spotlessly clean.

Aayanar wandered around, imagining the ways in which these rocks could be carved into temples. Mamallan and Sivagami were content to sit silently on a rock under the *magilam* tree.

Mamallan remembered the army he had left behind. *Gundodharan went in search of a boat this morning. Why hasn't he come back yet?*

The moon rose and climbed higher, like a golden pot of nectar rising from the ocean. Mamallan and Sivagami sat silently, their clasped hands speaking in secret. The fragrance of *magilam* flowers made them breathless with joy. They floated together in space.

A cool breeze shook the *magilam* tree and showered them with flowers, bringing them abruptly back to earth.

"Sivagami, why are you shivering? Is it the wind?"

Her voice shook. "No, my body is burning. I am afraid … will your love always be like this?"

Mamallan filled her hands with the flowers scattered on the rocks beside him. "Sivagami, my love is like the *magilam* flower whose fragrance grows stronger each day and endures even after it dries. Do you want me to promise again?"

"No, lord. I only want you to forgive me for believing the poisonous words of an evil cobra."

There was a rustle nearby. A snake slithered on the shadow-and-moonlight dappled ground near them.

Sivagami jumped up in fear. "Aiyo, snake!"

Mamallan held her close. "Sivagami, do not be scared. I am with you."

Sacrifice

THE SNAKE FROZE at Sivagami's cry and then slithered away. Mamallan and Sivagami moved to a brightly moonlit rock in the open.

"Lord, Naganandhi called you the 'Cowardly Pallava,' hiding in Kanchi Fort, scared to go to war. My heart said, 'These are lies. Mamallan is a good man.' But my pain over our separation made me believe his evil words. Lord, will you forgive me?"

"Sivagami, I am the one who should ask your forgiveness for the pain I have caused you. You will not believe such rumours about me in the future, will you?"

"Never! If I see that monk again, I will not let him off easily." She hesitated. "Lord, do you believe stories about men changing shape? Can a man take the shape of a snake?"

Mamallan held her close as she shivered. "Nonsense! And if any man threatens you in the form of a snake, I will become an eagle and kill him. Why should you fear anything when I am with you?" He paused. "My father said that your dancing skills belong to God and not to men. I understood when I saw you dancing at the temple. I am ashamed of my selfishness. I thought, *It is a sin to steal an offering which belongs to God …*"

Sivagami touched Mamallan's feet and pressed her fingers to her eyes. "If my dance belongs to God, you are that God. It is your love which gives my dance life. When I hold my *abhinaya*, it is you who stand before my eyes. Just say the word: I will throw my dance into this river for good."

Mamallan covered Sivagami's red-as-a-pomegranate-flower lips with his hands. "My heart aches to think that you will have to stop dancing—the Pallava empress cannot perform on stage. Sivagami, let me give up my claim to the kingdom. Let us take your father, Rathi and Shuka and live happily on some island. Say yes."

"Lord, I would never be so selfish as to accept such a sacrifice from you. You are born to rule the world and to destroy your enemies on the battlefield. Your hands are meant to hold the sword and the spear—I will never let you pick up a sculptor's chisel."

"Sivagami, when I go to war, you will be in my heart. Your love will give me endless courage …"

"Swami, you earned the title, 'Mamallan'-Great King. Do you need me to give you courage? I shiver at the sight of a spider. I was terrified to see the snake: look, I am still trembling."

Mamallan again held her close. "What foolishness, Sivagami! Why are you shivering?"

"I am scared. I feel danger looming over me. Do not tell my father this: when we were leaving the *matham*, Navukkarasar held back my father and spoke softly to him. I heard his words. 'Your daughter is blessed with a divine gift, but some great danger waits for her. Take care of her …'"

"What could be more dangerous than this flood? By God's grace, you escaped. Nothing more will happen …" Mamallan declared firmly.

"The flood gave me three heavenly days with you—I will not call it a danger. There is something more, but your love gives me courage. I will wait contentedly for you here—finish the war, get your father's permission and come for me."

"Have you decided to stay here? Lucky Mandagapattu!" It was clear that he approved.

"Yes, lord. I will live on sweet memories. And my father is eager to carve temples from these rocks. I am worried only about one thing: what if Naganandhi comes here?"

"Naganandhi will not come here."

Naganandhi slowly rose from hiding from behind the rock on which they sat and walked away.

The Moon Is My Witness

WHEN AAYANAR, SIVAGAMI and Mamallan returned to the village, they saw a crowd at the Navukkarasar Hall. Shields and swords glittered in the moonlight. The three of them stood cautiously by the temple wall at the street corner. *Who can these soldiers be?*

That morning, Mamallan had insisted that Gundodharan find a raft and row him to the other side of the river. But Gundodharan suggested that he would go by himself, gather news and come back to discuss their course of action. Mamallan agreed, as this would give him one more day with Sivagami. But now, he was worried. *How many days must I waste here? Gundodharan should have come back. Who are these men? Enemies? And if they are our men, they will cheer when they see me. The villagers will know about me.*

Aayanar knew that the prince was worried. Saying, "Lord, stay here with Sivagami. I will go and see who these men are," he went to the hall.

Mamallan heard Paranjothi's ringing tones above the commotion, and his doubts evaporated. "It is Commander Paranjothi! Come, Sivagami, let us go." He began to walk towards the hall.

Sivagami gently touched his hand. "Lord …"

In the milky light of the moonbeams, Mamallan saw the tears glistening like pearls on her face. "Why are you crying, my darling?" He lovingly wiped her tears with his stole.

"Once you heard your commander's voice, you do not need this foolish girl, do you?"

Mamallan was surprised. "My love, weren't you the one who bravely urged me to go to war?"

Sivagami held his hands to her eyes, drenching them in tears. "My heart is tormented by vague fears. I feel that my life's happiness is ending today. You will not forget me, will you?"

Mamallan looked up at the full moon. "Sivagami, I swear upon the moon which sails the sweet night skies: I will never forget you in this lifetime. There can only be one reason for your fear: I may die bravely on the battlefield …"

"Lord, do not say that! That will never happen!" Sivagami sobbed.

"One must be prepared for both death and victory. If I win the war and am crowned emperor, you will be seated by my side. If I die on the battlefield, will our love die in this lifetime? Never. Sivagami, is this promise enough? Do you want more?"

Sivagami heard cries of, 'There is the prince! Long live Mamallan Pallava!' She said, "I am satisfied. Go: the people are coming."

Row the Boat!

PARANJOTHI HURRIED FORWARD. "Lord, how could you do this? We were mad with worry."

Mamallan hugged Paranjothi. "Yes, I have given you all a lot of trouble. What did you do? Was our army badly affected by the flood?"

"By Lord Shiva's grace, we were warned in time, and there was no loss of life. I have much to tell you. Let us go into this temple."

They went into the temple, holding hands. The soldiers stopped others from following them.

Sivagami was sad to see Mamallan happily walking away. Aayanar came to her with Rathi and Shuka. Sivagami fondled the fawn and the parrot. *From now, you are my only true friends.*

It was past midnight when the feast prepared and served lovingly by the villagers ended.

Mamallan came to say goodbye to Aayanar and Sivagami. "Aayanar, I am sorry to leave you, but Pulikesi's army is marching on Kanchi. The emperor has asked me to go there at once."

Aayanar respected and loved the prince. "Lord, we are blessed to have had you with us. We must not ask for more. Go."

Mamallan looked at Sivagami, but her face was turned away. A screen had fallen between the two lovers.

Mamallan, Paranjothi and their company boarded the boat which stood ready on the Varaha River. Aayanar and Sivagami stood on the shore with the villagers. Gundodharan, who had suddenly come running from somewhere, stood behind them. There was no opportunity for Sivagami and Mamallan to speak. After climbing into the boat, Mamallan stared at Sivagami, who looked into his eyes. Mamallan longed to say something, but he was speechless.

The boat moved. Sivagami felt all her life's happiness leaving with the boat.

Argument

HEART FILLED WITH love, Mamallan was in a dream world through the crossing. *Once the war is over, on a moonlit night like this, Sivagami and I will drift on a boat in the Palar.*

He came back to earth when the boat thudded to a stop on the opposite shore. He saw the Pallava army in the distance. As he stepped out of the boat, Mamallan remembered Kannapiran and asked, "Commander, where is Kannapiran? Didn't he insist on coming with you?"

"He did, but I ordered him to stay and feed the horses. We must ride sixty miles non-stop."

Shouts of, 'Long live Mamallan!' rose from the camp. One soldier stepped forward.

Paranjothi asked, "Varadhungan, what news?"

"Two soldiers came here on horseback. They took Kannapiran with the chariot and ten soldiers. They said they had to go to Kanchi urgently."

"What?" Paranjothi exclaimed. "Who were these men?"

Varadhungan said, "One soldier said he was Vajrabahu. The other was the spymaster, Shatrughan. He had the lion signet ring. Here is the bull-and-spear scroll they left for you."

Mamallan and Paranjothi exchanged looks at the name Vajrabahu: both knew that it was the emperor. Paranjothi quickly took the scroll and read it in the moonlight.

From Emperor Mahendran to Commander Paranjothi. I am well. Dhurvineedhan is imprisoned in Mazlavaraya Fort. The Chalukyan army has crossed Tirupati. Bring Mamallan to Kanchi without stopping even for a second. If Mamallan refuses to come, show him this order, arrest him and bring him. The letter was sealed with the bull-and-spear emblem. A few lines followed. *If the fort gates are shut before you arrive, meditate on Lord Buddha.*

Paranjothi gave the letter to Mamallan. The prince read it and looked at the commander.

Paranjothi joked, "Prince, will you come with me, or shall I arrest you?"

Mamallan threw his dagger on the ground. "Commander, arrest me. I would rather be a prisoner than hide behind fort walls when the enemy invades."

Paranjothi immediately threw down his own scimitar and turban. "I would rather chant bhajans and wander from town-to-town than follow a prince who abandoned his soldiers and went running in search of a dancing girl."

Mamallan stared at the sky and then at the ground. Then, "Commander, this is not the time for us to quarrel. The enemy is near Kanchi. If we do not stop them, what is the point of our swords? I will insist to my father that the gates of Kanchi Fort must stay open. We must fight the enemy outside the fort. Will you support me?"

Paranjothi said, "Sir, Mahendran Pallava is your father, and you have the right to argue with him. But he is not only my father, my emperor and my war commander—he is my God. I cannot disobey him by word or deed. But if he allows you to fight the enemy outside Kanchi, I will be one step ahead of you. I will keep my promise as long as there is life in me."

The two friends jumped on their horses and galloped to Kanchi.

Saved Lives

AS SIVAGAMI STARED after the boats crossing the Varaha River, Aayanar turned to see who was panting behind them. Seeing Gundodharan, he asked, "My dear boy, where have you been?"

"Sir, I crossed the river, met the commander and told him that Mamallan was safe here. I hurried back to the bank, but my raft was missing. In the dim twilight, I saw someone steering it to this shore. I could make out the bald head and saffron robes of a Buddhist monk. *It is Naganandhi.* I was furious and loudly cursed all the monks in the world. Hearing my shouts, two men came to me. They were searching for Naganandhi. The three of us collected logs and creepers, built a raft and came here. I rushed to our hall. Sir, one must never trust princes: see how Mamallan left without saying goodbye to me!"

Sivagami said, "You are right, Gundodharan: one should never trust princes."

"Gundodharan, you said that Naganandhi was here. I have not seen him," Aayanar pointed out.

"Will a cobra show itself so easily? It will hide in a hole," Gundodharan muttered darkly.

"Gundodharan, do not talk like that. Naganandhi is a great man. I will be delighted if he stays here and advises me about carving rock temples." Aayanar paused. "You said that two men are searching for him. Who are they?"

"Master, they are very interested in sculpture. One of them said, 'What beautiful temples can be carved from these rocks!' I was surprised. 'My guru says the same thing,' I said. 'Who is your guru?' he asked. He was amazed to hear your name. I think he knows you."

"Who is this man who knows me? As far as I know, there is only one man who would think of carving temples out of these rocks. And there is no chance of him being here …"

"I will find the two men and bring them to you. You go ahead, master."

Aayanar and Sivagami went back with the villagers.

Gundodharan walked carefully along the shore in the bright moonlight. He was startled when two men rose from behind some rocks. On recognising them, he stood respectfully before them.

"Gundodharan, we began to doubt whether you were alive or in *Yamaloka*." It was Shatrughan.

"Master, if I had been a little careless, this dagger would have pierced my heart and sent me to *Yamaloka*." Gundodharan held out a marvellous dagger with a cobra-shaped hilt.

The Poisoned Dagger

AS SHATRUGHAN REACHED for the dagger, Mahendran, disguised as Vajrabahu, warned him: "Careful, Shatrughan!" He turned to Gundodharan. "How could you carry this dagger so carelessly at your waist? It does not have to pierce your heart: it is enough if its tip just scratches you. A man will die in a day once its poison mixes in his blood."

"Aiyo!" cried Gundodharan in horror.

"Where did you leave the monk? Tell us quickly. We should be halfway to Kanchi now," Shatrughan said impatiently.

"Master, the Buddhist monk aimed this dagger at the prince four or five times. I kept quiet because of your orders. Otherwise ..." Gundodharan gnashed his teeth.

While Mamallan and Sivagami sat under the *magilam* tree, lost in sweet words and silences, Naganandhi, hiding behind a rock, aimed his dagger. He hesitated, maybe fearing that the dagger would strike Sivagami. The cobra then slithered past, and the lovers moved to a rock brightly lit by the moon. The monk shifted to a new hiding place. Gundodharan watched from behind another rock. His hands itched to creep behind the monk and strangle him, but Emperor Mahendran's strict orders held him back.

When Mahendran, Shatrughan and Gundodharan crossed the Varaha River on their raft and came ashore, they saw Naganandhi standing on a rock in the distance, looking around.

The emperor said, "Gundodharan, I am giving you an assignment more important than anything you have done before. You must follow this monk. Do not let him out of your sight for even a second. You must not be seen by him. We have some work on the other bank. We will finish it, come back and wait for you here. When the moon is overhead, come and report to us."

"I will do exactly as you say, lord," Gundodharan said and followed the monk.

As Aayanar, Sivagami and Mamallan left the shore and walked to the village, Naganandhi followed them, hiding in the roadside bushes.

Gundodharan secretly followed the monk. When they reached the temple, Aayanar went ahead to check the crowd at the hall. Mamallan and Sivagami stood at a corner of the temple wall, whispering sweet nothings. Naganandhi, hidden at the other edge of the same corner, aimed his poisoned knife. But Sivagami was the one who stood within his reach. He waited for Sivagami to change places with Mamallan.

Gundodharan hid behind a fence opposite the temple wall and watched. Just as he prepared to jump on the monk, Paranjothi and his soldiers rushed there. Naganandhi immediately moved back. Gundodharan watched Paranjothi escort Mamallan away, followed by Sivagami and Aayanar. Naganandhi came back to stand at the corner of the temple wall. And then, the monk swung himself over the wall with the help of the overhanging branches.

Gundodharan rushed to the spot where the monk had stood. He jumped away when he saw a small snake slithering close to him. The snake remained motionless, and he laughed to himself. *It is not a snake; it is only a dagger with a snake-shaped hilt.* Gundodharan picked up the dagger, tucked it into his waist and looked up at the temple wall, preparing to climb over it.

Just then, the branches rustled. Gundodharan quickly hid behind the other edge of the wall's corner. He saw Naganandhi's head peeping over the wall. The monk jumped down and searched the ground. Knowing what he was looking for, Gundodharan quietly jumped over the temple wall. The temple kitchen was close by and Gundodharan hid behind its wall.

Soon Naganandhi also jumped back into the temple compound. He searched under a *paneer* tree there. Even the brave Gundodharan shivered when the monk gave up his search and hissed like a snake. Naganandhi waited under the tree, now and then going to look over the wall. They heard the soldiers' cheers and the villagers' excited shouts.

The noise ebbed around midnight, and they heard the temple doors being shut and padlocked. Naganandhi walked around the temple compound. Gundodharan saw him enter the kitchen through the open door. Gundodharan jumped across, softly shut the door and padlocked it. He then jumped over the temple wall and hurried to the Varaha River.

Who Is the Monk?

GUNDODHARAN PROUDLY ENDED his story: "I have locked the monk in the temple's kitchen, lord."

"Well done! Let us go—guide us to the village," Mahendran Pallava said.

Shatrughan said anxiously, "Lord, Gundodharan can deal with the monk. Come, let us go."

Mahendran Pallava said, "No, Shatrughan. This is even more important than stopping the Chalukyan forces. If we catch Naganandhi, we win half the battle."

"Lord, we could have easily arrested the monk earlier: even at Aayanar's house."

"Leaving him free all these days was essential. But if he remains free any longer, it will ruin my plans."

"Lord, leave him to Gundodharan and me. You go at once. Kannapiran is ready with the chariot on the other bank," Shatrughan said.

"Shatrughan, I must do this myself. Lead the way, Gundodharan."

The three men reached Mandagapattu at daybreak and jumped over the temple wall. The kitchen door was bolted from the outside. Gundodharan proudly opened the door—the kitchen was empty! The opening in the roof showed where Naganandhi had removed the tiles and escaped.

"As I thought, Shatrughan!" the emperor exclaimed. "Now do you see why I was reluctant to let you and Gundodharan deal with the monk?"

Shatrughan was furious. "Gundodharan, you have disgraced Kanchi's spy network!"

"Master, give me the poisoned dagger. If I do not find Naganandhi and stab him by daybreak tomorrow, I will plunge the knife into my own chest and die," Gundodharan declared.

As Shatrughan was about to hand over the dagger, the emperor took it. "Gundodharan, do not swear such foolish oaths! If you stab the monk, the dagger's point will bend: his body is as hard as diamond. Even if you hurt him, he is immune to this poison."

Shatrughan asked, "Is the monk a sorcerer, lord? Do not tell me you believe in magic!"

"There is no magic here—poison neutralises poison. For years and years, the monk has taken poisonous herbs and made his own blood toxic," the emperor explained. "As soon as they get wind of the Buddhist monk, all the cobras flee."

Gundodharan shivered. "Yes, master, I have seen this. Now I understand."

"Do you remember that terrifying cave of snakes we saw near the Kedilam River, Shatrughan? If they cannot capture Kanchi Fort, they plan to poison the city's drinking water."

"How evil! That too from a Buddhist monk in the name of the compassionate Lord Buddha—I can hardly believe it!" Shatrughan cried.

"The Buddhist monk is an imposter. He is an extremely skilled spy who uses saffron robes and the Buddhist *sangha* for his own evil purposes."

"How can we let such a savage, despicable killer live?"

"He is useless to us dead. If caught alive, he will be a powerful weapon in our hands."

"Lord, who is this monk?" Shatrughan asked.

"Once my suspicion is confirmed, I will tell you, Shatrughan. You and Gundodharan have served the Pallava kingdom well, but now comes your greatest task. If you carry out my instructions, we may win. What do you say?"

The golden moon paled and sank into the western horizon. Mahendran sat at the kitchen's entrance with Shatrughan and Gundodharan. The two spies listened carefully to his orders.

The Lion Seal

AT SUNRISE THE next day, Mandagapattu's streets were quiet. The Navukkarasar Hall was closed, but voices could be heard inside. The voices stopped when Gundodharan knocked on the door.

Aayanar came out saying, "It is you, Gundodharan. Where were you all night? If I depended on you ..." He stopped on seeing two other men. "Who are these men?"

"Didn't I tell you about two men, enthusiastic about sculpture, who came here last evening? I searched all night and brought them here: they wanted to meet you," explained Gundodharan.

"Is that so? Come in," welcomed Aayanar. "Sivagami, my dear, put out the chairs."

Aayanar and the two men sat down. Refusing to sit, Sivagami looked eagerly at the strangers.

"I hear that you are interested in sculpture," Aayanar said. "Where arc you from?"

"Guru, don't you know me?" Shatrughan asked. "I was your apprentice for a few days. To my bad luck, you left for Mamallapuram shortly after I came."

Aayanar sighed. "This wretched war brought work to a standstill."

Vajrabahu said, "Aayanar, the war will end soon, and you can go back to your forest house."

Startled by the voice, Aayanar asked, "Sir, who are you?"

Sivagami whispered into her father's ear, "It is the emperor, *appa*: can't you see?"

The astounded Aayanar jumped up from his chair. "Lord, Gundodharan told me last night that two men were here and that they discussed carving temples from the rocks on the riverbank. At once, I thought, *Who else but the emperor could be inspired by these rocks?* Finally, it was you! Lord, have you come here to see this poor sculptor?"

"Aayanar, I will not lie: I did not come to see you. I came here looking for my son, Mamallan."

Sivagami bowed her head in embarrassment.

Mahendran said, "By now, Mamallan and Paranjothi will be on the road to Kanchi. Since I was here, I thought I would meet you and thank you for saving Mamallan."

Aayanar protested, "Lord, it was the prince who saved us from drowning in the flood."

"Aayanar, do you see this?" Aayanar and Sivagami stared in horror at the dagger with the snake-shaped hilt. "This poisoned dagger was aimed at Mamallan. He escaped because Sivagami was by his side."

Sivagami trembled. She was overjoyed to hear that she had saved Mamallan but was confused as to how that had happened.

"Lord, which wicked man would aim a poisoned dagger at the prince? And how did Sivagami stop it? Sivagami, do you know about this?" Aayanar asked.

"Sivagami knows nothing. When the time is right, I will tell you everything. For now, the danger has passed. I must go. Aayanar, would you like to stay in this village until the war ends?"

"Yes, lord. The villagers are good people who appreciate art. They will help me with the temples."

"I will also order the district authorities to send you the money, men and tools you need."

"Lord, can you stay here for a day? We can see the rocks and decide on the temple designs."

Mahendran laughed. "The Chalukyan army is twenty-one miles from Kanchi. I must get there before them. Kannapiran is waiting on the other bank with the chariot."

Sivagami turned to Aayanar. "*Appa*, ask if Kamali is okay."

"Kamali is fine, my dear. Kanna wanted to come and tell you about her. I am the one who stopped him."

Sivagami found it hard to look the emperor in the face. She again turned to Aayanar. "*Appa*, ask them to send word when Kamali has her baby."

"I will ask them to send word to you, Sivagami. Let us go. Aayanar, we can look at the rocks on our way."

Aayanar stood eagerly. "Yes, lord."

Mahendran held out a hexagonal medal from his pocket. "Aayanar, only eleven people in the Pallava kingdom have this lion seal. I am giving you the twelfth one. With this, every official in the kingdom will help you. It will open the gates of any fort. You can use it to meet me and Mamallan whenever you want. Guard it, and use it only if absolutely essential."

Aayanar hesitated. "Lord, why does a poor sculptor need this?"

"Aayanar, to me, in all this vast kingdom, there is no greater treasure than you and your daughter. You may need the seal at some time. Take it and guard it."

Aayanar took the seal with devotion and said, "Sivagami, put this away carefully in your box."

Sivagami took the seal to the next room. The village women had gifted her a beautifully crafted box for her clothes and ornaments. Sivagami carefully put the seal in it.

Naganandhi, hiding behind a pillar, watched her.

The Monk's Change of Heart

AS MAHENDRAN, SHATRUGHAN and Aayanar left for the rocks, Sivagami stood at the entrance. The emperor casually said, "Sivagami, why don't you come with us?"

Sivagami hesitated.

Aayanar said, "Come, dear, let us go. What will you do here by yourself?"

Sivagami went with them, accompanied by Rathi and Shuka.

Sivagami had reason to hesitate. When she looked up after putting away the lion seal, she had glimpsed saffron behind a pillar. *It is Naganandhi. He was here before sunrise. When he heard voices, he said that he would leave by the back door. How did he come back? Why is he hiding?* Earlier, Sivagami would have screamed for help. But now, she was no longer suspicious of the monk.

Naganandhi seemed to have had a change of heart about Mamallan. "I feel like cutting out my tongue for calling Mamallan a coward. I saw him myself on the battlefield. How he whirled his sword, standing alone in the middle of a thousand enemies!" He continued, "He is also a good man: he does not even look at women."

Sivagami could hardly believe her ears; she began to respect Naganandhi.

When Aayanar questioned the monk about his sudden disappearance at Ashokapuram, Naganandhi said, "Kanga's Dhurvineedhan belongs to the Buddhist *sangha* and is devoted to me. Gundodharan's scroll said that Dhurvineedhan was marching on Kanchi with his army. I took Gundodharan's horse and rushed to stop him from doing such a stupid thing. But the battle was over before I got there. As I expected, Dhurvineedhan was thrashed by the brave Mamallan and had to run for his life. I have no idea where he ran or what happened to him."

Sivagami said, "Swami, why don't you stay with us here in this village?"

"Staying in one place is against my dharma. If it is Lord Buddha's will, I will meet you again after the war. Aayanar, the next time we meet, I will definitely bring you the secret of Ajanta's paintings. Sivagami, I long to stay here with you and enjoy your divine dance, but I must go ..." The tenderness in Naganandhi's voice melted Sivagami's heart.

Just then, they heard Gundodharan's knock at the door.

Naganandhi said, "Aayanar, Gundodharan wrongly suspects me. He will deliberately pick a quarrel with me. It also looks like there are other people with him. I will leave by the back door." He spoke tenderly to Sivagami: "Sivagami, I may not see you again. But wherever I go and whatever I do, I will never forget you ... or your dance." He left.

Sivagami was now surprised to see the monk hiding behind the pillar. *Does he want to tell me something? I will ask him after the emperor leaves.* She went back to the front room, rather pleased that Naganandhi was still there. When the emperor and her father asked her to join them, she could not refuse. She left with them. *Let the monk wait until we return.*

Trimurti Temple

AS THEY WALKED to the rocks, the emperor and Aayanar discussed sculpture and forgot the world: this rock can be an elephant … this one a camel … and this a lion … a chariot here … a pavilion there. They chose a huge rock to be carved into a temple and decided to start work on it first.

"Let us install the Trimurti in this one temple, Aayanar," Mahendran said.

"Lord, wouldn't it be better to build a temple for each of the three faiths?" Aayanar suggested.

"Aayanar, do not mention the words, 'Buddhist,' and, 'Jain,' to me for some time. My heart is filled with bitterness against them."

"Aiyo, what did they do to make your compassionate heart bitter?"

"I honoured the Buddhists and Jains, but it was useless. They let Dhurvineedhan hide in an underground cave at the Jain temple in Pataliputra. The Pallava army had to raze the temple to find him. Now they are saying that Mahendran Pallava destroyed a Jain temple. Aayanar, I must go. When I come back from the war, the temple must be complete. Shatrughan, where is our raft?" He paused. "Aayanar, could you go with him? If both of you search, we will find it sooner."

Aayanar and Shatrughan went in search of the raft, and Sivagami stood aside with Rathi.

The emperor went to her and sat on a rock. "Sivagami, I must talk to you. Sit beside me."

Sivagami bowed her head and remained standing.

"What I said about the dagger was a lie," Mahendran declared. "I do not want even your father to know the truth—that is why I sent him away. But you must know the truth. This knife, welded with poison, was meant for Mamallan's back."

Sivagami stammered, "But, lord … you said this was a lie …"

"I said you blocked the knife—that was a lie. Sivagami, you are an extraordinary, brave woman. That is why I am telling you the truth. Mamallan would be lying dead under this *magilam* tree. It was Lord Shiva who saved Mamallan."

Sivagami's head whirled. *Just last evening, Mamallan sat by me on this rock, murmuring sweet words of love.*

"Mamallan would have been stabbed in the back with this poisoned dagger. I would have lost my beloved son. The Pallava kingdom, and beautiful Kanchi, would have become defenseless. Do you know who is responsible for this?" The emperor sighed deeply. "You, Sivagami."

Thousands of flashes exploded in Sivagami's head.

Rain and Lightning

WHEN SIVAGAMI RECOVERED consciousness, she found herself sitting on the ground, leaning against a rock. The emperor sat by her, comforting her.

As she tried to jump up in respect, Mahendran held her hand. "My child, you fainted when you heard that you put Mamallan in danger—you have proved your love for him." He paused. "Sivagami, I want a promise from you: it is for Mamallan's good. You must not refuse me."

Sivagami's confusion cleared, and she became suspicious. *He wants to trap me. I cannot believe that I exposed Mamallan to danger. Why is he telling me all this privately?* She bowed her head. "My king, I do not understand—how did I put Mamallan in danger?"

"My child, I do not want to hurt you further. But now that you have asked me yourself, I will explain. I came to your forest home two days after your debut dance recital in Kanchi. Do you remember me saying that you have a divine gift which should be dedicated to God alone?"

Sivagami bowed her head. "I remember." *Why is he bringing this up now?*

"My child, if one tries to give man what rightfully belongs to God, it will only end in evil."

Sivagami sobbed, "You are talking in riddles. I am just a poor sculptor's uneducated daughter. Do not test me."

Mahendran Pallava stroked Sivagami's hair. His voice was tender. "Sivagami, you know my deep friendship for your father. His daughter is my daughter—I would not dream of harming you. You have no equal in dance. You must master dance and become famous throughout Bharat. Nothing must stand in your way. Even if my own son stands in your way, I will try to stop him."

The stunned Sivagami looked disbelievingly into the emperor's face.

Mahendran sighed. "My child, I will be frank for your own good. Forgive me if I hurt you."

Sivagami's heart shuddered at a coming disaster. Tears fell from her eyes.

"Sivagami, they say that when Brahma creates extraordinarily beautiful women, he weeps because he knows that these beautiful women will cause sorrow in the world. You are extraordinarily beautiful, and the most beautiful art in the world lives in you. When you were a child, I held you in my lap and petted you as my precious daughter. But once you became a young woman, every time I saw you, I was filled with pity. *Aiyo, do not let this girl cause tragedy in this world!* Two years ago, I saw the pure childhood friendship between you and Mamallan change into love. Even as I wondered how to end this ill-suited love without hurting you both, war broke out. To make sure that Mamallan could not meet you while I was away, I insisted that he stay in Kanchi Fort …"

Sivagami's tear-filled, dark eyes flashed with anger like lightning in dark, rainy skies.

"Sivagami, my instincts warned me that it would be dangerous for you and Mamallan to meet in my absence. I felt some mysterious power following you—either to guard you or to make you its own. That is why I made Mamallan stay away from you. As I expected, your love blazed stronger. I learned this from Mamallan's letters to you."

"What?" Sivagami looked at him in shocked disgust.

"Sivagami, I got the letters you hid in the tree. I was forced to be heartless for the good of the kingdom. My child, there is one dharma for commoners and another for kings. I would never stand between you if Mamallan was a trader's son, but it is my cruel duty to separate you …"

Sivagami gathered courage and said proudly, "Lord, fate, which is more powerful than kings, was on our side. It let the floods bring us together here."

"And the same fate supports my position. This poisoned dagger is proof of that."

Mahendran Pallava's Defeat

SIVAGAMI STARED AT the snake-hilt dagger. She stammered, "My king, which wretch held this dagger? Please tell me. If this happened because of me …"

Mahendran interrupted: "Sivagami, you caused this, but you knew nothing about it." He paused. "My dear, don't you know a man whose name itself has a snake in it?"

Sivagami was surprised and frightened. "Naganandhi? Why should Naganandhi hate Mamallan? I do not understand. Why should Naganandhi try to kill Mamallan?"

"Your beauty won the monk's hard heart, but you love Mamallan. That is why the monk hates Mamallan. Last night, when you and Mamallan sat on this rock, Naganandhi was hiding behind the same rock, holding this dagger. He followed you to the temple. Mamallan was saved by God's grace and Gundodharan's alertness."

"Gundodharan saved Mamallan?"

"Gundodharan followed you secretly. When the monk climbed over the temple wall, this dagger fell on the ground. Gundodharan picked it up. He locked the monk in the temple kitchen and reported to us. By the time we got there, the monk had disappeared." Mahendran noted the emotions flitting across Sivagami's face.

Sivagami kept seeing Naganandhi hidden behind the pillar in the hall. *If that wretched monk is still there, I will grab the dagger from the emperor's hand and kill him with my own hands.* "My king, I must go to the hall at once."

"You have not yet heard my request. This boon is not for me: it is for the Pallava dynasty. The power to save this empire is in your hands." He paused. "Write a letter to Mamallan saying that you release him … ask him to forget you."

"Lord, how can I let him go? How can I ask him to forget me?"

"Sivagami, I will tell you the truth plainly. The Pallava kingdom does not have the resources to fight the mighty Chalukyan army. The Pandyan forces are also marching on us from the south. If you agree to my request, the Pandyans will join us. If our two forces combine, we can defeat the Chalukyas. Sivagami, will you help the Pallava kingdom?"

"What have I to do with the Pandyan attack, lord? How can I help the Pallava kingdom?"

"I do not want to hurt you, but you are stubborn. Sivagami, when Mamallan turned down the proposal to marry the Pandyan princess, the Pandyans marched against us. All we must do is agree to the marriage and the Pandyan army will join us. If you release Mamallan, I will convince him to agree to this. What do you say? Will you save the Pallava kingdom?"

Sivagami fell to the ground and sobbed, "No, I can not! Plunge that poisoned dagger into my heart. Your son will be free and the Pallava kingdom will be saved. If you do not have the courage, give me the dagger: I will plunge it into my own heart!"

"Sivagami, you have won. I have failed," the emperor said.

Half an hour after this conversation, Aayanar and Sivagami were back at Mandagapattu village. Sivagami hurried inside the hall: Naganandhi was nowhere to be seen. She opened her box and searched inside—the emperor's lion seal was missing.

At the same time, on the other bank of the Varaha River, Naganandhi showed Kannapiran the lion seal and ordered him to take him to Kanchi. Kannapiran reluctantly let the monk climb into the chariot. The emperor and Shatrughan watched from their hiding place among some trees. When Shatrughan prepared to charge out and stop Kannapiran, Mahendran signalled to him to wait. They watched as Kannapiran disgustedly patted the horses and the soldiers rode behind the chariot. Shatrughan was furious; the emperor was smiling.

Kanchi in Uproar

MAMALLAN AND PARANJOTHI sped towards Kanchi. Every fourteen miles, fresh horses waited for them, and a hundred fresh riders were ready to replace the prince's escort.

Paranjothi said, "I have seen the emperor's advance planning during my time with him. That is why I do not even think of disobeying him." He told Mamallan about the strategies Mahendran had used to keep the enemy pinned down at the North Pennai for eight months.

Mamallan disagreed: "Commander, whatever you say, there is no glory in stopping the enemy by tricking them or retreating from them."

"In war, there is a time to retreat and a time to attack. You were upset by the emperor's orders not to chase Dhurvineedhan beyond the South Pennai. But wasn't the commander of Thirukkovalur Fort, Anandhan

Mazlavarayan, waiting on the opposite bank? Isn't Dhurvineedhan now in a cell in Thirukkovalur Fort? Lord, many men have triumphed with their mighty armies, but only our emperor has defeated a mighty enemy with just a small army."

Mamallan hated Mahendran mixing strategy and cunning with courage. "Isn't one Pallava soldier a match for ten Chalukyan soldiers? Didn't we see that at Pullalur?"

The two friends travelled all night and day and reached Kanchi Fort's southern gate at sunset. Triumphant horns, conches and drums blared from the terrace. There was a roar from inside, and the gates crashed open. Pallava soldiers stood in rows for as far as the eye could see. The people were excited by the news of Mamallan's great victory at Pullalur. Crowds lined both sides of the streets, ready to shower the victorious prince with flowers.

The Pallava army under General Kalipahai had also returned from the northern battlefield. Kanchi, deserted by the exodus of people, was now festive with the noise of one lakh soldiers. Mamallan entered the fort, followed by Paranjothi and the soldiers, and the gates shut behind them. Thousands of nandi flags fluttered in the wind along Mamallan's route. The crowd's excited murmur was like the waves of the seven seas crashing on the shore.

The council of ministers and General Kalipahai waited at the entrance. Mamallan and Paranjothi jumped off their horses. The chief minister garlanded Mamallan with golden *kondrai* flowers, and the general shouted, "Long live the great warrior Mamallan who defeated the Kanga king at Pullalur!" Shouts of "Long live Mamallan!" rose from thousands of throats.

Mamallan's face did not glow at this warm welcome. *What is the point of these cheers—the enemy is marching on Kanchi with a mighty army!*

Mamallan was eager to see his father, and Paranjothi and he galloped to the palace. Queen Bhuvanamahadevi stood at the entrance to the women's quarters, surrounded by her maids.

The queen welcomed her son with the *aarti*. "My child, I am so proud of your courage. But why are you sad? Are you tired after your long journey?"

"That is one reason, *amma* ... I also do not like this celebration of the Pullalur victory. The Kanga army was just a small pond: the Chalukyan army is a mighty ocean. And it is my father who is responsible for our victory. Leave that aside, *amma*. Where is the emperor?"

"I was going to ask you the same question. Where is your father? Isn't he with you?"

Mamallan was surprised. *He left before me. Has he met with some accident? What if he is not here when the enemy surrounds the fort? I must shoulder the duties of the kingdom and the war.*

Paranjothi did not seem surprised at the emperor's absence. He looked as if he had expected it.

Council of Advisors

AFTER THE FIRST watch of the night, Mamallan heard that the council of advisors was waiting for him. The Pallava emperor was assisted by the council of ministers and the council of advisors. In times of emergency, the district chiefs also participated in the councils.

The men stood in respect when Mamallan and Paranjothi entered the council chamber. The emperor's throne was empty. Mamallan sat on a throne beside it.

Paranjothi stood behind the prince. He was worried. *I prefer to stand. I feel that something unexpected is going to happen.*

Prime Minister Sarangadevan Bhattar opened the assembly. "The council meets today at the emperor's command, but the emperor is not here. He may have been delayed by important work, or he may have been stopped by force. We must decide whether to postpone the council." He paused. "When the emperor left for war nine months ago, he gave the prince all official rights over the kingdom. So, in my opinion, we can let the prince preside over the council."

"Hear, hear!" Everyone in the room seconded the prime minister.

Chief Minister Ranadheeran Pallavarayan said, "The Chalukyan army is now twenty miles from Kanchi. We cannot postpone the assembly until the emperor's return. We want to know the prince's thoughts and commands. General Kalipahai brought our Pallava army safely to Kanchi from the northern battlefield—we expect to hear his opinion too."

The commander of Senji Fort, Sadaiyappan Singhan, said, "We thought that the emperor was with the northern army. Can the general tell us when the emperor left and where he is now?"

General Kalipahai replied, "Ten days back, the emperor left with two thousand soldiers. He ordered me to march to Kanchi with the rest of the army. I have no news after that. I guessed that he was going to Pullalur. The soldiers who went with the emperor are back and confirm this."

Everyone's eyes turned to Mamallan at the word, 'Pullalur.' Mamallan spoke up. "My father came to Pullalur. But from the message he sent my dear friend, Paranjothi, I expected to see him in Kanchi. Commander, please tell them the details."

Paranjothi spoke about the Pullalur victory, chasing Dhurvineedhan, the emperor coming south from another direction, Mamallan being caught in the flood and washed ashore at Mandagapattu village, his search for the prince, the emperor catching and imprisoning Dhurvineedhan and sending him a scroll. He kept Aayanar and Sivagami out of his report.

The prime minister said, "Without the emperor, our responsibilities are heavier. An enemy force, greater than any seen in south Tamil Nadu, is marching on us. We wait for Mamallan's orders. The district chiefs must return to their homes before the enemy besieges Kanchi Fort."

Sunk in thought, Mamallan did not reply.

Seeing this, the chief minister said, "Let General Kalipahai give us his opinion first. He may know why the emperor convened this assembly."

General Kalipahai stood. "The emperor wanted to discuss the siege of Kanchi Fort. He expects it to go on for a year. During the siege, we cannot send or receive messages. The emperor wanted to give the district chiefs instructions, but I do not know what he wanted to tell them."

A district chief spoke up: "General, when do you expect the enemy forces to reach Kanchi?"

"They may be here at dawn tomorrow and surround the fort by

sunset."

"In that case, those who must leave should be out before sunrise, isn't it?"

"If the emperor is not back tonight, it will be best for the district chiefs to return to their homes. They can expect the emperor's orders to reach them there."

There was silence. Everyone looked at Mamallan.

Mamallan stood up with dignity and looked around the room. "When the emperor left Kanchi ten months ago, he commanded me to carry out all his duties until his return. The emperor has not yet returned. So I can exercise the authority he gave me, right? Do you all agree?"

"We agree!" many voices in the room shouted as one.

The prime minister said, "Prince, we have the right to advise; the right to command is yours."

"Good. Give me your advice. I will listen. But I have decided what is to be done. Hiding behind fort walls, frightened of an invading army, is a shame to the brave Pallavas descended from Thondaiman Ilanthirayan. There are almost one lakh Pallava soldiers in this fort, eager to fight. I have decided to attack the Chalukyan army outside the fort tomorrow morning. Commander Paranjothi will come with me. In his place, I appoint General Kalipahai to guard the fort. After you agree to this, I will issue my commands to the district chiefs."

The men were stunned. There was silence as the ministers and chiefs looked at one another.

The Emperor's Messenger

IN TRUTH, NONE of the men in the room had come to give his opinion about the conduct of the war. They were there to receive Emperor Mahendran's commands.

Mamallan looked at each of them in turn. "What is the meaning of this silence? Have I said anything to disgrace the brave Pallava dynasty?" he asked majestically.

Realising that they were caught in a moral dilemma, the men were quiet.

"Good. As no one objects, I will take it for granted that you agree with me. General, am I right?" Mamallan expressly asked Kalipahai.

General Kalipahai stood. "I am duty bound to obey the prince, but I do not agree. After much thought, the emperor has brought our army inside the fort. Emperor Mahendran is not a coward. He does not fear war. It is not good for us to go against his wishes."

Mamallan said passionately, "General, did I call my brave father a coward? I would rather cut out my tongue! My father has his war strategy and I have mine. In his absence, I have the right to follow my strategy. General, prepare the Pallava army to attack tomorrow morning."

Kalipahai said in a low voice, "The prince's decision is not a strategy—it is suicide. The Chalukyas have five lakh soldiers—we have less than a lakh."

Mamallan's eyes flashed fire. "General, does the strength of an army lie in numbers? Isn't it courage which gives victory? Have you not yet learnt this?"

"The Chalukyan army also has fifteen thousand war elephants," Kalipahai pointed out.

"It looks like our general does not know about the elephant which ran wild in Kanchi's streets, terrified of Commander Paranjothi's spear. Why should we fear Pulikesi's elephants when we have one lakh brave lions like Commander Paranjothi in our army?"

As the argument grew heated, the worried prime minister stood. Mamallan waited for the elderly man to speak. "There is still time for the emperor to return. Are the guards ready to open the gates for him at once if he comes tonight?"

Paranjothi replied, "Yes. I have also made arrangements in case the emperor sends a messenger."

Even before Paranjothi could close his mouth, a guard hurried in. "A messenger is here with a scroll from the emperor. He carries the lion seal."

Mamallan was stunned. The others were happy that God had intervened in time to save them from a very awkward situation.

Dreadful News

THERE WAS PIN drop silence in the room. The emperor's messenger was a gigantic man who seemed to have come straight from the battlefield. His head and face were bandaged, and his dress was bloodstained. Every eye in the room stared at him.

Paranjothi too stared at the messenger. *Where have I seen this man before?*

The messenger's eyes came to rest on the prince's face. "My prince, I bring dreadful news. But it must be said—the Pallava emperor has been captured ..."

It was a bolt from the blue for the men gathered there. Some cried, 'What?' Many jumped up from their chairs. Others stared at the messenger with open mouths.

Everyone's hair stood on end as Mamallan roared, "How? When? By whom?" His hand instinctively went to his sword.

"He was captured by Chalukyan soldiers last evening as he was riding north to scout the location of the enemy forces. Pallava prince, this is the message the emperor gave me for you. 'My son, the time has come for you to show your courage. It is your responsibility to destroy the Chalukyan army, humble Pulikesi and free me. Nothing is impossible for Mamallan.'"

Sparks flew from Mamallan's eyes as he thundered, "General, will you now agree to lead our forces outside the fort? What do you say? Have you all turned into lifeless objects?"

The chief minister stood. "What is the proof that this message is true?"

The messenger held out the lion seal. "This is my proof. My wounds are evidence."

Mamallan turned to Paranjothi. "The emperor is in the enemy's hands, and we waste time asking for proof! Commander, come, let us go."

But Paranjothi was thoughtful as he stared at the messenger with his bandaged head and face.

Sarangadevan asked, "Has anyone seen this messenger before this? Man, who are you?"

"I am the Pallava emperor's secret spy. I am second only to Shatrughan. Commander, don't you recognise me? I am the Naganandhi who brought you to Kanchi. Suspecting Aayanar and his daughter of knowingly or unknowingly being Chalukyan spies, the emperor assigned me to watch them. You went to the Nagarjuna Hills with Aayanar's secret scroll. The emperor took that scroll from you based on my information. Is all this true?" the messenger asked majestically.

Paranjothi's head whirled. *Maybe this messenger is telling the truth ...*

The messenger continued: "A Chalukyan spy named Gundodharan stayed with Aayanar. Yesterday, he took a message from Aayanar to the Chalukyas. As the emperor and I rode to stop him, we were ambushed by enemy soldiers. I escaped by God's grace. I must go in search of Shatrughan. I have said what I had to say—do what you think is best."

The messenger left. No one thought to stop him or question him. Everyone was turned to stone.

A thousand scorpions stung Mamallan. *Are Aayanar and Sivagami enemy spies? I rescued them from the flood ... I loved Sivagami ... Mahendran Pallava has been captured because of them ...*

Paranjothi was the only one in that room who understood Mamallan's pain. He gripped the prince's hand. "What are we waiting for? Come, let us go to battle. Let us destroy the Chalukyan demons and free the emperor. Remember Pullalur!"

At this, General Kalipahai came to himself. "Yes, the commander is right. There is nothing more to discuss. I will give orders for the army to march."

The men rose as one and cheered, "Long live Mahendran Pallava!"

There was a commotion at the entrance. They heard commands, horses' hooves, the clash of spears and swords and running feet. Just as Naganandhi had walked out, the emperor arrived there on horseback. At his orders, the soldiers on guard outside surrounded the messenger.

Bharavi Lights a Fire

THE ROOM ECHOED with cheers at Mahendran's entrance. Mamallan hugged his father. Forgetting tradition and custom, the commanders, ministers and chiefs surrounded the emperor.

Paranjothi alone stood a little away from the crowd, ashamed. *I too was fooled. Knowing the emperor so well, I still believed that he had been captured by the enemy.*

When the uproar subsided, Mahendran surveyed the room. "Why are you all so excited? Looking at you, one would think we had won the war! Only the commander seems dejected."

All eyes turned to Paranjothi, increasing his embarrassment.

Sarangadevan spoke first: "My king, we had just decided to lead our army outside the fort to attack Pulikesi. Maybe the fort commander is disappointed that there is no chance of that now."

"What? You planned to lead the army outside the fort? Whose stupid idea was this? General, how dare you disobey me? Have you too lost confidence in me?" the emperor roared.

Kalipahai spoke humbly: "Lord, after hearing of your capture, how could we stay holed up in the fort? If the Pallava army did not free you, who cared whether the army survived or died?"

To everyone's surprise, the emperor said, "I was captured by the enemy? What story is this?"

Sarangadevan gave a short account of the events which took place before the emperor's arrival.

"Naganandhi is cleverer than I thought. If I had been delayed, he would have ruined my plans."

"Lord, did the messenger lie? Weren't you captured?" General Kalipahai asked.

"It was a lie. And even if I was captured by the enemy, I would not need the Pallava army to rescue me. I can take care of myself. How could you believe an unknown messenger? Didn't Mamallan or Paranjothi tell you that Naganandhi is an enemy spy?"

"Lord, news of your capture addled my brains. The prince too was upset," Paranjothi explained.

"If he is a spy, how did he get the lion seal?" the chief minister asked.

"I gave it to him," Mahendran said. "I knew that Chalukyan spies were working here through the Buddhist *sangha.* I suspected Naganandhi from the day Commander Paranjothi came to Kanchi. I left him free all these days in order to round up his entire spy network, but I had to catch him before the siege began. Finally, I found him in Mandagapattu village."

The stunned Mamallan cried, "What? Mandagapattu?"

"Yes, Mamallan. Aayanar and Sivagami are well and happy. They told me that you had saved them from the flood. I have arranged for Aayanar to start work on a rock temple there."

Mamallan's face glowed. *Aayanar and Sivagami are not enemy spies!*

General Kalipahai was worried. He was skilled at warfare, but spies and devious plans only gave him a headache. "Lord, has the spy been arrested?"

"Yes, Vatapi's greatest spy has been caught. We have won half the battle," Mahendran declared.

Mamallan stood before his father with folded hands. "My king, you have won half the battle. Let me win the other half. Let me lead our brave soldiers to destroy the enemy."

Mahendran hugged Mamallan. "My son, I applaud your courage, but listen to me." He turned to the assembly. "I will tell you the root cause of this war." There was silence in the room as he went on: "My father, Simhavishnu, was known for his courage. Before I was born, he annexed lower Chola Nadu, making the Uraiyur Cholas Pallava vassals; he crushed the Pandyans; Kanga and Kadamba were his allies; the Vengi king was my maternal uncle. So I grew up with no thought of war. I spent my time on sculpture, painting, dance, music and poetry. I invited artists from various kingdoms here to encourage art in the Pallava kingdom.

"The Sanskrit poet, Bharavi, was the Chalukyan princes' friend. He came to Kanga to arrange a marriage between King Dhurvineedhan's daughter and Vishnuvardhan, Pulikesi's brother.

"When I heard of Bharavi's visit, I wanted to bring him here. My father sent word to Dhurvineedhan. Bharavi came here and fell in love with Kanchi. When Pulikesi became king, he urged Bharavi to return to Vatapi, but Bharavi refused. He wrote the verse, *Pushpeshu jati, purusheshu Vishnu, naarishu Rambha, nagareshu Kanchi* (As the Parijatham among flowers, Lord Vishnu among men and Rambha among women, Kanchi is the first among cities). I was proud to read this, but the fire lit by Bharavi has become the inferno of this war. In a letter, Pulikesi wrote, 'One day, I will come to Kanchi and see whether all you say is true.' I thought, *I will give Pulikesi a grand welcome.* But now, I must bar the gates and keep him outside …" Mahendran paused. "I personally saw Pulikesi's infatuation with Kanchi. How his eyes gleamed when I described Kanchi's beauty!"

There was an excited buzz.

Sarangadevan exclaimed, "What? You met Pulikesi in person? Where? When?"

"I met him in the middle of his army camp on the banks of the North Pennai."

"Lord, how could you take such risks?" Chief Minister Ranadheeran protested. "You are the Pallava kingdom's only hope!"

The Assembly Dissolves

EMPEROR MAHENDRAN WAITED for the commotion to die down. "This kingdom does not depend on me alone. My son, Mamallan, is here to immortalise the Pallavas' fame. I had an important reason to meet Pulikesi in person. Nine months ago, Naganandhi sent a scroll to Pulikesi through our brave young fort commander, who did not know its content. I took the scroll from him and went to Pulikesi's army camp. But the scroll I gave Pulikesi was not Naganandhi's: I exchanged it for one I wrote. It was because of this scroll, and General Kalipahai's courage, that we were able to hold Pulikesi at the North Pennai for eight months."

Sarangadevan asked, "Lord, what did Naganandhi's scroll say?"

"It said that if the Chalukyan army marched non-stop, it could capture Kanchi in just three days."

Angry growls filled the hall.

The emperor held out his hand. "What Naganandhi wrote was absolutely true at that time. If the enemy had marched here then, we could not have held out for more than three days. War elephants would have smashed our fort gates. Kanchi would have shared Vijayanthi's fate: the Kadamba kings' prosperous capital has been reduced to ashes."

He again waited for the murmurs to subside. "Kanchi city has flourished for a thousand years. Its fame has reached Rome, China, Java and Greece. I cannot shamefully let Kanchi be destroyed under my watch. My first duty is to guard Kanchi. Will you cooperate with me?"

The assembly roared in one voice, "Hear, hear!"

The emperor again held out his hands. "I told you the root cause of this war. I am the one who brought this war on Kanchi. Let me conduct and end this war in my own way."

Again there were cries of, "Hear, hear!"

The emperor spoke to the district chiefs: "You are in the villages outside the fort: you will suffer more than those of us inside the fort. Are you ready to do this to save Kanchi?"

The leaders shouted in one voice, "We are ready!"

"The enemy will reach Kanchi by dawn. You must leave the city before that. Go quickly to your towns. There will be no communication between us as long as the siege lasts. When Pulikesi's siege fails, he will vent his anger on your villages. Think well—are you prepared to endure his cruelty? Will you stand firm even when there is famine in the land and people die of hunger?"

The commander of Senji Fort, Sadayappan Singhan answered: "My king, Kanchi is the crown of the Pallava kingdom. If Kanchi falls, what does it matter who lives? We are prepared to make any sacrifice to save Kanchi. This is our unanimous opinion."

A messenger went to the emperor, bowed and said, "Lord, there is a cloud of dust in the east—and a roar like the sea crashing on shore."

The emperor thundered, "The Chalukyan army is here! The time has come for each one of us to prove his courage. This assembly is dissolved. From tomorrow until the siege is lifted, the council will meet here in the second watch of every night. Go now and do your duties."

The ministers hurried away.

Mahendran continued: "District chiefs, your promise gladdens my heart. If you stand by it, we will definitely defeat Pulikesi." He turned to Paranjothi. "Escort them to the southern gate. Once they have crossed the moat, break the bridge. You have implemented our other plans, right?"

"Yes, lord. Except the southern gate, the other entrances are closed. The bridges have been destroyed. Ten thousand soldiers stand on the fort walls, spears in hand," Paranjothi replied.

Mahendran and Mamallan were now alone in the hall. The prince's face was dull. The emperor placed his hand on his son's shoulders. "You too agree to let me wage this war in my own way, right?"

"*Appa*, why do you ask me this? I agree to whatever you want."

"I am glad, my son. Go to the palace and tell your mother that I have returned safely. There is one more important thing I must do before sunrise. I will finish that and come to the palace."

Mamallan left for the palace. The emperor rode to the Royal Monastery.

The Siege Begins

AT SUNRISE THE next day, Kamali sat sadly on her verandah, her eyes swollen with weeping. Kannapiran's father sat beside her, comforting her. The previous evening, on hearing of Mamallan's return, Kamali had expected Kannapiran to come home. But Asuvabalan had brought the news that his son had not come back with the prince.

In the third watch of that sleepless night, they heard that the emperor too had returned. They then heard that, as the Chalukyan army was near, the fort's gates had been shut and the bridges destroyed. Kannapiran could no longer enter the fort. Kamali was sunk in grief.

Just then, she saw Kannapiran. Kamali jumped up, crying, "Kanna!" and ran to embrace him. She stopped in shy confusion when she saw the emperor on a horse behind her husband.

"Kamali, I have brought Kannapiran safely back to you." Mahendran smiled. "Sivagami was concerned about you. She asked me to send word if you have a son." With that, he rode away.

Embarrassed, Kamali gave Kannapiran a sidelong glance and went in. Kannapiran greeted his father and followed her inside.

"Kamali, aren't you glad to see me? You went in without even looking at me. Are you blind?"

"Yes, I am blind with weeping all night long." Kamali shrugged away his hand. "Where was your concern yesterday? Why didn't you come last night?"

Kannapiran told Kamali all his adventures after leaving Kanchi. He then related his encounter with the Buddhist monk.

Naganandhi kept urging Kannapiran to drive faster. Changing horses twice on the way, they reached Kanchi's southern gate after sunset. Obeying the monk, Kannapiran drove on the path along the moat. The monk got down from the chariot and went into the forest. Kannapiran heard the sound of oars. In the dim moonlight, he saw two Buddhist monks go by in a boat. They got down on the other side of the moat and walked along the fort's walls. Suddenly, they vanished.

Kannapiran waited there for a long time, confused. *How did they disappear? Is there a secret way through the wall? The monk asked me to wait here ... he will be back. I will find out the secret then.* He kept his eyes glued to the spot where the monks had disappeared, but he fell asleep. Suddenly, he opened his eyes—he heard a sound like the roaring of the sea. Terrified, he climbed a tree. Far in the distance, in the moonlight, he saw a sea of elephants, horses, flags, canopies, swords and spears. *It is the enemy. I must get inside the fort.* He drove the chariot quickly to the southern gate, but although he shouted out to the guards, it was no use. *Maybe I can find the secret passage the monks used and get into the fort through it.* He returned to the same spot. *How do I cross the moat? I cannot swim: there are hundreds of crocodiles.* His blood froze. The sound of the approaching army was louder.

I would rather be food for the crocodiles than be caught by the enemy. Kannapiran prepared to jump into the moat. Suddenly, he saw a door open in the fort's wall across from where he stood. A young monk ran out. Kannapiran quickly hid behind a tree and watched the monk row the boat across the moat. When the monk reached the shore and began to sink the boat, Kannapiran jumped out of hiding. He threw the young monk into the boat, jumped in after him and slowly rowed the boat back across the moat.

The opening in the wall was still there. He pushed the monk into it and followed. He stopped abruptly. *The chariot!* He turned to go back, but a diamond-hard arm pushed him back inside. To his amazement, it was Mahendran Pallava.

"Kanna, this monk is the last of the enemy spies. You have served the Pallava dynasty well by stopping him from escaping. Come, let us go. Kamali will be worried and waiting for you."

The emperor entered the secret passage and closed the door behind him. It was soon clear that they were in the Royal Monastery.

"Kamali, it is the power of your *mangalsutra* which saved me last evening. I can hardly believe that I am still alive. Hold me in your soft arms and tell me if I am truly alive."

"No, Kanna, no! If I hug you, it will harm little Kannan!" Kamali gave him a suggestive smile.

PART 3

THE MONK'S LOVE

The Indestructible Fort

THE SIEGE OF Kanchi Fort by Pulikesi's Chalukyan forces is a well-known part of history. The Chalukyas expected to capture the fort in one savage attack. Countless foot soldiers rushed to cross the moat. They were sent to *Yamaloka* by showers of arrows from the fort's walls and by the crocodiles in the moat. Those who managed to cross the moat were caught in hidden traps along the walls. The water turned red as elephants and crocodiles fought in the water.

The Chalukyas then filled the moat and led their elephants to smash the gates. But the Pallava soldiers hidden in the upper terraces threw their spears at the elephants' eyes and vital body parts. The panicked beasts ran back, injuring the Chalukyan soldiers.

After great effort, the elephants smashed the outer gates. But the newly installed inner gates were studded with hundreds of spear heads. The elephants charged into these spears, trumpeted in terror and ran back, killing the Chalukyan soldiers behind them. The Chalukyan soldiers then brought huge battering rams to smash the doors. But behind these doors stood solid stone walls which completely closed off the entrances. After a month, Pulikesi gave up. He decided to lay siege to the fort and starve it into surrender. The Chalukyan army set up camp around Kanchi.

After six months, it was the Chalukyan army which faced a severe food shortage. Lakhs of soldiers and thousands of war elephants and bullocks must be fed. There was no food to be found anywhere from the North Pennai to Kanchi. The Pallava army had emptied the land of food as it retreated. The villages had been abandoned, leaving no food behind. The Chalukyan elephants ate all the forests and plantations around Kanchi within three months and then had to walk long distances in search of food. In that hot summer, there was no greenery to be found.

The greatest danger faced by the Chalukyas was the shortage of drinking water. The lakes within eighty miles of Kanchi had strangely breached their banks and flooded the countryside. By May, they were dry. The wells and ponds were silted after the floods. The few puddles were polluted and unfit for drinking. The dams across the Palar had been broken, and the river was dry. And so, the canals leading from Kanchi to the sea were empty. The moat around Kanchi filled with blood and flesh, becoming a sewer. The Chalukyan army depended on water drawn from holes dug in the Palar. Hunger and thirst drove the elephants into a frenzy: they stampeded and killed many Chalukyan soldiers.

One day in June, Pulikesi's war council met in a tent with the varaha flag fluttering above it.

Pulikesi sat majestically on an ivory throne with his war commanders sitting on a rug before him. "Like a fox hiding in its hole, Mahendran is hiding in his fort. How long can we wait?"

His army commanders were silent. No one dared to say a word.

Pulikesi sighed. "If only our monk was here ..."

"Lord, is there no news of the monk?" someone asked.

"The last message from him was through Vajrabahu. Maybe he met with an accident .... Maitraiyan, didn't I ask you to find the monk eight months ago? Is there any news?"

The spy chief bowed his head.

Pulikesi addressed the man who sat in the front: "General, what do you think? Should we prolong the siege? How long do you think it will take to bring Mahendran Pallava to his knees?"

"The Pallava soldiers on the fort walls are well fed, but our soldiers are on half-rations. In another month, we will not be able to give them even that."

Pulikesi was furious. "All you do is talk about food. Does no one have any constructive ideas?"

A commander said, "Lord, the Pandyan king has been waiting on the banks of the Kaveri for six months. Chola Nadu had a bumper harvest last year—Jayanthvarman Pandyan may send us food."

Pulikesi jumped up. "I will go mad if I sit here idly any longer. General, continue the siege. I will take one lakh soldiers and the elephant brigade and ride south to meet the Pandyan king. How thin our elephants have become! There will be plenty of food for them on the banks of the Kaveri."

Maitraiyan said, "Lord, you are taking a very small force. Can we trust the Pandyan king?"

"What does it matter? He would not dare to go to war with us—there is no fort near the Kaveri where he can hide. I do not fear any enemy who stands on the battlefield," Pulikesi declared.

The Elephant Bridge

WHEN PULIKESI AND his army reached the Kollidam after marching for two weeks, the water stretched from shore to shore. Jayanthvarman Pandyan's camp was on the opposite shore.

Jayanthvarman was furious with the Pallavas because Mamallan had refused to marry his sister. The Pandyan army camped between the Kaveri and the Kollidam a few days after the siege of Kanchi began. Jayanthvarman's vassals, Madhava Kalapan of Kodumbalur and the Chera chieftain, Ilancheralathan, joined him with their small forces. They planned to support Pulikesi as they hated the Pallavas. Only Parthiban Chola, the newly crowned king of Uraiyur, refused to join them, although he too resented Pallava dominance.

As the siege of Kanchi went on, Jayanthvarman's respect for Pulikesi decreased. When he heard that Pulikesi was on the opposite shore, he sent word that he did not have enough boats to cross the Kollidam to meet Pulikesi. Pulikesi sent a message saying that he would build a bridge across the Kollidam and come to meet Jayanthavarman himself.

Jayanthvarman was amused. "How can he build a bridge across the Kollidam? What madness!"

But the next morning, the elephants stood in a row in the river, with planks on their backs, forming a bridge. This extraordinary bridge restored Jayanthvarman's respect for Pulikesi. When Pulikesi and his escort crossed the elephant bridge, Jayanthvarman gave him a royal welcome.

The kings spent three days happily sharing their mutual complaints. They both agreed that the Pallava dynasty must be wiped out. The southern area up to Kanchi must be given to the Pandyans and the area north of Kanchi to the Chalukyas.

Jayanthvarman declared, "I will lead my army to Kanchi at once."

Pulikesi said, "Let me have the honour of capturing Kanchi. Come there as soon as you hear that the fort has been captured. For now, we need your help with food."

Jayanthvarman agreed to supply the Chalukyan army with provisions.

The Treaty

PULIKESI INVITED JAYANTHVARMAN to be his guest for a few days. The Pandyan king, along with his ministers, went to the Chalukyan camp. Pulikesi welcomed him royally and impressed him with a parade of his four divisions. A sumptuous feast was followed by a martial arts demonstration.

Jayanthvarman was intoxicated by the reception. *I must show Pulikesi Madurai and the glory of the Pandyans.* "Satyashraya, after you have captured Kanchi, you must come to Madurai."

Pulikesi sighed. "I have long wanted to see Madurai. The Buddhist monk wrote about it. But …"

Jayanthvarman interrupted him: "Where is the monk? I expected to find him with you."

"I wanted to ask you about him. What did he tell you before he left Madurai?"

"He was amazed to hear that your army was still on the shore of the North Pennai. He asked me to bring my army to the Kollidam and went ahead. Didn't he meet you after that?"

"No, it is very strange. I fear that that fool, Dhurvineedhan, has led them both into danger. Without the monk, I feel that my army is at half-strength," Pulikesi said.

"Yes, I developed a great respect for the monk even during our short acquaintance. In the confusion of my father's death, the monk was arrested. I released him after my coronation. The monk told me that in case Mahendran Pallava tried to escape, he planned for me to stop him on the Kollidam's shore while Dhurvineedhan blocked him in the west. So why did Dhurvineedhan rush to Kanchi? He gave the Pallavas a great victory at Pullalur."

Pulikesi's eyes flashed fire. "It is a mystery. I do not even know whether Dhurvineedhan is alive or dead. If we know about him, we may also get news of the monk. But in this wretched Pallava kingdom, every villager says, 'I do not know anything.' I want to burn every Pallava village."

"The Pallava people breached the lakes and did not cultivate summer crops. Every village hides grain and cries, 'We are starving!' Wicked people!" Jayanthvarman paused. "I vaguely remember one of my spies saying something about Dhurvineedhan—let me investigate."

Jayanthvarman's spy chief said, "When our army crossed the Kaveri, we heard of the Pullalur battle. I immediately sent a few men there. They reported that the defeated Kanga king fled southwards, chased by Mamallan. The Thiruparkadal Lake breached its banks and stopped Mamallan. King Dhurvineedhan reached the South Pennai and hid in a Jain monastery in Pataliputra. I have no clear report of what happened after that. There is some talk of the Thirukovalur district chief attacking the monastery and capturing Dhurvineedhan."

The two kings reached an agreement. Pulikesi would return to Kanchi and tighten the siege. The Pandyan king would provide the Chalukyan army with food. Once the Kollidam's water subsided, the Pandyan king would advance and capture all the territory up to the South Pennai. He would punish the Thirukovalur district chief and free Dhurvineedhan. In return for this, Pulikesi would recognise Jayanthvarman as the emperor of all the land from Kanyakumari to the South Pennai.

The Messenger from Vengi

AFTER JAYANTHVARMAN LEFT, Pulikesi said, "With the Pallava fox hiding in his hole, this Pandyan mouse dreams of becoming my equal. Just let Kanchi Fort fall! I will teach this upstart a lesson before I go back to Vatapi."

They heard the galloping of horses. The Chalukyan general had sent a messenger to escort a man from Vengi. The two men saluted Pulikesi.

The general's messenger said, "Lord, this man has an important message from Vengi. He was attacked on his way to Kanchi, but he escaped. The general asked me to escort him safely to you."

The Vengi messenger, who was covered with bandages, gave Pulikesi a scroll hidden in his sword's scabbard.

Sparks flew from Pulikesi's eyes, and he hissed like a cobra as he read the letter.

"To Emperor Satyashraya Pulikesi from his respectful brother, Vishnuvardhan. I have not heard from you since you reached Kanchi. As you commanded, I held a grand coronation here. But the Vengi army hides in the mountains and harasses us. The people are also defiant.

"Mahendran Pallava's nephew, Buddhavarman, has sprung out of nowhere with an army. He has camped on the southern shore of the Krishna to stop me if I try to come to your aid. The wounds I suffered in the Vengi war make me weaker by the day—I cannot even ride a horse.

"Before Mahendran Pallava went into hiding in his fort, he sent a message to Emperor Harshavardhan, asking for help. I hear that Harsha has decided to attack Vatapi and Asalapuram—now, when you are stuck in Kanchi and I in Vengi.

"I am ready to march at once if you say, 'Come with your army.' You are my beloved brother, father, guru and king. I am ready to sacrifice my life, body and soul in your service. I beg you to send me clear orders at once."

At the end of the letter, tears streamed from Pulikesi's eyes. He cried, "Vishnuvardhan, my dear brother, when will I see you again?"

No one came forward to comfort him. They were terrified of saying the wrong thing.

Pulikesi stopped crying and roared, "Where is the astrologer who gave the dates for this attack?"

"He did not come with us—he is in Vatapi," someone answered.

"The first thing I will do when I get back to Vatapi is have him trampled by an elephant!"

Just then, a man tied from head to toe was brought into the tent.

"Who is this?" Pulikesi roared.

The messenger from Kanchi said, "Lord, he is a Kanchi spy: we caught him on the way."

"The only thing this wretched Pallava kingdom has is spies! Good: instead of the astrologer, let him be trampled by elephants!"

The newcomer was none other than Gundodharan. He was no longer dressed as a villager. He wore modern clothes and did not seem troubled by Pulikesi's command.

The Kanchi Spy

MAITRAIYAN SAID, "MY king, let us question this man before we punish him."

"Bring him here," Pulikesi thundered. Gundodharan was brought forward. "Who are you?"

In the past eighteen months, the Chalukyan king had learned to speak and understand Tamil. It was easy, as the Vatapi language had much in common with Tamil.

"Sir, I am my mother's son. I am on my way to Thiruvenkadu to get medicine from a doctor."

"What medicine? What is wrong with you?" Pulikesi roared.

Gundodharan trembled. "It is for my mother, sir. When she was pounding dry rice, she swallowed the mortar."

Some of the men laughed; there was a faint smile on Pulikesi's face. He said threateningly, "What are you blabbering? Did your mother swallow the mortar?"

"No, no … the mortar swallowed my mother." Gundodharan trembled even more. "Sir, I am frightened to see you all. I have one thing in mind, but my tongue says something else."

"Now think calmly, and do not be afraid. State the facts," Pulikesi said.

"When my mother was pounding the rice, the pestle slipped and fell on her hand. Her hand is hurt. I am going to get medicine for her from the Thiruvenkadu doctor, Sivanesan."

"Is that all? Do you swear to this?" Pulikesi roared.

"Yes, sir. I swear it was the pestle which was hurt," Gundodharan blabbered.

Pulikesi burst out laughing and turned to Maitraiyan. "What shall we do with this mad man?"

"Lord, I suspect that he is not mad: he is a very brave man. Let me question him using my methods."

One of the soldiers stepped forward. "Lord, we found this scroll on him."

The scribe read aloud: "From the lord of the nandi flag to the lord of the fish flag. I hear that you met the tomcat from the north at the Kollidam. Do not be fooled by anything Puli says. Believe me—the Vatapi tiger cannot harm the Kanchi bull. Once the tiger starves to death in the swamp, there can be a lasting relationship between the Kanchi bull and the Madurai doe. But if you help the tiger, the doe will be in danger. Keep this in mind and do what is best."

Pulikesi understood the message and gnashed his teeth. "Take him away. Gouge out his eyes. Then behead him and throw him to the eagles," he roared.

As Pulikesi stared at Gundodharan, his anger turned to surprise. Gundodharan's head moved to make the sign of the swastika. This sign was used by the Buddhists and Jains of those times.

"Stop!" Pulikesi shouted. "I have some questions for this spy. Leave him here. All of you go."

The Monk's Message

AS MAITRAIYAN HESITATED, Pulikesi said angrily, "Go." Once they were alone, he turned to Gundodharan. "My dear fellow, who sent you? Have you brought any secret message?"

"Yes, great lord. I bring news from the monk," Gundodharan replied.

Pulikesi jumped up excitedly. "Tell me quickly: where is the monk? Is he well?"

Gundodharan's eyes filled. "Lord, my master is in that wretched Pallava's prison in Kanchi."

Pulikesi hissed, "What! Is the monk in jail even when I live? How was he arrested?"

"I saw my master last Friday in the underground dungeons. Mahendran Pallava, traitor to his religion, has imprisoned all the monks in his kingdom. King of kings, how many dangers I faced in the last week! I made many plans to meet you. Finally, I left Kanchi and purposely let myself be caught by our soldiers. Lord, the monk has given me four important messages for you."

Gundodharan listed four items for Pulikesi.

First, do not trust Jayanthvarman Pandyan. He is the one who imprisoned the monk in Madurai. Many secret messages have passed between Mahendran Pallava and Jayanthvarman. The monk suspects that the two kings are hatching a conspiracy.

Second, Dhurvineedhan betrayed the monk to Mahendran Pallava. Dhurvineedhan pretended to fight Mahendran Pallava and then went into hiding with his army. The Kanga king wants to make his son-in-law, Vishnuvardhan, the Vatapi emperor. Dhurvineedhan must be punished.

Third, Mahendran Pallava has sent Emperor Harshavardhan a message. Action must be taken on this. Mahendran Pallava has hoarded food and can comfortably hold the fort for at least another year. So it must be decided whether to continue the siege or attack the fort again.

Fourth, and most important, Emperor Harshavardhan was an art lover. Mahendran Pallava had begun work on exquisite sculpture at Mamallapuram just to show it to Harsha. If the Chalukyas harmed any sculpture in the Pallava kingdom, they risked becoming Harsha's enemies.

Saying, "I have fulfilled my promise to my master," Gundodharan burst into tears and sobbed.

"You, why are you crying?" Pulikesi asked.

"Sir, if the Chalukyan army enters Kanchi Fort, Mahendran Pallava has ordered all the captured Buddhist monks to be impaled at once. The monk asked me not to tell you this, but I cannot hide it from you. I cannot control my tears when I think of my master being impaled at the crossroads."

Pulikesi said, "How did you meet the monk? How did you get out of the fort?"

Gundodharan said, "As advised by the monk, I joined the Pallava spy brigade. I was assigned to gather information from the monks in the dungeon. By luck, I was asked to carry a scroll to the Pandyan king. I came out of the fort through a secret underground passage."

Pulikesi asked, "Can you go back to the monk and give him a message?"

"Lord, I risk my life by going back, but if you ask me to go, I will."

"My dear fellow, you must go back. Tell the monk that I will meet him personally in Kanchi in ten days. Tell him not to worry whatever happens or whatever he hears. Can you do this?"

Gundodharan was shocked at this message.

A week later, the guards at Kanchi Fort's southern entrance were also shocked to see two unarmed Chalukyan soldiers on horseback. Holding the varaha flag, the messengers blew their horns. It was clear that Pulikesi's men were there to discuss peace terms.

Mahendran's Magic

THE COUNCIL OF ministers was in session. The emperor and the prince sat on thrones, with General Kalipahai seated on a chair near them. There was no sign of Commander Paranjothi.

The food minister, Paranthaka Udaiyar, was standing anxiously.

The emperor frowned. "Udaiyar, you said that our granaries had enough food for fifteen months. It is only seven months since the siege began. How can there be food for only three months?"

Udaiyar's voice shook. "My king, many people who left came back after the Battle of Pullalur. You ordered all the sculptors in Thondaimandalam to be brought here. We planned to close schools and send away the teachers and students. At the last minute, you let them stay."

"Is that all? Is this the reason our food stock is reduced by five months?" the emperor asked.

"I also made a big mistake," the minister admitted. "I did not take into account the temple bulls, milch cows and horses. As there is no grass or hay, we have to feed the animals grains."

The emperor gave an angry, sarcastic laugh. "Excellent, Udaiyar. If Mahendran Pallava surrenders to Vatapi's Pulikesi, shall we blame the temple bulls and chariot horses?"

Mamallan jumped up and fell at the emperor's feet. "*Appa*, enough of hiding in this fort! Enough of the world laughing at us! At least now, order me to destroy the Chalukyan army."

The emperor turned away to hide his tears. He was stern when he faced the assembly again. He smiled sarcastically and lifted up Mamallan. "You are as hasty as a woman. A courageous man must not be hasty. You are a champion wrestler: must I tell you this?"

Mamallan's lips quivered. He was speechless.

"My child, be patient. You will have the chance to show your courage: I expect the Chalukyas to attack the fort soon." Mahendran turned to the food minister. "Udaiyar, from today, everyone in Kanchi, including the horses and cows, eats only two meals a day. This includes those in the palace. With this, we can stretch our food stock to four-and-a-half months, right?"

Sarangadevan said, "Lord, it looks like you expect the siege to end in four-and-a-half months."

"No, I want to reduce the food ration only as a precaution. I expect Pulikesi to attack the fort within a week …" He went on. "As far as food stocks go, Pulikesi is worse off than us. For the last three months, the Chalukyan army is on half rations. Pulikesi left Vatapi with five lakh soldiers and fifteen thousand elephants. Now there are only three-and-a-half lakh soldiers and eleven thousand elephants. Half of this force will die of starvation and disease in another month. So Pulikesi must attack the fort soon. There is no doubt that his attack will be savage."

Chief Minister Ranadheeran Pallavarayar spoke up: "My king, it is always the besieged people who starve and surrender. I have never heard of the besiegers starving!"

"By the grace of Lord Shiva, such a wonder has happened. The villagers refused to give the invaders even a handful of rice or *bajra*. They buried their grain stock. Even the lakes helped us by bursting their banks and destroying the coconut and banana groves. There was no summer cultivation. Because of all this, Pulikesi's soldiers and elephants have no food."

General Kalipahai stood. "The lakes burst their banks because of our emperor's magic."

The emperor choked with emotion. "I did nothing. Shatrughan and his spies did a brilliant job. The district chiefs have also been very clever. Even if it may bring famine to the land, they destroyed the embankments. I will never be able to repay them for their help."

Sarangadevan said, "The Pandyan king may supply the Chalukyas with food."

"I do not think so. And Pulikesi has other reasons to return quickly to Vatapi. At any moment, I am expecting important news from the south."

A guard entered, saluted the emperor and whispered into his ear. Mahendran's usually impassive face showed his surprise. "There is news which I find hard to believe. I will find out the truth. The council will assemble again tonight. I will give you the details then. Mamallan, you too can leave." Mahendran went to the entrance and jumped on a horse waiting there.

The Yoga Pavilion

ASUVABALAN, WEARING RUDRAKSHA beads and holy ash, stood in Kannapiran's house one evening, carrying a six-month-old baby. Kannapiran and Kamali watched happily as the robust baby cried loudly. The old man tried to give the baby to Kamali, who refused to take it.

"What can I do?" she said. "He is so fond of his grandfather that he refuses to come to me."

Just then, they heard the palace bells. The excited Asuvabalan abruptly laid the baby on the floor and ran into the garden.

Sparks flew from Kamali's eyes. "How can your father have the heart to put him on the floor!"

"Kamali, *appa* is not to blame. What can he do when the *Nada Brahma* calls?"

"To hell with the hypocrite! Why doesn't he go do penance in the forest? What work does he have in the ornamental pavilion in the palace garden? Is that the place for meditation?"

Kannapiran and Kamali both bent down to pick up the baby and banged their heads.

"Take your hands off the child!" Kamali said.

"I will pick him up—who are you to say no?" Kannapiran retorted.

As they quarrelled, someone quickly walked in—they were shocked to see Emperor Mahendran.

"Oh, a war here too!" the emperor said.

The embarrassed couple was speechless.

Mahendran walked to the baby. "He is a mirror image of Kanna. We will call him Kannan Junior. If Mamallan marries and has a child, the palace will be lively. It has been years since a child's cry was heard in it." Mahendran turned to Kannapiran. "Kanna, where is your father?"

"Lord, he just went to the garden pavilion," Kannapiran replied.

"Oh, the maharishi has gone to do his meditation, has he?" Kamali laughed at this. "Young people are amused by meditation and yoga. Once you are old and tired of the world, you will search for a road to travel. Continue with your war." He paused at the door. "Kamali, you will soon be able to meet your friend, Sivagami." He walked away.

"Kanna, he said I will see Sivagami soon! Is the war going to end? Have the Chalukyas run away?"

Kannapiran was thoughtful. "Kamali, come close. *Appa* talks about yoga and meditation and spends day and night in the garden pavilion. I suspect that there is a secret underground passage in that pavilion. It leads outside the fort. I think the emperor's spies come and go through it."

Meanwhile, the emperor walked to the pavilion. At the sound of footsteps, Asuvabalan peeped out. "It is you, lord. You are right on time—the bell just sounded."

Asuvabalan moved the Shiva lingam in the middle of the pavilion, revealing a hollow. In a few seconds, Shatrughan emerged from it.

"Shatrughan, what took you so long? Did you accomplish your mission?" the emperor asked.

Shatrughan replied, "Sir, your plans worked out. Gundodharan was captured by the Chalukyan soldiers and taken to Pulikesi at the Kollidam."

"Did you see Gundodharan after that? Any news from him?"

"Nothing. Swami, I hear that Pulikesi is a savage. I am worried about Gundodharan."

"Gundodharan will not be harmed, Shatrughan. Our plan has worked out: Pulikesi has asked for a truce. I rushed here to talk to you before I decide on my answer."

"Lord, can we trust Pulikesi? He is said to be very deceitful."

A cough came from the hollow. The men relaxed when Gundodharan's head emerged from it.

"Gundodharan, how did you suddenly spring up here?" the emperor asked.

"Lord, you have often told me, 'Follow Shatrughan.' That is very difficult. Although I ran behind him, I could not catch up with him in this dark passage," complained Gundodharan.

"Enough of your jokes. Tell me in detail what happened," the emperor said.

The Truce

THE WORRIED COUNCIL of ministers gathered again in the second watch of the night. Mamallan often gestured angrily to Paranjothi who stood beside him.

The emperor strode proudly to the throne. All eyes were fixed on the scroll in his hand. Mahendran said, "The Chalukyan emperor has sent a letter asking for peace and friendship."

The room broke into loud cheers. A grunt of objection came from Mamallan.

Mahendran continued: "Pulikesi, the Vatapi king with fifteen thousand elephants and five lakh soldiers, wants to end the war and be our guest in Kanchi. Shall we welcome him, or shall we strengthen the gates with more padlocks? Discuss this and give me a unanimous opinion."

The excited ministers spoke eagerly to each other.

The prime minister said, "My king, we have complete faith in you. What do you think?"

"We are comfortable enough in this fort, but the people in the villages are suffering. In a few months, there will be famine in our land. I do not want the war to continue for an instant longer than necessary. I think we must agree to peace."

Sarangadevan pointed out, "Pulikesi is a deceitful demon. Is it wise to let him into Kanchi?"

Mahendran Pallava smiled. "Pulikesi agrees to send his elephant brigade and infantry two miles away from Kanchi. He is willing to enter Kanchi unarmed, accompanied by about fifteen of his ministers. How can we suspect someone who trusts us? So tell me: do you want war or peace?"

The ministers again talked among themselves.

Finally, Sarangadevan said, "The council agrees on peace. We will go along with your wishes to welcome Pulikesi to Kanchi."

War of Words

MAMALLAN JUMPED UP angrily. "Pallava king, in this hall of peace lovers, can I also say a word?"

The emperor calmed him: "Mamallan, you are the crown prince. Speak your mind."

Mamallan glared at them. "You often speak of the courageous Pallava dynasty descended from Thondaiman Ilanthiraiyan. Has any Pallava backed away from battle or hidden in a fort? If you make peace with the enemy, our shame will live on until the end of the world."

There were whispers acknowledging the truth of the prince's rousing speech.

Mahendran Pallava interrupted in a majestic voice, his head held high. "My son, on the day I ascended this throne, I swore an oath to guard the people's lives and possessions and protect them from suffering. I cannot give up my oath out of empty pride."

But Mamallan had more to say: "Father, the Pallava people are brave and value honour above their lives and possessions. Do you know what the Mandagapattu villagers said? 'When he has a son like Mamallan and a commander like Paranjothi, why should Emperor Mahendran fear Pulikesi and hide in Kanchi Fort?' We have disappointed our people. There are one lakh Pallava soldiers in the fort, raring to fight. The swords forged by Kanchi's great smiths are thirsty for blood. Father, command me to destroy the Chalukyan army right now!"

Mahendran's heart melted at these brave words, but he was firm: "My son, spoken like a true warrior! But popular opinion is not always correct. I will not make the people suffer by listening to emotional words spoken impulsively." He turned to the ministers. "I have accepted Pulikesi's offer of peace and agreed to welcome him to Kanchi. I cannot go back on my words."

Mamallan was even more excited. "*Appa*, at least stop with ending the war. Let us even hide in the fort until the Chalukyan army leaves ... but that wicked Pulikesi must not set foot in our city."

"Mamallan, the Pallavas have never gone back on their given word. I must welcome Pulikesi."

Mamallan rushed forward with folded hands. "*Appa*, I cannot stay in this city with Pulikesi. Allow me to leave the fort when Pulikesi enters it."

Paranjothi stepped forward. "Lord, allow me to go with the prince."

"Oh, Lakshmana follows Rama! I had already decided to send you both out. Pick thirty thousand of our bravest soldiers and leave at once. Under cover of the Chalukyan invasion, the cowardly Pandyan king stole into the Pallava kingdom. We must teach him a lesson."

The Welcome

LATE THAT NIGHT, Bhuvanamahadevi protested to Emperor Mahendran: "Lord, I heard that you and Mamallan had a heated argument in the assembly. How could you argue in public?"

"*Devi*, Mamallan made me proud. But I had to hide my feelings and speak harshly to him."

"I do not like what you are planning to do. Is it wise to welcome our cruel enemy to Kanchi?"

"Won't the Pallava dynasty be praised for turning enemies into friends? There are three great dynasties in our sacred Bharat—Harshavardhan north of the Narmada; Pulikesi between the Narmada and the Tungabhadra; Mahendran Pallava south of the Tungabhadra. If we are allies, Bharat will be a paradise. Learning and art will flourish; people will live comfortably. When I was young, I dreamt of enjoying the wonders of Ajanta, visiting the Kannauj art festival and making Mamallapuram a dreamworld of sculpture. My dream will now come true."

"Lord, talking about friendship, why are you sending Mamallan to fight the Pandyans?"

"There can be friendship only among equals. Impudent men must be disciplined by force."

The next day, the cheerful people decorated Kanchi's streets and the thresholds of their houses. They once again wore their silks and gold. Contrary to Mamallan's expectation, they seemed happy that the Chalukyan king was coming to Kanchi.

On the fifth day after the truce, the fort's northern gate was opened, and musical instruments blared a deafening welcome. The Chalukyan emperor, who had wished to see 'Kanchi, the City of Learning,' in his youth, entered the fort. He was escorted by fifty of his men.

Mahendran Pallava welcomed Pulikesi. Mahendran's face was expressionless except for a slight smile, but Pulikesi's eyes showed his anger. *Is this the Mahendran Pallava who foiled my plans to defeat him? Where have I seen this majestic face before?*

After the heralds called their titles, the emperors dismounted from their horses and embraced.

Pulikesi searched the company standing behind Mahendran. "I have heard much about your brave son, Mamallan. Who is he among those standing here?"

Mahendran laughed. "Satyashraya, he is on an important mission."

Three Hearts

AS PULIKESI ENTERED Kaṇchi Fort through the northern gate, the prince left by the southern gate. An infantry division of thirty thousand, five thousand cavalrymen, a hundred war elephants and other army provisions waited a little distance from the fort. Mamallan and Paranjothi rode in Kannapiran's chariot which clanked across the half-filled, broken moat by a quickly built, makeshift bridge. Once they were across, the bridge was destroyed and the gates closed.

The sound of the bolts, locks and chariot wheels echoed the beat of the chariot riders' hearts.

Mamallan had said goodbye to his mother. Bhuvanamahadevi's eyes brimmed with tears. "Son, I do not like your father being friends with the Pallavas' mortal enemy. I do not like you leaving Kanchi at this time. My heart is troubled: what if something unfortunate happens?"

His mother's words made a deep impression on Mamallan. There was a sinking feeling in his heart. He tried to raise his spirits by thinking of the coming battle and of Sivagami in Mandagapattu. *If I take a short diversion, I can see Sivagami. I left her saying I would return after defeating Pulikesi. I will see her at least after destroying the Pandyans.*

Paranjothi's face was also stern. His heart was burdened with a great sense of responsibility. That morning, the emperor had met him secretly. "My boy, I am sending Mamallan to war only because I trust you. See that he does not rush into danger. He is the only heir to the ancient Pallava throne. The Pandyan *maravars* are great soldiers—you must be careful." He smiled. "Guard Mamallan from arrows on the battlefield ... and guard him from the sharp arrows of Sivagami's eyes. There must be no repetition of what happened last time. Come back straight to Kanchi."

As Paranjothi saluted him and turned to leave, the emperor said affectionately, "Commander, after defeating the Pandyans, go to Thiruvenkadu and visit your mother and uncle if you want."

What an extraordinary man the emperor is! I am lucky that he loves and trusts me. I must bring Mamallan safely back to Kanchi. Telling me to go to Thiruvenkadu shows the emperor's large-heartedness. But what will my mother and uncle think of my being a soldier? Will Umayaal be afraid to come near me?

Kannapiran, too, was worried. When leaving, he had put his cheek against his eight-month-old baby's face and cooed, "Goodbye, precious." The child laughed and held Kannapiran's long ears with its two soft hands. Kannapiran's heart melted. *When will I feel that touch again?*

He also remembered Kamali's words. 'Kanna, is Mahendran Pallava mad? Inviting Pulikesi here and sending Mamallan to fight the Pandyans! My heart is troubled. Kanna, whatever happens, do not forget my sister, Sivagami. Remind Mamallan about her.'

The three chariot riders worried about what the future might bring. Their hearts beat in unison.

The Royal Reception

PULIKESI'S ARRIVAL WAS celebrated for a week. The two emperors visited temples and monasteries, inspected Kanchi's schools and saw the art pavilions.

A friendship seemed to grow between them. Mahendran Pallava pointed out to Pulikesi that both their kingdoms would profit by an alliance. Mahendran explained that he had nothing against Buddhism or Jainism. He had embraced Shaivism because it respected all faiths equally. Pulikesi said that he had no strong religious feelings and favoured Jainism only for political reasons.

Pulikesi asked, "Can I meet Aayanar—the Pallava kingdom's great sculptor?"

Mahendran was amazed. "How do you know about him?"

"I saw his house in the forest. It was filled with lifelike, remarkable statues of dancing figures. I heard that a sculptor and his daughter, a dancer, lived there. Do you know where they are?"

"I have sent for them. They may be at court tomorrow," Mahendran said.

On the eighth day of Pulikesi's arrival, a valedictory function was held for him. The Pallava ministers, commanders, district chiefs, city leaders and wealthy merchants gathered in Kanchi's main hall along with ascetics, scholars, poets, sculptors, musicians and artists.

Important men were introduced to the Chalukyan emperor. Poets recited compositions in Tamil and Sanskrit, praising the two emperors equally. Musicians demonstrated their skills. Pulikesi was delighted to examine the seven-stringed *parivadini* veena designed by Mahendran.

Time passed pleasantly, but both the emperors seemed uneasy.

Mahendran's eyes often went to the hall's entrance. Finally, he exclaimed, "Here they are!"

Aayanar and Sivagami entered the hall. Sivagami stumbled as she crossed the threshold. *Ah, is this a bad omen?* She walked into the hall like a peacock with a deer's graceful steps.

Long May You Live, Peacock

PULIKESI WAS STUNNED. *Has one of the Ajanta paintings come to life? I have seen many beautiful women—but not one of them has this woman's exquisite walk.*

Sivagami walked as if floating in the air, oblivious to the fact that every eye in that assembly was fixed on her. With the natural modesty of a refined woman, her head was slightly bowed. She controlled her urge to see whether the man who filled her heart day and night was in that hall.

When they came to the two emperors, Aayanar and Sivagami greeted them with folded hands.

Sivagami looked at Pulikesi with lidded eyes. Her eyes then searched the area near the thrones. The handsome face they looked for was missing. *Ah, where is he? Has he met with some accident? No—in that case, Mahendran Pallava would not hold this ceremony.*

"Aayanar," Mahendran Pallava said. "Our friend, King Pulikesi, has heard of Sivagami's fame as a dancer. He wants to see her dance. That is why I sent for you. Can Sivagami dance now?"

"Lord, two great emperors sit here like two suns or two devas! What better place for Sivagami to showcase her talent!" Aayanar said.

"Good, Aayanar. The musicians are ready. I called this assembly just for you," Mahendran said.

As Sivagami walked to her dance circle her eyes happened to fall on Pulikesi's face. She shivered at the frenzy in his cruel eyes. There was something vaguely familiar about him. Sivagami shrugged aside her dark thoughts and prepared to dance. She could now openly look around the hall. She saw the empress and other women seated in the upper gallery. *Last time, he was sitting with the women. Maybe he is sitting out of sight and watching me now.*

All her disappointment, heartache and fear melted away, and she began to dance. *As my father said, this is a rare opportunity for me to showcase my dance on a great platform.* Sivagami also knew that art could melt Mahendran Pallava's heart. *I must win him over with my dance. It is my only weapon to make him agree to my marrying Mamallan.*

Once she began to dance, all thought vanished from her head. She lost herself in her dance. Her heart floated in ecstatic space and forgot beat, rhythm and order. Her body drifted in a flood of joy. Her spectators came back to earth from their happy dream worlds only when she ended the first segment of her recital. The hall was filled with loud claps: the two emperors applauded too.

Before Sivagami began her recital, Pulikesi had asked Mahendran, "Why do you give them so much respect? In my country, we whip the dancers to make them dance."

"Satyashraya, we are different. Here, we respect art and artists."

"What customs you have!" Pulikesi mocked.

When Pulikesi joined the others in clapping, Mahendran asked, "What do you say now? Have you changed your opinion about respecting artists?"

"Extraordinary dancing! I have never seen anything like this. But …" Pulikesi sank into thought.

For her *abhinaya*, Sivagami chose a song on the ancient Tamil god, Velan. Velan swears an oath on his spear to a female devotee, 'I will come back and make you mine.' But he does not keep his promise. The disappointed girl loses heart, but she does not become angry or criticise Velan. She blames his peacock instead.

I Do Not Fear Death

THE AUDIENCE WAS ecstatic, but Mahendran Pallava's face was dark. He understood that Sivagami was showing her love for Mamallan through the Velan song. *How bold she is! She thinks she can get her way by praising me. She has no idea who I am.* The emperor spoke to an attendant standing nearby. The man went to Aayanar and whispered to him.

"My dear, sing one of Navukkarasar's songs," Aayanar said to Sivagami.

Sivagami noted Mahendran's dissatisfaction. *What a fool I am to try to melt his hard heart!* Her shame blazed into anger. She began the song, 'We are no one's subjects, we do not fear death …'

The ecstatic mood in the hall changed. *Why sing this song now?*

This song had a history. When Navukkarasar converted from Jainism to Shaivism, Mahendran Pallava ordered him to come to Kanchi for a trial. Navukkarasar replied, 'Lord Shiva is my only God; I refuse to obey your king.' He inscribed this song on a scroll and sent it to the king. Mahendran wanted to meet the great man who had composed such a divine song. When he met the saint, the emperor too converted from Jainism to Shaivism.

Mahendran Pallava told Pulikesi the circumstances under which the song was composed.

Pulikesi said, "Ridiculous! A beggar's song defies your authority; a girl holds her *abhinaya* for this song in court; you rejoice over it. I can hardly believe it!"

"That is the glory of art, Satyashraya," Mahendran, the art lover, said. "When defiance was expressed in exquisite Tamil poetry, I wanted to meet the composer."

The *abhinaya* began and the engrossed spectators forgot the song's history, the world and themselves.

When the song ended, Mahendran asked Pulikesi, "How was that?"

The Chalukyan king stared at Mahendran. "What Naganandhi wrote was true."

There was no change in Mahendran's expression. "Who is Naganandhi?" he asked casually.

"Have you not heard of Naganandhi? He is a Buddhist monk on a pilgrimage through the south."

"What did this monk write?"

"I asked him to write to me about his pilgrimage. He once wrote, 'There is no greater sculptor than Aayanar and no greater dancer than Sivagami in Bharat.'"

"It looks like Naganandhi is an art lover. Where is he now?"

"I do not know. I heard that you imprisoned all the monks in your kingdom, suspecting them of being spies. Maybe you imprisoned Naganandhi too."

Mahendran was silent.

Sivagami's eyes took in the cheering audience, moved to Mahendran Pallava and then stopped at Pulikesi's angry face. Her vague memory took form. *That face! Can two men's faces resemble each other like this? Or is it one man? Is Pulikesi wandering around disguised as Naganandhi?*

The recital ended with Sivagami dancing to a song dedicated to Nataraja, the Lord of Dance. The audience cried in one voice, 'What a performance!'

Aayanar and Sivagami again stood before the thrones.

Mahendran said, "Sivagami, my dear, the Chalukyan emperor is captivated by your dance. He asks me to send you and your father to Vatapi. Do you agree to go?"

Sivagami's anger made her lose her self-control: "Lord, don't you want me in your country?"

Aayanar and everyone standing nearby was shocked and alarmed.

But Mahendran Pallava smiled at Pulikesi. "Satyashraya, see! Will artists want to go to a country where they are whipped?" Mahendran did not see Pulikesi's face darken and sparks fly from his eyes. He continued, "Sivagami, my dear, I do not even want to send you from this city. Aayanar, I must reward Sivagami for her extraordinary performance. You must stay in the city. Stay with Kamali. Kamali is eager to see Sivagami. I will come there later and talk to you leisurely."

Pulikesi's Departure

THE NEXT DAY, preparations were made for the Chalukuyan emperor's departure. Pulikesi wanted to see Kanchi one last time, and the two emperors went around the city on the royal elephant.

Pulikesi never tired of seeing Kanchi's wide avenues, palaces, art pavilions, dance stages, monasteries and temples. He said, "What a mediocre poet Bharavi was!"

"How can you say that?" Mahendran protested. "Haven't you read his beautiful *Kiratarjuniya*?"

"Ah, poets will describe forests and clouds, but Bharavi's description of Kanchi does not do the city justice. Pallava king, listen: I will give you my vast empire in exchange for Kanchi."

"King, take Kanchi. In exchange, just give me the Ajanta caves. Kanchi's buildings may turn to dust one day, but Ajanta's paintings will last forever. Sivagami refused to go to Vatapi, but if you tell Aayanar that you will give him the secret of Ajanta's paintings, he will go with you at once ..."

Memory flashed in Pulikesi's eyes. "Is Aayanar so interested in the Ajanta pigments?"

"Don't you remember him sending you a message about this?" Mahendran Pallava laughed. "How stunned you were!"

The brilliant Pallava emperor, who had no equal in strategy and foresight, forgot the proverb, 'Guard your tongue. Careless words cause grief.' He revealed the secrets buried in his heart.

Pulikesi hissed, "How do you know all this? You speak as if you were there."

"I was there."

Pulikesi stared at his face. "Ah, in that case, the messenger, Vajrabahu, was you!"

"Yes, it was me," Mahendran Pallava admitted. "Satyashraya, if you had received the true message given to that boy, there would be no Kanchi today. My friend, did you think of burning down this beautiful city?"

Not then. But now I am thinking of reducing this city to ashes. Aloud, Pulikesi asked, "Pallava king, what was the message in the true scroll?"

"Nothing but a division of the spoils. The monk said, 'Take the Pallava empire and beautiful Kanchi. Give me only the Dancing Queen, Sivagami.'"

Pulikesi was thoughtful. "Is capturing Kanchi so easy?"

"My friend, if you had come straight to Kanchi as the message advised, it would have been easy. At that time, the fort's gates would not have withstood even one of your elephants."

Volcanoes spewed fire in Pulikesi's heart.

Mahendran went on: "My friend, let us forget the past. I have now told you how I defended my country—keeping these secrets would have been a betrayal of our friendship. We will be friends for life. I will never betray you. It is the same for you, right?"

"Must you ask me that?" Pulikesi replied.

The elephant stopped at the northern gate. The emperors climbed down and embraced each other.

"Pallava king, I am a little disappointed to leave without seeing your brave son, Mamallan."

"You have not seen Mamallan or the young boy who brought you the scroll. Naganandhi helped the Pallava kingdom: he gave us a brave commander ..."

"Yes," Pulikesi interrupted him. "You have not yet told me where they are."

Mahendran laughed. "Mamallan and Paranjothi have gone to visit the Pandyan king."

"Ah, I thought so! There was a rumour about you making a marriage alliance with the Pandyans." Pulikesi paused. "Before I leave, tell me this: do you know who the monk, Naganandhi, is?"

"I can guess," Mahendran said and whispered to Pulikesi.

Pulikesi exclaimed angrily, "Knowing this, won't you free him and send him with me?"

"If the emperor so requests, it will be done," Mahendran replied.

Pulikesi declared majestically, "The Chalukyas of Vatapi do not make requests."

"The Pallavas of Kanchi do not grant wishes without requests," Mahendran replied.

"Till we meet again, Pallava king," Pulikesi said.

"Satyashraya, remember," said Mahendran.

"I will never forget," Pulikesi replied.

Little Kannan

MEETING AFTER ONE-AND-A-HALF years, Kamali and Sivagami hugged and wept and laughed and scolded each other. They did not know what to discuss first. Little Kannan solved their problem. The child awoke and wailed, and Kamali ran to pick him up.

Sivagami froze on seeing the boy ... every cell in her body throbbed.

Kamali asked, "Why are you standing there like a fool? Are you angry with little Kannan?"

Sivagami stretched out her arms. "Kamali, will he come to me?"

Little Kannan waved his arms and legs to show that he wanted to go to her.

Kamali laughed. "You have cast a spell on him like you did on Mamallan!"

Delighted and embarrassed, Sivagami took the baby and looked into its face. "Look, he is a mirror image of his father. Kamali, where is his father?"

"What a question! Wherever Mamallan is, that is where his father will be," Kamali replied. "Don't you know? Mamallan has gone to fight the Pandyans."

Sivagami jumped up, forgetting the baby in her lap. The baby fell to the ground and wailed.

Kamali shrieked, "You wretch, you dropped the child!" She rocked the baby and asked Sivagami, "Didn't you know that Mamallan has gone to fight the Pandyans?"

"No, *akka*." Sivagami choked with disappointment. *If he had been here, would he have let me dance before that wild cat?* She was furious with Mahendran Pallava. *He dared to make me dance before Pulikesi only because Mamallan was not there.* She had a sudden flash of understanding. *The emperor brought me here so that Mamallan could not meet me at Mandagapattu when he went south.*

Sivagami cried, "I have never known anyone as shameless as the Pallavas!"

Kamali was stunned. *Why is she talking like this? Is this the Sivagami who was ready to give her life for one sidelong glance from the Pallava prince?*

Sivagami fell on Kamali's neck and cried, "*Akka*, I am blabbering. Forgive me. When did Mamallan go to war? Did he know about the emperor calling me here to dance?"

Kamali said, "There is no chance of that: I myself heard about your dance only this morning."

"*Akka*, please understand. I have so much to say to you … and I will never tire of loving your precious baby. But I must go back to Mandagapattu at once. Let me tell *appa*."

Does Pulikesi Know?

THE NEXT EVENING, Aayanar, Sivagami, Kamali and Asuvabalan sat on the verandah of Kannapiran's house, discussing Pulikesi's stay in Kanchi.

Sivagami asked, "*Mama*, Pulikesi has gone. Won't they open the fort's gates now?"

Asuvabalan said, "I do not think so, dear. When Pulikesi left, his face was dark. I wonder what that demon plans to do."

Aayanar asked Asuvabalan, "Why was he angry? Do you know?"

"I believe the Chalukyas and the Pandyans are allies. Some say that Pulikesi is angry because Mamallan has marched to fight the Pandyans. Do you know what others say…" He hesitated.

"Come on, tell us," Aayanar urged.

"Pulikesi was captivated by Sivagami's dance and wanted to take her with him. He is angry because Mahendran refused."

"To hell with him!" Kamali exclaimed. "May he be struck by a thunderbolt!"

"Ahah, who speaks such a divine blessing?" a majestic voice asked.

They jumped up in surprise: Emperor Mahendran stood at the back door.

"Asuvabalan, Pulikesi did not ask for Sivagami. Do you know what he said? 'Why are you giving this girl so much respect? If you send her with me to Vatapi, I will whip her to make her dance.' See how much that fool appreciates art!" His eyes blazed with anger and hatred.

Sivagami stepped forward. "Lord, you made me dance before such a man—is that dharma?"

"My child, how was I to know that Pulikesi is a fool with no artistic sense? He camped outside the fort for months but did not visit Mamallapuram. He said, 'While there are living men and women, who wants to see stone figures?' And not just that. He said, 'What is so great about Ajanta? They are just paintings on the walls.' Aayanar, this is the man to whom you sent Paranjothi with a message, along with Naganandhi's, asking about the secret of Ajanta's pigments."

Aayanar was shocked. "My king, did Naganandhi send a scroll to Pulikesi? How did you ..."

"How did I know? I read the scroll myself. But, unlike Pulikesi, Naganandhi is a true art lover. He wrote, 'Come quickly and capture beautiful Kanchi. Give me only Sivagami.' Aayanar, your close friend, Naganandhi, was a serious threat to the Pallava kingdom."

But Aayanar was thinking about something else. He said softly to himself, "The monk's message was to the Chalukyan emperor ... does Pulikesi know the secret of Ajanta's pigments?"

At Mahendran's signal, Asuvabalan followed him to the garden pavilion.

The Underground Passage

SIVAGAMI SAID, "*AKKA*, the emperor wants to learn meditation now."

Kamali winked and whispered, "Nonsense! It is all a cover—I will explain later."

When Mahendran Pallava returned from the garden, Aayanar stopped him and said pitifully, "Pallava king, our work here is done. Can we return to Mandagapattu?"

Mahendran smiled. "Aayanar, I have not yet rewarded Sivagami for her performance. Be patient. And you need not return to Mandagapattu: you can go back to your house in the forest."

Aayanar said worriedly, "Lord, all the work I begin remains incomplete ..."

Mahendran interrupted him: "Human life is fleeting. Can any of us complete the tasks we begin? So what? Our descendants will complete them. A wedding will soon take place in the palace, and your daughter may have to dance for it." He paused at the threshold. "Aayanar, if you must go, leave when the fort's gates are opened. I will send for you if necessary." He hurried away.

After the emperor left, Sivagami lay face-down on the floor and sobbed.

Kamali lifted her head onto her lap. "Fool, you are crying because the emperor mentioned the wedding, right? Mamallan gave you his word—he will never agree to marry another woman."

Soon rumours of Mamallan's wedding filled the city. It was said that Mamallan was to marry the Pandyan princess in order to break the Pandyans' alliance with Pulikesi.

Sivagami sobbed, "*Akka*, once Mamallan defeats the Pandyans, he will go to Mandagapattu. He will hate me when he hears that I came here to dance for Pulikesi. The emperor has tricked me!"

Kamali was thoughtful. "Sivagami, the emperor said that you can leave once the fort's gates are opened ..."

"Ah, you do not know how cunning he is! He will not open the gates until Mamallan comes back."

"Do not worry. Even if the fort's gates stay closed, I will send you out," Kamali promised.

Sivagami stopped crying and sat up. "*Akka*, how will you send us out?"

Kamali whispered in her ear, "Through the underground passage."

Sivagami said eagerly, "Is there really an underground passage? Are you sure?"

Kamali whispered, "Do not shout. *Mama* only pretends to meditate. There is an underground passage from the pavilion. I have seen Gundodharan coming from there. The emperor too sometimes ..."

"Gundodharan?"

"Yes, the emperor has a spy called Gundodharan; Shatrughan is another. Both are wicked thugs."

"*Akka*, how did you find the passage?"

"*Mama* ordered me to never go near the pavilion, and so I often went there secretly. One day, I saw that the Shiva lingam in the middle had moved. There was a large opening in its place, and Gundodharan was coming out of it. My *mama* and the emperor were in the pavilion then."

Sivagami said, "Kamali *akka*, if you send us out through the passage, I will be your slave forever!"

"My slave forever, is it? You silly girl: you are going to be the queen of this entire kingdom." Kamali paused. "Be patient. By tomorrow, I will find out how to move the lingam. And what is the use of being in such a hurry? Your father must agree to come with you."

"He will be in more of a hurry to leave than I am."

Just then, Aayanar came to them and lamented, "How much longer must we stay locked up in this fort! If only I had known that Naganandhi sent Pulikesi a scroll about the Ajanta paintings! I would have begged Pulikesi and got the secret of the pigments from him while he was in Kanchi."

"How can you be sure that King Pulikesi knows the secret, *appa*?" Sivagami asked.

"He will know: I heard that Pulikesi spent his childhood in the Ajanta caves," Aayanar said.

Kamali and Sivagami exchanged looks and smiled.

The Kapalika Cave

THE FORT'S GATES stayed shut. Rumours spread through the city. Some said, 'The Chalukyan army is coming back to surround the fort.' Others said, 'Mahendran Pallava has imprisoned a Buddhist monk dear to Pulikesi. Pulikesi demands his release—otherwise he will attack the city.' Some insisted, 'Pulikesi wants Aayanar and Sivagami. If Mahendran refuses, there will be war again.'

For the first time in Mahendran's reign, the people criticised him. Some complained, 'It was wrong to let Pulikesi enter Kanchi.' Others asked, 'And even if he came, why give him such a grand welcome?' A few said, 'Our Sivagami should not have danced before that fool.'

Aayanar had just one thought. *If only the gates are opened before Pulikesi leaves! I can somehow meet him and ask about the secret of Ajanta's pigments.* He said, "There must be an underground passage from the city."

Sivagami's eyes flashed. "Really, *appa*? Can we go if we find the passage?"

"We can go. I worked on that underground passage for a few days, but I do not know where the entrance is," Aayanar said.

Sivagami said softly, "*Appa*, Kamali *akka* knows the entrance."

Aayanar rushed to Kamali. "My dear child, is this true? You must show me the way: I will be grateful to you all my life."

"*Chithappa*, I must find the opportunity to take you there. It is well guarded," Kamali said.

For three days, Asuvabalan spent most of his time in the yoga pavilion. The sound of the bell and excited voices often came from there. On the fourth night, the sleepless Aayanar saw a strange sight in the moonlight: two men dragged a huge, blindfolded Buddhist monk through the garden.

Is it Naganandhi? Is Pulikesi waiting for him to be released through the secret passage? Once Naganandhi is free, Pulikesi will leave. A great chance is slipping through my fingers! Aayanar too was struck by the resemblance between Pulikesi and Naganandhi. *Who is Naganandhi really?* Aayanar did not sleep at all that night.

Asuvabalan saw him when he came back from the pavilion at daybreak. "Hello, sculptor. It looks like you have not slept all night."

"Yes, sir. There was a commotion in your meditation hall all night. What is going on?"

"You must have been dreaming." Asuvabalan paused. "But last night, I had an extraordinary yogic experience—I must tell the emperor about it." He hurried out.

Minutes later, Kamali urged Aayanar and Sivagami to come quickly. They had their belongings packed in a wicker basket, ready to leave.

They went to the garden pavilion, and Kamali easily shifted the lingam. They saw the steps leading into the underground passage.

Kamali gave Aayanar the lamp she carried and said, "*Chithappa*, quick!"

Aayanar took the lamp and climbed down the steps. Sivagami and Kamali hugged and wept.

"Goodbye, *akka*," Sivagami said in a choked voice.

"Goodbye, *thangachi*. Come back to Kanchi as the crown prince's wife," Kamali blessed her.

Sivagami's heart beat fast as she stepped into the passage. She felt as if she had left a world of light and happiness for a world of darkness and fear. She braced herself and followed Aayanar.

Aayanar and Sivagami walked down the dark passage. They did not talk much.

Aayanar encouraged Sivagami, "The passage will end soon, my dear." After an hour, there was a chill in the air. He stopped. "We are crossing the moat. My child, this is the spot I worked on. It needed skilled work to see that the water did not come in."

After walking for another hour, they saw light shining from above.

"Ah, it is the end of the passage!" exclaimed Aayanar.

They climbed up the steps leading to the light. They were in a small Jain rock temple. A Kapalika sat there with closed eyes. His ash-smeared body and garland of skulls were frightening, but luckily, he was in a trance. Without giving him a second glance, Aayanar and Sivagami quickly walked away.

After a short distance, Sivagami asked, "*Appa*, what is a Kapalika doing in a Jain temple?"

"The Jains, angry with Mahendran Pallava, have left the kingdom. The Kapalikas must have occupied the empty cave when they were sent out of Kanchi before the siege."

Talking, Aayanar and Sivagami walked through the forest. They heard a crowd. Soon a large group of Chalukyan soldiers appeared, carrying the varaha flag.

The Volcano Erupts

WHEN PULIKESI LEFT Mahendran Pallava, a volcano simmered in his heart, waiting to erupt in smoke and flames. He was jealous of Kanchi's beauty, the people's refinement and wealth and the luxurious palace. Sivagami's dance and Mahendran's pride in art fanned the flames of his envy. Above all, Pulikesi was furious to find out that Mahendran had fooled him.

He cheated me at the North Pennai with a false message. And how many cunning tricks after that! If I had marched straight here, Kanchi would now be mine. The brave tiger, who makes the jungle beasts tremble, has been caught in the web of a wily fox: what a disgrace!

Pulikesi did not say a word until he reached the Chalukyan army camp about twelve miles from Kanchi: then, the volcano erupted. His army commanders and spies burned in the fire.

Pulikesi roared, "I will have half of you trampled by elephants ... and the other half impaled!" The tent was silent. "Are your mouths blocked?" He blamed them for all the Chalukyan defeats.

"You fools! Kanchi Fort initially had doors of single-layered wood. A single elephant could have smashed a door. There were less than ten thousand soldiers to guard the walls. Our men could have entered the fort in one day. If Mahendran Pallava had not fallen at my feet in surrender, I would have burned Kanchi to the ground. That Pallava insulted me before a mere sculptor and a dancing girl! It seems I do not appreciate art—what arrogance!" Pulikesi gnashed his teeth and stamped the ground. "While the Pallava was strengthening his defenses, you were sleeping on the shores of the North Pennai." He laughed wildly.

Maitraiyan picked up courage. "Lord, Naganandhi's message is the cause. I objected then ..."

Sparks flew from Pulikesi's eyes. "Are you trying to blame Naganandhi for your stupidity? The scroll we got was not from Naganandhi. That thief, Mahendran, robbed Naganandhi's scroll, prepared a false scroll, disguised himself as a messenger and delivered it to me. Our clever spies could not see this. Ah, if only Naganandhi had been with us then! He would never have been fooled by the Pallava fox's tricks ..." Talking about Naganandhi, Pulikesi's heart melted and his voice softened.

Using this chance, the Chalukyan general said, "Lord, let us forget the past. We must now think about taking our army safely back to Vatapi. As the days pass, it will become more difficult ..."

Pulikesi thundered, "General, when I was young, Naganandhi looked after me like a mother. He risked his life to save mine and put me on the Vatapi throne. Naganandhi is now in Kanchi's dungeons, and you are telling me to abandon him. That will never happen. Attack Kanchi Fort. We will capture it, burn the palace to the ground, cut off Mahendran Pallava's head and tie it to my chariot wheel. We will free Naganandhi and take him back to Vatapi with us on the royal elephant." There was silence in the tent. "Why are you silent? Have you become dumb?"

The commanders spoke up: "Our starving elephants are wild. Soon they will break their chains and attack our own soldiers. Our men will not attack. They are unhappy and tired and want to go home. We will all starve to death soon. We do not have weapons to mount an attack."

Pulikesi dared not ignore their unanimous opinion. "To think that I started this invasion trusting you!" he said disgustedly. "Get out! I will think it over."

Pulikesi's Command

PULIKESI WAITED FOR three days. His determination to take revenge on Mahendran Pallava grew until it encompassed the earth and the sky.

Finally, Pulikesi reached a decision. The emperor and his chief commanders would leave at once for Vatapi with the major part of the army. Fifty thousand of the fittest soldiers would stay behind. They would form groups and plunder and burn all the villages within twenty miles of Kanchi. They would capture young women, kill young men and mutilate the old. Most importantly, they would destroy all sculpture, and cut off a hand and a leg of every sculptor they came across.

Pulikesi left for Vatapi with the larger part of his army. It was one of the Chalukyan companies left behind which found Aayanar and Sivagami.

When she saw the varaha flag, Sivagami shivered and her heart sank. The hundred enemy soldiers seemed fifteen thousand to her.

But Aayanar was excited. He asked a soldier, "Sir, can you tell me where your emperor is?"

The soldier could not understand Aayanar.

Sasangan, the company commander, came up on horseback and exclaimed in surprise. He had accompanied Pulikesi to Kanchi and watched Sivagami dance in court. He was delighted to recognise the pair. Sasangan stared at Aayanar and asked, "What did you say?"

Aayanar said excitedly, "Sir, where is your emperor? I must meet him."

Sasangan raised his eyebrows and smiled sarcastically. "Why do you want to meet him?"

"It is confidential." When the man laughed mockingly, Aayanar explained, "Your emperor knows the secret of Ajanta's pigments. I came to learn the secret from him. Please take me to him."

Sasangan laughed even louder and ordered his soldiers, "Blindfold them."

Aayanar was shocked. "Blindfold? But why?"

"Emperor Pulikesi has ordered us to arrest all young women in the Pallava kingdom. Every sculptor will have a hand and a leg cut off. If you are blindfolded, the girl will be spared the sight."

Sivagami fell to the ground with an anguished cry. When she regained her senses, she walked in a daze, supported by two soldiers. Her heart ached when she saw that her father was not with her. Suddenly, a figure darted out from the thick forest—it was Naganandhi. She shook herself free and jumped to him. She fell at his feet and cried, "Swami, you are my only hope. Save me!"

Promise of Refuge

NAGANANDHI WAS AMAZED. "Sivagami, is it really you? Are my eyes playing tricks?"

"Swami, it is me, the orphaned Sivagami. Save this poor sculptor's daughter!"

"My dear, you are not a poor orphan. Aren't you the lucky woman the Pallava prince loves? I am just a saffron-robed beggar. How can I save you?" He paused. "How did you get caught by these men? Why did you leave the fort? How did you come out?"

"Swami, my foolishness brought me here. I led my beloved father to his death."

Commander Sasangan, who resented the monk's influence over Pulikesi, rode up to them and greeted Naganandhi. "Which hole has the cobra been hiding in all these days?"

A frightening hiss came from Naganandhi. Someone shouted, "Snake!" and the soldiers scattered. A cobra slithered across Sasangan's horse's leg and disappeared into the bushes.

"Careful, commander," the monk warned. "A cobra usually does not bite. But if it does, its poison is fatal."

Sasangan clenched his teeth. "I do not have the time to talk to you. Hey you! Tie this woman."

"Commander, you are lucky to have captured the famous dancer of the south. I will soon give the emperor this good news. I just met him in another part of this forest ..."

"Lies! The Chalukyan emperor would have reached the North Pennai by now."

"We will soon know what is true and what is a lie. But remember: if a cat wants the deer which the tiger has marked as its prey, there will be trouble," Naganandhi warned majestically.

Sasangan growled.

Naganandhi turned to Sivagami. "Girl, if you do as I say, you will not be harmed. Go with these men. As a dancer, your legs are strong. You are not afraid of walking, are you?"

Sivagami, who had stood like a statue, now came to life. "Swami, I am not worried about myself. Your friend, Aayanar, is in danger because of me. Save him!"

Naganandhi asked, "Commander, where is her father?"

Sasangan laughed cruelly. "Let me tell you. The emperor has ordered one hand and one leg of all Pallava sculptors to be cut off. Her father is a great sculptor: so I am honouring him by cutting off both his hands and both his legs. I have asked them to take him right to the top of that rock, cut off his limbs and roll them down so that the Pallava soldiers on the fort's walls can see."

Sivagami turned to Naganandhi with indescribable anguish in her eyes and wept, "Swami …"

"Girl, trust me. I will save your father. Go peacefully with them," Naganandhi said.

"The monk knows the penalty for interfering with the emperor's orders, right?" Sasangan asked and turned to Sivagami. "Girl, follow the monk's good advice and come with us."

Atrocity

AAYANAR COULD NOT believe his eyes or ears. *Is this a dream? Emperor Pulikesi's kingdom has the Ajanta paintings—would he order his soldiers to cut off the hands and legs of artists? Did that commander say, 'Take him to the summit of that rock, cut off his limbs and roll them down?' Is this a nightmare? Ah, but I see Kanchi Fort. The fort is real. I am really standing on the rock's summit. The demons raising their swords to chop off my hands are real. Ah, Sivagami, my beloved daughter, I have sacrificed you to my Ajanta madness. Aiyo! My daughter!*

A soldier raised his sword and Aayanar closed his eyes—but the sword did not come down.

"Stop!" said an authoritarian voice.

Aayanar opened his eyes. *It is Pulikesi! How did he come here?*

Shocked to see the emperor, the soldiers released Aayanar. Aayanar stumbled into a hollow, rolled down the rock and fell to the ground. He lost consciousness. When he came back to his senses, he heard a commotion nearby: men shouted and stonework fell.

The same authoritarian voice commanded, "Stop!"

Aayanar opened his eyes. He found himself in his old home in the forest. He saw Pulikesi majestically signal with his hand, 'Out!' The savage Chalukyan soldiers crowded to the entrance. He saw his precious statues of dancing figures lying broken around him. The unbearable pain in his right leg did not let him stand. *My leg is broken.* His sister came running to him, trembling and weeping. Once all the soldiers had left, Pulikesi walked calmly to where Aayanar lay.

Aayanar wailed, "Lord, how could your soldiers commit such a crime?"

Imposter

EMPEROR PULIKESI SAT by Aayanar. "Great sculptor, forgive me. Without even waiting for you to come to your senses, I tied you to my horse and rushed here to save your statues. But many of them were destroyed. Be thankful that at least some have survived."

Aayanar stared at him with a vague suspicion in his heart. *How can the Chalukyan emperor speak such fluent Tamil? Is this really the cruel Pulikesi who sits talking so casually with me?*

Aayanar remembered Sivagami. "Aiyo, how could I forget my Sivagami and talk about my statues! Lord, your soldiers took my daughter with them. Save her," he wailed.

Pulikesi said, "Aayanar, your daughter will not be harmed. She will reach Vatapi safely."

"Aiyo, is Sivagami going to Vatapi? Then why should I stay here? Take me too."

"That is what I planned. But you have broken your leg: any movement will endanger your life."

"Lord, if you care for my life, bring my daughter here."

"That is impossible."

Aayanar shouted angrily, "You are an emperor: do you only have the power to command your men to maim sculptors, destroy statues and capture virgins?"

Pulikesi pointed to Sivagami's terrified aunt. "Aayanar, please ask your sister to go inside."

Aayanar signalled to his sister, who left them.

"Aayanar, if I rush after your daughter, I may find her and be able to send her here. But, just as they broke these statues, a force is on its way to destroy Mamallapuram. If I go there, I can stop them. Shall I save your daughter? Or shall I save Mamallapuram's statues?"

Aayanar's suspicion grew stronger. "Sir … you …" He hesitated. Pulikesi removed his crown and put it down. "Ah, it is you, Naganandhi!"

"Yes, Aayanar. I assumed this disguise to help my friends."

"What an uncanny resemblance! It is identical! Swami, who are you? Maybe you are …"

"No, Aayanar. Naganandhi and Pulikesi are not the same person. God made us identical through some strange trick of creation. Using this, I was able to save your life." He paused. "Aayanar, it is up to you. Shall I go in search of your daughter? Or shall I go to Mamallapuram?"

Aayanar wailed, "Swami, God will save my daughter. Hurry to Mamallapuram."

The disguised monk went out.

The aunt came and sat beside Aayanar. "*Thambi*, how are you feeling?" Aayanar did not reply. Suddenly, she panicked. "The child! Where is Sivagami?"

Aayanar sat up and screamed, "*Akka*, where is Sivagami? Where is my daughter?" He hung his head and sobbed.

Pride is Humbled

MAHENDRAN PALLAVA WAS in Kanchi's secret council chamber with General Kalipahai, Prime Minister Sarangadevan, Chief Minister Ranadheeran, Spy Chief Shatrughan and Gundodharan.

Mahendran's face was radiant. "Gundodharan, did you see this with your own eyes? Did the Chalukyan forces really spare Mamallapuram? Are you sure the sculpture was not harmed?"

"My king, two thousand Chalukyan demons came running with crowbars and iron rods. My heart sank. *Aiyo, the statues painstakingly carved by thousands of sculptors will be destroyed in minutes!* The next instant, Emperor Pulikesi appeared on the summit of the rock. He gestured majestically with his hand. That was it! The charging soldiers stopped in their tracks. Lord, I was so stunned, I froze like a statue. I came to my senses only after everyone left."

"Lord, how did this miracle happen? How did you save Mamallapuram?" Ranadheeran asked.

The emperor said, "Pulikesi begged for Naganandhi. For a second, I was moved. But I kept Naganandhi safely in custody, expecting that the monk would be useful at some time. Mamallapuram has been saved because of that."

Shatrughan said, "I was confused when you said, 'Keep the underground passage open and wait. Do not be surprised by anyone you see going out. Remain in meditation.' I was stunned when Naganandhi came out. I felt like strangling that wicked monk. I controlled myself, remembering your strict orders."

General Kalipahai complained, "We are still confused. Are you saying that Naganandhi brought Pulikesi back to save Mamallapuram?"

Mahendran said, "Naganandhi did not bring Pulikesi ... he became Pulikesi." There was a gasp of surprise from everyone. "Didn't you see the resemblance between Naganandhi and Pulikesi? When Pulikesi was here, I asked our goldsmiths to copy his crown and ornaments. I gave them to Naganandhi yesterday and asked him to go straight to Mamallapuram."

"But how could you trust that deceitful monk?"

"Naganandhi is a demon in human form, but he is an art lover. I was confident that he would save Aayanar's masterpieces in Mamallapuram. After that, I did not care what happened to him."

The men listened to this in stunned silence. A woman's wail suddenly split that silence.

A guard rushed in, saluted and said, "Lord, Kannapiran's wife, Kamali, insists on meeting you."

"Send her in," Mahendran commanded.

Kamali, hair uncombed, rushed in and fell at the emperor's feet. "My king, forgive this traitor!"

That morning, Asuvabalan had asked Kamali, "Where are Aayanar and his daughter, my dear?"

Kamali replied casually, "They are bored, and they cannot bear this baby's crying. They have gone to visit all the temples in the city. After all, they are crazy about sculpture."

"Thank goodness. Do you know what would have happened to them if they went outside? Pulikesi's men are burning down all the towns and villages. They are chopping off the legs and hands of sculptors. They are capturing and taking away all the young girls ..."

On hearing this, Kamali wailed, "Aiyo!" and confessed to Asuvabalan.

Asuvabalan scolded her and cried, "Go! Run and tell the emperor what has happened."

The emperor's proud smile became a look of sorrow. He turned to Shatrughan. "Is this true?"

Shatrughan's voice shook. "Yes, lord. Soon after Naganandhi left, Aayanar and his daughter followed. I sat quietly as you had ordered me not to be surprised by whoever came."

Mahendran said, "I boasted of my cleverness: God has humbled my pride. I cannot look Mamallan in the face if I lose Sivagami. Assemble the army at once."

The Victorious Hero

THIRUVENKADU WAS IN a happy uproar—the Pallava crown prince, Narasimhavarman, was expected there, along with his friend, Commander Paranjothi. The villagers knew about the battle between the Pallavas and Pandyans on the bank of the Kollidam two days ago. Although the Pandyan army was bigger, Mamallan and Paranjothi had bravely defeated it.

Navukkarasar was staying at the village, and it was rumoured that Mamallan and Paranjothi were coming for his blessings. Only Doctor Sivanesan's family knew the truth. The normally calm doctor ran in and out of his house a hundred times that day. His wife took more care over her daughter's dress and ornaments than she ever had before. Umayaal's heart was like a stormy sea. Paranjothi's mother eagerly looked forward to seeing her only child.

About ten miles from the village, Mamallan teased Paranjothi: "Commander, your horse is lagging behind. Shall we exchange horses? Why is your face like this? Are you going to see your sweetheart, or are you going to your execution? Do not worry: I will see that Umayaal does not scold you."

"Sir, you convinced me to come here, but I now regret it. Let me go back. Meet my mother on my behalf and tell her that I am fine but could not keep my promise to her. Tell her that I am ashamed to see her."

Mamallan was shocked at this outburst. "Commander, what did you promise your mother?"

"Lord, my uncle, Sivanesan, did not want to give his learned daughter, Umayaal, to an uneducated boy like me. I came to Kanchi to join Navukkarasar's *matham* and return home a scholar. But I am coming back as uneducated as when I left ..."

Mamallan burst out laughing.

A grand reception was held for Mamallan and Paranjothi. Mamallan was reminded of the reception at Mandagapattu village. *How much has happened since then! Kannapiran must have reached Mandagapattu and told them about our victory over the Pandyans. How Sivagami must have rejoiced! How eagerly she must be waiting for me!*

A Village Girl

AFTER THE RECEPTION, Mamallan and Paranjothi went to Sivanesan's house. The family was silent: they were awed to see the Pallava prince in their humble home. Paranjothi was too shy to speak.

Mamallan understood the situation. Guessing that the old woman with tears in her eyes was Paranjothi's mother, he spoke to her: "I have been waiting to pay my respects to the fortunate woman who gave us our brave commander." He turned to Paranjothi. "Commander, greet your mother. Everyone will say that you have forgotten your manners after going to Kanchi."

Paranjothi touched his mother's feet in respect. Vadivazlagi longed to raise him up and kiss his forehead, but Mamallan's presence and Paranjothi's war dress made her hesitate. Paranjothi respectfully greeted Sivanesan and then went back to sit beside Mamallan and stare at the ceiling.

Sivanesan spoke to Mamallan: "Our humble home is honoured by your presence."

Mamallan said, "You must be Doctor Sivanesan. The girl standing by the door is your daughter, right? She looks harmless, but she has terrified the Pallava army's greatest commander. I had to drag Paranjothi here by force! *Amma*, ask your son if this is true."

Vadivazlagi looked at Paranjothi with proud, loving eyes. "My child, is Lord Mamallan saying the truth? You did not want to see us, is it?"

"The prince always speaks the truth, *amma*. Let him tell you why I did not want to see you all."

"It seems that your beloved son could not keep his promise to come back from Kanchi as a scholar. So he is embarrassed to look you all in the eye. What do you say to that?"

Vadivazlagi sat beside Paranjothi and stroked his face. "My dear boy, it is enough for me that you have come back safely by Lord Shiva's grace."

Paranjothi said, "Lord, ask my uncle if he is willing to let his daughter marry an ignorant fool."

Sivanesan said, "Why ask me? Ask the girl he is to marry. If she agrees, I will agree too." He continued. "We have heard of Paranjothi's great feats. He has brought glory to Chola Nadu. We were worried that he might not come back here. With you and Navukkarasar here, let us have the wedding on the next auspicious day. Take Umayaal with you."

Mamallan said, "Sir, the Pallava kingdom's commander must be married in the capital before the emperor. As soon as we are back in Kanchi, we will send an escort for you all. And if your daughter insists that she will marry only a scholar, I have a solution. Rudracharya, our family guru, is only ninety. There is no book he has not studied. If you want, I can get your learned daughter married to him." Mamallan laughed and stood. "Come, commander, let us go meet Navukkarasar."

When Mamallan and Paranjothi returned, Paranjothi's mother took him to the inner room where Umayaal lay sobbing on the floor. "Do you know what she says? You went to Kanchi and became the emperor's friend. Now you do not want to marry a village girl."

Paranjothi's heart melted. "Aiyo, no, never, *amma!*"

"In that case, console her. She refuses to listen to me." Vadivazlagi left the room.

It was not easy to console Umayaal. She was a village girl, ignorant of city life, but she knew how to get her way. She would be comforted but again break into sobs. When she could no longer stretch her tears, she made Paranjothi promise to marry her.

Paranjothi said, "Uma, you may have a long wait—I will not marry before Mamallan."

"If you wish, I will wait for ages," Umayaal replied.

Even the Wind Stopped

THE NEXT MORNING, Mamallan and Paranjothi left Sivanesan's house. They marched with their victorious army to the South Pennai by sunset. Mamallan was worried and thoughtful.

The previous day, Navukkarasar had affectionately blessed Mamallan and congratulated him on his victory over the Pandyans. He was delighted with the Chalukyan emperor's truce and promised to return soon to Kanchi. "Prince, how is Aayanar? Is his daughter, Sivagami, well?"

Mamallan said, "They are in Mandagapattu village. I may see them on my way back."

"Give them my warm regards. My heart melts when I think of Sivagami. Prince, I told Aayanar this: I fear that danger hovers over her. May Lord Shiva be merciful."

Like a mantra, Mamallan's heart chanted, *Let no harm fall on Sivagami*. Every atom of his body yearned to see her at once. Leaving the cavalry far behind, Mamallan galloped ahead.

Paranjothi had to stop him often with the warning, "Lord, do you want to kill your horse?"

Mamallan was worried. *I sent Kannapiran to Mandagapattu two days ago. Why have we not met him on his way back?* Soon after they crossed the South Pennai, he saw Kannapiran speeding towards them on the chariot. *Is there anyone with him? No, that is too much to expect.*

Mamallan was disappointed to hear that Mahendran Pallava had asked Aayanar and Sivagami to go to Kanchi two weeks ago. The prince consoled himself—*she is safe in Kanchi.* He built castles in the air. *Why did the emperor call them to Kanchi urgently? Why did he order me to return to Kanchi without chasing the defeated Pandyan army? Does he by any chance know about my love? Has he decided to have my wedding soon?*

They camped on the bank of the Varaha that night, and the prince confided his dreams to Paranjothi. They left early the next morning, excited at the thought of reaching Kanchi that night.

About ten miles from the Varaha, two riders galloped towards them and saluted Mamallan. One of them took a scroll from a bull's horn and said, "Lord, from the emperor."

The other man gave Paranjothi a scroll.

After reading a few lines, Mamallan inspected the scroll to check the secret sign. *There is no doubt: this message is from my father.* His heart raced; he frowned; sweat beaded his forehead.

'To my beloved son, the brave Mamallan, from your father, Mahendravarman, whose pride has been humbled. I write with tear-filled eyes and a sad heart. All my strategy has come to nothing. I have brought great sorrow on myself by refusing your honest advice. Pulikesi has betrayed me. He has ordered that Thondaimandalam's villages be burnt, sculpture destroyed and people tortured. Aiyo, my son, how do I tell you this … the Pallava kingdom's greatest art treasure is lost.

'Mamallan, forgive me. I go now to make amends for my mistakes. I go to save our people from the savage Chalukyas. General Kalipahai comes with me. My son, you and Paranjothi must defend beautiful Kanchi. I doubt whether I will return or live to meet you again. I will be lucky to die bravely on the battlefield. My son, never forget that you are the Pallava dynasty's only hope.'

Paranjothi finished reading his own short message long before Mamallan read his.

'My beloved Paranjothi. You often asked me, 'Have you made any mistakes?' In my pride, I said, 'No.' Now, I have made the most terrible mistake of my life. I tried to make my enemy my friend—the result is the opposite. I am leaving for the battlefield to make amends.'

Mamallan was speechless. He gave his scroll to his friend.

Paranjothi quickly read it. "Sir, I will go ahead with the cavalry. You follow with the infantry."

"Nonsense, commander! My body is here, but my spirit is with my father. There will be no more stopping on the way. Let the infantry follow. We will go ahead with the cavalry."

The earth shook with the galloping hooves of thousands of horses. A storm of dust stretched into the distance.

Where Is Sivagami?

AAYANAR FELT THE torments of hell. His broken right leg gave him unbearable pain and his heart ached with Sivagami's loss. His old sister devotedly cared for him and saved his life, but her repeated question, 'Where is Sivagami?' rubbed salt into Aayanar's wounds.

They constantly heard the beat of drums, war cries, the sound of men and horses, weeping and laments and the clash of weapons. At night, they saw clouds of smoke and the glare of fire. The forest birds were unnaturally silent.

One evening, four or five Pallava soldiers, covered with blood, barged into Aayanar's house, shouting, "Water! Water!"

Aayanar welcomed them and told his sister to bring water. He asked them how they had been wounded. One of the soldiers told Aayanar everything that had happened from the time Pulikesi left Kanchi until the terrible battle near Manimangalam that day.

Hearing of the Chalukyas' atrocities, the emperor left Kanchi with his small force. That morning, the Pallava and Chalukyan armies met near Manimangalam. Although the Chalukyas, led by Pulikesi, were stronger in numbers and weapons, the Pallava army, personally led by Emperor Mahendran, fought bravely. The two emperors battled each other one-on-one. Just as the Pallavas were on the verge of defeat, horses' hooves were heard and the Pallava soldiers shouted, 'Here comes Mamallan!' The Pallava cavalry fell on the Chalukyas like a thunderbolt, and the Chalukyas ran away. The demon Pulikesi also fled, but as he ran, he threw his dagger at Emperor Mahendran who fell unconscious. Mamallan and Paranjothi then chased the enemy.

Aayanar was broken-hearted to hear that Mahendran Pallava was mortally wounded. But he was glad that Mamallan and Paranjothi were chasing the Chalukyas. *They will free Sivagami.*

A week passed as Aayanar waited eagerly for good news. He finally heard two horses stopping at the door. With a racing heart, Aayanar stared at the door. Mamallan and Paranjothi came in, but Aayanar's happiness vanished when he saw the question in Mamallan's eyes. To stop Mamallan from asking his question, Aayanar wailed, "Lord, where is my Sivagami?"

Pulikesi Runs

MAMALLAN AND PARANJOTHI reached Manimangalam with their cavalry just as Mahendran Pallava's force was about to be wiped out. Quickly the tide of war changed, and the Chalukyan soldiers retreated. As Mamallan prepared to chase and destroy them, news came that Mahendran Pallava was mortally wounded and was being treated at the palace guest house near the village. Mamallan and Paranjothi hurried there.

Mahendran opened his eyes. His face was radiant on seeing his son. Then his happiness changed to pain and anxiety. He murmured, "Son, I have betrayed you. Will you forgive me?"

Even as Mamallan said, "*Appa*, do not worry. The Chalukyas broke ranks and ran ..." the emperor sank back into unconsciousness.

After arranging for the emperor to be taken safely to Kanchi, Mamallan and Paranjothi analysed the situation. They learnt that most of Mahendran Pallava's small force was dead, including General Kalipahai. Small Chalukyan groups roamed the countryside, burning villages and torturing people. The friends decided that their first duty was to deal with these bands of savages. They would wait for the infantry's arrival before they went after Pulikesi.

In three days, they destroyed the roaming Chalukyan bands. The infantry arrived and they marched north. Pulikesi had left Commander Sasangan to hold the ground while he crossed the River Vellar. A great battle took place at Sooramaaram village, thirty miles from Kanchi. Sasangan, and a major part of the Chalukyan army, died in this battle, while the remaining soldiers retreated. Mamallan wanted to cross the Vellar and go after Pulikesi.

Paranjothi, now general, objected: "Lord, what if anything happens to the emperor while we are away? Kalipahai is dead. Who will see to the villagers who are suffering from Pulikesi's torture?"

Mamallan's resolution faltered. "General, you are right. The Chalukyas are laying waste to the villages they cross. If we advance now, how will the villagers feed us? Let us go back to Kanchi."

The people shouted and lamented when they saw Mamallan and Paranjothi. In village after village, houses, huts and fields ready for harvest had been burnt. There was ash everywhere. It was as if the entire Pallava kingdom had become one huge crematorium. Mamallan felt that his heart would burst in anger as he heard about sculptors being mutilated, young girls being taken prisoner and cows and goats being slaughtered. He could not speak even to Paranjothi.

They hurried to Mamallapuram to find its exquisite sculpture relatively unharmed. One thing comforted Mamallan: *Thank goodness Aayanar and Sivagami are safe in Kanchi.* Aayanar's forest house was on the way from Mamallapuram to Kanchi. *I must see whether those statues of dancers are safe. And going via Aayanar's house is a shortcut to Kanchi.*

Both of them were startled to find the house's open door and heartbroken to see the shattered statues. Aayanar's pale face and wild eyes terrified them. When he asked, 'Where is my Sivagami?' Mamallan felt as if a mountain had shattered and fallen on his head.

Blood Flowed

THE FRIENDS STARED speechlessly at Aayanar. Paranjothi held Mamallan's arm. *He is going to fall.*

Aayanar continued in a frenzy, "Pallava prince, where is my beloved daughter?"

A storm raged in Mamallan's heart. *I must control myself and find out what has happened to Sivagami.* He clenched his teeth and said softly, "Sir, please be calm. It is I who should be asking you, 'Where is Sivagami?' What has happened to Sivagami? Tell us."

Aayanar sobbed, "Yes, lord. It is I who lost my treasure. Oh, my daughter! Your father himself became your enemy!" He tried to stand but stumbled and crashed to the floor.

Mamallan realised that Aayanar was lame, and his heart melted. He sat beside Aayanar and spoke gently, "Sir, I came here straight from the battlefield. I thought that you and Sivagami were well in Kanchi. When did you leave Sivagami? What has happened to her?"

Aayanar stammered and sobbed and told them everything as Mamallan listened. The prince took his dagger from its sheath. The fingers of his left hand stroked its sharp point, making cuts in his flesh. The blood flowing from those cuts fell in drops and pooled on the ground.

Darkness Falls

THE SUN BLAZED in a cloudless blue sky when Mamallan left Aayanar's house for Kanchi, but darkness shrouded Mamallan's heart. *To Sivagami, honour is greater than life—she must have died after being captured. This earth and I were not worthy of her divine beauty, goodness and talent. Our fathers caused her death—and ruined their own lives. But how can I be angry with them? Aayanar is mad and lies with a broken leg; my father is fighting for his life. I cannot bear to live without Sivagami, but I must live to take revenge on those Chalukyas. Rivers of blood must flow in Vatapi. Their wails of grief must echo through the generations.*

Mamallan's spirits rose with thoughts of revenge, but sorrow again enveloped him. *I will never see Sivagami again.* The horse's reins almost slipped from his nerveless fingers. His memories brought a lump to his throat. *Sivagami was always in my thoughts—she was like water in the wellspring of my heart.* He saw Sivagami smiling, laughing, frowning, frightened, tired, playful, eyes half-closed in bliss. During the busy day, Sivagami had always been at the bottom of his heart. In bed at night, he had delighted in images of her dark eyes rolling at him in mock anger. And when he fell asleep, Sivagami had been in his dreams. *How many imaginary dangers I rescued her from! But when danger really came, I was not there to save her. She must have sensed danger. That is why she often asked, 'You will not forget me, will you?'*

Sivagami, my precious! I will never forget you in this lifetime or after. I will take revenge on the wicked men who separated you from me. After that, I will come in search of you. I will not give up. No one can separate you from me, wherever you may be—Yamaloka or Brahmaloka or Vaikundam or Kailash. I am coming, Sivagami, I am coming. I will soon be with you.

Who Is This Girl?

A STRANGE SILENCE fell upon Kanchi. The people expected to hear the announcement, 'The Emperor is dead,' any minute. They heard about the Chalukyas' atrocities while retreating from the battles at Manimangalam and Sooramaaram. Pained by the news of Aayanar's broken leg and Sivagami's capture, the emperor went down in their esteem.

The palace had the dark, lifeless look of a haunted house. A deep, frightening silence enveloped it. The royal physicians struggled day and night to save Mahendran Pallava. After Mamallan returned from Sooramaaram, the emperor opened his eyes and recognised the people around him. The physicians said that the emperor was out of danger but advised Mamallan not to meet his father, as the emperor became emotional on seeing him.

Mamallan's pain increased. There was no one in whom he could confide, as Paranjothi was busy leading battalions to help the surrounding villages.

Bhuvanamahadevi wept and kept saying, "I warned your father not to invite Pulikesi to Kanchi … and you should have married the Pandyan princess. What a big mistake we made!"

Mamallan felt that his heart would burst if he did not talk about Sivagami to someone. *Who can I talk to? Aayanar is the only one who shares my love for Sivagami.*

Mamallan went alone to Aayanar's house. As he rode through the forest, he longed to see the lotus pond. He turned away from the main path and rode slowly to the pond. He saw a girl coming towards him on the narrow trail. Startled to see him, she stood to one side. Mamallan, with innate chivalry, rode past without looking at her face, but the girl's face seemed familiar. *Who is she? Where have I seen her before?* He reached the lotus pond.

The Pond

AH, IS THIS the pond where Sivagami and I spent so many happy days? It has changed completely. It now reflected Mamallan's heart. The pond which had once brimmed with crystal clear water was now largely mud. There was no sign of lotuses. A few leaves lay trampled into the mud by elephants. Lotus stalks with wilted leaves were scattered around. The trees were half-bare, with broken branches. One half of the bench lay smashed to pieces on the ground, while the other half was cracked and standing on its edge. The broken-hearted Mamallan sat on it.

Memories filled his aching heart. Sivagami and he had sat here silently when the air was filled with birdsong, speaking with their eyes and hearts and hands. *I will never be so happy again.*

He rode to Aayanar's house, filled with hatred for the Chalukyas. He was furious with Aayanar for his foolishness. He was suspicious about the Buddhist monk. *Why didn't he save Sivagami?* His anger turned to his father. *The Pallava kingdom is in this sorry state only because of Mahendran Pallava's tricks and disguises! It made me lose Sivagami.* A dangerous suspicion came to him: *Was it Mahendran Pallava himself who conspired to have Sivagami captured? Is Kamali his accomplice? Did everyone join to betray me?*

Mamallan decided to talk to Aayanar about Sivagami's mysterious capture. He reined in his horse and walked into the house. He was surprised to see Shatrughan talking to the sculptor.

The face of the girl he had seen on the forest trail flashed into Mamallan's mind. *What an extraordinary resemblance! Can it be ....* Mamallan saw a woman's clothes and ornaments lying on the ground by Shatrughan's side.

Shatrughan's Story

AAYANAR SAT UP. "Welcome, lord. Shatrughan brings good news—Sivagami is alive and well."

Mamallan's head whirled. "Shatrughan, is this true?"

"Yes, lord." Shatrughan stood with folded hands and said, "My prince, forgive me for not speaking up when I met you on the forest trail. Seeing you suddenly embarrassed me."

"Were you the girl? Excellent disguise!" said Mamallan.

Shatrughan told his story. "When the emperor heard that Aayanar and Sivagami had left the fort by the underground passage, he took me aside and said, 'Shatrughan, I must go to war for the Pallavas' honour. I trust you to find Sivagami and bring her back. If you cannot bring her back, stay and guard her.' I said, 'Lord, if Sivagami is a Chalukyan prisoner, what can I do?' 'Shatrughan, you have assumed many disguises. There is one disguise which is more effective than all those—that of a woman.' I assumed that disguise, left Kanchi and came here.

"Sivagami was not with Aayanar. I went around Kanchi Fort. I hid and watched the savage Chalukyas. I saw a large Chalukyan force marching north and heard women crying. I went closer and saw that these women were from our villages. There was a palanquin in the middle—Sivagami was in it.

"I quickly let my hair loose, wailed and ran towards the group. Then I pretended that someone was chasing me and ran away. The Chalukyas mocked me and took me to join the group. The commander of that force, Sasangan, planned to take Sivagami to Pulikesi and claim a reward. I was confident that she would not be harmed, but it was impossible to rescue her. I considered many plans and rejected them all.

"We continued northwards. We camped on the bank of the Vellar. News came of the battle between Mahendran Pallava and the Chalukyan emperor at Manimangalam. Sasangan knew that Pulikesi had marched ahead from Kanchi. He had assumed that the emperor would have reached the North Pennai by then. He was stunned to hear that Pulikesi was behind him, fighting at Manimangalam. He was frightened that Pulikesi might be angry with him for going ahead.

"The next day, Sasangan sent his female captives across the river, along with a small group of soldiers. This was a good opportunity to rescue Sivagami. As there were only a few guards, we could escape at night and hide in the nearby hills. I managed to get near Sivagami. After the others fell asleep, I used sign language to tell her who I was. She was amazed and then asked about Aayanar and you. But at that time, I had no news of you. So I only told her that Aayanar was alive. Then I whispered my plan to her. Lord, I was disappointed …"

Pulikesi and Sivagami

ANGRY SPARKS FLEW from Mamallan's eyes. "What? You left Sivagami with Pulikesi and escaped, didn't you? Shatrughan, tell me the truth at once," he roared.

Aayanar interrupted excitedly, "Lord, let Shatrughan tell the story his way. Please be patient."

Shatrughan continued: "I expected Sivagami to happily agree to my plans, but she burst into tears and said, 'I am in danger because I did not obey him. How will I ever look him in the face?' She said much more. I feared that she was mad.

"She then spoke about the Chalukyan atrocities she had seen in our villages. 'Lady, Mahendran Pallava and Mamallan will take revenge on them for this,' I said. 'Yes, Shatrughan, we must take revenge!' she shouted. I was terrified that the guards would be alerted. Thank goodness, among all the murmurs and cries of the sleeping women, her shout did not draw their attention.

"I calmed her and again told her my escape plan. She stared at me and said, 'Sir, there are a thousand girls like me. Some of them have left their husbands and infants behind. How can we leave them all to the Chalukyan demons and go? I have no husband or child. What does it matter what happens to me? Take one of the women who has an infant at home.' My heart melted. I hardened myself and said, 'Lady, Emperor Mahendran ordered me to rescue you. I must carry out his orders.' I knew this would not make her change her mind. So, I said, 'Lady, you have a father. Won't you think about him?'

"Sivagami's eyes brimmed with tears. I said, 'Lady, if you want him to live, come with me at once.' She covered her face and sobbed. She then said, 'Sir, I am tired in body and spirit. I cannot take a single step now. I will tell you my decision tomorrow.' Thinking it best to give her time, I said, 'Okay, lady. Nothing will be lost in a day.'

"But the next evening, Pulikesi unexpectedly joined us with a small army. As I guessed, he let Commander Sasangan make a stand there while we went ahead. We marched north through that night. I cannot tell you how disappointed and sorry I was! When I had the chance to go near Sivagami, I said, 'Lady, how could you do this!' She replied, 'It is fate.'

"We camped at the foothills of the Venkata Hills. Pulikesi did not come near us for the first two days. On the third day, Pulikesi and a few men rode up to the rock near us. In the blink of an eye, Sivagami jumped forward, blocked the emperor's horse and shouted, 'Emperor, a request!'

"Even the stone-hearted Pulikesi was moved by her cry. He asked, 'Girl, what do you want?' I do not know from where Sivagami got her courage. She looked up at the majestic Pulikesi and spoke firmly.

"'Sir, you kings fight wars to prove your courage and for glory. Why must we poor girls suffer for it? Be merciful and send us back. Some of the women have left crying infants behind; others wear the *kanganam* on their wrists. Let a thousand women bless you—let us go home.' That fool, Pulikesi, said, 'Girl, keep your *abhinaya* for your dance recitals. Do not waste them on me.'"

Mamallan said angrily, "Ah, Aayanar's daughter fell at that evil man's feet and begged, didn't she? Serves her right!"

Shatrughan continued: "Sivagami bowed her head. That merciless wretch then said, 'Girl, I am not fooled by your emotional *abhinaya*, but I will grant your request on one condition. You say that these women have been separated from their husbands and children ... but you have no husband or child. Will you come with me to Vatapi? If you agree, I will release all the others this instant and send them back.'"

Mamallan interrupted in a hate-filled voice, "Did Sivagami agree?"

"Yes, lord. She immediately lifted her head and said, 'I agree, emperor.' She looked divine ..."

"Shatrughan, your rapture can wait. What happened then?" Mamallan asked.

"The emperor ordered our release and assigned some soldiers to escort us up to the North Pennai. The women praised Sivagami, but I was stunned. I fell at Sivagami's feet and begged, 'Lady, ask the emperor to let me stay with you.' But she was stubborn. 'Go and give my father the news.' Finally, I had to leave. I was afraid that if I stayed, the enemy would see through my disguise, and I would not be able to carry her news back here. She said, 'Tell my father not to worry about me. Tell him that when I return from Vatapi, I will bring him the secret of Ajanta's paintings.'"

Aayanar squirmed in excitement. "My beloved daughter will fulfill my heart's desire. And we must change our opinion of Pulikesi. He appreciates art: otherwise, would he have released a thousand women and kept only Sivagami? Lord, I will recover … and go to Vatapi myself."

Mamallan's pure love was corrupted by a drop of poison. *I cannot bear the thought of Sivagami agreeing to go to Vatapi with Pulikesi.* He wanted to be alone. *Let me go to the lotus pond.* He jumped up. "Is that all, Shatrughan? Sivagami did not send any other message, did she?"

Shatrughan said softly, "Lord, Sivagami asked me to remind you of the oath you swore on your spear. She said that she will wait for you in Vatapi like Sita waited for Rama in Lanka."

Just a short while ago, the world had seemed a barren desert to Mamallan … now he saw a living oasis in that desert.

The Road to Vatapi

PULIKESI'S ARMY MARCHED on to Vatapi. It was reduced to half its original size but was still a large force with about three lakh soldiers and seven thousand war elephants. The hungry, vengeful Chalukyas plundered towns and villages, destroyed embankments, burnt houses and haystacks and ruthlessly killed or mutilated those who tried to resist. Their starving, wild elephants destroyed groves and trampled fields. It looked like a tempest had roared down the road taken by the Chalukyan army. Wails and laments were heard along its way.

Sivagami felt that relentless fate was carrying her palanquin. Her fear was gone. *The cruel Pulikesi of Vatapi, whose empire is larger than the Pallava kingdom, obeyed me!* This made her proud and confident. *I will not be forced into anything; I will not be harmed.*

Sivagami thought that she had discovered a secret. *Pulikesi's face is a copy of Naganandhi's. Ah, Emperor Pulikesi and Naganandhi are one and the same! Mahendran Pallava goes about the kingdom in disguise—Pulikesi is doing the same.* She remembered the Buddhist monk's love for her dance. *Maybe Pulikesi attacked Kanchi just for me.*

She thought of Mamallan with love and anger, sorrow and hatred. *Mamallan could not stop the Pallava women from being captured, but I freed them. What will he think of that? He despised me for being a sculptor's daughter and let his father insult me. If he truly loved me, he would have openly declared his love and married me. Then all this would never have happened.*

I will teach him a lesson. A great emperor, whose empire is thrice as large as the Pallava kingdom, wants to please me. Let Mamallan come and see this. But what if he never comes? Sivagami's blood froze in her veins. Then she recovered her courage. *He is not so shameless. He will definitely come, at least to keep the oath he swore on his spear.*

Sivagami shored up her courage. *If he does not come, why should I grieve over a man who only pretended to love me? My father has given me the precious gift of dance ... the vast Vatapi empire is there ... and beyond that lies Harshavardhan's kingdom ...*

But even as she argued like this, her heart melted. *Why fool myself? To hell with dance! I live for his love. If he does not come for me, what is there for me in this world? I will kill myself ...*

Emperor Pulikesi did not come near Sivagami after releasing the Pallava women. *He is afraid that I will see through his Buddhist monk disguise. I must not let on that I know his secret.*

Pulikesi's smaller force joined the larger Chalukyan army camped at the North Pennai. That night, Sivagami had a strange experience: she could not decide whether it was a dream or real.

Sivagami's palanquin was a little distance away from the camp. The beautiful countryside was silent. The milky-white full moon lit up the sky and the earth. A sweet breeze blew. Exhausted by the long journey, Sivagami lay under a tree. Her eyes closed and soon, she fell asleep. Voices disturbed her slumber. With great effort, she half-opened her eyes.

The Buddhist monk and Pulikesi stood close together. The same height, figure, face, nose, eyes … only their clothes were different. One wore the emperor's crown and ornaments; the other's head was shaven, and he wore a monk's saffron robes. *How can this be? Aren't Pulikesi and the monk the same person? This must be a dream.* Her eyes closed again, but she heard the men.

"*Anna*, you wrote, 'You take Kanchi, give me Sivagami.' I cannot understand what you see in this girl. I have seen Vatapi girls more beautiful than this."

"You should see her dance: you will change your mind."

"I saw her dance at Mahendran Pallava's court. I did not see anything extraordinary in it."

"Only those who appreciate art can see it. After all, you are the one who looked at the Ajanta paintings and said, 'What is so wonderful about this?'"

"One art devotee in our dynasty is enough. Our invasion has failed—I am pleased that at least you got what you wanted."

"*Thambi*, take care of her. The divine art which lives in her must not be harmed."

"Do you know what I told Mahendran Pallava? I said, 'Why give these second-class people so much respect? In our country, we whip them to make them dance.'"

"See? How can I trust her with you? I am not going to Vengi."

"*Anna*, I was just teasing you. Have I ever done anything against your wishes? I will see that she is happy. Go in peace."

With that, Sivagami fell into a deep sleep.

When she woke up the next morning, this conversation came back to her. *No two people can look so alike. And even then, one cannot be an emperor and the other a monk. It must be a dream. Pulikesi and Naganandhi are one.*

But she was confused and worried.

Brothers

PULIKESI SAT ALONE in his tent, tired and depressed. *All my plans were ruined by Mahendran Pallava. There is no news of Naganandhi who can match Mahendran's cunning and defeat him.*

Pulikesi's only consolation was that he had left Sasangan behind to teach Mahendran Pallava a lesson. *Let that Pallava fox come out of its hole. He will know what a mistake he made when he betrayed Pulikesi of Vatapi.* Pulikesi camped at the North Pennai, waiting for Commander Sasangan. *Why is Sasangan taking so long to carry out my orders and come here?*

Pulikesi heard that an army was coming from the south. *Sasangan is here.* A horse stopped outside his tent, but it was not Sasangan who came in. It was a tall, majestic figure wearing an emperor's crown and ornaments. *Am I mad? Or am I dreaming? How can I, seated in my tent, enter the same tent from the outside?*

The man who came in smiled. "*Thambi*, why are you so scared? Don't you recognise me?" He removed his crown, showing a monk's bald head.

Pulikesi jumped up in delight. "*Anna*, is it you?" He ran to embrace him but stopped short. Jealousy and hate flashed in his eyes. "What is the meaning of this disguise? You promised ..."

Naganandhi said, "*Thambi*, this disguise once saved your life. Now I have used it to save mine. I promised you that I would never use it in your kingdom. We are not yet in your kingdom, right?"

Pulikesi replied angrily, "But why is this country not yet a part of our kingdom? Why has our mighty army been defeated by Mahendran Pallava's little army? It is all your fault."

"*Thambi*, who has been defeated? Neither you nor the Chalukyan army has been defeated. And it is not my fault. First give me two sets of saffron robes. This disguise will cause confusion. As it is, when I came here, the soldiers on guard stared at me."

"They would have wondered, 'When and how did the emperor leave the camp?' I myself was confused for a second." Pulikesi walked to the tent's entrance and ordered the guards there, "Go to the spies' tent and get two sets of saffron robes."

Naganandhi changed his clothes, and the two brothers sat close together on the same chair.

Naganandhi said, "Now tell me all that happened from the time you left Vatapi." He listened attentively. "Mahendran Pallava is cleverer than I thought. He has been fooling us for a long time. I made a single mistake in the beginning which grew into a great danger: Paranjothi."

"You sent a message trusting that scoundrel."

"It was because of you, *thambi*. I was returning to Kanchi when I saw a tired boy sleeping by the lake shore. He reminded me of you the first time we met, and so my heart melted with affection for him. I saw greatness in his face and wanted him to join us. I sent you a scroll through him. If you had received that scroll and marched straight to Kanchi, you could have captured the fort in three days. Mahendran Pallava would have fallen at your feet."

"But, instead of your message, I got one written by Mahendran Pallava. I wasted eight months at the North Pennai because of it. With a small cavalry brigade, Mahendran Pallava fooled us with skirmishes. My siege of Kanchi failed. This is my first defeat after ascending the throne ..."

"My dear boy, don't you understand the first lesson of political science? One must never admit defeat. If you do, the whole country will say, 'Emperor Pulikesi has been defeated.' It will reach Harshavardhan's ears. Mahendran Pallava's false message may come true—Harsha's army may cross the Narmada and invade our kingdom. Do not say the word, 'defeat,' again, *thambi*."

"If I do not say it, will defeat become victory, *anna*?"

"Think. You set out to conquer the south. You destroyed Vijayanthi. You wiped out the Pallava army at the North Pennai. You besieged Kanchi Fort. You went as far south as the Kollidam. You freed Dhurvineedhan from the Pallavas' dungeons. The three kings of Tamil Nadu—the Cholas, the Cheras and the Pandyans, paid tribute to you on the banks of the Kaveri."

"But *anna*, the Cholas never came."

"If the Cholas were not there, the Kalambharas were. Who is going to dig into these details? When you returned to Kanchi, Mahendran Pallava surrendered to you. You put your foot on his head and said, 'I give you your life as alms to a beggar.' You took his tributes and left … when you spread this news all over Uttar Pradesh, will they say that you have returned triumphant from your tour of conquest? Or will they say that you ran back after being defeated?"

"*Anna*, you are a genius! You can turn even defeat into victory. After listening to you, I myself feel that I have won. But how will news of this victory spread in the north?"

"What are the Buddhist *sangha* and Jain *mathams* for? We must send a messenger to the Nagarjuna Hills at once."

"*Anna*, you must go. You have work in Vengi. Vishnuvardhan lies there, wounded. The Vengi kingdom which he captured last year is in turmoil. You must go there and advise him."

"*Thambi*, the full moon has risen. Why stay cooped up in this tent? Come, let us go out."

"Yes, yes. Nature's beauty is being wasted," Pulikesi mocked. He stood up.

"What is the use of all your good fortune? You are not fortunate enough to appreciate beauty."

The two brothers held hands like soulmates and walked out.

The Ajanta Foothills

PULIKESI AND NAGANANDHI sat on a bare rock outside the army camp.

The full moon rose on the horizon and shone between two tall palm trees, like the beautiful face of a young girl peeping through a latticed window. Naganandhi saw Sivagami's face in it. He said, "*Thambi,* do you remember the last time I dressed like you? Twenty-five years have passed. I wondered whether you had forgotten."

"I will never forget: not only in this lifetime but in all the lifetimes to come."

"Do you remember our first meeting?"

"I escaped from my uncle, Mangalesan's prison. Hiding from his soldiers, I wandered in the forests for many days. I ran until my legs and body ached. I learnt how cruel hunger and thirst could be. One day, I fainted from exhaustion. When I regained consciousness, I was lying on your lap. You were squeezing the juice of some green leaves into my mouth. *Anna*, why did you take so much effort to save me?"

"*Thambi,* for as long as I remember, I lived with the Buddhist monks at the Ajanta caves. I learned sculpture and art, but I longed to see the outside world and meet young people. Sometimes, without the abbot's knowledge, I would follow the Waghora River and leave the hills. But there was no sign of men. One day, I found you at the foothills. I lavished all the pent-up affection of twenty years on you. I loved you with the love that young men usually have for their sweethearts. I brought you back to consciousness with herbal juice."

"*Anna*, I too felt the same affection for you. I love my younger brother, Vishnuvardhan, but my love for you is many times greater."

"For three days, we wandered the forest, holding hands like two lovers. You told me about your life. We planned to chase Mangalesan from Vatapi and take over the kingdom."

"And then, Mangalesan's men came there searching for me."

"Frightened, you hugged me tight and said, '*Anna,* do not abandon me!' You promised to do as I said. I wore your clothes, and you put on mine. I told you the way to the Buddhist *sangha* at Ajanta and how to behave there. I told you to hide in a tree a little distance away."

"I had just hidden myself when Mangalesan's men came there. Their leader pointed to you and ordered, 'Tie him up!' What a narrow escape I had! I am eternally grateful to you."

"*Thambi*, I had already noticed our resemblance to each other. I saw it in our reflections when we bathed in the river and ponds. It came in useful when I had to save you."

Pulikesi's voice shook, and his eyes brimmed with tears. "*Anna*, how can I ever forget that you were willing to sacrifice your life for a stranger like me!"

The full moon seemed to ask, 'Tears in the cruel Pulikesi's eyes! Can this be true?'

In the Ajanta Caves

NAGANANDHI STARED AT the full moon on the horizon and continued: "Those cruel men mistook me for you, but when I struggled to get on a horse, they became suspicious. You wore earrings. When they saw that my ears had not been pierced, they knew that I was not you. They took out their anger on me. I still have the scars from their beating ..." The monk touched his face.

"Aiyo, *anna*, how many sleepless nights I have suffered thinking about those scars!"

"*Thambi*, when one suffers for another, that suffering will soon pass. I rejoice over it. But if these memories trouble you, I will not talk about them."

"*Anna*, they are happy memories for me too."

"Very well. When I could no longer bear their torture, I told them that I belonged to the Ajanta Buddhist *sangha*. I said that I had found the clothes I was wearing on the bank of the Waghora River and just wanted to see myself in them. They took me back to the river and searched the surrounding forest. Finally, they decided that some wild animal must have killed you. They let me go and went away. I returned to Ajanta, worried if you had found your way safely there."

Pulikesi interrupted: "I followed the river which wound on and on. I would often come up against a rock wall and wonder whether I had taken the wrong path. I had a frightening thought: what if you betrayed me? What if you planned to come to terms with Mangalesan and rule the kingdom? I finally reached the marvellous Ajanta caves. As you had instructed, I remained silent and pretended to be a sculptor's apprentice. You came back after a week ..."

"One day, the abbot saw us both together when we were bathing in a secluded part of the river. I told him the truth, but the abbot did not punish me for breaking the rules and bringing a stranger to Ajanta. That evening, he called us to his monastery. *Thambi,* your heart blazed with jealousy when you heard his story ..."

"Yes, *anna,* that is true. At the same time, I was ashamed of myself."

"The abbot revealed that we were twins, and I was the elder one. As soon as we were born, our father hid me. When I was five, he sent me to the abbot. He ordered the abbot to reveal the truth of our birth and make me the heir to the kingdom only if you died. The abbot marvelled that fate had made me save your life—he praised me. You were born about twenty minutes after me; our father chose you to be his heir because of your horoscope. My love for you increased, but you hated me from that minute. I was not surprised or angry with you—it was only natural for you to resent me as I was the rightful heir to the Vatapi throne. I decided to kill your suspicions. I fell at the abbot's feet and begged him to make me a monk. He finally agreed. I shaved my head, put on saffron robes and became a monk. I swore to renounce worldly affairs. The fire of jealousy in your heart died, and you loved me once again."

"*Anna*, from that day, you have been my God. I have never disobeyed you."

"*Thambi*, you have profited by your obedience. I left you in Ajanta and wandered through the kingdom for three years. I brought government officials and army commanders to your side. I stirred up the people against Mangalesan. When the time was ripe, I sent for you. You marched to Vatapi at the head of a large army. Mangalesan died in the battle and you ascended the throne."

"*Anna*, for my sake, you gave up the throne which rightfully belongs to you and became a monk. Only because of your sacrifice could I kill Mangalesan and become king. Since then, for twenty years, you have been my father and mother, my prime minister and army commander. It is because of you that the varaha flag flies from thc Narmada to the North Pennai. But why are you reminding me of these old stories? Is there some way in which I can show my gratitude to you?" Pulikesi looked eagerly at the monk's face in the moonlight.

The monk's face, withered by years of hard fasting, showed a new tenderness. "Yes, *thambi*, there is something you can do for me in exchange for all that I have done for you."

"Tell me at once. Let me repay at least a small part of my debt of gratitude to you."

"*Thambi*, I sent you a message: 'You take beautiful Kanchi, give me beautiful Sivagami.' You have not taken Kanchi, but give me Sivagami. I have brought her here."

"What? Really?"

"*Thambi*, I disguised myself as you for her sake. For her sake, I led our forces at Manimangalam and fought with Mahendran Pallava. I stopped the battle and retreated for her."

Naganandhi told Pulikesi everything that had happened since he came south three years ago.

"*Anna*, are you telling me that you truly love that dancing girl?" Pulikesi asked in disbelief. "But what about your oath of celibacy?" *All his love was mine. Now, after all these years, a dancing girl has found a place in his heart. He loves her more than he loves me. She must be a dangerous woman!*

The Monk's Love

IGNORANT OF THE jealous snake spreading its hood in Pulikesi's heart, Naganandhi began his story.

"*Thambi*, I grew up in the Buddhist *sangha* in Ajanta. I never saw a flesh and blood woman until I was twenty. But I saw women whose eyes could penetrate the secret depths of a man's heart. I saw women whose beauty was beyond mortal reach. I saw serene women, compassionate women and seductive enchantresses. I saw them in the brilliant paintings on the walls of Ajanta's temples. To me, they were real. They welcomed and praised me; they asked about my health.

"There was one particular woman who captured my heart. Her blue silk dress and fawn-coloured stole highlighted her golden beauty. The red of her smiling lips rivaled the red water lily in her black hair. When her black, lotus-petal-like eyes stared into my heart, I felt a painful pleasure. Those eyes seemed to follow me. Although that painting was more than three hundred years old, its colours glowed as if it had been painted just the previous day.

"The curve of her waist and her arched neck and hands puzzled me. I could not understand what she was doing. Finally, I asked an artist monk. He said, 'That girl is doing Bharatanatyam.' I got the book on the *Natya Shastra* and studied the various aspects of Bharatanatyam.

"All day and night, she ruled my heart. I longed to meet real women.

Maybe there is a girl like this somewhere. That is why I wandered in the forests. When I saw you, the girl faded from my heart, and you took her place. Once I knew you were my own brother, my own blood, she disappeared completely.

"*Thambi,* we left the Ajanta caves, and you became the emperor of Vatapi. Together, we fought and won many wars. The Chalukyan kingdom spread from the Narmada to the Tungabhadra. Even Emperor Harshavardhan of Uttar Pradesh feared the varaha flag.

"I found it easy to stay true to my monk's oaths. I met many women in Vatapi and on my travels, but when I compared them to the beautiful paintings on Ajanta's walls, these women seemed ugly. *Thambi,* when you married six women, one after the other, I pitied you."

There was a trace of mockery in Pulikesi's voice: "Yes, *anna,* I came to my senses after foolishly making mistakes. But you realised the foolishness of lusting after women right from the start."

The monk did not notice the sarcasm. "I do not deserve your praise. After being celibate for many years, after losing my youth, I have fallen in love with a woman. Let me tell you how …

"After our treaty with Emperor Harshavardhan, by which he agreed not to bring his army south of the Narmada, I went south to prepare for our invasion. This was easy because of the Buddhist and Jain *mathams.* Even in Kanchi's Royal Monastery, there were monks ready to work for us.

"*Thambi*, even when I was busy with affairs of state, my heart hungered for art. I heard about the work going on in Mamallapuram and went to see it. The sculptures were wonderful! Hearing that the chief sculptor lived in the forest, I went to meet him.

"I was captivated by Aayanar's statues of dancers. They reminded me of the dancer on Ajanta's cave wall. While I was admiring the statues, a girl walked in. She was a flesh and blood woman, but there was not an iota of difference between her and the girl in the Ajanta painting. A face like the full moon; golden-hued body; clothes of the same colour; long eyes which penetrated one's heart; the same hairstyle. I was stunned. *Is it a dream?* Only after the girl asked, '*Appa*, who is this swami?' did I realise that she was real. Aayanar said, 'This is my daughter, Sivagami. I have made these statues from her *abhinaya*.'

"I saw the world through new eyes. I realised that there are more important things than war and politics. Sivagami captured not just my heart but every atom of my life, body and soul. Yes, *thambi.* I fell in love with Sivagami, but my love is not of the body.

"I do not love her for her golden-hued body—one can find a more brilliant gold in the moon right here. I am not bewitched by her beautiful eyes—the eyes of her fawn, Rathi, are more beautiful. My love for Sivagami is not of the flesh. And so Sivagami is not a threat to the vow of celibacy I took twenty-five years ago for your sake."

Pulikesi saw an unnatural glow on Naganandhi's face. *Is this a kind of madness? Has he lost his mind because of his long imprisonment in Mahendran's dungeons?*

Naganandhi guessed Pulikesi's thoughts. "No, *thambi,* I am not mad. I have never been so clear in my mind. I have no sexual desire for Sivagami. I am bewitched by her art. When Sivagami loses herself in dance and drifts on an ocean of bliss, I too lose myself. Nothing in this world makes me as happy as I feel then. *Thambi*, I hate Mahendran Pallava, but I agree with him about one thing. Hiding behind the Buddha statue, I heard him tell Aayanar that Sivagami was not born to be a common man's wife; her art is meant to be dedicated only to God. You can be sure that Sivagami will not affect my monk's vows."

Pulikesi's Promise

PULIKESI SMILED. "SIVAGAMI may not be a threat to your celibacy, but our southern invasion was ruined by that goddess."

Naganandhi was angry and surprised. "What is the connection between Sivagami and our invasion? It was Mahendran Pallava's cunning which defeated us."

"If you had not been bewitched by Sivagami, would you have been captured by Mahendran Pallava? Examine your heart and tell me the truth."

Naganandhi bowed his head in embarrassment. "Forgive me for the sake of my work over the years. I am no longer fit to serve the kingdom. Let me go."

"*Anna*, is this a joke? Where do you plan to go?"

"I will find a lonely place like Ajanta and spend the rest of my life watching Sivagami dance."

"What madness! I will send Sivagami back to Kanchi ... or let her marry one of our commanders."

Angry sparks flew from the monk's eyes. "*Thambi*, if anyone dares to go near Sivagami with sexual thoughts, I will send him to *Yamaloka*."

Pulikesi asked sarcastically, "*Anna*, has Mamallan gone to *Yamaloka*?"

"I decided to kill that fool with my own hands. I had the opportunity, but I changed my mind at the last minute." He paused. "This is Mamallan's punishment: he will be tormented all his life by the thought that the Chalukyas have taken the love of his life."

"Alright, *anna*. What now?"

"I have worked for you and the kingdom for twenty-five years. Let me live for myself for a few years. *Thambi*, let me go."

"*Anna*, you can retire from affairs of state, but you do not have to go in search of forests and hills. Choose a palace in Vatapi, build a dance pavilion and watch Sivagami dance blissfully there."

"*Thambi*, do you mean it? Will you do this for me?"

"I will definitely do it—but I beg you to do this one last thing for me. Vishnuvardhan is mortally wounded, and Vengi is in turmoil. You must go and save him. Vishnu too is your brother."

"Yes, but he hates the sight of me. He has never forgiven me for separating him from Bharavi."

"*Anna*, why did you do that? How much trouble that caused!"

"I did it for his own good. He was wasting all his time reading and writing poetry ..."

Pulikesi smiled. *One of my brothers is mad over poetry; the other is mad over art. I am the only one who is sane. Just as I saved Vishnu then, I must save the monk now.* "I sent Bharavi from the kingdom as you wanted, but what happened? Bharavi went to the Kanga kingdom and got Dhurvineedhan's daughter married to Vishnu. He then went to Kanchi and sent me bewitching descriptions of beautiful Kanchi."

"Why are you telling me all these old stories now?"

"We have not captured Kanchi. If Vishnuvardhan too is defeated in Vengi, our dynasty will be disgraced. Help me this one last time. Take half of our forces with you."

Naganandhi thought for a while. "Okay, *thambi*, but you must make me a promise."

"I must guard Sivagami, right? I give you my word. I agree to keep her safe in one of Vatapi's beautiful palaces until you return."

"Sivagami is the goddess of art. Anyone who nears her with evil intentions will be destroyed."

"I will keep that in mind. But, as you go on talking about art, I find myself getting interested in it. Can I ask Sivagami to dance?"

"I do not mind—as long as she does it of her own free will."

"Good! I swear to guard Sivagami and give her back to you."

In the second watch of that night, Pulikesi and Naganandhi went to the spot where Sivagami lay half-asleep and watched her in the moonlight.

Journey at Midnight

MAHENDRAN PALLAVA WAS unconscious for a month after the Battle of Manimangalam. It was found that the dagger thrown at him on the battlefield was poisoned. The court doctors did their best but could not cure him. General Paranjothi sent for Doctor Sivanesan from Thiruvenkadu. Sivanesan's treatment was effective, and Mahendran regained consciousness.

Mahendran first asked about Aayanar and Sivagami. He was heartbroken to hear about Aayanar's leg and Sivagami's capture by the Chalukyas. They feared that he would have a relapse. When Mamallan came to see him, Mahendran asked, "Narasimhan, where is Sivagami?"

In a pained voice, Mamallan said, "*Appa*, why worry about that now? You must first recover."

"Narasimhan, was your love for Sivagami just empty words? I will go and find her ..." Mahendran tried to get up from his bed.

Mamallan was embarrassed. "*Appa*, I was worried about what you would say ..."

"What else would I say, Narasimhan? Sivagami is famous for her dance from the Himalayas to Kanyakumari. If the Chalukyas have taken her, what a disgrace for the Pallavas!"

"Father, the general and I were waiting to get your permission. The army is ready."

"If you march with the army, you will not bring Sivagami back. You too will not come back." He paused. "Here is my plan. Let Paranjothi and Shatrughan go to Vatapi in disguise and bring back Sivagami. They can also gather information for our future attack on Vatapi."

Mamallan begged, "*Appa,* please let me go with the general."

The emperor agreed after Mamallan promised to consult Paranjothi before doing anything.

Two days later, at midnight, six horsemen stood in the palace courtyard. Sporting beards and mustaches, the disguised men were Mamallan, Paranjothi, Shatrughan, Gundodharan, Kannapiran and Asuvabalan.

"Come back victorious," Mahendran said from the palace terrace.

The men saluted and urged their horses into a gallop.

Mahendran's Secret

MAHENDRAN AND HIS queen sat talking on the terrace, under the star-spangled sky.

"*Devi*, the stars above once sang my praise: 'Mahendran, can anyone on earth be more just, more virtuous, a more formidable enemy and a greater art lover than you?' Now the same stars mock me: 'Mahendran, see how fate has made dust of your pride!'" Mahendran smiled sadly. "Fate came in Sivagami's form to ruin my plans."

"Why are you blaming that poor girl?" the queen asked in a compassionate voice.

"I tried to separate Narasimhan from Sivagami. Fate won finally."

"I am confused. Fate helped you by sending her to Vatapi. Why must you bring her back?"

"Sivagami's fame has spread from Lanka to Kannauj. I have invited Harshavardhan to see Mamallapuram and Sivagami's dance. As long as Sivagami is in Vatapi, the world will believe Pulikesi's lie that he defeated the Pallavas. What greater disgrace can there be for the Pallavas?"

The queen became emotional: "Swami, the phrase, 'royal burden' is so true!"

"I carried that burden happily, but now my heart is suffocated by its weight. *Devi*, I criticised my ancestors for wasting time on war and bloodshed. I wanted to make this earth a paradise, but Pulikesi shattered my dreams. The Pallava army must fight and defeat Pulikesi to restore our honour. If this does not happen in my lifetime, it must happen in Narasimhan's."

"Lord, my son will restore the Pallavas' honour," Bhuvanamahadevi declared proudly.

Vatapi

AS SIVAGAMI TRAVELLED to Vatapi, a fire blazed in her heart. *I must tell the emperor to stop torturing the villagers.* She asked her guards to take her to Pulikesi, but they ignored her. Every night, she was startled by a devilish laugh and vaguely saw the Chalukyan emperor walking away. *It is my imagination.*

As a child, Pulikesi was tortured by his uncle, Mangalesan. After becoming king, he focused on destroying his enemies. This made him cruel, with no sympathy for others. Naganandhi had cared only for the Chalukyan empire and for Pulikesi. Now a Pallava dancing girl had captured the monk's heart. Pulikesi's defeat and jealousy increased his cruelty. He vented his anger on the innocent people in his way and plotted to ruin Sivagami.

Sivagami was ignorant of all this. *If only I meet him once, I can stop his army's atrocities.*

They reached Vatapi. Sivagami was taken to a large, beautiful palace with two women as companions and servants. They spoke a combination of Prakrit and Tamil which Sivagami understood. She learnt from them that the emperor had specially arranged the palace for her and ordered that she have every comfort. She had expected this. *Emperor Pulikesi will soon come to see me.* She spent all her time planning what to say and how to behave with him.

She thought of Sita being kept a prisoner by Ravana. *Just as Rama defeated Ravana and freed Sita, Mamallan will come one day, defeat this wretched Pulikesi and take me away.*

Sivagami was furious with Pulikesi over his army's cruelty, but she was proud to think that she had power over such a tyrant. *Pulikesi captured me because he loves my dance. I can use the power of my dance to make him do as I want. I will not let that wicked monk get away easily. Let him come.* She still believed that Naganandhi and Pulikesi were one.

Eight days after her arrival in Vatapi, the servant came running and cried, 'The emperor is here!' Sivagami excitedly prepared to welcome Pulikesi. But when he stood before her, looked her up and down and gave the devilish laugh she had heard in her sleep, she was scared speechless.

"Dancing Queen, Mahendran Pallava's art treasure ... does Vatapi's air agree with you?"

Sivagami shivered. *Is this the monk who delighted in my abhinaya? Naganandhi was respectful when he granted my wish to release the women. Has he changed because he is now back in Vatapi?* Confused, Sivagami could not answer Pulikesi.

"Girl, why are you silent?" Pulikesi asked. "I have given you a palace worthy of the Pallava kingdom's Dancing Queen. Are you comfortable? Tell me if you need anything."

Sivagami steeled herself and said, "Lord, I have every comfort. Thank you."

"Ah, you speak! I wondered whether you were a living woman or one of your father's dancing statues. If you truly wish to thank me, there is a way ..."

The frightened Sivagami was silent. *I wonder what he is going to ask for ...*

"Girl, that stupid Mahendran Pallava accused me of not being able to appreciate art. The Parasika delegation is coming here with gifts of friendship from their emperor. There is to be a grand assembly to welcome them. Queen of Art, you must dance in the coronation hall."

Sivagami's confusion disappeared. She looked Pulikesi boldly in the face and declared, "No."

Pulikesi clenched his teeth to control his anger. "I will give you three days' time. Think."

"There is nothing to think about. Lord, you want me to dance in your court to proclaim to the world that you have defeated Mahendran Pallava. You can enslave my body, but you cannot enslave the art which lives in me. I will not dance in fear of authority or by command."

Pulikesi's eyes reddened. He laughed fiendishly. "If you do not want to dance, don't. This palace is not your prison—you can go out whenever you want. Although Vatapi is not as beautiful as your Kanchi, we too have sights to see. The men at the gate are not your jailers. Whenever you wish, they will arrange a palanquin for you. If you wish to see me again, send word through them." With her head bowed, Sivagami did not see the jealousy and vengeance in Pulikesi's eyes.

Sivagami was proud that she had defeated the cruel Pulikesi. That evening, she asked the guards to be taken around Vatapi and climbed into the palanquin. *Let me see if I am truly free.*

Through the Streets

A THOUSAND YEARS ago, Vatapi was one of the three great capital cities in Bharat, along with Kanchi and Kannauj. Pulikesi's conquests and plundered wealth made Vatapi prosperous, and trade flourished. Jewel merchants and pilgrims came from distant lands. Festive crowds thronged the streets. The air was filled with the sound of carriages and carts.

Sivagami saw the difference between ancient Kanchi and newly rich Vatapi. Kanchi's citizens did not flaunt their jewels and silks; here, there was a vulgar show of wealth. Kanchi's citizens greeted friends with respectful affection; in Vatapi, there was loud laughter. Kanchi's employers treated servants with firm affection; here, they used crude, abusive language. Sivagami saw one other difference—there were no monks or beggars in Vatapi. *The people here are not generous.*

Sivagami saw a crowd of men and women standing in a corner of a crossroad with their hands tied. A group of thugs stood around them, holding whips. Sivagami's heart raced. *These men and women are from Tamil Nadu. Shall I stop the palanquin and go to them?* But she could not find the courage to do that, and the palanquin moved past. Sivagami turned back—some people in that pitiful crowd pointed to her palanquin with their tied hands and stared after it with tear-filled eyes. Sivagami turned away and ordered the bearers to take her straight back to the palace.

As soon as she was back home, Sivagami sent her servant to enquire about the sight she had seen. The woman came back with terrifying news: Emperor Pulikesi had brought many prisoners from the Pallava kingdom. Some tried to escape; others refused to be slaves; a few went on hunger strike. Pulikesi had ordered all these rebels to be whipped at the crossroads for two months. Every evening, the pedestrians on Vatapi's streets could enjoy this spectacle.

Sivagami did not sleep a wink that night. She felt the blow of the whip on her own body. *The women I made Pulikesi release were just a small part of the Pallava prisoners. Many more were captured by the army which marched ahead.*

Sivagami now understood the meaning behind Pulikesi's words and his permission to see Vatapi. *That merciless wretch wants me to fall at his feet and beg him, but that will never happen.*

The next day, she trembled as the sun set. *By now the Pallava men and women would have been taken to the crossroads. Those guards will soon start whipping them.*

Sivagami went to the crossroads in her palanquin. Many of the prisoners cried out to her, "Mother, save us!" Sivagami's heart ached. *How I wish I had the power to save them!* She stopped the palanquin and walked towards the prisoners. Her head whirled and her stomach churned when she saw the prisoners' wounds and the bloodstains on the ground. She controlled herself and asked a woman near her, "Lady, how can I save you? I too am a prisoner."

"Mother, you have the power to save us. Ask that Chalukyan demon," the woman replied.

Sivagami went to the soldiers' captain. "Sir, why are you torturing these people? Stop it."

Virupakshan, the captain, laughed. "What can I do, lady? It is the emperor's order." He paused. "We will stop if you say so—but on one condition."

Sivagami was startled. "What condition?"

"You must dance for us here. As long as you dance, we will not whip these people. If you dance until the sun sets, you can go home, and we will take the prisoners back to their cells."

Sivagami stood rooted to that spot, her face flaming with anger. *Ah, this is the evil man's revenge. He wants to insult my precious gift.* She looked the captain in the face. "Are you asking me to dance at the crossroads? Never!"

The captain smiled and commanded the men waiting with whips: "Begin your work."

Dance at the Crossroads

AT THE CRACK of the whips, Sivagami's resolve melted, and she began to dance. She danced exquisitely. She danced as if to show that happiness can be born from suffering. She forgot place and time. She was a beautiful goddess dancing in a frenzy.

The people in the streets froze and watched the magic. The tied prisoners were rooted to the spot. The men with whips stood motionless.

The sun set over the hills and the drums beat a tattoo for closing the city gates. The sound broke Sivagami's trance. She stopped dancing and looked around. She remembered where she was and what she had done. In the middle of her shame and sorrow, she felt proud and happy. She saw the gratitude in the Pallava prisoners' eyes. Without a word, she climbed into her palanquin.

The Monk's Arrival

SIVAGAMI DANCED AT the crossroads every evening for more than a month. Virupakshan often changed the venue. People thronged all the important crossroads in Vatapi to see Sivagami dance. Officials came in chariots, and queens and concubines in their palanquins.

The news spread like wildfire: the dancing girl Pulikesi captured from Kanchi is dancing in the streets. People came from the surrounding towns and villages to see the spectacle.

Vatapi's citizens were stunned by Sivagami's dance. They pitied and loved this gifted girl who had left her country and family for a distant land. Many wanted to befriend her and welcome her to their homes. But Sivagami's exhaustion, mingled with bitterness, stopped her from talking to them.

Soon the people said, 'The Tamil dancer is arrogant!' Their pity turned into hate, and they mocked Sivagami. Those who had called her dance, 'Divine!' now called it, 'The mad woman's dance.' Children ran howling behind Sivagami's palanquin, throwing mud at her.

Sivagami's heart turned to stone. She was indifferent to praise and criticism. She was like the lotus leaf floating on water, detached from the world and reaching for the divine.

One day, Sivagami stopped dancing at sunset, paused to recover her breath and turned to leave. She stopped in shock: Naganandhi stood staring at her in angry surprise. His pitying eyes seemed to beg, 'Forgive me!' Confused, Sivagami bowed her head and walked to her palanquin.

The palanquin made its way to the palace. *Is Naganandhi really the Vatapi emperor in disguise? The appearance is the same … but what a difference between Pulikesi's cruel face and the monk's loving, compassionate eyes!* Seeing the monk made Sivagami think of home. *It is not even a year, but it feels like ages.*

Back at the palace, Sivagami's heart raced in excitement. Her eyes kept going to the door and lit up when Naganandhi came in at the end of the night's first watch. They stared at one another and tried to penetrate the secrets in each other's hearts. The room was silent.

The monk broke the silence in a trembling voice: "Sivagami, forgive me."

Sivagami's Oath

SIVAGAMI JUMPED TO her feet. Her eyes flashed lightning. She hissed, "Sir, are you a monk who has renounced worldly life? Or are you the Chalukyan emperor who uses these saffron robes as an evil disguise? Do you truly love sculpture and dance? Who are you? Naganandhi? Pulikesi?"

Naganandhi was calm. "My dear Sivagami, you have reason to be suspicious of me. But I am truly a Buddhist monk who has lost his heart to your Bharatanatyam. I am not the foolish Pulikesi who made you dance before savages. I am his wretched brother. Sivagami, you begged me, 'Save my father.' To do that, I took off my saffron robes and dressed as Emperor Pulikesi."

Sivagami ran to the monk. She knelt before him with folded hands and cried, "Swami, forgive me for my angry words. Did you save my father? Is he alive? Where is he? How is he?"

"My dear, I saved your father. I kept my promise to you. I will tell you all the details."

The monk told her how he had saved Aayanar from mutilation, how Aayanar had broken his leg, how he had taken the unconscious sculptor to his home and left him after he regained his senses.

Tears flowed down the grateful Sivagami's cheeks. *How could I have doubted him?* She said, "I am indebted to you for saving my beloved father's life. I thought you and the Chalukyan emperor were the same man. I was furious because I thought you were the one who brought me to Vatapi and made me dance at the crossroads. Swami, forgive me!"

Naganandhi choked with emotion. "Sivagami, you are the one who must forgive me. I am the cause of you being a prisoner here." Sivagami wiped her tears and stared at him in amazement. "Sivagami, my brother, Pulikesi, planned to invade Vengi with the entire Chalukyan army. I am the one who asked him to march to Kanchi with half our forces. I wrote telling him it was enough to send our brother, Vishnuvardhan, to Vengi. Vishnuvardhan is now dead. I brought his widow and infant son safely to Vatapi only today ..."

"Swami, weren't you in the city all these days?"

"Sivagami, if I was here, would I have let your sacred art be mocked in the marketplace? If I had known that Pulikesi would do this, I would not have left you with him at the North Pennai."

Sivagami remembered her dream. "But it was near Kanchi that I asked you to save my father."

"After acting like Pulikesi and saving your father, I fought with Mahendran Pallava in the same disguise. I defeated him at Manimangalam and followed you. You saw me at the North Pennai and asked me to free the Pallava women. I could have freed you too and let you go back to your father, but I cheated you and brought you to Vatapi. I never dreamt that fool, Pulikesi, would insult you like this when I was away. Now you know why I ask for your forgiveness."

"Many things are now clear to me. But you have renounced the world—what use am I to you? What have you gained by separating me from my father and keeping me a prisoner here?"

"I will tell you. The Chalukyas delayed attacking Kanchi and lost half their army. Vishnuvardhan defeated Vengi but died without consolidating his victory. You are the cause of all this ..."

Naganandhi told Sivagami his story. He described his childhood in the Ajanta Hills and his fascination for the Bharatanatyam dancer painted on the wall. He related his visit to Aayanar's house and his amazement at seeing that painting come alive to dance for him.

"Sivagami, I became a new man. I forgot my dreams of greatness for the Chalukyas. I forgot my plans to bring all of Bharat under the Buddhist *sangha* with myself as the chief abbot. *To hell with the empire and the sangha! I will spend the rest of my life watching Sivagami dance.* From that day, my only thought was how to bring you to Vatapi ..."

Sivagami swung between pride and sorrow. *Ah, two great empires went to war because of me! Aiyo, all the cruelty I saw between Kanchi and Vatapi was because of me!*

"Sivagami, I caused a great war because I was bewitched by your dance and wanted to save you from that cowardly nobody, Mamallan. But that fool, Pulikesi, insulted you and your art by making you dance in the streets. Forgive me. I will make amends for your pain. I have arranged for you to go back to your father. I fought with the emperor and made him agree."

The dictates of fate, or the strange workings of a woman's heart, made Sivagami think deeply.

"Sivagami, why are you silent? When can you leave? I will send you in a palanquin with women to serve you and soldiers to guard you. They will take you up to the North Pennai ..."

Sivagami stood and swore a terrible oath: "The brave Mamallan, whom you called a coward, will attack Vatapi. Like a lion falling on a pack of foxes, he will wipe out the Chalukyan army and send the wicked Pulikesi to *Yamaloka.* Rivers of blood will flow on the streets where Tamil prisoners were paraded. Vatapi will be reduced to ashes. Mamallan, wearing the garland of victory, will hold my hand and take me with him. Only then will I leave—not when you send me."

Naganandhi smiled. *My trick has worked once again.*

Pillar of Victory

TWENTY MILES WEST of Vatapi, there was a hill surrounded by thick forests. Two half-finished caves stood side by side on the hillslope—the work of Buddhists or Jains who, for some reason, had moved on. A small waterfall splashed from one cave, spraying water like pearls before it flowed down and disappeared into the shadows of the huge trees. This beautiful landscape was ruined by scattered human skulls and bulls' horns. The bloodstained rocks showed that they had been recently used as sacrificial altars by Kapalikas.

As the evening light turned the green trees to gold, four men sat on a bare rock near the caves, exhausted by their long journey. They had thick beards, wrinkled skin and hollows under their eyes. Their clothes were dirty and their hair tangled. But their eyes glowed with determination and courage. A fifth man stood on the summit of the hill, scanning the four directions.

Suddenly the man on the summit shouted excitedly, "There!" It was Gundodharan.

The four men on the rock stared eagerly in the direction he pointed to. Shatrughan came out of the dense forest. He was clean-shaven and was obviously coming from the city.

The five men crowded around him. "Shatrughan, success or failure? Tell us, quickly!"

"Success of course," Shatrughan said and opened a cloth bag. Fruits tumbled out. The hungry men scrambled after them.

One man ignored the fruits—it was Mamallan. "Shatrughan, did you see Sivagami?" he asked.

"Yes, lord, I saw her," Shatrughan said and was quiet again.

"Why are you silent? Tell us more. Where did you see her? How is she?"

"Lord, she is well. There is no need to worry."

They sat on the rock and Shatrughan told his story. "I went to Vatapi last evening, posing as a bangle merchant. It is not hard to enter the fort. People move in and out easily. They guard the fort only when they expect an enemy attack. When Vatapi's brave army was on its victorious campaign ..."

Paranjothi interrupted: "Nonsense, Shatrughan! What victorious campaign? The Chalukyas lost and came running back with their tails between their legs. Their invasion of Vengi too failed."

Shatrughan said respectfully, "General, these are not my words. I saw a Pillar of Victory at the crossroads of Vatapi's four main streets with a message etched on it in Prakrit. I will repeat it as closely as I can remember. The great Emperor of Emperors, the Demi-god, the Pride of the Chalukyan dynasty, Emperor Pulikesi, went on a conquest of the south. He defeated Mahendran Pallava at the North Pennai. Mahendran ran and hid in Kanchi Fort. Emperor Pulikesi continued his victorious campaign and crossed the Kaveri on an elephant bridge. There he blessed the Chera, Chola, Pandyan and Kalambhara kings who asked for his protection. He then attacked Kanchi Fort and made Mahendran Pallava fall at his feet, begging for his life. He mercifully spared his life, accepted Mahendran Pallava's tributes and returned to Vatapi to the triumphant beat of drums and blowing of conches. In the fourth year of the era of Salivahana, month and date. May the city of Vatapi, this Pillar of Victory and the Chalukyan line live forever."

Shatrughan's listeners cried, "What lies! What arrogance! Smash that pillar!"

Shatrughan continued: "Lord, I was about to kick the stone, but I remembered my mission. I pretended to stumble and covered up my mistake. What if anyone had noticed!"

"Shatrughan, tell us about the purpose of your visit to Vatapi," Mamallan said angrily.

"Lord, I went past the pillar of lies. *How do I find Sivagami in this vast city? Whom can I ask?* God answered my prayers: I saw Sivagami dancing at the next crossroads ..."

There were cries of, "What? Shame, shame!"

"Lord, when I saw Sivagami dancing in the middle of a crowd, I was angry and ashamed. My ears burned to hear the people's insults. But I noticed the Tamil men and women standing behind her with their hands tied. Thugs stood among them, holding whips. Once I learnt the truth, I was proud ..." Shatrughan explained the reason for Sivagami's dance.

His listeners were thrilled to hear that Sivagami had danced to save the Pallava prisoners from being whipped. They listened eagerly to what happened after that.

"Sivagami finished dancing and paused to take breath. Suddenly she was surprised. I followed her eyes. Who do you think was standing there?" He paused. "It was our old friend, Naganandhi."

The Bangle Merchant

SHATRUGHAN'S LISTENERS WERE shocked to hear Naganandhi's name.

Mamallan looked at Gundodharan. "The Buddhist monk? Then is Gundodharan's news false?"

Shatrughan replied, "Gundodharan's news is correct, lord. Naganandhi did go to Vengi. Unfortunately, he returned yesterday. His arrival makes our task ten times more difficult ..."

"Did the monk return only yesterday? How do you know, Shatrughan?" Paranjothi asked.

"The city is buzzing with talk of it, general. Pulikesi's brother,

Vishnuvardhan, died a few days ago. Naganandhi brought back his widow and six-month-old son from Vengi."

"How did Vishnuvardhan die?" Paranjothi asked.

"The Vengi forces retreated and hid in the forests. There were uprisings throughout the land after Vishnuvardhan's coronation. Vishnuvardhan was badly wounded in a fight with the rebels ..."

"Why bother about all this now, Shatrughan? Tell us what happened after that," Mamallan said.

"Sivagami hid her shock and hurried to her palanquin. I followed her to a beautiful mansion on a quiet street. I went to the two guards at the gate. 'Does the dancing girl from Kanchi live here?' I asked. 'Yes,' they replied. 'I am a bangle merchant. I have beautiful bangles to show her.' 'No one is allowed to enter the house at night. Come back tomorrow.' I chatted with them and gathered information. Sivagami lives in that house with a companion and a cook. No one visits her. Pulikesi came there once and asked her to dance in his court. She refused and so, Pulikesi is punishing her by making her dance in the streets. I cursed that demon in my mind. I saw a palanquin coming. I hid and watched—it was Naganandhi."

They heard Mamallan grind his teeth.

Paranjothi cut in: "Shatrughan, did you meet Sivagami? Tell us that."

Mamallan glared at Paranjothi. "Shatrughan, leave out nothing. Did Naganandhi go to Sivagami's house?"

"Yes, lord. He was inside for about half an hour. From the gate, I heard Sivagami scolding the monk. I slept in a guesthouse on the same street. Early the next day, I met Sivagami. She was amazed to see me. She sent her companion out and said, 'Shatrughan, didn't you go to Kanchi?' I said, 'Lady, I went to Kanchi and gave Mamallan your message. He is here—and so is the general.' She asked excitedly, 'Where is the army camped?' I said that there was no army and that Mamallan was waiting near the fort. I told her that tomorrow was a new moon day and that we would come for her at night. I asked her to be ready to leave with us."

"Shatrughan, what did Sivagami finally say?" Mamallan asked.

"She just said that she would expect us on the night of the new moon and sent me away."

Suspicion

SIVAGAMI SAT ALONE in her mansion on the night of the new moon. She had sent her companion home to visit her ailing mother. A single lamp burned in the room. *Mamallan is coming.* Her heart rose to her throat and choked her. *If only I had loved and married a sculptor's son—I would not be in this sad state. Why did Mamallan come and drive me mad? He is the cause of all my grief.* As time passed, her anger changed to longing. *Aiyo, why is he not here?*

At midnight, Sivagami sat up in fright to see two men with thick beards and mustaches suddenly standing before her. But their faces were familiar. She asked, "Who are you?"

"Sivagami, don't you recognise me?" Mamallan asked.

Sivagami's beautiful face lit up in joy, but Mamallan's face fell. *Ah, she is happy in this place.*

"Lord, is it you?" Sivagami's voice was choked with emotion. She stood.

Mamallan said sternly, "Yes, it is me. When you are living luxuriously in the Vatapi emperor's palace, why would you remember old friends?"

His cruel words shocked Sivagami. *Is this really Mamallan, or is it an imposter?*

As they both stared at each other, Paranjothi realised that he was an intruder. He said softly to Mamallan, "Lord, we do not have much time," and went out to wait at the entrance.

"Do you at least remember your father, Sivagami? Or have you forgotten him also in all your dancing and singing?" Mamallan asked.

Sivagami frowned and controlled her fury. "Prince, how is my father? Where is he?"

"He is fine. He asks everyone, 'Where is my beloved daughter?' Sivagami, come. Let us go."

Sivagami's eyes brimmed with tears, but she did not move.

Mamallan mocked her: "After living luxuriously in the Vatapi emperor's palace, it looks like you do not want to come with me to Kanchi."

Sivagami laughed. "Pallava prince, you are right. I do not want to leave this luxurious palace. Go."

Angry sparks flew from Mamallan's eyes. "What a fool I am! To think that I came a thousand miles in search of you!" He paused. "Sivagami, come for your father's sake. Come for your friend, Kamali. I promised them that I will return with you."

"I too have taken an oath, lord. Only when the city of Vatapi burns to the ground, when its streets run with blood … only then will I leave this place. This is my oath."

"What a cruel oath! Why did you do this?"

"Lord, you would not ask me this if you had seen Tamil men and women being whipped at the crossroads while the Pallava kingdom's Dancing Queen danced before them."

"Sivagami, I know this. Even then, you should not have sworn such a cruel oath."

Sivagami stared at Mamallan. "Lord, years ago, a prince swore on his spear that he loved me. He promised to make me his queen. Near the lotus pond, under the light of the full moon, he swore, 'In this lifetime, and every lifetime to come, you will be my wife.' I swore my oath based on his promise." Her look was a spear which pierced his heart.

Disaster

MAMALLAN LOOKED LOVINGLY at Sivagami. "I am here to keep my promise to you. I have come a thousand miles across forests, hills and rivers. Forget my harsh words. I was angry with someone else and took it out on you. Come, let us go. There is no time to lose."

"Prince, fulfill my oath. Kill the wicked Pulikesi, burn Vatapi and then take me with you."

"Sivagami, I will fulfill your oath. But we must muster a large army. It may be many years …"

Sivagami was bitter: "Is it so difficult for the brave Mamallan to defeat Vatapi and kill Pulikesi? Pallava prince, go to Kanchi and do your royal duties. What do you care about my oath!"

"Sivagami, is it you who talks like this? Are you the old Sivagami?"

"No, lord, I have changed. My life is bitter and my heart is empty. Forget this new Sivagami."

"I am still the old Mamallan. I did not forget you for even an instant while we were apart. I swear on my love for you: I will fulfill your oath. Now come with me."

Sivagami's experiences had hardened her heart. "I do not want your love. I want only revenge. I want Pulikesi to die and Vatapi to burn. I want its people to scream in terror. Fulfill my oath."

"Sivagami, do not be stubborn. I will tell you one last time: I will fulfill your oath. The men of the Pallava dynasty have never gone back on their words."

"Prince, Sculptor Aayanar's daughter too has never gone back on her words."

"What arrogance!"

"Is it only Pandyan and Chera princesses who can be arrogant? I am only a sculptor's daughter, but I was born in the land of Goddess Kannagi."

"If you do not come with me now, you will lose my love."

Paranjothi hurried in and whispered to the prince. Alarm flashed on Mamallan's face. He said, "General, it looks like this stupid girl's stubbornness will ruin all our plans." He turned angrily on Sivagami. "Girl, are you coming or not? There is no time to argue with you."

Paranjothi cut in: "Lady, you must not waste time arguing. Only four of us have come into the fort. Kannapiran and his father are waiting on the wall with a rope ladder. Kapalikas are searching for us outside to use us as their sacrificial offerings. That deceitful monk knows we are here—he is at the street corner. *Devi…*"

Sivagami said, "Sir, I did not know that the Pallava prince and his beloved friend would run for their lives from Kapalikas and monks. I am not stopping you: go."

Mamallan erupted with rage and hissed, "You wretch! You will suffer the consequences for this!" He turned to Paranjothi. "General, this wicked woman wants to betray us to the evil monk. Let us go." He pulled Paranjothi by the hand.

Paranjothi said, "Lord, I heard everything. Aayanar's daughter will not betray us. She refuses to come only because she stands by her oath. We will just have to carry her away by force …"

Sivagami broke into goosebumps. *Won't Mamallan hold me close and carry me?*

Mamallan said, "No, general, I will not take a woman by force. I will fulfill my promise to her one day. Let her come then if she wants. Until then, let her stay with that monk."

Shatrughan and Gundodharan ran in.

Shatrughan stammered, "Lord, the monk is at the corner. Half the soldiers who came with him are going to the back entrance!"

Paranjothi again went to Sivagami and said hurriedly, "Lady …"

"General, stop. This pitiless woman wants the monk to trap us. Let us go!" Mamallan dragged Paranjothi and ran towards the mansion's back entrance. The four men disappeared.

The Dagger Flies

SIVAGAMI STARED AFTER Mamallan. The next instant, she fell flat on the ground. A mountain pressed down on her heart and darkness swallowed her. The house and the lamp whirled. She was falling down, down, down into a bottomless pit.

'Sivagami, Sivagami,' someone called. She heard a cobra's hiss and opened her eyes. *Aiyo, a cobra with its hood spread! No, it is Naganandhi. I feel his poisonous breath on my face.*

With a great effort, Sivagami sat up. She moved away from the monk and shivered.

Naganandhi looked compassionately at her. "Girl, what happened? Why did you faint? Where is your companion?" He looked around.

Sivagami was alarmed to see Mamallan's turban and stole lying on the ground.

Not noticing them, Naganandhi turned back to Sivagami. "Girl, listen to me. What I say is for your own good." The monk took one of Sivagami's hands in his iron clasp.

Sivagami felt as if a hooded cobra was lunging forward to bite her. She shuddered and pulled back her hand.

The monk's voice shook. "Sivagami, why do you tremble? I have not harmed or insulted you in any way. I have loved you truly and saved your father's life. Why do you hate me?"

"Swami, I do not fear or hate you. You have been good to me."

"I am glad, Sivagami—these words are enough for me. Why do you shiver? Are you ill?"

"Yes, swami, I am ill."

"I will send a doctor here tomorrow. But where is your companion?" The monk looked around and saw the garments lying behind a pillar. "Ah, it looks as if someone has been here." He examined the clothes. "Congratulations, Sivagami! You have quickly found lovers. Are they from the city or from outside?" He laughed mockingly. Sivagami was silent. "You will not answer. Very well: I will find out." He walked to the entrance.

Mamallan's words came back to her. *She wants to betray us to the monk.* She looked around wildly—something glinted under the prince's stole. She dashed to pick up the dagger and hurled it at the monk's back. The monk shrieked and fell ... blood gushed from his wound.

The monk turned to Sivagami and said in a pitiful voice, "Sivagami, what have you done? I hurried here to reunite you with your lover, Mamallan."

Mahendran's Last Wish

MAMALLAN AND HIS companions returned to Kanchi to find that Mahendran's health had worsened. When he saw them come back without Sivagami, he became weaker.

One day, Mahendran Pallava summoned his son, his commanders and the council of ministers. Lying in his bed, he saw their devoted faces and their tears. The men who had heard the emperor roar like a lion were shocked by his weak voice.

Mahendran Pallava said, "It has been twenty-five years since I ascended the glorious Pallava throne. When Kanchi shone in all her glory, you stood by me—my word was law. That was nothing remarkable, but when Kanchi's fame dimmed, you stayed loyal. I invited King Pulikesi to Kanchi as a guest, against your advice. You put up with the consequences of that blunder. In my last days, I want to thank you and ask your forgiveness for my mistakes ..."

As some men sobbed, the prime minister spoke up: "Lord, I beg you, do not talk like this. You hurt us by asking for our forgiveness and shouldering all the blame. It was all fated to happen."

"Sarangadevan's words make me even more grateful to you," Mahendran Pallava continued. "I am dying. Very soon, my spirit will leave this crushed body. My beloved son, Narasimhan, will perform my last rites according to the Vedas ..."

Overcome by anger and grief, Mamallan wailed, "*Appa, appa!*"

Mahendran lovingly embraced him and kissed him on the forehead. "My child, this must be said." The emperor turned to his ministers. "But my soul will be at peace only if you grant my last wish."

"Lord, just say the word—all of us here swear to fulfill your command, whatever it may be," the prime minister declared.

"The Pallava dynasty has lost its glory because of my mistakes and the Chalukyan king's treachery. You must do what I have left undone. Our army must go to war, kill Pulikesi and burn Vatapi. There must be a majestic Pallava Pillar of Victory in Vatapi. This is my wish—will you fulfill it?"

There was a chorus of, "We will! We will!"

The prime minister asked, "Lord, why are the crown prince and the general silent?"

"Narasimhan and Paranjothi have already sworn their oaths to me—you must support them. I must discuss an important matter with Narasimhan. Could you please excuse us?"

A Royal Dynasty's Dharma

THE MINISTERS AND the general moved away from the emperor's bed.

Mahendran looked at Mamallan. "My child, I have made sure that you can fulfill Sivagami's oath: the council will support your Vatapi invasion. The ministers have granted their emperor's dying wish. You, my beloved son, will also grant me my last wish, won't you?"

"*Appa*, whatever it is, command me. I will do it. It is not a request or a wish."

"Son, the heavy burden of ruling this empire will soon be yours. You will sit on the throne of Kanchi, a city celebrated for a thousand years ..."

"*Appa*, I do not want the throne or the crown: I want only you. You must live long ..."

"Narasimhan, I will not live much longer. Even if I live, I will not be strong. I cannot carry the burden of the empire for another minute. You must take it from me ..."

"I will take on the responsibilities of governance. You only need to sit on Kanchi's throne and command me."

"Okay, my son, but I have one important condition."

"Tell me your condition, *appa*." There was a vague ache in Mamallan's heart.

"My child, you are my only son: the ancient Pallava dynasty must not end with you. Narasimhan, marry the Pandyan princess. I want to see you married before I die—or I will not die in peace."

Mamallan was silent. Then, "*Appa*, you know that I love Sivagami. When I love one woman, how can I marry another? Won't I ruin three lives? Why do you test me? Are you ordering me to do this?" Every word came from the bottom of his heart and was drenched in his blood.

Mahendran Pallava lovingly stroked him. His voice was filled with pity. "Yes, Narasimhan, I am asking you to do this. I know the good that will come from this. In this world, common men can consider their personal joys and sorrows. But royalty must consider only the kingdom's welfare. Narasimhan, think: can you marry Sivagami now? Can you attack Vatapi tomorrow? It will take years for you to be ready. After that, God only knows how many years the war will last. Will you stay unmarried? Will the Pallava subjects agree to that?"

Mamallan sighed. He was furious with Sivagami. *If only that wretch had come with me!*

Mahendran read his mind. "Son, if you had brought Sivagami from Vatapi, I would have married her myself—for the sake of the kingdom ..."

Mamallan screamed, "*Appa!*"

"Forgive me—it was the only way to stop you from marrying Sivagami. Your mother agreed. Luckily, Sivagami refused to leave Vatapi and spared me from doing this terrible thing."

Thank goodness she refused to come with me!

"Son, am I asking you to sacrifice more for the kingdom than I was ready to? Think how your marriage to the Pandyan princess will strengthen the Pallava kingdom. Defeating the Chalukyas will not be easy. Can you do it without the Pandyans' support? Can you march north leaving an enemy behind you? You must marry the Pandyan princess ..."

Seeing the emperor struggling to breathe, Bhuvanamahadevi intervened: "Lord, hasn't the doctor ordered you not to talk much?" She turned to Mamallan. "My child, your father ..."

Mamallan clenched his teeth and said, "*Appa*, say no more. I will marry the Pandyan princess."

Mahendran's face was radiant. At the emperor's signal, Paranjothi and the ministers came close. "I have good news. The crown prince and the Pandyan princess are to be married. At the same time and place, General Paranjothi too will be married."

The hall filled with cheers. 'Long live Mamallan! Long live General Paranjothi!'

PART 4

SHATTERED DREAMS

The Forest House

AAYANAR'S HOME WAS again surrounded by tall, green trees, thick with tender sprouts and buds or heavy with clusters of flowers. Fragrant blossoms fell in the soft breeze and carpeted the ground. The birds sang out, breaking the forest's silence. The lotus pond brimmed with water. Water droplets shone like pearls on the lotus leaves. But no mortal eyes saw this beauty.

A single chisel was heard inside the house: it was Aayanar at work. More than nine years had passed since Aayanar lost his beloved daughter. His hair was now as white as the *thumbai* flower. With sunken eyes and wrinkled skin, he had become an old man. He clung to life only because of his sculpture. His house now had more statues of dancing figures than before. Every statue resembled Sivagami. The paintings on the walls had faded—Aayanar had not yet learnt the secret of the Ajanta pigments. Engrossed in his work, Aayanar did not notice the chariot which stopped at his door.

Emperor Narasimhan and his two children walked in. Mamallan too had changed. The glow of youth had given way to a majestic, mature radiance. His eyes shone with intelligence and determination, instead of wild daring. The two children resembled Mamallan. The boy was eight and the girl, six.

"*Thatha*," the children cooed and ran to Aayanar.

"My precious ones, come!" He hugged and fondled them. His eyes brimmed with tears. Were they tears of joy on seeing the children or tears of regret over what might have been?

After a while, Mamallan said, "Mahendran and Kundavi, play outside for some time. I will come after talking to *thatha*." He led them out. "Kanna, keep an eye on the children."

Kannapiran stood outside, holding the horses' reins. He now sported a black mustache.

Aayanar looked up at Mamallan and said, "Lord, I have carried out your order. I will finish the hundred-and-eighth dancing statue today."

Watching Aayanar going mad in Sivagami's absence, Mamallan had commanded him to make a hundred-and-eight dancing figures. Once he started work, Aayanar's mind had steadied.

"Aayanar, my preparations too are made. I leave for war next week, on Vijayadashami."

"Sir, Gundodharan told me about the huge army assembled at the Kazhugukundram Hills. And still more soldiers are arriving. Swords, spears and lances lie heaped in mountains."

"That is only a part of our army. A huge force, under General Paranjothi, is waiting at the North Pennai. And the Pandyan army is marching here from the south: it is now near the Varaha River." He paused. "Aayanar, I thought that I would invade Vatapi in three years. It has taken Paranjothi and me nine years to do what we had planned to do in three."

"Pallava king, those nine years have been nine ages to me."

"I feel the same, but what could I do? For two years, there was famine in the land. One year, there was damage from heavy rain. I had to help the Lankan prince, Manavanman. I had to broker a peace when war broke out between the Pandyans and the Cheras ..."

"Lord, I do not know how many more years I will live. Let me come with you and see Sivagami before I die."

Mamallan wiped away his tears. "Do not talk about dying. You must live for your daughter. If you must come, I will take you. Be ready to leave on Vijayadashami."

Manavanman

THE PALLAVA ARMY was camped on the vast plains around Kazhugukundram. Looking northwards from the summit, all one could see were elephants, elephants and more elephants. Turning to the west, one saw fifteen thousand tall, thoroughbred horses imported from Arabia and Parasika through Mamallapuram. To the south were horse-drawn chariots, bullock carts, and load-bearing bulls, camels and donkeys. The carts were packed with sacks of grain, cloth bundles, knives, shields, swords, spears, lances, tridents, bows, piles of arrows, cords, rope ladders, hooks, sickles, spades, torches and many other things. Countless soldiers buzzed about like flies.

In all the four directions, the nandi flag fluttered over the camp and reached skywards.

As Mamallan reached the army camp on his chariot, a mighty shout rose from thousands of strong throats: 'Long live Mamallan! Down with Pulikesi!' The earth and the sky trembled.

A majestic figure rode forward to meet Mamallan: it was the Lankan prince, Manavanman.

Manavanman's father and Mahendran Pallava had been friends. When Manavanman's father died, Attaduttan, a chieftain, seized the Lankan throne. Manavanman asked Mamallan for help. Although Thondaimandalam was then reeling under a famine, Mamallan sent a small force to Lanka. But by the time this force reached Lanka, Manavanman had been defeated and was hiding in the jungle. Seeing that Mamallan's small force was not enough to fight Attaduttan, Manavanman returned to Kanchi with the Pallavas.

Mamallan's pity for Manavanman matured into a deep friendship. Manavanman occupied the place in his heart which he had once wanted to give Paranjothi. Mamallan and Paranjothi did not become close friends because Paranjothi did not consider himself the prince's equal. After their return from Vatapi, Paranjothi was busy mustering and arming the Pallava army, recruiting and training soldiers and building up a stockpile of weapons. Manavanman filled Mamallan's need for an intimate friend.

When Manavanman came to Kanchi, Mamallan offered him a large army. But the prince realised that the Pallava army was being mustered for the Vatapi invasion and refused. He said that he would stay until the war with Vatapi was over and then go to Lanka with a Pallava force. Mamallan was delighted with Manavanman's consideration. *I was afraid that Paranjothi would object to sending a large force to Lanka at this time.*

Manavanman was particularly useful in training the Pallavas' elephant brigade. He asked Mamallan to let him accompany him to Vatapi.

But Mamallan had other plans. *Manavanman has come to me for sanctuary: it is wrong to take him to war. And once Paranjothi and I leave for Vatapi, someone must govern the kingdom and send provisions to the battlefield.* Deep in his heart, Mamallan had another reason for wanting Manavanman in Kanchi. *If I die in battle, I need someone clever enough to hold the Pallava kingdom together and put Prince Mahendran on the throne. I can trust Manavanman to do this.*

Mamallan did not trust his brother-in-law, Jayanthvarman Pandyan. *He once dreamt of ruling the whole of Tamil Nadu.* And so, Mamallan asked Manavanman to stay in Kanchi. Manavanman insisted on going to Vatapi. They had not yet reached an agreement.

Mamallan and Manavanman now embraced. Manavanman pointed to Aayanar. "*Anna*, why have you brought this old man?"

"This old man was the first to say that he is going to go to war. Competing with him, Prince Mahendran too wants to go to war. And Kundavi says, 'If *anna* goes to war, so will I!' Did it stop with that? Last evening, Kannapiran's son, Little Kannan, stole into the garden with a knife. Saying, 'This is how I will cut off the Chalukyas' heads!' he cut down many plants."

Manavanman interrupted him: "Take the brave warriors, old Aayanar, Little Kannan, Prince Mahendran and Princess Kundavi to war. Leave useless men like me in Kanchi."

That evening, in private, Manavanman asked Mamallan, "Are you taking Aayanar to Vatapi?"

"Yes, *thambi*. If we rescue the person for whom we have mustered this huge army, we must have someone who will take charge of her. If we give her to her father, our responsibility ends."

Mamallan's deep sigh pained Manavanman.

Rudracharya

EMPEROR MAMALLAN'S CHARIOT stopped at the entrance to Kanchi's famous Sanskrit school which was housed in a large building. Students recited the Vedas, enacted classical dramas and heard the *Bhagavad Gita*.

Mamallan and Manavanman went to a pavilion in a silent corner of the campus. An old man lay on a cot. His beard, white as the *thumbai* flower, flowed to his naval; his hair was a shining white. It was none other than the famed Sanskrit scholar, Rudracharya.

"Pallava king, I am too weak to rise and greet you. Forgive me," Rudracharya said. "You are leaving on Vijayadashami, right?"

"Everything is ready for our departure," Mamallan replied.

"Lord, the planetary alignment on this Vijayadashami happens only once in a thousand years. You will return victorious." Rudrarcharya paused. "I will not be lucky enough to see it … but even after I die, I will not forget Kanchi. Mamallan, when you return from Vatapi, your father and I will stand above this school and welcome you with a shower of divine *parijatham*."

Mamallan's eyes overflowed with tears.

Navukkarasar

AT THE SHAIVA *matham* near the Ekambar Temple, Navukkarasar and Aayanar sat together, talking.

"Sculptor, ten years back, your daughter danced here ..."

"Your warning that day came true." Tears streamed from Aayanar's eyes. "Swami, how she has suffered! When Sivagami was an infant, her mother died. Until she was eighteen, I guarded her as my treasure. We were not apart for even one day. I have now been separated from my child for nine years. Sir, why does God, the ocean of compassion, make innocent people suffer?"

"Aayanar, mortals cannot read the secrets in God's heart. Let me tell you a truth—joy and sorrow are because of worldly desire. Once we get rid of desire, only the bliss of God's grace remains."

Aayanar sobbed, "Swami, whenever I pray, I can only think of my daughter as a prisoner in a distant land. I can only pray, 'Shiva, be compassionate—let me see Sivagami before I die.'"

The saint consoled him: "Mamallan has gathered a huge army. By God's grace, Sivagami will come back. Until then, why don't you stay here with me? Why live by yourself in the forest?"

"Revered sir, forgive me. I am going to Vatapi with the Pallava army..."

Navukkarasar was surprised. "Aayanar, do you want to see the horror of war? Do you want to see corpses cut and pierced, without hands and legs and heads?"

Aayanar was embarrassed. "I am going to see my daughter and bring her back."

General Paranjothi came in with his mother, Vadivazlagi, his wife, Umayaal, and Doctor Sivanesan.

The doctor said, "Swami, I came to say goodbye. I am going north to Vatapi."

"What! It looks like there will be no one left in Kanchi … why are you going, doctor?"

"I am going as the head of the army's medical team. The wicked Chalukyas use knives and swords dipped in poison. You know about the poisoned dagger which killed Emperor Mahendran. While I was treating the emperor, I found the antidote for that poison. And so, the general has ordered me to accompany the army." Sivanesan looked proudly at Paranjothi.

Navukkarasar stared at Paranjothi. "Is this the famous general? His face shows his *sattva guna*. He is devoted to Lord Shiva. Why is he involved in this murderous expedition?"

His amused listeners smiled among themselves.

Doctor Sivanesan said, "Swami, I sent him to Kanchi twelve years ago to join your *matham* and study Tamil. Fate brought him here. It is now dragging me to the battlefield with him."

Navukkarasar stared at Paranjothi. "He is a man who will change fate itself."

Paranjothi touched Navukkarasar's feet. "Gurudeva, I will take your words as a blessing."

Vadivazlagi stood with folded hands. "Swami, please bless Umayaal to have a child."

Navukkarasar looked at Paranjothi and Umayaal with a radiant face. "A great soul who will be celebrated in stories and poems will be born to them as their son."

Mamallan's Fear

MAMALLAN AND MANAVANMAN sat on a marble bench on the palace terrace, under a sky embedded with diamond-like stars. An unnatural silence lay over Kanchi.

Mamallan sighed. "This great city sleeps peacefully tonight. Tomorrow, at this time, there will be a great commotion as the soldiers prepare to leave. Ah, nobody will sleep tomorrow night."

Manavanman said, "Rudracharya said that two princes would help you capture Vatapi ..."

Mamallan laughed. "My friend, you are one of them. You will stay in Kanchi and help me ..." He went on. "My beloved friend, what if you die on the battlefield? The Lankan kingdom will permanently belong to the man who took it from you. Princes must give importance to the continuity of their lineage. I have a son to continue the Pallava dynasty. You do not."

Manavanman smiled. "I will go and fight with my wife, Sujatha, for not giving me a son. Because of that, I cannot take part in the Battle of Vatapi which will go down in the annals of history."

"My friend, after I leave for Vatapi, you can fight with your wife daily at leisure."

Manavanman said, "Lord, it is past midnight. You must sleep for a while at least."

"I have not slept for twelve years. When that sculptor's daughter lived nearby in the forest, she robbed me of my sleep. Now, when she is a thousand miles away, she still keeps me awake ..." Mamallan raised his eyes to the sky. "Sivagami, do you sit alone all night in that house in Vatapi and curse me? I have not forgotten my promise to you. You have been patient for so long: just be patient a little longer."

The Lankan prince was frightened by Mamallan's wild speech. "My king, calm down!"

"I made a mistake ten years ago. When the general and I went to Vatapi, Sivagami refused to come with us, saying that she had taken an oath. The general advised me to ignore her angry words and carry her away. If only I had listened to him!" Mamallan paused. "I eagerly waited for the day when I would march on Vatapi. But now, as the day comes, I am afraid …"

Manavanman was surprised. "I do not believe you are afraid."

"I am not afraid of the battle. I am frightened of what happens after I kill Pulikesi and capture Vatapi. Sivagami has waited ten years, keeping faith in our love—but I am married and the father of two children. How do I look her in the face? What do I tell her? When I think of this, I am frightened. It would be better to die on the battlefield!"

Manavanman's voice shook. "If you die on the battlefield, what will happen to me? What will happen to your promise to seat me on the Lankan throne?"

Ekambar Street

PEOPLE CROWDED THE Ekambar Temple's entrance. The sanctuary was brilliantly lit with silver lamps.

Emperor Mamallan stood majestically in front, wearing the six-hundred-year-old crown of his ancestors. General Paranjothi and Prince Manavanman stood on either side of him, followed by other noblemen and relatives. Further back, Prime Minister Sarangadevan, Chief Minister Ranadheeran and other ministers and district leaders were crowded together.

On the other side stood the beautiful women. In front was Bhuvanamahadevi, her face calm and devout. Beside her stood Vanamadevi, Mamallan's wife and daughter of the Pandyan king.

Standing with her was Princess Kundavi, whose black eyes darted here and there.

The temple bells clanged; the drums beat an excited tattoo; the sound of conches, horns, *melams* and cymbals filled the air. As the *aarti* was performed for Lord Ekambar, loud shouts of, 'Hara hara Mahadeva!' and, 'Nama Parvathi Pathayae!' rose from the devotees.

The priest carried the plate of *vibhuti* from the sanctum. He stopped before the emperor and said loudly, "May you triumph by the grace of the Three-eyed Lord who burnt the Tripuras with a smile. May you kill Pulikesi, destroy Vatapi and come back victorious!"

As Mamallan devoutly applied the *vibhuti* on his forehead, a lamp in the sanctuary suddenly flared into dazzling light. A spark flew from the wick and sizzled to the ground. It flared for a second and died out. Everyone there took this to be a good omen.

The news that Lord Ekambar had approved of the Pallava emperor's campaign spread to the waiting crowds. Rousing shouts of, 'Hara hara Mahadeva!' filled the streets.

Kannapiran, Emperor Mamallan's charioteer, did not join in the cheers.

Kannan's Anxiety

KANNAPIRAN TOOK BHUVANAMAHADEVI and the others from the temple to the palace and went home. He saw his ten-year-old son whirling a sword. Kamali sat watching her son playing at war.

Kannapiran said angrily, "Murugayya, stop this game! Why does a charioteer's son need a sword? If you want, play with the horses' whip."

Stunned by his father's angry voice, the boy dropped the sword, ran to Kamali and sobbed.

Kamali was shocked. "What is wrong with you, Kanna? Why are you making the child cry? You are leaving for the battlefield tomorrow. God knows when you will return ..."

"Kamali, the emperor has ordered me to stay in Kanchi."

Kamali's face fell. "Why is the emperor cheating you like this? I heard that he is even taking the broken-legged Aayanar to the battlefield."

"If Manavanman dies on the battlefield, it will be the end of the Lankan dynasty: he does not have an heir. And so, the emperor has commanded him to stay behind—and I am to stay for him."

"Do not worry, Kanna. You and the Lankan prince can soon leave for the battlefield. The Lankan princess is to have a child soon."

Kannapiran folded his hands and turned in the direction of the temple. "Lord Ekambar, please let the Lankan princess's baby be a boy."

Vanamadevi

THE CITIZENS OF Kanchi turned that night into day. The streetlights blazed. Elephant brigades, cavalry, infantry and horse-drawn chariots stood in formation, ready to march at daybreak. Banana plants, bunches of tender coconuts, ornamental arches and clusters of tender coconut flowers hung everywhere. The nandi flag flew from the top of every house.

The women painted colourful *kolams* on the thresholds, depicting armed soldiers on elephants and horses, along with war scenes from the *Ramayana* and the *Mahabharata*.

There was great excitement in the palace. The entrance and the courtyard were decorated with arches and banana plants. Swords and spears were rubbed with ghee until they dazzled the eye with their brilliance. Saddles for horses and elephants were polished to a shine.

In the palace's women's quarters, the maids went about their tasks quietly and spoke in whispers. Everyone knew that the emperor was there to say goodbye to his queen.

The emperor sat on an ivory bed, ornamented with a blue silk canopy and strings of pearls. His queen stood respectfully before him. Through the open door to the next room, Mahendran and Kundavi could be seen sleeping peacefully on golden beds.

It was nine years since Vanamadevi, the Pandyan princess, had married Mamallan and become the Pallava queen. She was the embodiment of beauty. Her red-lotus-like complexion delighted the eye. Her eyes were like the black beetles which hover over the lotus.

"*Devi*, I go to war at sunrise tomorrow. I may not return … you must raise Mahendran and Kundavi carefully. You must guard the Pallava throne until Mahendran comes of age."

At this, Vanamadevi sat at Mamallan's feet and wept.

Mamallan said, "*Devi*, you are from the brave Pandyan dynasty—are you reluctant to send your husband to war?"

Vanamadevi looked up at him. "Lord, the astrologers in Madurai emphasised the power of my *mangalsutra*. There is no doubt that you will destroy Vatapi and come back a hero."

"Then why are you crying? Be frank."

"Swami, the astrologers also predicted that I will die a *sumangali*, with the *mangalsutra* around my neck and vermillion on my forehead. I wept at the thought that I might die before seeing your triumphant return to this city."

Mamallan seated her beside him and wiped her tears. "*Devi*, I will also make a prediction: I will kill Pulikesi, destroy Vatapi and come back with the garland of victory. I will ride in a triumphant procession through the streets of Kanchi in a golden chariot, drawn by white horses. You will be by my side. Mahendran will be seated on your lap and Kundavi on mine."

"Lord, I will be satisfied just to see you return victorious. I will make way for the person who has the rightful claim to sit by your side. I will stay in this palace if you let me. If not, I will go back to Madurai."

Mamallan was stunned. "You have said nothing in our nine years of marriage ..."

"Must I say it with my own tongue? You are going to free Sculptor Aayanar's daughter …"

"Ah, how long have you known? How did you know?"

"I have known for years. When I came to this palace nine years ago, everyone looked at me with pity. Slowly, I realised that there was another woman in your heart …"

"You knew that I married you, with the fire as my witness, after giving my heart to another woman. But you have not questioned or criticised me even once in nine years. *Devi*, I have heard of many virtuous women in stories and poems—but none can match you!"

"Swami, you married me for the good of the Pallava kingdom—you needed alliances with the southern kings to help you fight Pulikesi and your father wanted it. I learnt all this within a few days of coming to this palace ..."

Yet you never asked me about this even once! How deep a woman's heart is! Mamallan examined his wife's face and saw only endless trust, calm, love and determination.

Vanamadevi looked at Mamallan with tear-filled eyes. "Swami, I never worried about your reason for marrying me. I have lived happily in your palace for nine years. But others must also have the chance to be happy, isn't it? On the day you return to Kanchi, I will give up the Pallavas' ancient throne and this ivory bed."

War Drums

MAMALLAN'S VOICE SHOOK. "Light of the Pandyan dynasty, you are not only my wife—you are also the mother of the crown prince who will ascend the throne after me. As soon as you came to Kanchi, the years of drought ended; you brought the rain. For that, my subjects proudly call you Vanamadevi. No one in the world has the right to remove you from the Pallava throne ..."

Vanamadevi interrupted him: "Swami, have I the right only to the Pallava throne? Is there no room for me in your heart?"

Mamallan was shocked. He gathered himself and looked lovingly at her. "Ah, you have lived with me for nine years with this question in your heart! Any ordinary woman would have made her husband's life a living hell with hundreds of questions daily."

"Lord, in that case, is what I heard false?" Vanamadevi asked eagerly.

"*Devi*, what you heard is true, but it belongs to my past." Mamallan looked within himself. He then sighed deeply and said, "Yes, it is a faded, old dream. When I was young and carefree, I fell in love with a sculptor's daughter. I was ready to sacrifice my life and soul and this Pallava kingdom for her. But one day, she let her anger overpower her love. I travelled a thousand miles to bring her back, but she stubbornly refused to come with me. On that day, I stopped loving her. I cannot forget her because I have not kept my promise to her. Sivagami's ghost haunts me and keeps me awake at night. On the day I defeat Vatapi, free her and give her to her father, that wretch's ghost will stop haunting me. I will uproot the very thought of her from my heart. There will be room in my heart only for you, our precious children and the Pallava kingdom. Do you believe me?"

Vanamadevi stood and touched her husband's feet. "Lord, I will never doubt you."

Mamallan compared Sivagami's love, which was filled with anger and doubt, with Vanamadevi's pure love. "It is good that we discussed this now. You have lifted a great burden from me. In my absence, the council of ministers will consult you on important matters."

Vanamadevi said eagerly, "Lord, I will consider it a privilege to help you in any way."

A great roar shook the palace walls and engulfed the bedroom, making one's hair stand on end.

Mamallan jumped up. "Ah, it is midnight. I hear the war drums!"

The drumbeats brought to his mind images of the dreadful battlefield. War elephants trumpeted savagely and crashed against each other. Speeding chariots made the earth tremble as they collided and shattered. Horses flew like the wind and met in the middle of the battlefield. Eyes were blinded by the lightning flashes of spears. Soldiers cut and slashed with their swords. Dead elephants, horses and headless and limbless human corpses floated on a river of blood. In the middle of this cruel scene, Mamallan saw a woman's furious face—it was Sivagami.

The Army Marches

THE NEXT DAY was Vijayadashami. The rising sun seemed to stop in its tracks at the sight of Kanchi. Emperor Mamallan stood at the Pallava palace's entrance, performing the *yatra dhanam*, *graha preeti* and other rites prescribed for a voyage. Rudracharya and other elders blessed him. Saying goodbye to his mother, Bhuvanamahadevi, and his queen, Vanamadevi, he climbed on the royal elephant and left for the battlefield. War drums beat a loud tattoo.

The ranks of elephants, horses and chariots moved towards the fort's northern gate. Women stood on the terraces and showered flowers on the emperor, shouting, 'May you be victorious!'

The emperor's martial procession reached the fort's northern entrance in forty-five minutes. A little distance from the open gates, a sea of soldiers stretched as far as the eye could see.

On the other side of the moat, Mamallan said goodbye to his beloved children. His eyes filled with tears as he lifted and hugged Mahendran and Kundavi. *Will I ever see these children again?* He put them down and turned to Manavanman. "My dear friend, I leave these children, their mother and the Pallava kingdom in your care. Guard them until I return. On Paranjothi's advice, I am leaving behind a part of our army. If there is any threat to the Pallava kingdom, use it."

Manavanman said, "Lord, do not worry about things here."

"I was worried that you would stubbornly insist on coming with me at the last minute. This is the beauty of real friendship!" Mamallan said with a happy heart.

He climbed his war elephant and the immense army surged forward like a sea. The storm of dust raised by it hid the sky and the earth. Manavanman, Mahendran and Kundavi stood staring after them until the army was lost in that dust storm.

Friends

THE FULL MOON'S milky light made the earth a beautiful dream world. The North Pennai shone like molten silver as it splashed sweetly on its way. White sand stretched on both sides of the river. A great silence enveloped the earth. One could lose oneself in the bliss of nature's beauty.

But now there was a great commotion as countless rows of elephants, horses, chariots and carts crossed the river. The elephants' gold headplates and the silver knobs on their tusks, the horses' ornamental saddles and the gold-plated chariots glittered in the moonlight.

On the opposite bank, the infantry stretched as far as the eye could see. Sharp spears glinted like flashes of lightning, blinding the eye. Thousands of nandi flags fluttered in the breeze.

A single tent stood a short distance away from the riverbank. Emperor Mamallan, General Paranjothi, King Adityavarman of Vengi and Spy Chief Shatrughan were seated on the rich carpet spread on the grass. A dozen armed soldiers stood guard within calling distance.

Adityavarman was Mamallan's distant cousin. His dynasty ruled the northern Vengi kingdom as independent chieftains. When Pulikesi invaded the Pallava kingdom, his brother, Vishnuvardhan, defeated the ancient Vengi dynasty and crowned himself king of Vengi. Adityavarman was responsible for Vishnuvardhan's later defeat and death. When Pulikesi invaded Vengi a few years later, Adityavarman retreated south with his small army and waited for his opportunity. When Mamallan marched on Vatapi, Adityavarman joined him.

Paranjothi was narrating the story of his capture by Pulikesi's forces twelve years ago and Mahendran Pallava following him in disguise to the North Pennai and releasing him.

Adityavarman was amazed. "How I wish I had met Emperor Mahendran!"

Mamallan said, "It is not because he is my father that I say this: it was a privilege to know him. He took me on a three-year journey through the south. We passed the time happily, sitting in the open on moonlit nights like this. He always brought his *veena* with him on his travels. When he played, it seemed as if the earth and the sky stood still to listen."

"*Anna*, stop! If you talk like this, I wonder, why choose war and bloodshed? Why not learn the *veena* and live happily?" Adityavarman said.

Mamallan laughed. "My father said, 'If kings gave up their hunger for land, the world would be a paradise. There should be no war. Smiths should make only plows and chisels.' But he changed his mind when the Chalukyas invaded the Pallava kingdom." Mamallan smiled at Paranjothi. "And it was a young boy who threw his spear at a mad elephant who captured his heart."

"You are talking about the day our general arrived in Kanchi, right?" Adityavarman said.

"My father has never loved anyone the way he loved Paranjothi," Mamallan declared. "Sometimes I was jealous of him. I was even afraid that my father would crown him emperor instead of me. I was prepared for that too: even now, if the general agrees …"

Paranjothi cut in: "Lord, why do I need a kingdom? I was born in a poor family in a village. I promised my mother to become a scholar and came to Kanchi. Even after twelve years, I am ignorant. Once this war is over, I am going to keep my promise. If you must give the throne to someone, give it to that man from Lanka who is waiting."

Mamallan signalled Adityavarman and Shatrughan with his eyes, and they smiled in understanding. Mamallan knew that his affection for Manavanman bothered Paranjothi. This was the main reason for him to insist on Manavanman staying in Kanchi. "Nonsense! Are you asking me to give Mahendran Pallava's kingdom to that fool? I ordered him to stay behind, but he is on his way here. I am furious with him. I think I will chase him back to Lanka. What do you say, general?"

Paranjothi did not personally hate Manavanman. He was unhappy only because Mamallan was so fond of the prince. Now the general supported Manavanman. "Manavanam trained the elephant brigade. That is why it is not fair to send him back. Won't he want to lead the elephants to battle?"

"What new training has the Lankan prince given the elephants?" Adityavarman asked.

Mamallan explained, "Elephants were used to ram fort gates and break them. Mahendran Pallava made sure that this tactic did not work during the siege of Kanchi. We embedded spear points in the gates—the elephants went mad and stampeded after butting the gates once. Now Manavarman has trained our elephants to shatter the gates with iron rods, break the fort walls with crowbars and throw flaming torches into the fort."

The peepal tree near them rustled loudly. Thousands of birds which had settled in it for the night flapped their wings and circled the tree before going back to the branches with loud cries.

Shatrughan stared at the tree. He clapped and one of the guards came running. "Someone is climbing down the peepal tree. Catch him and bring him here."

The guard brought back a man and bowed. "Lord, here is the Vatapi spy."

Mamallan and Paranjothi burst out laughing—it was Gundodharan.

Paranjothi asked, "Why did you say that you were a Vatapi spy, Gundodharan?"

"General, I meant, 'The spy coming from Vatapi.' At once those soldiers grabbed me and dragged me here. Ah, I am still aching from their grip!" Gundodharan complained.

"Yes, but what were you doing on that tree? How long were you there?" the emperor asked.

"Lord, I came here last night. I woke up in the morning to find our army here. I climbed the tree, estimated our army's strength and was judging whether it is enough to defeat Pulikesi."

"What do you think? Is this army enough?" Mamallan asked.

"Lord, I have no doubt about that at all. My only worry is that, by the time we reach Vatapi, Emperor Pulikesi may not have returned from the Ajanta Hills."

Pulikesi's Art Infatuation

GUNDODHARAN'S LISTENERS ERUPTED with surprised questions: "Really? Pulikesi is not in Vatapi?"

"Quiet, everyone. Gundodharan, describe your journey from the beginning," Mamallan ordered.

Gundodharan saluted the emperor. "Lord, Emperor Pulikesi has gone to Ajanta with a traveller from China. I can hardly get my tongue around his name … 'Hiuen Tsang.' This man praised Emperor Harshavardhan. Pulikesi wants to show that he is as good as Emperor Harsha, and so he has personally taken the traveller to see the Ajanta paintings. Lord, Pulikesi is now infatuated with art. He has made Mamallapuram-like sculpture from the rocks in Vatapi. I saw some of our sculptors, who were captured without being dismembered, working on this. Listen to this joke: when Pulikesi showed Huien Tsang these sculptures, Pulikesi said, 'It was only after seeing this that Mahendran Pallava started work on Mamallapuram. I set him a good example.' My blood boiled to hear this! Vatapi is not preparing for war. It seems that they never expected our invasion this year. Their army is split between the Narmada in the north and Vengi in the east."

Mamallan said, "Even we did not expect our scheme to work out so well!"

Adityavarman asked, "I do not understand what you are talking about. What scheme is this?"

Mamallan said, "You will understand how well Mahendran Pallava has trained us. Over the past nine years, as Paranjothi and I prepared for war, Shatrughan and his spies worked cleverly. Some of our spies sold our war secrets to the Chalukyas. At first, we sold them true facts … and so Pulikesi began to trust these men. Three years ago, they said, 'The Pallava army will invade Vatapi this year.' Believing this, Pulikesi prepared for war, but he was disappointed. When this happened continuously for three years, Pulikesi rejected all the old spies. This year, the new spies said that the Pallava army was preparing to secure the Lankan throne for Manavanman and had no intention of marching on Vatapi. Pulikesi believed this. He divided his force into two and sent them to the Narmada and to Vengi. Gundodharan now says that Pulikesi has gone to Ajanta. Shatrughan's scheme has succeeded."

"It looks like the Lankan prince has helped us in this too. It is only because Manavanman came to Kanchi that Shatrughan was able to mislead Pulikesi," Adityavarman said.

Mamallan's voice was stern. "However much Manavanman may have helped us, I will never forgive him if he is martyred on the battlefield—the Lankan royal dynasty will end."

Adityavarman said, "But Manavanman's wife had a baby boy five days after we marched …"

The others burst out laughing as Mamallan said, "Even Shatrughan did not tell me this …"

Gundodharan said, "Lord, when I was on the peepal tree, I saw a great cloud of dust in the south. It is the Lankan prince rushing here."

"Oh, is he already here?" Mamallan's face was radiant in the moonlight. He turned to Paranjothi. "General, shall I forgive Manavanman and let him come with us?"

"Yes, lord. We might as well take him with us," Paranjothi said reluctantly.

"In that case, the three of you cross the river and prepare for our camp tonight. Gundodharan and I will wait here for Manavanman," Mamallan said. After the others left by boat, Mamallan looked questioningly at Gundodharan.

Gundodharan said, "My king, I met Aayanar's daughter in Vatapi. She is well. She waits day and night for our arrival."

"That wretch is well. It is I who have lost my happiness and my peace," Mamallan murmured.

The *Parijatham* Blooms

SIVAGAMI WAS IN good physical health—but her mind was without a moment's peace.

In her first year in Vatapi, Naganandhi told her that *parijatham* trees bloomed in Ajanta in August and September, spreading their fragrance far. Sivagami asked for a plant. The monk brought her a *parijatham* sapling from the Ajanta Hills. Sivagami planted it by the well in her courtyard and raised it with water and tears.

Sivagami celebrated the plant's first green sprouts. When the first bud appeared and bloomed, she forgot her sorrow and drifted on an ocean of joy. She rejoiced over the beautiful petals and coral-red stems. As the soft petals shrivelled and fell, her heart too dried.

Sivagami began to measure the years and seasons with the tree. When the winter chill penetrated to men's bones, the *parijatham*'s leaves dried and fell. In early summer, the tree sprouted new leaves. As summer peaked, the leaves matured and buds appeared. From mid-August to September, clusters of flowers hid the bright green leaves. Sivagami sat on the courtyard steps and stared at the tree for hours. She remembered that during *Navratri*, the temple deities in Tamil Nadu wore skirts of *parijatham* blossoms. *It is one Vijayadashami since I came to Vatapi.* By this calculation, it was now nine years since Sivagami had come to Vatapi.

The Chinese Traveller

SIVAGAMI'S SHAME AT being made to dance at the crossroads dimmed with time. The Tamil captives found suitable occupations and started families. Some of them visited her now and then. She saw that there was no anger or malice in their hearts. *I swore my oath out of anger and ignorance. I sent Mamallan away through my foolishness.*

But, in tune with a woman's nature, she continued to blame Mamallan. *I was just an ignorant girl. Why didn't he carry me away as General Paranjothi advised?*

As the years passed, her confidence in Mamallan weakened. She sometimes felt like sending him a message: *My oath was a mistake ... ignore it. Just come and take me with you.* Naganandhi's mocking words stopped her from doing this.

When Sivagami threw the knife at his back, that cunning pretender had said, 'What have you done? I thought of sending you with them!' Sivagami's anger evaporated, and she pitied the wounded monk.

Naganandhi took full advantage of her sympathy. He assured her that he would personally escort her to Kanchi. When Sivagami told him about her oath, Naganandhi mocked, "What an impossible oath!"

Sivagami defiantly said, "Just see whether it is fulfilled or not!"

Living among strangers in a distant land, caught in a prison of her own making, Sivagami found comfort in the well-travelled, learned monk's company.

He sometimes tempted her: "If you do not want to go back to Kanchi, don't. I will take you to Ajanta. You can see for yourself and learn the secret formula your father longs for."

"I will not leave Vatapi before my oath is fulfilled," Sivagami insisted.

Three years ago, Sivagami had been overjoyed to hear rumours of a Pallava invasion. It turned out to be a lie. When Naganandhi mocked her for it, she hid her feelings and defended Mamallan. "Patience, revered sir, patience! If not this year, then the next," she said. Three years had passed since her proud declaration. Nine years had passed since she came to Vatapi. *How many more years can I fool myself and endure this sad life? Enough! The well by the parijatham tree calls out to me: 'Come. Come and find sanctuary in me!'*

It was then that Naganandhi brought the Chinese traveller to meet her. Hiuen Tsang, a world-wide traveller, was in Bharat to visit its three greatest kingdoms. He came to Vatapi after visiting Harshavardhan's kingdom. He planned to visit Ajanta and go on to the Pallava kingdom.

Knowing this, Naganandhi brought him saying, "The daughter of the famous Pallava sculptor lives here. She is an expert Bharatanatyam dancer."

Sivagami lost herself in Hiuen Tsang's tales of his travels. He was amazed to hear that Sivagami's father had carved statues of her dance postures. He insisted on seeing some of these poses. After nine years, Sivagami was once again enthusiastic about dance. She demonstrated some dance postures and *abhinaya* for Hiuen Tsang who watched in delight. Naganandhi was in bliss.

The monk explained how Sivagami had come to Vatapi and the details of her oath. "I offered to take her back to Kanchi with the emperor's permission, but she refused. I am pained to see her talent wasted in this house. I sometimes feel like burning down Vatapi myself to set her free."

Hiuen Tsang closed his ears and exclaimed, "By the grace of Buddha, that will never happen!" He spoke about the greatness of *jeevakarunyam* and the evils of war. He narrated the story of Buddha stopping a yagna to save the sacrificial goat.

Sivagami interrupted him: "Sir, you have no idea of the Chalukyas' atrocities in Tamil Nadu."

Hiuen Tsang replied, "My dear lady, war makes all men animals. The Pallavas are waging war in revenge for the Chalukyan invasion. The Chalukyas will again wage war on Kanchi in revenge. Evil will keep growing like a tree from a seed and a seed from a tree. Someone must forgive and forget. Only then will the world prosper. My dear lady, no good will come from your oath. How many thousands of houses there are in Vatapi! How many of the people are old or children or helpless women like you? If the city is burned, how many innocent people will suffer!"

Sivagami was confused by his words.

Using this opportunity, Naganandhi said, "Sivagami, what is the point of revenge? Isn't nine years long enough for your oath? In two days, I am going to Ajanta with this man and the Vatapi emperor. A great art festival is to be held there. Come with us. You will see wonders there which you will find nowhere else in this world."

Sivagami's artistic soul was tempted to say, "Yes, sir, I will come." But a voice whispered in her heart, "Sivagami, what a betrayal! After refusing to go with Mamallan, you want to go with this Buddhist monk? What if Mamallan comes here when you are in Ajanta? His heart will break."

Sivagami said, "Monk, thank you for your concern. I agree with this great man from China—I will not ask for my oath to be fulfilled. Let Vatapi and its people prosper. Let no harm come to them through me. But I will spend my life in this house. I will not leave this city for any reason."

The Coral Merchant

AFTER NAGANANDHI AND Hiuen Tsang left, Sivagami was lost in her memories. It seemed like yesterday that the Thiruparkadal Lake breached its banks. *I survived that great flood only to die by jumping into a well in a courtyard. What will I think when I am struggling for breath? Will I remember the raft overturning at Mandagapattu and Mamallan saving me?*

A loud cry came from the street: "Corals! Corals for sale!"

Sivagami broke into goosebumps. *I have heard this voice before!*

The coral merchant came into the house and asked, "Lady, do you want coral? Beautiful coral which puts even Ajanta's colours to shame?"

At the mention of Ajanta, the startled Sivagami looked closely at the man's mature face with its thick beard and mustache. *Ah, the devotion and affection in these eyes ...*

"Lady, don't you recognise me?" the merchant asked as he sat and opened his bundle.

Unable to believe her eyes and ears, Sivagami said, "Gundodharan, is it you? Years have passed since you promised to return." Sivagami was a little harsh.

"Lady, what is the use of coming back empty-handed? We must be ready to fulfill your oath."

"Stupid oath! I have had my fill of oaths, Gundodharan. I have given up the oath I swore."

"Do not say that, lady. Your oath is Tamil Nadu's oath. We are all obliged to fulfill it. Lady, I come to you as Hanuman went to Sita as a messenger. Lord Rama is coming with a huge army."

Sivagami trembled. *Is Mamallan coming for me after nine years? Will I cheat the well which is waiting to swallow me?*

"Lady, a Pallava army, the likes of which has never before been seen in the south, is ready. It is led by Emperor Mamallan and General Paranjothi."

Sivagami was startled. "Emperor Mamallan?"

"Mamallan is now the Pallava emperor. It has been many years since Mahendran Pallava reached Kailash."

Sivagami wept. She had been angry with Mahendran Pallava, but the love and devotion she had for him since her childhood was not dead. She stopped sobbing. "Gundodharan, I beg you, I cannot stay in this city for another instant. Take me with you. This is the right time. Pulikesi and the false monk are leaving for Ajanta in two days. There is not much security at the house. We can escape easily. If you do not want to take me with you, there is a well in the courtyard. Be merciful and throw me into it before you go …" She burst into sobs again.

Mahendran Said It

GUNDODHARAN WAITED FOR Sivagami to recover. "Lady, there is a Tamil proverb which says, 'When you have the patience to cook, have the patience to wait for the food to cool.' After being patient for so many years, will you give up just on the threshold of success?"

Sivagami was furious. "Gundodharan, are you preaching about patience to someone who has lived for nine years in an enemy city, helpless and friendless?"

"Lady, I am telling you that I am helpless. When Hanuman met

Sita in the Ashoka Garden, he told her that he would take her safely to Rama. But Sita refused to go with Hanuman …"

"Gundodharan, why are you comparing me with Sita? I am a poor sculptor's daughter …"

"Lady, I am no Hanuman, either. Maybe I resemble him a little in appearance … but I do not have the strength to burn down Vatapi single-handedly and take you away. What can I do?"

"You are talking about my wretched oath again! Didn't I tell you that I have given it up? Am I not asking you to take me with you?"

"Mamallan stood in this same spot and urged you to come with him. You stubbornly said, 'Fulfill my oath and take me.' Now Mamallan is coming to fulfill your oath. Lady, the Pallava army marches tomorrow. If everything goes as planned, our army will besiege Vatapi Fort a month from today. You will see your oath fulfilled before your eyes. Be patient and brave …"

"Gundodharan, I do not want to be the cause of another terrible war. I was angry at that time, and so I swore that foolish oath. How many men will die! How many innocent people will suffer! Can we predict victory or defeat? That is why I am asking you to take me with you."

Gundodharan was stunned. "Lady, even if you change your mind, Mamallan cannot stop the invasion. He must fulfill Mahendran Pallava's dying wish."

"Oh, and what was Mahendran Pallava's wish?"

"He commanded that your oath must be fulfilled at any cost. He insisted that only if Mamallan burned Vatapi and brought you back would the Pallavas' honour be redeemed."

"How compassionate the emperor was! How mistaken I have been about him!" Sivagami wept. She asked Gundodharan about Mahendran's death and the happenings at Kanchi over the past nine years. Gundodharan told her everything except one thing: he did not dare tell her that.

When it was time for Gundodharan to leave, Sivagami said longingly, "My dear fellow, will Mamallan really come—or are you just fooling me?"

"He will definitely come, lady. He will come to reclaim the Pallavas' honour."

"He values the Pallavas' honour more than anything. That is why he is coming after so many years. If he came out of love for me, he would have come earlier."

"Lady, didn't Mamallan come here in disguise to show that his love for you meant more to him than the Pallavas' honour? Didn't he beg you to come with him?"

"I made a great mistake then. Tell Mamallan that I have been punished enough—I have stayed alive all these years just to see him again and ask for his forgiveness."

Luckily, Sivagami did not know the other cruel punishment waiting for her.

Gundodharan hesitated.

Sivagami reassured him: "Do you have anything else to say? Do not hesitate."

"Lady, do not be angry ... they say that women cannot keep secrets. No one must hear about my visit or Mamallan's invasion."

Sivagami smiled sadly. "Gundodharan, would I betray Mamallan to these evil wretches? The only person I know here is Naganandhi ... and he is going to Ajanta. So you can go back in peace." She paused. "Gundodharan, you compared yourself to Hanuman. Be worthy of his name—stay with Mamallan and guard him. These wretches have poison in their hearts and kill with poisoned daggers. Aiyo, must my stubborn foolishness again lead him into danger!"

It was now clear to Gundodharan why Sivagami did not want war. *She is afraid that Mamallan may risk his life on the battlefield.* His respect for her increased.

The Birth of Neelakesi

SIVAGAMI'S ANXIETY GREW, and time passed slowly. She worried over Gundodharan's visit again and again. *Did I speak to him properly? What will he tell Mamallan?*

Three days after Gundodharan's visit, Emperor Pulikesi left for the Ajanta art festival. Sivagami watched the procession through her windows. Pulikesi rode majestically on the royal elephant. Naganandhi and Hiuen Tsang followed in palanquins. Pulikesi's three young sons sat in a golden chariot. The emperor's advisors, ministers, chieftains and army commanders proudly went by in various vehicles. The people's cheers and the sound of musical instruments was deafening.

Sivagami was reminded of Mahendran Pallava leaving Kanchi for Mamallapuram. The angry Sivagami consoled herself. *Pulikesi's pride will soon be humbled. Mamallan will arrive before these men come back from Ajanta. What a shock they will get when they hear the news! Maybe I was wrong to tell Gundodharan that I do not want war.*

There was another reason for Sivagami's growing anger. Naganandhi had not come to see her before he left on his voyage. *What arrogance!*

She was amazed when the monk came to her house that evening. "Swami, I thought you were on your way to Ajanta!"

"I am going, Sivagami. I will be at the emperor's camp tonight. I have important work in Ajanta which concerns you, and I hurried back to tell you about it." Without giving her time to reply, he went on. "Did you see the emperor's procession this afternoon?"

"Oh, yes. It reminded me of Mahendran Pallava leaving Kanchi for Mamallapuram. It looks like Emperor Pulikesi will put Mahendran to shame!"

"The Vatapi emperor is not the old, bloodthirsty Pulikesi. He is now infatuated with art."

"In that case, the Ajanta festival will be magnificent."

The monk said proudly, "No doubt about that. Ajanta's monks have prepared a grand welcome for Pulikesi. Famous Buddhist *acharyas* from Nalanda and the Nagarjuna Hills have arrived there. The Ajanta *sangha* gave Pulikesi sanctuary when he was a boy. But, for many years, the Jain monks insisted that all royal aid should go only to Jain temples. The emperor has now changed his mind: any faith which fosters art receives aid from the treasury. Because of this, the Chalukyan kingdom has overtaken Kannauj and Kanchi to become Bharat's greatest in art." He paused. "Sivagami, do you know who made the bloodthirsty, war-crazy Pulikesi an art lover?"

"Can there be any doubt, swami? It is the great art expert and devotee, Naganandhi!"

Naganandhi's features had become refined over the past nine years. He no longer looked cruel. His handsome face glowed at Sivagami's reply. He looked at her lovingly. "Goddess of Art, you are right. But who made me mad about art? Can you tell me?"

"How would I know, swami?" *He is referring to me.*

"I have never told you until now. There are many beautiful paintings on the walls of the Ajanta caves. One of these paintings shows a Bharatanatyam dancer. It is that painting which inspired my love for art. You must see that extraordinary painting someday …"

"I will not be lucky enough to see Ajanta's wonders in this lifetime."

"Do not say that. In a way, I am glad that you are not coming with us this time. If you had come, both of us would not have been satisfied. But things will change soon."

Sivagami felt a pang at these words. She stared at Naganandhi. "How will things change?"

"The time may soon come for you to leave this cage and soar singing into the sky." He paused. "Don't you believe that your oath will be fulfilled?"

Sivagami clenched her teeth. "It has been years since I lost hope." She was confused and frightened. *Does this wicked monk suspect anything? Has he caught Gundodharan?*

"Sivagami, you have lost hope. At the same time, you will not leave this city without your oath being fulfilled. Am I right?"

Sivagami replied without hesitation, "Yes, swami. You are right."

"Ahah, I will have to do what I told the Chinese yesterday: if Mamallan does not come to fulfill your oath, I will I do it. I will set fire to this city myself!"

"Why must you do something so cruel because of a madwoman's stubbornness?"

"Then you must give up your empty oath."

Sivagami tried to change the topic. "Swami, enough of talking about me. Tell me about yourself. Tell me about Ajanta."

"Yes, I came here to talk about myself. I will be reborn in Ajanta. When I return, I will no longer be a saffron-robed monk. I will come back dressed in cloth of gold as Maharaja Neelakesi."

The surprised Sivagami looked questioningly at him.

Heart's Fire

NAGANANDHI STARED AT Sivagami with his glowing, hypnotic snake's eyes. "Sivagami, if I could open my heart to you … if I could tear open this hard heart and show you the fire which burns in it day and night …" The monk loudly beat his chest. Suddenly, he drew the dagger tucked into his waistcloth and tried to pierce his chest with it.

Sivagami held his hand and stopped him. Nine years ago, when Sivagami had looked upon the monk as a father, she had sometimes touched his hand by chance. *What a hard body! It seems as if his body is not made of flesh, blood, skin and nerves … it is made entirely of bone.* Now she realised that the monk's body had become soft.

Naganandhi stared wide-eyed at Sivagami with the dagger in his hand. Then he came back to his senses and dropped the dagger. Sivagami let go of his hand.

"Sivagami, I lost my mind. Please tell me what I was saying before I drew the dagger."

"Swami, you said that you were renouncing your monk's vows. You said that you were going to become a king."

"Yes, Sivagami. Thirty-five years ago, I became a monk on the shore of the Waghora River. I am going to wash away my vows in the same river. I will get my release from the same guru who initiated me into the Buddhist *sangha*. Do you agree?"

Frightened and confused, Sivagami asked, "Swami, why should you renounce the Buddhist dharma you have followed for so many years? Won't the world mock you? Won't all the fasting and penance of these years be wasted? What will you gain from this?"

Sivagami's instinct warned her: *My questions are a mistake. I have fallen into his trap.*

Naganandhi laughed loudly. "I will tell you. I am giving up the vows I kept for thirty-five years for you, Sivagami. Only for you! At Ajanta, I will give up my vows in public according to the traditional doctrine and with my guru's permission. But I already violated my vows on the day I visited your father's home and saw you standing as a living statue among his sculpture. I have no regrets: I am ready to suffer ten thousand years in hell to live a single day with you. I am ready to forever lose my chance of *moksha* for the blessing of a single moment of your love ..."

Sivagami trembled in fear. What she had suspected in her heart for many years had now been proved. *But why did this deceitful monk keep this buried in his heart all these years? Why did he leave me free without troubling or forcing me in any way?*

"Sivagami, nine years ago, if you had gone with Mamallan, or if you had given me the chance of taking you to him, I might have kept my vows. You could have kept your happiness. But you wrongly suspected me and wounded me with a poisoned dagger. The knife did not kill me. If the same knife was to pierce me now, I would not survive even for half an hour. Sivagami, when you held my hand a short while ago, you were surprised that my hand, which was as hard as iron nine years ago, is now so soft. You are the cause of this change. I did severe penance to harden my body. I ate poisonous herbs to change my blood into poison. In those days, even if I was bitten by the most venomous snake, I would not be harmed—the snake would die. If my sweat mingled with the air, all the venomous snakes nearby would scatter. You have seen this yourself ..."

Both of them remembered a moonlit night in the open, ten years ago at Mandagapattu village.

Naganandhi went on. "For nine years, I have used herbal antidotes and other treatments to soften my body and neutralise the poison in my blood. Sivagami, I am now as good as a young, thirty-year old for married life. You cannot refuse me now .... you cannot make me suffer."

Sivagami's head was spinning. *Is this a dream? No, the monk is really staring at me with blood-shot eyes.* Her mind cleared. *There is only one way to escape from this cruel madman. I must somehow buy time. By God's grace, Mamallan will rescue me before this mad monk comes back from Ajanta. If not, I must use some other trick. And I have the well if nothing else works ...*

The monk stopped her before she could say anything. "Do not say anything now. I had planned to tell you all this only after I returned from Ajanta. But I thought it best to open my heart to you before I left. This will give you time to think it over and make a decision. I will not force you. I will never ask you to do anything you dislike. I will tell you what I have to say in one go. Be patient and hear me. You can give me your answer after I return from Ajanta."

Sivagami calmed down.

Naganandhi continued his story. "From the minute I saw you, you replaced my brother and the Chalukyan kingdom in my heart. Because of my mistakes, the Vatapi emperor's southern invasion failed. If you knew how I suffered, your tender heart would melt. On one hand, my heart burned with love for you. On the other hand, my body burned with jealousy towards your family, friends and loved ones. I wanted to kill your entire family, but I realised that I would lose your love if you came to know of this later. I had many opportunities to kill Mamallan and Mahendran Pallava, but the thought, *What if she comes to know?* stopped me. Paranjothi saved you from the elephant, and so I rescued him from jail and brought him to your house. But I could not bear to see you thanking him. Goddess of Art, I was even jealous of your father, Aayanar. But, because he was the lucky man who gave birth to you, I stopped the soldiers from killing him."

Sivagami's heart melted at these words. *This Buddhist monk may be a ruthless demon with the cobra's poison in his blood. But didn't he save my father's life because he loves me?*

The monk sensed her feelings and went on frenziedly, "Sivagami, I saved Aayanar because he was your father. I will give you an example of how I destroyed your enemies. All these years, you have been living safely in Vatapi because you are under my protection. The queen's sister became jealous of you. She tried hard to seduce me. When that did not work, she criticised you one day: 'Am I not as beautiful as that Goddess of Art from Kanchi?' I held her hand and scratched her with my nail. When she saw herself in her mirror the next morning, she went mad: her appearance was horrible! She left this city and wandered in the forests and hills for years. Now she sits on the Kapalikas' sacrificial altar and lives on the offerings ..."

Sivagami was again terrified. *Why can't this mad monk go away quickly?*

"Sivagami, a few days ago, I happened to meet that madwoman. Do you know what she said? 'Swami, one day or another, you will have to give me your lover, Sivagami. My hunger will be satisfied only if I eat her.' She does not know that my hunger for you is a hundred times greater than hers. I want to swallow you whole whenever I see you!"

Naganandhi changed into a python. The snake opened its mouth and stretched out its forked tongue, ready to swallow Sivagami. She screamed and moved back. She shut her eyes.

Naganandhi laughed. "Sivagami, did you get scared? Open your eyes: it is the Buddhist monk."

Sivagami opened her eyes. *It was a delusion*. But she was still frightened.

Naganandhi stood. "Sivagami, by the time I come back, you must tell me your decision. If my love for you is not satisfied soon, I will go mad. Then I do not know what I will do. I am going to make a sacrifice for you which is even greater than all that I have sacrificed for you all these years. You will hear about it soon … and you will not be able to stop yourself from pitying me."

Naganandhi stared longingly at Sivagami before he turned abruptly and went to the door. Sivagami continued to shiver long after he had gone.

Festival and Conflict

TWO THOUSAND YEARS ago, in a hidden region of the Ajanta Hills not easily accessible to men, Buddhist monks carved the black granite into monasteries. For six hundred years after that, they created immortal stone sculpture and indelible paintings in those secret caves. Gods and goddesses, heroes and warriors, handsome men and gem-like women touched and spoke to the viewer's heart.

As kingdoms and dynasties changed, a religion's influence grew or weakened. Now and then came men who viewed all religions as one and patronised art for the good of all. Harshavardhan, Mahendran Pallava and Mamallan were such great kings. Pulikesi, on his return from Kanchi, became like them. He gave generous donations to Ajanta's Buddhist *sangha* and encouraged art. The grateful monks decided to hold a grand art festival at Ajanta for the first time to honour Emperor Pulikesi in the thirtieth, and last, year of his reign.

A wide road was laid across the forests and hills for the emperor and his company. Ministers, advisors, generals, famous Chalukyan artists and poets and special guests from abroad arrived by elephant, horse and palanquin. The monks gave them all a royal welcome. The guests spread out into the monasteries and temples and delighted in the sculpture and painting. As the cave paintings could be seen only in broad daylight, arrangements were made for the guests to spend the night there, continue to view the art the next day and then leave.

It was evening. The sun sank behind the western hills. The shadows of those hills lengthened eastwards. The waves of the Waghora River, which split the hill into a crescent, sang and danced and leaped as it flowed rapidly. As far as the eye could see, *parijatham* trees were bursting with flowers and buds. *Kondrai* trees dazzled the eye with golden showers of blossoms. Two majestic men sat talking on a rock near the river—Emperor Pulikesi and Naganandhi.

The two men sat on the same rock on which they had sat as brothers thirty-five years ago, talking about their dreams and their plans to seize the Vatapi throne and make the Chalukyan kingdom great. There was a great difference in their appearance and speech from then and now. The passage of years, along with their personal experiences, the fierce conflicts in their hearts, their desires and passions, had carved cruel lines and wrinkles on those innocent, young faces.

Naganandhi was furious. "*Thambi*, you ask me what I want. Shall I tell you? I want a thousand thunderbolts to strike all these monasteries, the monks, you and your company, and me."

Pulikesi smiled and replied calmly: "Coming to Ajanta has been useful. You were changing into a harmless innocent. Only today are you the Naganandhi of old. I am delighted."

The monk hissed, "Yes, I have become the old Naganandhi—watch out! Tonight, while you sleep, I will plunge this poisoned dagger into your heart."

Pulikesi burst out laughing. "And what will you do with my corpse?" he asked mockingly.

"I will throw it into this river."

"And after that? How will you answer those who ask how the emperor disappeared overnight?"

"No one will know." Naganandhi paused. "Once I wore your clothes, was beaten and tortured, and saved your life. Another time, I disguised myself as you and fought and killed Mahendran Pallava with a poisoned dagger. The same resemblance will help me again. The people will not know about your disappearance, and no one will notice Naganandhi's absence. The Chalukyan kingdom is mine by right. I gave you this kingdom. For the past thirty-five years, I put you above everything. But today, without any pity, affection or gratitude, you insulted me in public. Ah, how is it that the earth has not split open and swallowed you!"

"*Anna*, how can you have the heart to curse me? How did I insult you?"

"You commissioned a painting of Sivagami falling at your feet and begging for mercy. How can there be a greater insult to me than that? Is this why you brought me here? Ah, you evil beast!"

"*Anna*, what has that Pallava dancing girl done to you? What power allows her to separate brothers who are two bodies with one life? *Anna*, look me in the face. Think of our thirty-five years of friendship; think of the dreams we made come true. With this sacred Waghora River, these mountain peaks and the sky and the earth as your witnesses, tell me: does that woman from Kanchi mean more to you than I do? Is it for her that you are cursing me?"

The monk's voice was harsh. "Yes. I tell you this with Lord Buddha's lotus feet as my witness. I swear upon the *sangha* and dharma: Sivagami means a thousand times more to me than you do. You and your kingdom, and your sons and friends, are not worth the dust under her feet. Do you know what happened to the artist who painted that picture of surrender?" The monk gave a terrible laugh. "Wait and see. Soon, someone will bring you the news."

"*Anna*, it is a big mistake to make vows of celibacy when young. One should experience the joys and sorrows of married life before becoming a monk. Those like you, who renounce worldly pleasures when they are young, will later be trapped by a seductress and go mad."

"Pulikesi, if you say another word about Sivagami, I will not tolerate it!"

"Respected sir, you love Sivagami Devi so much. You guard her honour so strongly. But does Sivagami Devi love you? Does she have for you even a fraction of the love you have for her?"

Naganandhi's expression showed that Pulikesi's words cut through his heart like a sword. He hid his pain and steadied his voice. "You have no right to ask me that question, but I will answer you. Sivagami is not hard-hearted like you ... she is fond of me."

"*Anna*, I never dreamt that you would be fooled like this!"

"*Thambi*, I am not a fool. On the night we left for Ajanta, I was about to strike myself with this poisoned dagger. Sivagami held my hand and saved my life." The monk's eyes filled with tears.

Pulikesi smiled. "Aiyo, how could your brilliant mind become like this! Do you know why Sivagami saved you? That stupid girl still dreams that you will die at the hands of her lover, Mamallan."

That afternoon, Pulikesi, Naganandhi, Hiuen Tsang and other dignitaries had viewed Ajanta's wonderful art. The inner walls of the caves showed scenes of Lord Buddha's divine life and avatars. Two incidents in Emperor Pulikesi's life were depicted on the outer walls. One scene showed Pulikesi seated majestically on his throne with envoys from Parasika paying him tribute. Naturally, everyone appreciated this painting.

But the second scene made the viewers uncomfortable. That perverse painting showed a Bharatanatyam dancer begging forgiveness with her head on Pulikesi's feet. Pulikesi's handsome face showed righteous fury. The artist had brilliantly captured the grief and pleading on the dancer's face. In the picture's background, a worried Buddhist monk was hurrying forward. It was clear that he was rushing to save the dancer from royal punishment.

As the guide began to explain the implications of this painting, everyone turned to Naganandhi. The monk's face looked like a cobra with its hood spread. Realising that a hundred eyes were on him, he changed his expression and smiled. "Extraordinary! What feeling! What imagination! Who is the master who created this painting? He must be given his due reward."

Traitor

THE ARGUMENT BETWEEN the brothers became heated. The more Pulikesi tried to dispel the monk's infatuation with Sivagami, the angrier Naganandhi became. Just as the brothers reached the point where they were ready to come to blows, a cruel scene caught their attention.

A man came running, shouting, "Aiyo, aiyo!" in a terrible voice which stopped his listeners' hearts. He stood on the Waghora's steep bank, again screamed, "Aiyo!" and jumped into the river. He sank into the water. Seconds later, his head came up a short distance to the east. A shriek, loud enough to split the rocks, was heard. He sank again and did not come up. There was no sign of him at all. The Waghora flowed on. The scene began and ended in seconds.

Pulikesi felt as if his heart was caught in an iron vise. He stared at the spot where the man had disappeared and then turned to Naganandhi. He broke into goosebumps when he saw the smile on the monk's face. "*Anna*, what did you do to that monk?"

Naganandhi laughed wildly. "I blessed him for having created a masterpiece. When he bowed his head to receive my blessing, I just scratched him on the neck with the nail of my little finger. When the poison in my nail entered his blood, his entire body would have been on fire. His brain would have burned. He jumped into the river to cool his body and brain …"

"Aiyo, *anna*! When did you become such a cruel demon?"

Naganandhi hissed, "Oh, only now do you realise that I am a ruthless demon! Haven't I done crueler things for you and your kingdom? Have you forgotten how happily you agreed when I suggested that we poison Kanchi's drinking water and kill the people?"

"That was a different time." Pulikesi sighed. He stared into the river for some time and then looked Naganandhi in the face. "*Anna*, I have not forgotten all your help. I want to repay you. My life and my kingdom are yours. I enjoyed being king for thirty-five years, but I have had enough. From now, the duties and pleasures of the throne are yours. I will wear the robes you have worn all these years and spend the rest of my life here. You spent your childhood in these Ajanta Hills where beautiful nature and art rule. I will spend my old age here …"

When Naganandhi realised that Pulikesi was sincere, the monk's angry face glowed with sweet dreams of the future.

Pulikesi went on: "*Anna*, I swear on our grandfather, Satyashraya's name, I mean what I said. I am ready to do this at once. I will take a monk's vows today. I will ask the abbot to release you from your vows. But I have one condition—you must give up that Kanchi woman."

Naganandhi glared at his brother. "I thought there would be some evil trick in your offer—I was right."

"*Anna,* can I let a sculptor's daughter sit on the throne once occupied by Satyashraya Pulikesi of the Chalukyan dynasty? Chase away that seductress who has sowed hatred between us, ascend the Vatapi throne and rule for the rest of your life," Pulikesi said in melting tones.

Naganandhi again hissed like a snake, "You wretch! You will be ruined. Your capital will become ashes. Your kingdom will be destroyed. I cannot give up Sivagami even for *Devaloka*. Are you asking me to give her up for this trifling Chalukyan kingdom? Never! From this second, all our bonds are broken. I will never again set eyes on you. I will take Sivagami and leave your kingdom forever. Look at those men: they bring news of your ruin."

Some ministers and generals hurried into view on the opposite bank of the river. It looked as if they had urgent news for the emperor. The men crossed the river by a bamboo bridge and came to the emperor. Naganandhi took two steps and then hesitated—obviously, he wanted to hear their news.

Seeing their anxious faces, the emperor asked, "What has happened? Any important news?"

The Vatapi prime minister said, "Yes, lord. It is hard to believe, and I am hesitant to tell you."

"Why are you all dying of fright? Is some enemy marching on Vatapi? Tell me quickly."

"Great lord, you said it … the enemy is marching on Vatapi …"

"Who is this enemy? It cannot be Harshavardhan from the north: I recently got a friendly letter from him. I do not have any other enemies in the west and east. If an invasion comes, it must be from the south. Is Kanchi Mamallan marching on us?"

"That is what we hear, lord."

"I do not believe it. And even if it is true, why are you so worried?"

"Lord, the larger part of our army is on the shores of the Narmada. Another part is in Vengi …" the prime minister said hesitantly.

"So what? Can't we bring our forces back to Vatapi before Mamallan comes?"

"Lord, Mamallan is not in Kanchi. It is one week since the Pallava army crossed the North Pennai. By now, they will be near the Tungabhadra."

"What! Who brought this news?"

The prime minister stood two messengers before the emperor. "These men have rushed here non-stop from Vatapi."

Pulikesi was dazed. "Who sent you? Do you bring any scrolls?"

"No, lord, there was no time to write a message. The Vatapi Fort commander sent word through us. Six of us left Vatapi four days ago. Four fell by the way. Only two of us reached here."

"Minister, can this be true? Didn't we hear that Mamallan was building ships to invade Lanka?"

"Yes, lord. It is hard to believe, but these men have the commander's signet ring. I believe more messengers are coming with a detailed scroll. If what they say is true, the Pallava army would have crossed the Tungabhadra by now. We sent the forces stationed on the Tungabhadra shore to Vengi only recently because of the famine in the Tungabhadra region."

Pulikesi was stunned. He looked at Naganandhi standing a short distance away, listening to the conversation. He turned back to the minister. "What was our spy network doing? Why did we not hear of Mamallan's invasion earlier?"

The prime minister said, "Lord, our spy chief was dismissed a year back. The monk took over his job … you must ask him."

All eyes, including the emperor's, turned to Naganandhi.

"*Adigal*, did you know about Mamallan's invasion? Did you deliberately hide it from me?" Pulikesi asked.

"*Thambi*, do you want me to reply before all these men?"

"*Adigal,* you said that there is no longer any bond between us: why celebrate a relationship now? The truth at once!"

"In that case, let me tell you: I knew about Mamallan's invasion. I did not tell you because I wanted an ungrateful wretch like you to be punished," Naganandhi roared.

"Catch this traitor and tie him," Pulikesi commanded.

The eight men there surrounded the monk.

Naganandhi drew his dagger. "The first one to come near me will go straight to *Yamaloka!*" The men drew their swords. Naganandhi mocked them. "Let eight brave heroes cut down one monk. Emperor Pulikesi's fame will spread throughout the world. The awed Mamallan will go back."

"Stop!" Pulikesi cried. "Do not stain your swords by killing this disgusting traitor. Stand back."

The men moved back, but they stayed alert in case the monk jumped at the emperor.

Pulikesi spoke in a furious, quavering voice: "*Adigal*, killing you is not punishment enough for betraying your country and your brother. You monster! Go to Vatapi, take your seductress and go. Keep your word at least in this—do not let me see you as long as I live. You wicked man—you sold your country out of lust for a woman. Go! Live long and weep over your betrayal."

Naganandhi stood like a statue. Then, without saying a word, he turned and walked eastwards.

Pulikesi stared after the monk until he disappeared from sight. He wiped his tears. "The news must be true. I did not believe your warnings about the monk. Now we are going to pay for it. But all is not lost. Let us teach Mamallan that it is dangerous to put one's head into a tiger's mouth. We will see that not a single Pallava soldier who crosses the Tungabhadra goes back alive. The Pallava kingdom will become part of the Chalukyan empire."

The Great Vatapi War

THE PALLAVA FORCES from the south and the Chalukyan forces from the north raced to reach Vatapi. The Pallavas won—their army surged forward like a mighty ocean, reached Vatapi and surrounded the great fort while the Chalukyan army was still sixty miles away.

Proud of Pulikesi's conquests, the people of Vatapi never dreamt that their kingdom could be attacked. The Pallava invasion stunned them like a bolt from the blue. Knowing that Vatapi was not securely guarded, the citizens were terrified. A rumour spread that the Ajanta art festival was a Buddhist conspiracy. Bhimasena, the Vatapi Fort commander, had to guard the city's Buddhist monasteries from the people's anger.

Emperor Pulikesi sent the people a scroll by urgent messenger. He promised that he was leading a huge army to Vatapi from the Narmada and that another huge force was rushing there from Vengi. He urged the people to stay calm if, by chance, the Pallava army besieged Vatapi before he reached the city. He promised to destroy the Pallava army and lift the siege at once. Bhimasena had this royal order read out at all the city crossroads, and the people gained courage.

When Emperor Pulikesi, with his army from the Narmada, was forty miles away from Vatapi, he heard that the Pallava army had surrounded the city. He also heard that his Vengi army was delayed by the difficult terrain. Pulikesi decided to set up camp and wait for the Vengi army to join him before launching a blistering attack on the Pallavas.

The Pallava War Council debated whether to besiege Vatapi Fort or attack Pulikesi's army. Manavanman and Adityavarman felt that, since their aim was to capture Vatapi, they should immediately attack the fort. Paranjothi said that Pulikesi must be destroyed before the Vengi army joined him. He insisted that Vatapi Fort was not going anywhere and the longer the siege lasted, the easier it would be to capture the city. Spy Chief Shatrughan supported the general, and Mamallan agreed with them. Leaving a small force outside Vatapi, the Pallava army marched north.

To uphold the honour of the Chalukyas, Pulikesi refused to retreat and prepared for war. The two great armies met thirty miles from Vatapi. The savage battle raged for three days and nights. Tens of thousands of soldiers were killed. Dead elephants lay here and there like dark hills. Dead horses and dead men were heaped on each other. There was an unbearable, frightening roar—the pitiful cries of dying men, the terrified trumpeting of elephants and the sad neighing of horses. Rivers of blood flowed through the battlefield. Limbless, headless corpses were piled high.

Right from the start, the relative strengths of the two armies was clear. The Pallava army, which had camped and rested near Vatapi, attacked with full strength and spirit. The Chalukyan forces, exhausted after their non-stop march, could not withstand the attack. They were further weakened by the fact that their main elephant brigade had been in Vengi and could not join them.

On the morning of the third day, the Pallava army's victory was certain. That afternoon, the Chalukyan generals urged Pulikesi to retreat safely for the good of the kingdom, and wait until the Vengi forces arrived. Seeing no other way out, the emperor agreed. It was decided that Pulikesi would retreat after sunset, defended by the remaining cavalry. But they did not get the chance to carry out this plan. That evening, the Pallavas finally used the elephant brigade specially trained by Manavanman which they had kept in reserve.

Five thousand elephants in rut whirled iron rods in their trunks and charged the Chalukyan cavalry. The poor horses panicked and scattered. That night, the Pallavas hunted and killed the fleeing Chalukyan soldiers. At sunrise the next day, Chalukyan corpses littered the battlefield: there was no sign of a single living Chalukyan soldier.

Drums beat a tattoo of victory, conches blared, and triumphant cheers reached the sky. Mamallan and his commanders exchanged congratulations and celebrated their great victory by garlanding each other with *vaagai* flowers. But there was a niggling worry in their hearts: where was Pulikesi? No one knew whether the Chalukyan emperor had fought to the end and died on the battlefield or whether he had fled. If he had fallen on the battlefield, his corpse must be given the respect due to a great emperor. If he had run away, he would again muster an army and fight. Finally, it was decided that further argument was a waste of time. Ordering Shatrughan to organise a search of the battlefield, Mamallan and the others turned their attention to Vatapi.

The Monk's Oath

ON THE DAY after the battle, the rays of the setting sun reached through the trees to fall on the bare rocks around the Kapalikas' sacrificial altar near Vatapi. The rocks and their dark shadows took on monstrous shapes. A woman walked along the edge of the rocks, carrying a corpse on her shoulders. In the moonlight, the woman's shadow was that of a huge demon carrying its prey. She was hideous, with blackened, swollen skin, short brown hair and burning eyes. But the male corpse she carried showed majestic, royal features.

The woman turned a corner and was startled to see a man coming towards her. She stopped.

The man came closer and asked, "Ranjani, is it you?" It was Naganandhi.

The woman was the beautiful Ranjani, who had once delighted men's eyes and bewitched their hearts. Naganandhi had changed her into this hideous Kapalika.

Ranjani froze. Then her shock wore off. "*Adigal*, is it really you?"

"Who else would come searching for you at midnight? Which wretch's corpse are you carrying?"

The Kapalika dropped the corpse with a thud and laughed wildly. "What a joke! *Adigal*, I walked twenty miles weeping for you. What a waste!"

"Why should you weep for me? And what is funny about it?"

"It is very funny. Let me tell you from the beginning … I stood on a hillock near the battlefield and watched the war. What fun! The Kapalikas make a human sacrifice once a month. There, they sacrificed lakhs of men and thousands of horses and elephants. The sacrifice went on for three days and nights. Finally one side ran, and the other chased them. Afraid that they might catch me, I too ran. I ran through the day, hiding in the forest. In the evening, I heard a horse behind me. *Someone is coming to catch me!* I ran faster. When it was dark, I hid behind a tree to see who it was. The horse chasing me fell suddenly, and its rider lay still. When I went near, the horse was dying, and the rider had been dead for a long time. His legs were caught in the horse's bridle, and so he had been hanging on without falling off. I bent to see his face—it looked like yours. Thinking it was you, I carried the corpse on my shoulder and wept all the way here …"

Naganandhi was struck by a sudden thought. He bent and stared at the face of the corpse in the moonlight. His cry, "*Thambi* … Pulikesi!"

echoed through that vast rocky clearing. "Ranjani, go. Leave me alone for some time," he sobbed.

Frightened, the Kapalika moved away and waited in the shadow of the rocks.

The monk sat with Pulikesi's corpse on his lap. "*Thambi,* what a way to die!" The monk beat himself on the head and chest. "It is because of this wretch that this happened! Aiyo, *thambi!* You died thinking I had betrayed you. Would I betray you … the brother who is dearer to me than life … the brother who shared my mother's womb with me for ten months? I was conspiring to take a terrible revenge on Mamallan. Now I will never be able to tell you about it …" He beat himself on the chest again. "*Thambi,* I did not betray you or our kingdom. If only we had been patient with each other in Ajanta, I would never have let this war take place. I would have starved the entire Pallava populace. I would have sacrificed Mamallan alive. Aiyo, how could this happen?"

The monk gently placed the corpse on the ground. He stood and raised his hands to the skies. Even the Kapalika's hair stood on end as he howled, "*Thambi,* Pulikesi, I swear an oath on Lord Buddha's lotus feet. I swear an oath on Rudra, the destroyer who carries the skull. I swear an oath on Kali who asks for blood sacrifice. I will take revenge on your killers!"

The Kapalika's Love

THE MONK AGAIN sat down with Pulikesi's corpse on his lap. "*Thambi,* you are not dead. Your life has become one with mine. From now, you are me and I am you. We are one." He said this in melting, loving tones and then broke into shuddering sobs.

The night passed quickly, and the moon rose higher. The shadows of the trees and rocks shortened. The Kapalika finally lost patience. She came out from behind the rocks and walked softly to the monk. She stood behind him and gently touched his shoulders.

The startled monk turned back. "Ranjani, it is you. Haven't you left yet? In this wide world, you are the only one who loves me."

"But there is no one who loves me."

"Ah, Ranjani, don't I love you?" The sorrow in his voice was now replaced by a pretense of love.

"*Adigal*, do not try to fool me. How can anyone love this hideous, ugly body?"

"Haven't you heard that love is blind? However ugly you may be, you are beautiful in my eyes."

"You wicked monk! You are the one who made me like this. Would you have done this if you loved me?"

"Ranjani, if you had stayed at the Vatapi palace looking as beautiful as an Ajanta painting, some handsome prince would have carried you away. That is why I did this."

"Why didn't you carry me away? Would I have refused?"

"I will tell you once again: there were certain things I had to do. Most importantly, I had to get my release from the Buddhist *sangha*."

"You have been saying this for years. When on earth will you be released?"

"Ranjani, I am free … the obstacle to your love is gone. Are you happy?" the monk asked sweetly.

"Are you telling me the truth?"

"The whole truth. The Buddhist *sangha* itself excommunicated me." He paused. "It is a long story: I will tell you later. We must burn this body at once. If anyone knows, our plans will be ruined. Come, Ranjani, let us see you gather logs and build a funeral pyre here."

Ranjani was not convinced. "How did the *sangha* dare to excommunicate the powerful Naganandhi? Tell me that and I will help you."

"I will tell you briefly, listen. I knew in advance about Kanchi Mamallan's invasion. For some reasons, I hid it from my brother. When he found out, the fool thought that I had betrayed him and my country. The brother I guarded with my life and raised to such heights said, 'Do not let me see you again as long as I live.' Because of that, he lies here an orphaned corpse. We must cremate him." The monk sighed. "As soon as the Ajanta Buddhist *sangha* heard that the emperor was angry with me, they forgot all my help over the years and excommunicated me. They faced the consequences. Ranjani, no one can defy Neelakesi and get away with it."

"How have the Ajanta monks suffered?" the Kapalika asked.

"They had to run for their lives. A rumour spread through the land: the Ajanta art festival was a Buddhist conspiracy to help Kanchi Mamallan. I am the one who sowed the seeds of that rumour. The people wanted to go to Ajanta and destroy the *sangha* and the art. Hearing this, the monks blocked and hid all the paths to Ajanta and ran to Harshavardhan's kingdom. After that, even I could not find my way to Ajanta. It looks like I came back here at the right time. Ranjani, build the pyre at once. Bring fire." Naganandhi paused. "Ranjani, you must not tell anyone about the emperor's death and cremation. You must keep it a secret, do you understand?"

"You deceitful monk! I know why you want it to be kept secret. You will burn this corpse and go to Vatapi through the secret underground passage. You will say that you are the emperor. You will ascend the Chalukyan throne with that nobody from Kanchi by your side."

Naganandhi said angrily, "To hell with you! From now …"

Ranjani fell at his feet. "*Adigal*, forgive me! I will do as you say." She paused. "If you want me to trust you, give me that dancer."

Naganandhi's eyes flamed in the moonlight. "Ranjani, you have been patient all these years—be patient a little longer. Wait until the siege of Vatapi ends. As soon as I have taken revenge on Mamallan, I will give you Sivagami. After that, I will be the emperor of South India, and you will be my empress. Chalukya, Pallava, Chola, Pandyan, Chera … all these kingdoms will be ours."

Ranjani brought logs of wood and built a funeral pyre. She murmured to herself, "Deceitful monk! You are trying to cheat me again, but you will not succeed. Even if you offer her *Devaloka* as the reward, Sivagami will not even look at you. Finally, you will have to fall at my feet."

War Council

AFTER THE WAR, one half of the Pallava army marched twenty miles south and camped there, ready to face the coming Vengi army. The other half prepared to attack and capture Vatapi Fort. Mamallan was in a rush to attack the fort. He hurried the general and the others. He rode around the fort, giving the soldiers instructions.

Paranjothi was angry and hurt. "Why don't you leave all this to me? Don't you trust me?"

Mamallan was in a hurry to attack the fort because he was afraid that the fort would surrender first. A week after the Pallava victory, what he feared happened. Just when they had decided to attack the fort the next morning, the white flag of surrender was raised at the fort's entrance. Two men climbed down a rope ladder, gave General Paranjothi two scrolls and went back.

One scroll was a message from the fort's commander, Bhimasena, to Emperor Mamallan. It said that the city officials had decided to surrender without a fight. They would surrender all the wealth in the palace, along with the elephant brigade and cavalry stationed in the city. They were also willing to accept any other conditions laid down by Mamallan. They asked Mamallan to be merciful and to spare the city and the lives, homes, property and freedom of its citizens.

The people of Vatapi had watched the battle between the Pallavas and Chalukyas from the fort's terraces. The Pallava victory was clear. Everyone knew that there were not enough soldiers to guard the fort. There were no stockpiles of food to face a long siege. Within a month, the people would starve. If the enemy attacked the fort, the citizens could expect no mercy. Lakhs of women, children and old people would suffer. And so, Bhimasena sent his message of surrender.

Mamallan was furious as the message was read out. It was clear that, for some reason, he disliked the offer to surrender. In spite of that, the council of ministers agreed that it was best to accept the surrender and save the city and people.

As each man recommended accepting the surrender, angry sparks flew from Mamallan's eyes.

Manavanman and Paranjothi remained silent.

"Why are you standing there silently? General, what do you think?" Mamallan asked.

"Lord, I too think we should stop fighting. What is the point of making innocent people suffer?"

Mamallan spewed fire: "General, have you too begun to talk about dharma? Have you forgotten Pulikesi's cruelty? What is wrong with all of you? Are you afraid of blood? Do you fear death? Manavanman, do you at least support me? Or have you too renounced violence?"

Manavanman knew Mamallan's heart. *Mamallan wants to fulfill Sivagami's oath at any cost. If he accepts the surrender, he will not be able to do that ... and there will be no chance to use the elephant brigade I have specially trained for the attack.* He said, "Lord, I hesitate to disagree with the brave Pallava commanders. Above all, I do not want to contradict the general."

Mamallan said, "Anyone here can boldly state his opinion. There is no need to be afraid."

"Lord, I think we should refuse this offer of surrender. After committing every grievous crime, is it enough to just surrender?"

Paranjothi interrupted him: "What crimes have the citizens of Vatapi committed? How can they be held responsible for Pulikesi's crimes?"

Manavanman said, "Did these people try to stop Pulikesi? Aren't they the ones who gave him his power and shared his plunder? Aren't they the ones who made the Tamil captives work for them? Didn't they make Aayanar's daughter dance at the crossroads? Has our general forgotten this?"

Mamallan gave Paranjothi a look as sharp as a sword.

"My king, I remember everything. I wanted to talk to you privately but, since Manavanman has brought up Sivagami, I will speak now. The messengers who brought the scrolls brought a private message for me from Sivagami." Paranjothi gave Mamallan a scroll.

Mamallan's bloodshot eyes reddened further as he read the message. His hands shook in anger. Once he finished reading, he began to tear the palm script.

Paranjothi stopped him. "My king, that scroll is mine. Please give it to me."

Sivagami's Message

THIS WAS SIVAGAMI'S message to Paranjothi.

'From Aayanar's daughter, Sivagami, to the brave Pallava army's general and my loving brother, Paranjothi. I hear that you and the prince, without forgetting me for nine years, are leading an invasion to fulfill my oath. News of the great war fought to the fort's north has also reached us. People here say that the Vatapi emperor must have died in that war.

'Bhimasena, the fort commander, asked me to send a message, and I write this wholeheartedly. The purpose of your invasion has been achieved. The Chalukyan army and the Vatapi emperor have been ruined. I beg you to stop the war and accept Vatapi's surrender. I no longer want the Pallava prince to fulfill my oath. The innocent people of this city will lose their homes and suffer. I do not want to do that to them. What will anyone gain from it?

'Both sides have suffered heavy casualties in the war. I grieve to think that I am the cause of this. My beloved brother, living alone for nine years, I have been thinking constantly. I realise what a great mistake I made by refusing to go with you and the prince when you came for me. I realise how foolish I was to insist that I would come only after my oath was fulfilled. What madness it is for intelligent men to kill each other in the name of war!

'Is it right for man to kill beings created by God? When we cannot create even the smallest life form, what a sin it is to take thousands of lives! The all-knowing God is there to punish or forgive sinners. We should leave it to him.

'Brother, let us forget the past. Let us stop the bloodshed. Forgive me for all the trouble I have caused through my foolish stubbornness. Tell the prince that I beg him to stop the war. The fort's citizens show me great respect since the siege began. They are ready to carry me out in a palanquin with every honour if the prince accepts their offer of surrender. Please tell the prince all this. My heart beats eagerly to see you all. I hope that I will be lucky enough to see you and the prince by sunset today. I pay my respects to the lotus feet of my beloved father.'

The furious Mamallan said, "Here, take your scroll, general. Keep it and worship its sermon on dharma!" He threw the scroll.

Paranjothi picked it up with respect. "My king, I am lucky to receive Sivagami's spiritual instruction."

Mamallan had never mentioned Sivagami in public, but now he lost his temper before all those men. "General, I have made two mistakes in my life. First, I tried to make a sculptor's daughter a queen. Second, you came to recite Tamil and learn sculpture: I made you a general. The sculptor's daughter has proved that she is not worthy of a throne. You have proved that the son of a doctor who reads one's pulse is not worthy of being a general who guards the kingdom …"

Paranjothi's eyes filled. Choked with anger and shame, his voice shook. "My king …"

"General, stop!" Mamallan roared.

Paranjothi was silenced. The emperor had never before said a word to disrespect or hurt him.

Mamallan went on: "Who does this sculptor's daughter think I am? How dare she write such a message! When this foolish woman stubbornly insists, we must prepare for war. When she reconsiders, we must bow to her command and stop the war, is it? She dared to write this message only because she thinks that the Pallava citizens and the Pallava emperor are her slaves. Be clear—I did not work for nine years to gather this great army and launch this invasion to fulfill the foolish oath of a sculptor's mad daughter. I came for the Pallavas' honour. I came to fulfill my father, Emperor Mahendran's, dying command. I came to ensure that the world does not mock Narasimhan Pallava who earned the title, 'Mamallan,' at the age of eighteen. I did not come to listen to a sculptor's daughter's sermons on dharma and attain *moksha.* As it is clear that you do not want to continue the war, I relieve you of your position as general right now."

Mamallan turned to Manavanman and roared, "Manavanman, I brought you along because I knew that the general would leave me in the lurch. Prepare to attack the fort tonight."

There was silence. Everyone was shaken and stunned by Mamallan's harsh words to Paranjothi.

Manavanman was silent. *What have I done! I started out with the best of intentions, but everything went wrong. Have I made a permanent enemy of the general?* He stood sadly.

Mamallan threatened, "Manavanman, why are you standing here?"

Manavanman looked at Paranjothi.

Paranjothi, as stunned as the others, stepped forward. "My king, you and I stood at the crossroads in Vatapi and swore an oath. We promised that we would return with an army, free Sivagami, break the false Pillar of Victory and erect a new pillar proclaiming the Pallava victory. We worked day and night for nine years to keep that promise. As a reward for serving the Pallava dynasty for twelve years, let me continue as general until we fulfill our oath."

Mamallan's expression softened, and he smiled. "General, that is what I want. Attack at once."

"Forgive me, lord—another small request. Once we begin our attack, we must finish it within a day and a night. Please give me three days to prepare for it," Paranjothi said respectfully.

Mamallan's silence was a sign of his reluctant consent.

Vatapi Ganapati

SOME MEN BECOME accustomed to cruelty; their initial pity disappears, and their hearts harden. Others become increasingly troubled by cruelty; their hearts ache, and they become determined to uproot injustice and evil. Paranjothi belonged to the second type. During the Battle of Vatapi, he saw flowing rivers of blood and mountains of corpses. He heard the hideous shrieks of wounded and dying men. *What is all this for? Why must men kill one another?*

In this state of mind, Sivagami's words rang true in his heart. *God speaks to me through Sivagami. When Sivagami herself says that there is no need to fulfill her oath, Mamallan should agree. What will anyone gain by taking revenge on the people of Vatapi for Pulikesi's cruelty ten years ago? And how do we know that it will end with this? A few years later, someone from the Chalukyan dynasty may take revenge on the Pallava people. When kings want to redeem their honour through war, it is the innocent people on both sides who suffer.*

Paranjothi was wounded by Mamallan's harsh words. *I was a fool to think that Mamallan and I were of one heart and mind. He insulted me. Royalty is fickle-minded. And Mamallan has changed ever since that Lankan prince arrived. He is the cause of all this trouble.*

Paranjothi's request for a three-day interval was indeed to prepare for the attack. He knew from experience that good preparation shortened wars. But he also had another reason. *Sivagami may be in danger once we attack the fort. I must bring her out before we attack.* Mamallan and Paranjothi had considered sending in a few men in advance. Shatrughan and Gundodharan were looking for secret passages into the fort. Paranjothi wanted to give them time.

At sunset on the third day, the Pallava general rode along the fort's walls. *If Mamallan gives the command, I must attack. There is still no sign of Shatrughan and Gundodharan. What can I do?*

Paranjothi stopped outside the fort's main entrance. *We can capture the city while it sleeps. Everything is ready, but let me examine the gates one last time before I order the elephant brigade to advance.*

He dismounted from his horse and went to the gate. His attention was drawn to the exquisite figure of Ganapati sculpted on the threshold. Paranjothi stood before it with folded hands and prayed: *Lord Vinayaga, remover of all obstacles, grant us success. Help me return Sivagami safely to her father. If you do this for me, I will guard you during the battle. I will take you to my hometown, build a temple for you and worship you daily.*

Just as Paranjothi finished his prayer, the Pallava soldiers stationed a short distance from the entrance shouted, "General, the white flag has been lowered!"

Paranjothi looked up—there was no sign of the white flag of surrender which had fluttered above them for three days.

Victory or Death

ALL ALONG THE fort's walls, lines of soldiers stood on the wide ramparts which had earlier been empty. Their iron helmets, copper breastplates and sharp spear points sparkled in the setting sun.

Thousands of voices cried, "Long live Satyashraya Pulikesi, King of Kings!"

Paranjothi stood stunned.

"There!" one of the soldiers standing near him shouted, pointing to the terrace above the main entrance. A tall, majestic figure stood there, looking around.

It is Pulikesi! He survived the battle. He must have entered the fort through an underground passage or slipped past the Pallava guards. There will be no more talk of peace. We must fight. The blood of thousands must flow like rivers. Vatapi must burn.

Suddenly, an arrow whizzed straight at Paranjothi from the upper terrace. The soldiers shouted in alarm. Luckily, the arrow missed the general's head by inches and fell to the ground behind him.

Paranjothi smiled and calmly ordered the men to pick up the arrow. He read the message tied to its shaft: 'Victory or Death.' A great burden was lifted from his heart. *Pulikesi is responsible for continuing the war and spilling more blood. I can attack the fort with a clear conscience.*

Paranjothi spoke to a soldier standing by him. "Sadaiyan, do you see the Ganapati on the fort's threshold?"

"I see it, swami. I noticed it when you were standing by the entrance."

"I have a very important task for you. When night falls, take ten soldiers and go to the entrance under the cover of darkness. Without damaging the statue, remove it from its base and bring it to my tent. Our victory in this final battle depends on you bringing that statue carefully to me."

"It will be done, general. I will guard the Vinayagar and bring him to you."

Paranjothi rode to Mamallan's tent. The other commanders were already gathered there to receive their final orders. Mamallan chatted casually with them, waiting for Paranjothi.

Paranjothi entered the peaceful tent like a tornado and saluted the emperor. "Lord …"

Mamallan interrupted him: "General, why are you so excited? After thinking it over for three days, I have decided to take your principled advice. I will accept Vatapi's surrender."

Paranjothi's eyes brimmed with tears. "Lord, my advice was foolish.

You were right. It was a great mistake to delay for three days. Lord, the white flag has been taken down. There are armed Chalukyan soldiers on the ramparts."

The emperor jumped up from his chair. "What is the reason for this?"

"Pulikesi did not die on the battlefield. He survived and somehow entered the fort. I saw him standing on the ramparts, inspecting his troops. And here is Pulikesi's scroll. It was tied to an arrow and sent to me." Paranjothi showed the emperor the 'Victory or Death,' message.

"Excellent! All Vatapi's suffering will be on his head." Mamallan was enthusiastic. "General, no more doubts, right? We can attack the fort."

"No doubts, lord. Everything is ready. Within an hour, our elephant brigade will attack the gates. Our soldiers will cross the ramparts and enter the fort." He turned to the other commanders. "Go to your posts. Be ready to move as soon as you hear the war drums."

The commanders enthusiastically saluted the emperor and the general and left. Only the emperor, his two bodyguards, Manavanman and Paranjothi remained.

"General, what orders have you given our soldiers about the city?" Mamallan asked.

"Lord, women and children will not be harmed. Men who resist will be killed, while those who surrender will be arrested. Every single house in Vatapi will be burnt to ashes. Anyone who tries to put out the fires will be killed. Those fleeing the city may go but cannot take any possessions. Our soldiers can collect as much wealth as they can from the city. They will be allowed to keep half as their own share. Is there anything you wish to add?"

"General, you have left nothing for me to add."

"Lord, with your permission, there is an important task I have assigned to our Lankan prince."

Before Mamallan could reply, Manavanman said, "I wait for the general's orders."

Paranjothi spoke to Mamallan: "I hear that the Vatapi emperor's palace has unique treasures and the accumulated gold of thirty years. Manavanman must take the treasure and only then burn the palace. I have reserved five thousand soldiers to help him."

Mamallan asked softly, "General, there is another treasure to be safeguarded in Vatapi … what arrangements have you made for that?"

Paranjothi looked at the emperor. *He is asking about Sivagami.*

Shatrughan's Fear

THE WAR DRUMS sounded an hour after sunset. The Pallava army marched towards the fort's walls like an ocean about to engulf the city. The earth shook as the Pallava elephant brigade advanced to the four entrances with iron bars and hard logs in their trunks. Clouds of dust hid the sky. The smoke from flares and torches created a terrible world of sorcery.

Paranjothi paced restlessly outside his tent until Sadaiyan and four other soldiers arrived with the Ganapati from Vatapi Fort's threshold. The general followed them into his tent and said, "Sadaiyan, you and your men must stay here and guard this Vinayagar. If Sivagami is rescued from the fort, I have sworn to build a temple for this deity in my village." He paused. "Sadaiyan, if you stay here, you will not get a share of the plunder. I will compensate you for it."

"Swami, as you command," Sadaiyan replied.

Paranjothi closed his eyes in prayer. They heard running feet outside the tent. The next instant, Shatrughan charged in. His hair disheveled, he looked as if he had seen a ghost.

Paranjothi said, "Shatrughan, why are you so terrified? Is there danger? Did you fail?"

"General, I have been in many deadly situations, but I have never faced anything more dangerous than what happened yesterday and today …" He stopped and looked at the men there.

Paranjothi sent the soldiers outside. "Shatrughan, we have started the attack. There is no time to lose. Tell me briefly what happened. First tell me whether you succeeded in your mission."

"General, I found a secret underground passage, but it is not easy to enter the fort through it. And the attack has begun. What is the use of the passage now? I came here for your advice …"

Shatrughan began his story.

The Cave of Horrors

"GUNDODHARAN AND I searched the area around the fort for hidden underground passages. Thinking that a passage might start from the rocks around the Kapalikas' sacrificial altar, we examined that area carefully. One night, as we searched, we saw a man and a woman near a fire. We recognised Naganandhi. The woman was a hideous Kapalika. We eavesdropped on their conversation but could not make any sense of it. We often heard the names Pulikesi and Sivagami. It was clear that the monk was asking the Kapalika for help. At daybreak, they rolled a rock from a cave entrance and went in. The cave's mouth closed behind them.

"After a long wait, Gundodharan and I saw the rock moving—we hid quickly. The Kapalika came out alone. She did not budge from the entrance all day. When she finally went away in the evening, I entered the cave, leaving Gundodharan to stand guard outside. What horrors! Human skulls and bones were heaped there. The stink was unbearable. The cave was pitch dark and I could not find any underground passage. Suddenly, the little light there was, disappeared. I looked for the opening through which I had entered—there was no sign of it. I was terrified: the Kapalika had blocked the entrance! I do not know how long I stayed in that stinking darkness with the skulls and bones. However hard I tried, I could not find the entrance.

"Then the cave's mouth opened, and the Kapalika came in. I hid in a bend in the cave. She carried a human skull and bones. She put them safely in a corner, sat in the middle of the cave and shifted a huge rock. When she climbed down there, I guessed that the underground passage was at that spot. I was glad that all the time I had spent there, hungry and thirsty, had not been wasted. It seemed that the Kapalika soon changed her mind: she came up again, closed the passage's entrance and lay there talking to herself.

"I learnt some important things from her. She loved Naganandhi and hated Sivagami because of that. Pulikesi was dead: it was his skull and bones she had carried into the cave. Naganandhi had disguised himself as the Vatapi emperor. He planned to ascend the Chalukyan throne and make Sivagami his empress. The Kapalika was determined to stop this. After a long time, she was quiet. Thinking that she was asleep, I tiptoed to the cave's mouth and jumped out. At that instant, someone in the cave gripped my hand. I looked back: standing inside the cave, the Kapalika held my hand and growled. My heart stopped. *This is the end*. Making a last attempt to save my life, I shook my hand—but I could not free myself from her iron clasp.

"The Kapalika cried, 'Lambodhara, Lambodhara.' I was stunned when Gundodharan came running from the nearby rocks saying, 'Coming, lady.' Gundodharan signalled to me with his eyes and went to her. 'Lambodhara,' she said. 'Hold this deceitful spy while I get my knife. You won't let him go, will you?' 'Never, lady. I will make him my first sacrifice.' Gundodharan held me tightly. As soon as the Kapalika went inside, Gundodharan loosened his hold and winked at me. I ran. Gundodharan shouted and chased me. When we came to the cover of some rocks, Gundodharan said, 'Swami, in order to find out what had happened to you, I became this Kapalika's disciple. Do not worry about me. I will stay here and calm her. Go quickly. It looks like the attack on the fort has started.' I said, 'Gundodharan, the secret passage begins in the cave. I will go to the general and come back with men. Keep this demoness occupied until I return. Do not let her use the underground passage.' I came running to you. I do not know what happened to Gundodharan after that."

Paranjothi was worried. "Shatrughan, there is no time to think. The attack has begun. We will be inside the fort by tomorrow morning. Take a hundred soldiers and go to the Kapalika cave's entrance. See that no one escapes through the underground passage. If possible, you and Gundodharan come to the fort by the passage. I am going straight to Sivagami's house as soon as the fort's gates are opened. By Vinayagar's grace, we will be fortunate enough to rescue Sivagami and hand her over to her father."

Vatapi Burns

EMPEROR MAMALLAN STOOD outside his tent, watching the Pallava attack. *This is the most important day of my life. My name will go down in the annals of history as 'Vatapi's Destroyer, Narasimhan.' I will definitely fulfill my promise to Sivagami—within three days, Vatapi Fort will fall, and the city will burn. But poor Sivagami can never go back to the happy past. All her dreams are shattered. And my life will be an endless desert with only mirages to cool my eyes.*

Mamallan was surprised to see Paranjothi coming back to his tent. "General, what news?"

"Lord, Shatrughan is back." Paranjothi gave a brief report of Shatrughan's adventures.

"Does this make any difference to our strategy?" Mamallan asked.

"Not much, lord. It is even more important to speed up our attack on the fort. The snake slithering at our feet is more dangerous than the tiger which pounces on us from the front."

"Do you believe that it was Naganandhi who challenged you to war? In that case, we have more to worry concerning Sivagami. Shall I come into the fort with you?"

"Lord, I think it best that you stay here." Paranjothi could not forget that Mamallan's last meeting with Sivagami had been a disaster. *It is my duty to see that nothing like that happens this time. Come what may, I must meet Sivagami first.*

Mamallan had his own reasons for not wanting to see Sivagami first. "Okay, general. Remember—show Naganandhi no mercy. We cannot live in peace as long as that deceitful monk is alive."

Seeing the general hesitate, Mamallan asked, "Do you have anything else to say?"

"Yes. You commanded that the city be burnt after the fort fell ... I want to burn Vatapi first."

"Why do that?"

"I have promised our soldiers that they can take half of their plunder. When they see the city burn, their hunger will increase ten times. Lord, I must enter the fort by dawn tomorrow. If there is any delay, we may not be able to rescue Sivagami. Be ready at sunrise. Stay awake tonight, and watch Vatapi burn." Paranjothi hurried away without waiting for the emperor's reply.

Siege towers were positioned around the fort's walls. Specially trained Pallava soldiers stood on these towers and flung flaming torches and Sulphur bombs into the city. By the third watch of the night, Vatapi city, with its lakhs of people, was burning. The wind fanned the flames which swallowed Vatapi's storied mansions and towers. Clouds of smoke hid the sky.

At the same time, Pallava soldiers climbed the fort's ramparts. The Chalukyan soldiers there tried to stop them. Thousands of Tamil soldiers fell to their swords, spears and arrows, but wave after wave of attackers swarmed over the ramparts.

Elephants shattered the fort's four gates with iron bars and wooden logs. By the fourth watch of the night, Pallava soldiers entered the burning city. The soldiers attacking the ramparts also began to jump in from all sides. The rising sun stared in surprise at Vatapi falling to the flames.

Turmoil

FROM THE DAY the Pallava army surrounded Vatapi Fort, Sivagami's mind smoldered like a volcano. She was angry that, although Mamallan and Aayanar were just across the wall, she could not meet them. She worried about the result of the war. She wondered what to say and how to behave when she met Mamallan. Her heart burst with pride when she heard of the Pallava victory north of the city. She also worried how this victory would affect her position.

When Fort Commander Bhimasena asked her to write to Mamallan, Sivagami was prouder than she had ever been. She also sent a message to Paranjothi, expressing her feelings. But at the bottom of her heart, she still wanted to take revenge on the people who had insulted her and her art. After sending the scroll, she had regrets. *After making such great preparations for war, what will Mamallan and the general think of me? Will they mock my foolishness?*

The people of Vatapi, who had almost forgotten Sivagami, now remembered that she was the cause of their suffering. Crowds gathered in front of her mansion. Hearing the buzz in the street, Sivagami looked out from her window: the crowd booed and mocked her.

The anger which had died down and cooled years ago once more flared up in her heart. *If Mamallan is truly a brave warrior, he will tear my foolish message and invade Vatapi. He will make these uncultured beasts howl and run. Only then will my anger die.*

As the days passed, the crowds grew larger and their jeers louder. Some thugs threw stones at her house and roared with laughter when the stones thudded on the door. That evening, the crowd suddenly fell silent. War drums beat a tattoo.

A voice thundered, "The emperor is in the fort. He will destroy the Pallava forces and raise the flag of victory. Go home. All men who can fight, gather at the palace with your weapons."

The crowd broke into cheers of, "Long live the Vatapi emperor! Death to Mamallan!" As if by magic, the street before Sivagami's house emptied. Soon, twenty Chalukyan soldiers came and took up guard at the house and at the two ends of the street.

Sivagami heard all this from her companion. *Since Pulikesi has survived and entered the fort, it will certainly be war. I do not care what happens after I see my oath fulfilled. If my chastity is threatened, I will kill myself. I have my dagger ... and there is always the courtyard well.*

Once the attack began, the roar of a tempest filled the air. The beat of war drums, the shouts of soldiers and the loud clamour of people echoed from the towers and ramparts and assaulted the ears, squeezed the nerves and maddened the heart. By sunset, the ten lakh people in the city were in a daze.

Sivagami was even more affected than others. She could not stay still or leave the house. She paced the house and peeped through the window. She went up and looked out from the house's terrace. From there, she could see the ranks of soldiers marching down the streets and the panicked people running around.

She came down again and sent her companion to gather information. The frightened girl brought news that the Pallava army would attack the fort that night. She also said that she wanted to spend the night with her family. Sivagami pleaded with her, but it was useless. The girl left, taking the other servant with her. Sivagami overheard the guards complain at being made to guard that house. She closed and padlocked the huge doors. One door had a wicket gate: a small door, just wide enough for one person. This door had its own padlock.

That night, the anxious Sivagami did not sleep at all. *What will happen?* She sighed and her heart raced. She had butterflies in her stomach. At midnight, from her upper terrace, she saw houses burn. *My oath is being fulfilled after nine years.* She felt a great satisfaction.

The fire spread in all directions. The jubilant cheers of the evening changed into lament. The people's proud walk became a panicked run. As time passed, the cries and the running of women and children grew louder. Sivagami's satisfaction gave way to pain. Finally, unable to bear the cruel sight, Sivagami climbed down from the terrace. *What a disaster I have caused! How will it end? Will this big city be completely burnt? Will all these lakhs of men, women and children die? Aiyo, what will happen to me?* She did not have the heart to climb to the terrace again: instead, she paced the hall. Her legs ached. She lay face down on the bare floor. *It would be a relief to weep.* But she could not cry. It was as if her tear ducts were blocked.

The first flush of sunrise fell on the courtyard. There was a great commotion at the entrance. *Is it Mamallan? Has he come to take me away? Good! I can fall at his feet and stop the destruction of the city.* Sivagami jumped up and ran to the door. She hesitated. *Let me look through the wicket gate.* She was terrified to see a furious mob. Some of the men were arguing with the guards.

When they saw Sivagami's face at the wicket gate, the mob roared angrily. Men pushed aside the guards and rushed towards the entrance. Sivagami hurriedly closed the wicket gate—in her fright, she forgot to lock it. Instinct gave her feet strength and made her run to the back. *I must escape from this savage mob.*

When she reached the courtyard, Sivagami's blood froze in her veins. She saw the hideous figure of a woman in the dim sunlight, wearing a garland of skulls and bones.

The monster laughed. "Sivagami the beauty! Sivagami the goddess of art! The wicked devil who trapped Mamallan and Naganandhi in her seductive web! How will your beauty help you now? Can your intoxicating eyes and sparkling face save you?" She laughed again. "Hey, Sivagami, once I too was as beautiful as you. Because of you, I am now like this. I have waited all these years for my revenge." The Kapalika clenched her teeth and raised her dagger.

Sivagami was stunned and did not have the strength to think of escape. She instinctively moved back. In that instant, a figure appeared behind the Kapalika and gripped her knife-holding hand. The grip forced the Kapalika's fingers to loosen, and the dagger fell to the ground.

The Kapalika turned back in fury. "You wretch! You are here!"

Sivagami stared at the man whose timely arrival had saved her life. It was none other than Emperor Pulikesi. *They said the emperor was dead. Is this his ghost? Or ... or ... is it once again the monk in disguise?*

Here Is Your Lover

THE MINUTE AFTER Sivagami ran inside, the gallop of horses was heard. Most of the crowd ran away. The Chalukyan guards were stunned to see Emperor Pulikesi. On seeing their king, the few people who remained wept and lamented.

The emperor spoke to one of the guards who announced loudly, "Great people, the emperor thanks you for your loyalty. Treachery has brought this evil upon us. The emperor promises to avenge this at the right time. He knows that the Pallava woman living in this house is one of the causes of this disaster. He asks you to leave her punishment to him, and save your own lives. The ruthless Pallava demons are burning your houses. Go save your women and property!"

The people cried louder, shouted their curses and dispersed.

The emperor turned to the guards. "You have done your duty. Now look to saving your lives. All those who escape, come to Nasikapuri. I will meet you there." The soldiers' eyes filled with tears as they saluted their emperor and left. The emperor turned to the leader of his cavalry escort. "Dhananjayan, do you remember everything I said?"

"Yes, lord," Dhananjayan replied.

"Let me tell you once again. Shout, 'Long live Emperor Mamallan!' and leave the city. Come to the Kapalikas' sacrificial altar in the forest. I will be there before you." He bent to the man's ear. "You will find a mad Kapalika woman in the cave near the altar. Show no pity—kill her."

Dhananjayan and his company rode away. The street was now empty.

Naganandhi, disguised as the emperor, went to Sivagami's door and knocked softly. He pushed the wicket gate and found it open. He went in and locked it. Finding the front section of the house empty, he went to the back. He was just in time to save Sivagami's life. He stared at the Kapalika with his glowing eyes. He said, "Ranjani, come here," and moved away.

Sivagami was amazed to see the savage Kapalika following him obediently.

Naganandhi took Ranjani behind a pillar and spoke softly: "Why did you try to kill her?"

"Monk, it was to help you escape. How do you know that she is not dangerous? She is from the enemy kingdom after all."

"Fool! What danger can come to me through her?"

"Monk, love is the greatest danger of all."

"You are as foolish as ever. When you are here, would I even look at another ..."

"In that case, what does it matter to you if I kill her?"

"Fool! How many times have I told you that I am keeping her safe only to take revenge on Mamallan? Ranjani, if you help me now, I will obey you for the rest of my life."

"Monk, do you mean this?"

Naganandhi whispered instructions to the Kapalika. "Do you understand? Will you do this?"

She smiled cruelly. "Monk, once you have had your revenge, I can have mine, isn't it?"

The monk said, "How many times have I said, 'Yes?' Go quickly—I hear a chariot and horses."

The Kapalika walked to the front door. She unlocked the wicket gate and stood aside. She hid her right hand with the dagger behind her back. She waited like a tigress ready to pounce on an unsuspecting goat. A murderous frenzy blazed on her face and in her eyes.

Naganandhi came to Sivagami. "Sivagami, don't you trust me yet?"

The monk's tender voice confused Sivagami. "Emperor ..." she hesitated and stopped.

Naganandhi removed his crown.

Sivagami's confusion cleared. "Swami, it is you! This disguise ..."

"Yes. If I had come a second later, that demoness would have killed you—she would also have killed the extraordinary art which lives in you."

"But …" Sivagami hesitated. "What power you have over the Kapalika!"

"That is the power of love, Sivagami. That female monster loves me." He went on. "Once, she was the most beautiful woman in Vatapi's palace. One day, she insulted you—and so she became like this. Do you remember me telling you about this earlier?"

"Aiyo, what a cruel punishment!"

"She got away lightly. Do you know what happened to the artist who showed you surrendering to Pulikesi? I touched his neck and blessed him. That is all. His body began to burn. He threw himself into the river and never came up again."

Sivagami's heart throbbed in anguish. "Aiyo, how cruel! Why did you do all this?"

"Ah, is this all I have done for you?" The monk beat himself on his chest. "Sivagami, when I left for Ajanta, I knew about Mamallan's invasion. But I hid it from my brother, Pulikesi, and took him to Ajanta. Do you know why? Just for your happiness. Just for you to leave this city after seeing your oath fulfilled. I am a traitor to my country and my clan—the wretch who is responsible for the Vatapi emperor's death!" Naganandhi again beat himself on the chest.

Sivagami shuddered. She held the monk's hands tightly and stopped him from beating himself.

Naganandhi calmed down at the touch of her petal-soft hands. "Sivagami, forgive me. I have frightened you."

"What is there to forgive, swami? You saved my father's life and mine too. I am indebted to you."

"Sivagami, I have not yet saved you. You must trust me, and come with me."

Suddenly, Sivagami was suspicious. "Where do you want me to come? Why?"

"Sivagami, you are still in danger. In less than an hour, the fire will spread here …"

There was a commotion at the entrance. A door opened and closed, followed by a shriek and a thud. Sivagami shivered.

"You heard the mob. Do you want to stay here and be killed by those savages? Come with me."

Sivagami believed Naganandhi. "*Adigal*, where will you take me?"

"Prepared for danger, I built an underground passage from here in advance. If you trust me and come with me, I will take you outside the fort in half an hour." He paused. "Sivagami, my only concern is to take you safely to your father. I will hand you over to him and go my way."

Sivagami considered this. "Swami, I trust you completely, but I will not leave this house. If he comes and takes me by my hand, I will go from here. Otherwise, I will stay here and die."

Naganandhi's expression changed. Sparks flew from his eyes. He laughed angrily. "You think your lover, Mamallan, will come and take you from here. It will never happen."

"Why not?" Both of them turned towards the voice.

It was the Kapalika. She threw down the body she was carrying. "Sivagami, do not believe the monk. Here is your lover."

Sivagami stared at the body from which the hilt of a dagger protruded. It was Kannapiran. *Anna!*" she shrieked and went to him.

Kannapiran's eyes opened, and he looked at her for an instant. He murmured, "My dear, Kamali and Little Kannan are waiting for you." The next instant, he was dead.

Sivagami fainted.

Ranjani's Betrayal

NAGANANDHI JUMPED TO Sivagami, held his long fingers under her nostrils and felt the pulse at her forehead. He was furious with the Kapalika. "You wretch! What have you done!"

The Kapalika laughed like a ghoul. "*Adigal*, I followed your instructions. You told me to kill her lover, Mamallan, as soon as he entered the house. What can I do if this Queen of Chastity falls down dead on seeing her lover's corpse?"

"Fool! This is not Mamallan. He is Mamallan's charioteer, Kannapiran. Can't you see the difference between a king and a charioteer?"

"You said, 'Mamallan will walk in first: kill him.' I obeyed. Now you tell me it is not Mamallan, it is his charioteer."

They heard the door being smashed with axes.

"Ranjani, forget the past. Help me one last time. This woman must stay alive until I take my revenge. If I have a little time, I can save her. As long as she is in our hands, Mamallan will come looking for her. I will go ahead with her. The Pallava soldiers are breaking down the door. Stay here and hold them back."

"*Adigal*, I can manage one or two men. But how can I handle all of them?"

"Use your wits. Say that you are Sivagami and give some excuses. All I need is half an hour."

"Ah, you cunning monk! Are you trying to get me killed by the Pallava soldiers?"

"Ranjani, I promise that you will not be killed by them. They will say you are mad and spare you. Go quickly! Help me just this once. I will never forget you all my life."

The Kapalika's jealous, angry eyes went from Naganandhi to Sivagami and back again. She turned back reluctantly towards the entrance. In the blink of an eye, the monk drew the poisoned dagger at his waist and plunged it into her back with all his strength.

Ranjani howled and turned back. "Sinner! You betrayed me!" She jumped at Naganandhi. He moved back, and she fell face down on the ground. At lightning speed, Naganandhi lifted the unconscious Sivagami and hurried to the courtyard.

At sunrise, Paranjothi entered Vatapi Fort by the western gate. Like an arrow released from the bow, he headed straight for Sivagami's house, but it was not easy. The panicked people ran around like madmen, screaming and lamenting. The frenzied Pallava soldiers charged about, plundering the city and killing anyone who stood in their way. Burning roofs collapsed, blocking the streets. Clouds of smoke billowed and spread.

The confusion made it difficult for Paranjothi to find his way to the house based on his memory of the streets nine years ago. He stopped often to consult Kannapiran, who followed him with the chariot. When they finally reached the street, it was dawn. They saw a big crowd dispersing. When these people saw the nandi flag, they scattered in fright.

The street was empty when Paranjothi reached Sivagami's house. A sudden fear gripped his heart. The outer door was locked. The house was silent. *Our preparations, the invasion ... everything was to fulfill Sivagami's oath and rescue her. Will I be lucky enough to find her alive and give her to her father who is waiting at the fort's entrance?* Just then, some Pallava soldiers, holding the nandi flag, came galloping from the opposite direction. *They have important news for me.* Paranjothi turned to Kannapiran who stood by the chariot. "Kanna, knock on the door. When the door is opened, go in and tell Sivagami that we have come for her."

Kannapiran knocked on the door. The wicket gate opened. He went in and the gate closed behind him.

The captain of the Pallava company brought Paranjothi a message from Manavanman. He had evacuated the palace's treasures before the palace caught fire. But even after a thorough search, Pulikesi was not to be found anywhere. When questioned, the palace guards said that the emperor had urged all the Chalukyan soldiers at the palace to save themselves and go to Nasikapuri. He was last seen riding towards the fort's western gates. But the Pallava soldiers guarding those gates insisted that Pulikesi had not come that way.

Paranjothi's alarm grew. *That evil monk is more dangerous than a venomous snake. He might try to take revenge on the Pallavas through Sivagami. Is he torturing her or planning to hide her somewhere?* The general rushed to the door and heard a woman's wail of grief. In a frenzy, Paranjothi tried to open the door. He roared, "Hurry, smash the door with your axes!"

The soldiers attacked the door with their axes. In five minutes, the door crashed open and Paranjothi ran inside. He saw a man and a woman lying dead, stabbed by knives. The man was Kannapiran. *Aiyo, why did this have to happen to Kamali's husband?* But there was no time for emotion. He turned to the woman's body lying face down nearby. *Is it Sivagami? Has that wretch killed them both and ...?*

Paranjothi turned over the corpse and was relieved to see the hideous face. *It is not Sivagami.* He was startled when the body moved. The woman sighed. Her bloodshot eyes stared at him.

"Ah, so you are Mamallan," she mumbled.

Eager to learn what he could from her, Paranjothi said, "Yes, I am Mamallan. Where is Sivagami?"

"I am Sivagami." Her cruel smile heightened her hideous expression.

Paranjothi was stunned. *Has Sivagami lost her mind and become this crazy woman over the long years of imprisonment? Chi, never!* He remembered Gundodharan's meeting with Sivagami just a month ago and Shatrughan's account of the Kapalika. *It is that Kapalika from the cave.* "You liar! You are not Sivagami. If you tell me where Sivagami is, I will save your life."

"Ah, it is impossible for you to save me—he stabbed me with a poisoned dagger."

"Poisoned dagger? Then it must be Naganandhi who stabbed you. Tell me quickly—how did Naganandhi go? By which path? If you tell me, I will take revenge on him for you."

"What is the use of taking revenge on Naganandhi? It is true that the deceitful monk killed me. But it was that wicked Sivagami who goaded him. Pallava, that nobody, Sivagami, does not love you. She is infatuated with that dry, emaciated Buddhist monk. When she heard you coming, she ran away with Naganandhi. Thinking that I might stop them, she made him kill me. If you want to avenge me, take revenge on Sivagami. Do not harm that foolish monk."

Paranjothi could not bear to hear more. "Where are they? How did they go? Tell me quickly."

Thinking that her plan had worked, the Kapalika said, "Climb into the courtyard well. The underground passage is there. Take revenge on Sivagami. Do not forget!"

She fell silent. Her breath stopped.

Buddha's Sanctum

ORDERING FOUR OF his soldiers to follow him, Paranjothi hurried to the courtyard and looked into the well. The well's walls were made of brick for a short distance. Below that, it was rock. The water level was very low.

His heart beating loudly, Paranjothi used the bricks as handholds and climbed into the well. His men followed him. Once they reached the rock, the cracks and crevices made the going easier. Three quarters of the way down, Paranjothi exclaimed in surprise—there was a large hole in the rock wall which opened into the darkness. Paranjothi signalled to his men and entered the hole which was just wide enough for one person to crawl into. After a short distance, the passage widened. He could now sit up and push himself along. His feet touched some steps. After climbing down four steps, he reached level ground and could stand. It was pitch dark. When his eyes grew accustomed to the dark, he saw a little of his surroundings.

Paranjothi found himself in a corner of a wide, underground hall carved out of rock. There was a large Buddha statue opposite him. There were two rows of huge, beautifully carved granite pillars. Paranjothi and the soldiers searched behind the pillars and in the corners. No one was there, but there were some clothes and ornaments lying beside a pillar. *These are an emperor's clothes. Naganandhi must have left them here and put on saffron robes. Where are Naganandhi and Sivagami? How could they disappear?*

Paranjothi's eyes fell on the Buddha statue. He had a sudden brainwave. *There was a secret passage behind the Buddha statue in Kanchi's Royal Monastery.* He charged to the statue, but the statue stood against the rock wall. There was no room for any opening or passage. *Something tells me that this statue is the key to the secret passage.* He prayed, "Lord Buddha, if you are truly Mahavishnu's avatar, show me the way. I surrender at your lotus feet."

Paranjothi touched the statue's feet. A miracle happened—the Buddha statue shifted a little to one side. The secret passage was on the rear rock wall. Paranjothi was overjoyed. *Ah, Buddha has shown the way!* Signalling to his soldiers, he entered the passage and took a step forward. He stopped short at what he saw.

Rows of torchbearers, like black, fire-spitting demons, were moving down the narrow passage towards him. A shaven-headed monk, carrying a woman on his shoulders, came running ahead of them. *When the monk was halfway down the passage, Shatrughan and his men must have come from the opposite direction. The monk is now running back here to escape from them.*

Paranjothi immediately backed out of the passage. He and his men hid behind the pillars. Soon, Naganandhi emerged from behind the Buddha statue with Sivagami on his shoulders. Paranjothi held his breath and waited. Naganandhi laid Sivagami on the floor near the statue. He walked to the statue and was lost in thought. He looked around. Then he went and sat beside Sivagami.

He plans to shut the passage entrance. Paranjothi signalled to his men and leaped at the monk. His men joined him and held the monk's hands tightly.

The monk turned and looked up at them. He could not see their faces in the dark, but his words showed his keen intelligence. "My dear Paranjothi, I was expecting you. If I must lose, I prefer losing to you." He stood.

They all moved to the center of the hall.

Naganandhi pleaded with Paranjothi: "My dear boy, why are they holding me? Where can I escape to? Your men are coming from that side … my time is over. Ask them to release me. I am ready to obey you."

Moved by Naganandhi's plea, Paranjothi commanded his men, "Release the monk."

The soldiers released him and moved away.

"Paranjothi, on the day you arrived in Kanchi, I saved you from being bitten by a snake. That very night, I helped you escape from prison. Do you remember all this?" Even as he spoke, in the blink of an eye, Naganandhi drew his dagger from his waist.

Paranjothi jumped back and drew his sword. *Ah, this is the end. Just at the point of success, I made a mistake! Why is he turning that side? The deceitful monk is aiming his dagger at Sivagami!*

Naganandhi hesitated—in that split second, Paranjothi brought his sword down on the monk's shoulder. The dagger missed its mark and fell far away. The monk dropped like an uprooted tree.

The Final Prize

SIVAGAMI FLOATED UP slowly from a bottomless ocean. Glimmers of light swirled in the darkness. There was a soft sound which grew into a roar. The roar became human voices. *There are two voices. One is familiar ... but who is it?* She sighed deeply and opened her eyes. She saw a strange sight. *Is it a dream? Or have I lost my mind?* She was lying on the ground in a rock-cut Buddhist temple. The uneven stone chilled her to the bone. A man lay a little away from her. Another man stood majestically over him like Shiva the Destroyer, holding a sword. Many soldiers stood further away, armed with swords and spears. The sparks and smoke from their torches made that hall a scene from hell. A huge statue of Buddha, seated in meditation, looked on with a smile.

Sivagami shut her eyes and opened them again. Her mind cleared. *It is true.* She saw that it was Naganandhi on the floor and Paranjothi who stood over him, sword in hand. *The men must be Pallava soldiers. How did they all come here?* The voices cleared.

Naganandhi was saying, "My dear Paranjothi, how grateful you are! This hand saved you from a cobra's bite. This hand released you from a Pallava prison. This hand saved the life of Aayanar, your guru. This hand saved Sivagami from the Kapalika's dagger. You have cut off that hand."

Paranjothi cut in: "You cunning monk! Wasn't it that hand which threw the poisoned dagger at Mahendran Pallava? Wasn't it that hand which helped you to carry Aayanar's daughter down this passage? Wasn't it that hand which tried to throw a poisoned dagger at Sivagami?"

"My dear boy, everything you say is true. But why did I try to carry away Aayanar's daughter? Ah, Paranjothi, you think that you care more for Sivagami than I do. Your master, that fool, Mamallan, thinks that he loves her more than I do. My dear boy, do you know the meaning of love? I am the cause of Vatapi burning. I sacrificed my own brother for Sivagami. I dedicated the mighty Chalukyan empire to her. What do you know about love!"

"*Adigal*, I just learnt that one must throw a poisoned dagger at a woman to show one's love for her. You deceitful monk! I have no time to waste on you. If you were in your royal disguise, I would have killed you. But I do not have the heart to kill a monk in saffron robes. I will let you live on one condition. Ten years ago, Aayanar sent me to learn the secret of Ajanta's pigments. I gave him my word. If you tell me the secret, I will let you live. Otherwise … if an evil man like you has a God, pray to that God."

"My dear boy, I have only one God: Sivagami. I will pray to her. I wanted to take Aayanar and Sivagami to Ajanta and show them the secret, but that did not happen. Listen. We usually take the juice of leaves, roots, fruits and seeds, boil them and use them as pigments. These plant-based dyes fade quickly. But some rocks produce natural colours which do not fade under the sun or rain. The pigments made by powdering, treating, grinding and liquidizing these rocks never fade. Ajanta's paintings use these coloured rocks. I have told you the secret known only to Ajanta's Buddhist *sangha* for five hundred years. Can I go now?"

"Go at once before I change my mind. Use the secret passage. Quick! Quick!"

Naganandhi stood with great effort, holding his wounded hand with his good hand. "Paranjothi, you are a good boy. You have spared my life. It would have been better if you had cut off my neck instead of my hand, but I still want to live. I will go at once. I know that you want me gone before Mamallan comes. I have one request: Sivagami will soon regain consciousness. You must tell her that I tried to kill her with my poisoned dagger. Tell her that it was my love's final gift to her." Naganandhi turned towards Sivagami. He saw her leaning against a pillar, as still as a statue.

"Ah, Sivagami, you are up. Did you hear what I said to Paranjothi? Yes, I tried to kill you with my dagger. I thought of your future and wanted to do this for your good. The general stopped me. Sivagami, in the future … no, leave it. Forget this false monk who offered his life, body and soul at your feet. Forget me, and be as happy as you can. But I will never forget you. I will not forget Paranjothi and Mamallan too. Goodbye, Sivagami, goodbye. May Lord Buddha guard you." Naganandhi stumbled to the Buddha statue and disappeared behind it.

Everyone stood watching the monk escape. Sivagami stared at him until he disappeared. *Is he a demon, a man deranged by grief, or a ruthless murderer?*

Paranjothi said, "Shatrughan, you came at the right time. See if there is an easy way out of this damned Buddhist temple. It will be difficult for all of us to get out through the well."

"General, I already found the main entrance. I will get it cleared at once," Shatrughan replied.

Paranjothi had a sudden thought. "Shatrughan, where is Gundodharan?"

"Ah, general! The Kapalika killed my best and dearest disciple. Not finding that demoness in her cave, we came looking for her by the secret passage. Have you seen that wicked woman?"

"She and Kanna lie dead in the house. I do not know how Kanna died. We must go and see."

Paranjothi went to Sivagami and said respectfully, "My dear lady, by Lord Ekambar's grace, all the danger is past. Rest for a while. We will leave this cave once the entrance is cleared. Your father and the emperor wait outside the fort."

Choked with grief, Sivagami stammered, "General, I must see Kamali's husband once more. Take me to the house."

The Lion Flag

SIVAGAMI SOBBED OVER Kannapiran's lifeless, peaceful face.

Paranjothi said, "Lady, Kanna will not come back to life. This is war. Is Kannapiran the only one who died? Sixteen thousand soldiers are dead. Please come. The fire is nearing this house."

Sivagami sobbed, "General, I sent you a message saying no to war …"

"I tried my best to stop the war, but that fake monk ruined everything."

"Sir, I am the wretch responsible for all this. I foolishly refused to leave with you …"

"Lady, many things could have happened differently. What is the use of thinking about all that now? Please come. Mamallan and your father are waiting eagerly for you."

"General, how will I look them in the face? Let me stay here and die. Tell them that I beg their forgiveness a thousand times."

There was a loud noise at the entrance. Mamallan came in, followed by Aayanar.

"Ah, here they are!" Paranjothi said. *With this, my responsibility ends.*

Sivagami broke into goosebumps. She looked up at the door. Her eyes met Mamallan's for an instant. Unable to control her emotion, she bowed her head again. Something blocked her chest and throat—she could not breathe or weep. She had no idea of what was happening around her.

She came back to her senses when she heard her father's voice. "Ah, is it Kannapiran? Aiyo!"

Mamallan said, "Yes, it is Kanna. He came to rescue Kamali's friend, and now he lies dead with a poisoned dagger in his chest. Aayanar, ask your daughter: has her oath been fulfilled? Has her anger cooled? Ask her, Aayanar."

Mamallan's words were like molten lead being poured into Sivagami's ears. *How many sweet words this voice once said! What cruel words it says now! Ah, is it for this that I patiently stayed alive for nine years?*

Paranjothi was pained by Mamallan's harsh words. "Lord, Sivagami is heartbroken ..."

Mamallan cut in: "Why must Sivagami be heartbroken? Hasn't her oath been fulfilled? Let her rejoice over the burning houses, the corpses, the people weeping as they run. Sculptor Aayanar, take your daughter and go at once."

Sivagami's heart shattered into a thousand pieces. Her head whirled.

Aayanar went to her and said with pity, "My dear child, don't you recognise me?"

"*Appa*!" Sivagami shrieked and sobbed as she hugged him.

From the time Paranjothi had entered Vatapi, Mamallan's anxiety grew. *Danger looms over Sivagami. I must go to her*. Once Manavanman sent word that Pulikesi had not been found at the palace, Mamallan could no longer wait. He took Aayanar and went into the city. *I must speak lovingly to Sivagami when I see her.* But when he saw Kannapiran, whom he greatly loved and respected, lying dead, Mamallan's heart hardened.

Aayanar and Sivagami went ahead in the chariot, while Mamallan and Paranjothi rode behind them, talking. Paranjothi related everything that had taken place from the time he reached Sivagami's house.

Mamallan was furious that Paranjothi had spared Naganandhi's life. The monk had said that he had tried to kill Sivagami to save her from suffering in the future. In his heart of hearts, Mamallan had to admit to the truth of this. His hate blazed stronger.

Sivagami leaned on her beloved father. Unable to bear the cruel sights in Vatapi's streets, she closed her eyes. But the noise of burning houses, the wails of infants and the laments of women filled her ears and forced her to open her eyes again. Once, when Mamallan happened to come forward and ride by the chariot, she looked up at him eagerly.

Mamallan ignored her and looked at Aayanar. "Sculptor, it may be a month before we can all leave. If you want, I will see you and your daughter escorted safely to Kanchi. I heard that Naganandhi wanted to take you and your daughter to Ajanta. If you want, you can do that too."

Even in the middle of all the suffering and terror of war, the word, 'Ajanta,' roused Aayanar's longing. Aayanar did not yet know that Paranjothi had got the secret of Ajanta's pigments from Naganandhi. He asked Sivagami, "My dear, shall we go to Kanchi or Ajanta?"

Sivagami's heart turned to stone. "*Appa*, I am not going to Kanchi or to Ajanta. In the name of the love he once had for me, ask the prince to plunge his sword into my chest and send me to *Yamaloka*." Sivagami again fainted and fell on her father's lap.

Having vented his anger on Sivagami, Mamallan was pacified. He went back to Paranjothi. "Friend, there is Pulikesi's false Pillar of Victory. We have kept the promise we made as we stood by it nine years ago. Knock it down and let a Pallava Pillar of Victory stand in its place. Let the triumphant flag of the Pallava army fly on the new pillar, reaching up to the sky. As a sign of this great victory, let the nandi be replaced by the lion on all our flags and medals."

The Full Moon

FROM THE DAY of earth's creation, the full moon rises once a month and rides in state among the stars sparkling like diamonds in the sky.

Nothing surprises it. But on that December night in 642 BC, the full moon must have stopped for an instant above Vatapi and sighed before moving on.

A month ago, Vatapi's towers and mansions stood majestically as if reaching out to touch the moon. The blazing city lights competed with the stars. Men and women proudly walked the streets, dressed in silks and jewels. Caparisoned elephants, beautiful horses, ivory palanquins and golden chariots glittered in the moonlight. The sound of temple bells and music and tinkling anklets was heard. The fragrance of incense and sandalwood and flowers spread in the air.

Now only a few broken walls remained of that paradise. The rest was charcoal and ash and blackened stone and sand. A few men, looking like animated corpses, wandered about mindlessly. Others sat sifting the ashes and sand. Who knows who or what they searched for?

On the other side of the shattered fort's walls, the full moon saw a different sight. Lakhs of Pallava soldiers celebrated their victory and guarded their share of Vatapi's plunder. The thought of leaving this desolate land and marching back to their homes the next day made them stay up all night in noisy celebration.

Mamallan inspected the camp, talking with the men. He congratulated those who had performed extraordinary feats of courage, wanting to keep these soldiers permanently in his service.

After Mamallan and his escort moved away, the soldiers praised the emperor. There was also gloomy talk: why did General Paranjothi not accompany the emperor? The soldiers were proud that a commoner had risen to become a general, and the emperor's close friend, through his courage and virtue.

Now it seemed as if that friendship was ruined. Was it because of the argument over attacking Vatapi Fort or Mamallan's harsh treatment of Sivagami? Had Manavanman and Adityavarman poisoned the emperor's mind? Was the general exhausted and resting in his tent?

Siruthondar

PARANJOTHI WAS IN good physical health, but his mind was troubled. He sat alone in his tent, sleepless. In his mind's eye, he saw Vatapi burning, women, children and old people wailing, Pallava soldiers plundering the city, dismembered corpses and rivers of blood.

He saw Naganandhi hurling his poisoned dagger at Sivagami; he heard Mamallan's cruel words to her; he saw the dead Kannapiran's expressionless face. Above all, he saw Navukkarasar, with holy ash on his forehead and *rudraksha* garlands on his body, looking lovingly at him. "My dear boy," he heard him say. "Where are you? What are you doing? Enough. Come. How long must I wait for you?" He heard himself reply, "Gurudeva, just another forty-five days. I will come to you."

After rescuing Sivagami, handing her over to her father and sending them on ahead, Paranjothi and a company of hand-picked soldiers rode west. They joined Adityavarman, who was waiting for the Chalukyan army from Vengi. The Vengi army, made up mostly of elephants and cavalry, was there three days after Vatapi fell. When its commanders heard of Pulikesi's death and the burning of Vatapi, they tried to retreat, but Paranjothi outflanked the Chalukyas and blocked their retreat. Surrounded, the Chalukyan army surrendered. The Pallavas got ten thousand elephants and thirty thousand horses.

Paranjothi gave Mamallan this gift and asked to be relieved of his post. After serving the kingdom for so many years, he now wished to serve Lord Shiva and his devotees. Mamallan was not surprised—he had noticed Paranjothi's increasing detachment from worldly desire.

Mamallan said, "General, please hoist our lion flag in Vatapi. After that, you may leave."

The next day, at sunrise, armed Pallava soldiers stood in rank upon rank in Vatapi. Behind them, caparisoned war elephants and horses stretched as far as the eye could see. In the middle of this army, like a ship's mast among the waves, stood a brand new, majestic Pillar of Victory. There was pin-drop silence.

War drums beat a tattoo, announcing the emperor's arrival. The soldiers shouted in one voice, 'Long live Mamallan, Destroyer of Vatapi!' The cry rose to the sky and echoed everywhere.

Followed by Paranjothi, Manavanman and Adityavarman, Mamallan stopped by the pillar. Once the cheers died down, Mamallan said, "Nine years ago, General Paranjothi and I came here in disguise and stood by another Pillar of Victory. It was inscribed with the lie that Pulikesi had defeated Mahendran Pallava. The general and I swore to knock down that pillar and erect a Pallava pillar in its place. We have kept our promise. General Paranjothi, instrumental in our great triumph, is the right person to raise the Pallavas' flag of victory over the pillar."

The Pallava soldiers were delighted to see Mamallan and Paranjothi together. As Paranjothi raised the Pallavas' lion flag, the deafening sound of war drums, musical instruments and cheers filled the air.

Mamallan waited for silence. "I have some sad news for you. General Paranjothi, who worked day and night all these years to give us this great victory, has asked me to release him. His mind is filled with Shiva bhakti. It is wrong to make a Shiva devotee serve as an army general, and so I have agreed to release him. Tomorrow morning, he leaves us to go on a pilgrimage of the sacred rivers. I ask you all to give him a rousing send off."

Silence fell over the army. Mamallan sensed the soldiers' unhappiness. Suddenly, the tall, sturdy Emperor Mamallan hugged the shorter General Paranjothi. At this, the men broke into cheers.

All that day, Mamallan gave out awards to the Pallava soldiers and commanders. With the help of a thousand soldiers, the hundred goldsmiths who had accompanied the army melted the gold bars and ornaments taken from Vatapi Palace and the Chalukyan treasury. They poured the molten gold into molds and made lakhs and lakhs of treasury coins bearing the lion emblem. In addition to their share of the plunder, each soldier was given ten gold coins. The commanders, and those men who had performed exceptional acts of courage, were rewarded with all the treasure that an elephant or a horse could carry.

Adityavarman was given complete authority to rule over the vast region between the Krishna and the Tungabhadra, with his capital at Vengi.

Manavanman said, "Lord, the only prize I ask from you is the Lankan throne. I do not want anything else."

Finally, Mamallan turned to Paranjothi. "My friend, this great victory and the immense wealth from this war are yours. I would like to give you five thousand elephants, ten thousand horses and all the wealth they can carry …"

Paranjothi stopped him: "My king, all I want is a small place in your heart. I ask for only one prize in addition to that."

"Ah, what is this special thing?" Mamallan asked in curiosity.

Four soldiers brought a covered palanquin with the Vatapi Vinayagar. Paranjothi told Mamallan about his prayer and his desire to take the deity with him and consecrate it at Sengathankudi village. He firmly refused to take anything else from Vatapi.

Mamallan was forced to agree. But he insisted that Paranjothi take a company of two elephants, twelve horses and hundred infantry soldiers on his pilgrimage.

Mamallan and his army would march back to Kanchi the next afternoon, taking the same route they had used earlier. Paranjothi and his small company would leave that morning to visit Srisailam and other important temples. When Paranjothi went to Mamallan's tent to say his final goodbyes, the soldiers threw discipline to the winds and gathered there. They were stunned by Paranjothi's new appearance. He had thrown aside his dagger, shield, sword, spear, armour, turban and tunic. With holy ash on his forehead and *rudraksha* beads around his head and neck, he stood before them as a mature Shiva devotee. His face glowed.

The soldiers cheered, "Long live General Paranjothi! Long live the hero who destroyed Vatapi!"

Paranjothi folded his hands and waited for silence. "Friends, I am no longer a general. I am just a siruthondar (small servant) in the company of those who serve Lord Shiva's devotees."

The soldiers heard him in wonder. One of them raised the divine cry, "Long live the Siruthondar of Shiva's devotees!"

Hundreds of men took up the cry, "Long live Siruthondar!"

Paranjothi left with his small company and the Vatapi Vinayagar. The sea of soldiers continued to shout, "Long live Siruthondar!" until he was lost to view.

Talk by the Pond

IT WAS A cloudy morning in late *Thai*. The red lotuses in the brimming pond spread their fragrance in the air. Blue beetles with red-striped wings circled the flowers, buzzing happily. Large carp swam in groups in the crystal-clear water. Pearl-like droplets of water crawled over the lotus leaves. The tall trees around the pond rose skywards, their branches spreading dark shadows over the pond. Green parrots, little multicoloured birds, singing cuckoos and mynahs pecked the tender leaves and scattered the flower petals.

A woman sat sadly by the pond. It was Sivagami–Sculptor Aayanar's beloved daughter, the lover who had captured the brave Emperor Mamallan's heart, the Queen of Dance.

The last ten years had not changed her appearance, but how much her heart had changed! What had happened to the sweet pleasure she had once taken in her dreams as she sat alone by the same pond? Why was she not able to delight over the lovely lotuses and the blue beetles buzzing over them? Where was the pride she had once taken in her beautiful reflection? *Am I still imprisoned in that Vatapi mansion—is this beautiful lotus pond just a daydream?*

Sivagami was lost in vague thoughts for a long time. She came to herself when the sky cleared, and the sun blazed on her. She walked towards Aayanar's house. Suddenly, she heard a horse: every hoofbeat was a pang of pain in her heart. *How many times Mamallan came looking for me by the lotus pond! Who is coming now? Can it be him? Ah, how can I face him? His fierce, accusing eyes will say, "You wretch, how much suffering you have caused!"*

There were two horses. *I cannot face him alone: how can I even think of facing him in someone's company?* Sivagami hid behind a dense thicket near the pond. The two horses approached. Mamallan was on the first horse. *How stern his face is! What a change from the loving, innocent face of the past! The other man is a stranger. He must have made many new friends.*

The horses stopped at the pond, and the men dismounted. They stood under the very tree in which Sivagami used to hide Mamallan's lyrical love letters. She could hear Mamallan. *Yes, he is talking about me.*

"How happy I once was to see this lotus pond! How my heart beat, wondering whether Sivagami was here! Now, I do not have the heart to look her in the face. I went up to the house's door and came away. This pond is even more beautiful than it used to be, but it gives me no joy. Manavanman, look at this bench under the tree: we sat here many times, blissfully holding hands. The bench lies in pieces. This shattered bench is a symbol of my ruined life."

Sivagami did not catch Manavanman's words but heard Mamallan's reply.

"Ah, Manavanman, I cannot even think of that! A withered flower which falls from the plant can never be fused with the plant again. I remember what my father said: 'Sivagami and her special gift must be dedicated to God. They do not belong to common men.' His words have come true."

Mamallan and his friend walked down the bank to the shore of the pond. They soon came back, mounted their horses and rode away.

As Sivagami walked home, pleasure and pain warred in her heart. *Mamallan's love for me is as strong as ever, but there is an unbridgeable chasm between us. What is it? I must meet him. I must tell him that my heart has not changed. I must insist that I will always belong to him. Even if he pushes me away, I cannot leave him.*

That afternoon, Aayanar said hesitantly, "My child, I do not like living here anymore. I want to go to our house in Kanchi. What do you say?"

"*Appa*, I too do not like living alone in the forest. I feel like meeting and talking to people. In Kanchi, I can at least pass the time with Kamali *akka*. Shall we leave tomorrow, *appa*?"

"I have sent word asking for the palanquin. There will be great excitement in Kanchi tomorrow. The emperor will make his triumphal entry into the city."

"Has the emperor returned?" This was the last time Sivagami deceived her father in her life.

"Yes, my child. The Pallava army and the emperor returned the day before yesterday. I believe they have camped near the fort's northern entrance. Tomorrow is marked as an auspicious day for the emperor's triumphal entry into the city. Sivagami, I think I am losing my mind as I grow old—I am imagining things. This morning, I thought I heard horses. I thought it was the emperor coming here as he used to do in those days. But when I went to the door, there was no one there."

Sivagami's eyes filled. *I do not have the heart to tell him that the emperor was here.*

Seeing her tears, Aayanar turned away silently. Then he looked at her and said lovingly, "My dear child, I must tell you something."

"What is it, *appa*? Tell me."

"Like every woman, you must marry a good man and have children. My child … I want to cherish and play with my grandchildren."

"*Appa*, isn't it enough that I was born a girl and made you all suffer?" Sivagami asked in a heart-breaking voice.

"What pain have you caused anyone, my dear?"

"You are lame because of me. Kamali *akka* lost her husband because of me …"

"What can you do, Sivagami? Fate's dictate was written on Kannapiran's forehead. And Little Kannan is there to continue his lineage. Mustn't my line continue too?"

"*Appa*, those born into royal dynasties need to worry about heirs to ascend the throne and rule after them. Why must poor, simple people like us worry about heirs?"

Triumphal Entry

AT THEIR PREVIOUS meeting, Kamali had been full of tears and anger, as she had just heard of Kannapiran's untimely death. She scolded Sivagami: "You wretch! You have ruined yourself and me along with you! Why didn't you die first?" She was a little consoled when Sivagami remained patient, weeping with her and blaming herself for everything.

This time, Kamali was loving and kind to Sivagami and was calmer. She insisted that Sivagami tell her all about her life in Vatapi. She also heard a detailed account of Kannapiran's death. The two friends spoke continuously about Kannapiran's goodness and his love for Kamali.

Little Kannan came running from outside, crying, "*Amma, amma*!"

Kamali hugged him and said, "This child is all we have. He must grow up and support us."

Sivagami felt a pang. *Why must I become like her? Must I give up Mamallan and his sweet love?*

Just then, the sound of music and cheers came from the street.

Sivagami was eager to see the emperor's triumphal entry. "*Akka*, let us watch the procession through the window."

"What do you and I have to do with the triumphal entry? Be quiet!"

She is bitter about losing Kannapiran. "How can you say that, *akka*? How much effort the emperor took to fulfill my oath! When the whole city is celebrating his triumph, how can we …"

"You and your oath and your emperor! You madwoman, don't you have any self-respect? Did you lose it in Vatapi?" Kamali went on, her eyes filled with tears. "I dreamt of you and Mamallan getting married. I longed to see you both going in procession in a golden chariot, with your brother at the reins. That wish is dead!"

Sivagami was confused and silent. *She is bitter about Kannapiran's death.*

As the procession came closer, Sivagami could not control her eagerness. She ran to the window, followed by Kamali.

The emperor's triumphal entry was a delight to the eye. The procession was led by huge bulls, carrying victory drums. Then came caparisoned elephants, horses and camels, followed by Pallava soldiers with musical instruments, flags and prizes. The people showered the emperor with flowers and turmeric-coloured rice as his golden chariot came down the street, drawn by white Arabian horses.

Cheers rose to the sky from ten thousand throats: 'Long live Mamallan, Destroyer of Vatapi!' 'Long live the brave king, Narasimhan Pallava!'

Sivagami's heart raced as the emperor's chariot came near. She looked at the white horses. Then she turned her eyes to the gem-studded throne. Her head whirled. *What is this? Who is the queen sitting beside the emperor?* Sivagami held the wall tightly and looked again. *It is true, my eyes are not fooling me. A queen is sitting by Mamallan. Ah, how beautiful she is! She looks like Rathi or Mahalakshmi.* Sivagami asked softly, "Who is that, *akka*? The one seated by the emperor?"

"That is the Pandyan princess—Mamallan's queen. Who else would sit beside him?"

"*Akka*, is he married? When?" Sivagami's surprise and dashed hopes were clear.

"You poor thing! Did nobody tell you? I thought you knew. It has been nine years since Mamallan's marriage. That schemer, Mahendran Pallava, got his son married before he died."

"Why do you criticise him, *akka*? Mahendran did what was right. Only now do I know the truth—and realise my foolishness," Sivagami murmured.

She stood staring at the royal couple. The golden chariot moved on, followed by the royal elephant. She saw the two children seated on the elephant. "Who is that?"

"Who else? The lucky ones born to ensure the Pallava dynasty's prosperity. The children born to Mamallan and the Pandyan princess: Mahendran and Kundavi. Didn't you know any of this?"

Sivagami was silent. *Ah, there is no need to worry about heirs to the Pallava dynasty!* Her heart broke. She stared at the children on the royal elephant. Once the elephant moved on, she left the window. She sat like a statue in a corner of the courtyard, as if in a trance.

Kamali joined her when the procession ended. "Why are you sitting like this? Cry, for heaven's sake! So what if you love the emperor? Don't you at least have the right to weep?"

Sivagami lay on Kamali's lap and sobbed. After an hour, her tears dried. She felt as if a great burden had been lifted from her heart. Her mind was filled with a peace she had never before experienced.

Her Beloved's Feet

THAT EVENING, SIVAGAMI went to Aayanar. "*Appa*, didn't you say you wanted me to get married? Make arrangements for it."

Aayanar thought that he would die of happiness. He examined Sivagami's radiant face. "That is easy, my child. I will soon find a husband worthy of you."

"*Appa,* I have accepted Lord Ekambar as my husband."

Aayanar was worried. *Has my precious girl gone mad?* He spoke to her again and realised that she was clear in her mind. *This is not madness—it is bhakti.*

Hearing that Navukkarasar was at a nearby Shiva temple, Aayanar went to consult him.

Navukkarasar heard him patiently. "Aayanar, your daughter has experienced more sorrow than any woman. Now a bliss equal to that sorrow waits for her. Didn't you name her Sivagami? She has lived up to that name in her love for Lord Shiva. Do not stand in her way—grant her wish. That is the greatest gift you can give her."

Three months later, Aayanar, Sivagami and a few others came to Lord Ekambar's sanctum. The temple priests performed the pooja and came with the tray of *prasadam.* Along with the fruits, flower garland, holy ash and vermillion, Aayanar had arranged for a *mangalsutra.* Sivagami took the garland and the *mangalsutra* and devotedly wore them around her neck. She then began to dance before Lord Nataraja's sanctum.

For some time, she danced in bliss. Then, she sang Navukkarasar's verse *Munnam avanudaya namam kettal* and held the *abhinaya* for it. People slowly gathered there and lost themselves in bhakti as they watched her dance.

Emperor Mamallan arrived there unexpectedly.

The last time Sivagami had danced to this song, she had seen Mamallan coming and had danced with him in mind. Now Sivagami did not notice the emperor's arrival. Lord Ekambar had captured her heart and her entire being. Her eyes saw nothing but God; there was room in her heart only for him.

Mamallan stood there for a while, lost in her dance. His eyes filled with tears. He controlled himself. *I am the Pallava emperor. People are looking at me.* He quietly moved away.

As Mamallan crossed the threshold of the Ekambar Temple's main entrance, he heard Sivagami's sweet, passionate voice sing Navukkarasar's line—

She fell in surrender at her beloved's feet.

Glossary

aarti	Hindu ritual in which lighted wicks are waved in a circular motion before a deity or person
abhinaya	conveying expression through the face, limbs or body movements in dance
acharya	teacher or spiritual guide
adigal	a respected ascetic
Agama	traditional Hindu religious text
Aippasi	mid-October to mid-November
akka	elder sister
amma	mother
Ananda tandavam	Shiva's dance of bliss
anna	elder brother
appa	father
appam	pancake
archakar	temple priest
arugam	Bermuda grass or *Cynodon dactylon*
Arugan	god in Jainism
bajra	pearl millet
bhakti	devotion
Bharatanatyam	classical dance form
Bharata Shastra	ancient Indian treatise on dance and drama
bhiksha	alms
Buddham saranam gacchami	I take refuge in Buddha

chithappa	uncle
deeparadhana	worshiping a deity with lamps
Devaloka	abode of the demigods
devi	Hindu goddess or a title of respect for a woman
dharma	religious and moral duties
dosai	crisp, savoury pancake
Gandiva	Arjuna's bow
gandharva	celestial musicians and dancers
graha preeti	propitiating the planets
guru dakshina	gifts offered to a teacher
hastha	hand gestures in dance
jeevakarunyam	compassion
Kalaivani	goddess of art, Saraswathi
Kaliyugam	the fourth, decadent age of the world
kamandalam	oblong water pot
kanganam	sacred thread tied around wrist during marriage
Karthigai	mid-November to mid-December
Kiratarjuniya	epic Sanskrit poem by Bharavi
Kondrai	Indian laburnum or *Cassia fistula*
Kovai	ivy gourd
kozlukattai	sweet dumpling
kundalam	earring
kungumam	vermillion
Magizham	Spanish cherry or *Mimusops elengi*
mama	father-in-law
mangalsutra	auspicious thread around a bride's neck
Maravar	a caste
matham	Hindu monastery for spiritual studies
Mattavilasa Prahasana	a one-act Sanskrit play by King Mahendran Varma
melam	percussion instrument
moksha	release from the cycle of rebirth
Munnam avanudaya namam kettal	she first heard Lord Shiva's name
Nada Brahma	transcendental cosmic sound

Nandi	sacred bull
Navratri	nine-day festival celebrating Goddess Durga
paati	grandmother
Padmasana	lotus pose in yoga
Panchajanya	Lord Krishna's conch
Panchakalyani	Kathiawadi breed of horse
Paneer tree	temple tree or *Plumeria rubra*
paniyaram	fried dumpling
Parijatham	coral jasmine or *Nyctanthes arbor-tristis*
Parivadini	musical instrument with seven strings
prasadam	offering to god
Punnai	Indian laurel or *Calophyllum inophyllum*
Purasu	Flame of the forest or *Butea monosperma*
rudraksha	dried seeds of the *Elaeocarpus ganitrus* tree
sangha	Buddhist monastic order
sattva guna	state of harmony and goodness
Shaiva	Shiva devotee
Shenbagam	Champak or *Magnolia champaca*
sumangali	a woman whose husband is alive
swami	term of respect for a religious leader or person in authority
Thai	mid-January to mid-February
thambi	younger brother
thangachi	younger sister
Thondai	a thorny creeper or *Capparis zeylanica*
Thumbai	*Leucas aspera*
Vaagai	Indian siris or *Mimosa speciosa*
varaha	wild boar
veena	stringed musical instrument
vibhuti	holy ash
Yamalokam	abode of Yama, the god of death
Yatra dhanam	ritual performed before travel